OUT OF
THE DEEP

And Other Supernatural Tales

OUT OF
THE DEEP

And Other Supernatural Tales

WALTER DE LA MARE

This collection first published 2017 by
The British Library
96 Euston Road
London NW1 2DB

Copyright © 2017 The Literary Trustees of Walter de la Mare
Introduction copyright © 2017 Greg Buzwell

Cataloguing in Publication Data
A catalogue record for this book is
available from the British Library

ISBN 978 0 7123 5675 6

The texts of these stories are taken from the
critical edition of Walter de la Mare's short stories
published by Giles de la Mare Publishers

Text designed and typeset by Tetragon, London
Printed in England by CPI Group (UK) Ltd, Croydon CR0 4YY

CONTENTS

INTRODUCTION

W HAT QUALITIES CONTRIBUTE TO THE MAKING OF A REALLY good ghost story? A deftly crafted air of unease and suspense is essential. A well-defined sense of place is also an advantage – the isolated mist-shrouded mansion, or the forest landscape never penetrated by the sun. Then you need a protagonist, someone who is haunted as much by loneliness and doubt as by the spirits of those departed. All these qualities help to shape a good ghost story, but the best ghost stories, and those by Walter de la Mare are certainly among the best, have something else in their favour – an enduring sense of mystery and a solution or explanation that remains tantalisingly out of reach. Take for example the most famous ghost story of them all, Henry James's *The Turn of the Screw* (1898). James's tale certainly has the atmosphere, the location and the troubled protagonist, but it also raises numerous tantalising questions. Are the ghosts in the story 'real', or do they only exist within the mind of the governess? Do the children within her care see the ghosts but refuse to admit it, or are they totally innocent and merely bewildered by events? Is the governess malevolent or mad, or is she rather the only hope of salvation in a story that deals almost exclusively with evil? James's ability to weave ambiguity into the fabric of the tale makes it a sublime ghost story. As the stories in this collection reveal, Walter de la Mare possessed a very similar ability to create narratives in which many interpretations are possible, something which – taken together with his perfectly pitched sense of place and his elegant prose – made him one of the finest writers of supernatural tales in the language.

Walter de la Mare (1873–1956) was born in Charlton, Kent, the sixth of the seven children of James Edward Delamare (as the name was originally spelled), an official at the Bank of England, and his wife Lucy Sophia. He was educated at St Paul's Cathedral School, from which perhaps his love of ecclesiastical buildings derives. Like the work of his near-contemporary M. R. James, the ghost stories of Walter de la Mare often feature cathedrals, churches and churchyards. The layers of history, antiquity, legend and ritual associated with such places makes them ideal settings for tales in which the seemingly safe and traditional often harbours something altogether more mysterious. Later, between 1890 and 1908 he worked in the statistics department of the Anglo-American Oil Company, a dreary and ill-paid job that he made bearable by writing stories and poems in his spare time. In August 1899 he married Constance Elfrida Ingpen and the couple had four children, the eldest of whom, Richard, became chairman of the publishing house Faber and Faber.

De la Mare's career as a writer began to take flight in the mid-1890s, just as a taste for Gothic and supernatural tales was beginning to flourish. Oscar Wilde's *The Picture of Dorian Gray*, for example, had been published in 1891, while Bram Stoker's *Dracula* and Henry James's *The Turn of the Screw* would appear in 1897 and 1898 respectively. M. R. James's first collection of ghost stories – *Ghost Stories of an Antiquary* – was published in 1904, although some of the stories including 'Lost Hearts' and 'Canon Alberic's Scrap-Book' had first appeared in the mid-1890s. For someone with an interest in writing mysterious and haunting tales there were few better times to embark upon a literary career than the Victorian fin de siècle. De la Mare's first published story, 'Kismet', appeared in the *Sketch* in 1895 under the pseudonym Walter Ramal. The story, which opens with two lone travellers, one on foot and the other with a horse and cart (a cart in which there is a coffin) owes something to Thomas Hardy. Like Hardy's work, the stories of de la Mare reveal a great love of the English countryside, with its buildings and its people, its folklore and its customs. Like Hardy, again, de la Mare's stories often feature a strong undercurrent of melancholy. The protagonists, particularly in the later stories, are often men who find themselves suddenly faced with old age, gloomily left to reflect upon distant youthful days and the path not travelled. Perfect, in many ways, for ghost stories – a genre in which the past is frequently more alive than the present.

Walter de la Mare's literary output was huge. He published over a thousand poems and rhymes, about a hundred short stories and four novels, including the sinister *The Return* (1910), a tale of possession from beyond the grave, and the splendidly titled and surreal *Memoirs of a Midget* (1921). Although accomplished in every literary form to which he turned his hand, he is especially well known today for his ghost stories. The reasons for his success in the field are many, but one comment that sheds particular light on his success occurs in a letter he wrote to Naomi Royde-Smith, the literary editor of the *Saturday Westminster Gazette*, in August 1911: 'Now and again over one's mind comes the glamour of a kind of visionary world saturating this'. This observation gives us an insight into the faintly hallucinatory quality possessed by many of de la Mare's ghost stories, that sense of meaning being ever so slightly beyond our grasp and the feeling that events are running marginally out of kilter with reality. A particularly good example of this occurs in his story 'Winter', in which a figure glimpsed in a snowy churchyard appears not so much as an illusion or a ghost but rather as a visitor from an alternate world existing just beyond that which our senses normally perceive.

Walter de la Mare's prolific output makes the task of selecting just a few of his finest ghost stories a difficult one. Some tales, such as

'Seaton's Aunt', 'Out of the Deep' and 'All Hallows', have been much anthologised over the years, but their quality means they deserve another outing. 'Seaton's Aunt' in particular is a work shrouded in such mystery, and open to so many interpretations, that few supernatural tales can rival its air of enigmatic menace. Other tales in this volume are much less well known. 'A:B:O.', for example, owes something to M. R. James, featuring as it does a box containing a creature that bears some (but disturbingly not quite enough) resemblance to a human being. 'The Riddle', meanwhile, is a short tale that perfectly captures de la Mare's ability to turn expectations upside down – initially the story appears to centre upon a group of children, but it is the old lady with whom they are staying who carries the weight and the meaning of the story. 'The Green Room', meanwhile, is a brilliant example of descriptive writing with its perfectly evoked setting of a book-lined room in which the shadows play upon the walls as the seasons change outside. As a descriptive writer, and a writer with a poet's eye for the perfect word, de la Mare has few equals.

Finally, to return to where we started, perhaps it is worth adding one more quality to the ingredients of an excellent ghost story. Along with atmosphere, suspense, place and mystery we should add – as with all the best fiction – the ability to bear repeated rereading. Indeed one could argue that de la Mare's ghost stories *demand* rereading. They do not rely on a single twist ending for their dramatic impact – something which, no matter how brilliantly executed, tends to work only on a first reading. De la Mare is much more subtle than that, and with each rereading of his stories new details emerge, deft descriptions take on a new significance, and the seemingly throwaway comments made by a character gain a new depth. And yet each newly revealed detail only serves to deepen the surrounding mystery and makes the story itself more sinister, and more profound.

KISMET

THE MAN IN THE CART, WHEN HE REACHED THE TOP OF THE
long hill up which the old mare had been steadily plodding, was
rejoiced to spy against the whiteness of the road beyond the figure of
a man walking. For, although he was of a taciturn disposition, and
cared little for company, yet on this night he felt lonely. At times, even,
he had peered timorously between the trees that overshadowed the
roadway, and had started in affright when the ring of the hoofs on the
frozen ground had roused some bird from sleep, and the sound of its
swift flight could be heard, growing gradually fainter, till hushed in
the distance. Uncanny stories had flocked up from forgotten stores
of memory, and, with the creeping of his flesh, haunting fancies had
come that grim shapes were gathering behind him. With a shudder
at the dread thought, he had pulled the collar of his heavy coat about
his ears, and so had sat, almost fearful to breathe.

But now, as he leisurely drove down the steady decline, the sight
of the lonely figure in the distance restored his usual stupidity;
defiantly he hummed under his breath a song brimming over with
blasphemy against all midnight loiterers other than those of the
flesh, to which song the mare put back her ears, and hearkened in
astonishment.

As he drew slowly nearer to the traveller, suddenly a great, deep
voice came leaping through the cold air, roaring out the swinging
chorus of some song of the sea; the man in the cart stopped dead
in his crooning, and listened in amazement to the intense happiness
that rang in every note. The music in the song seemed to run in his
blood – a shudder shook him from head to foot. The song ceased

as suddenly as it had begun; the traveller had heard the noise of the approaching cart, and was now waiting at the side of the road till it should come up with him.

The driver pulled up near at hand, and eyed the stranger with some curiosity; the mare also turned her head to gaze wonderingly at him for a moment, then shook herself, till every scrap of metal on her harness rang again. The stranger startled the man in the cart when he spoke, so intent was his stare.

'How far might it be to Barrowmere?' inquired the man on foot.

'Nigh on seven mile,' replied the driver, with wonder in his brain at a man possessing the courage to walk alone at midnight through the still country lanes.

'Thanks,' said the stranger shortly, in a bluff, hearty voice, then turned as if to continue his tramp.

The driver watched him a few paces. 'He's a seaman,' he muttered to himself, 'and I don't make no doubt but he's going home,' after which reflection he was about to gather up the reins to continue his interrupted journey, when his whole face lit up at the brilliant charitable idea that, as he was taking much the same way as the other, he should offer him a lift in the cart. His plump cheeks grew hot with virtuous pride as he shouted, 'Hi! Was it Barrowmere you said?'

The man wheeled round smartly. 'Barrowmere it was!' he sang out in answer.

'I be going to Barrowmere,' said the driver. 'There's room enough behind if you want a lift.'

The stranger with the joyous resonant voice strode back, and swung himself into the cart with a muscular jerk.

'P'raps you'll sit there,' said the driver, pointing with the butt of his whip to a tarpaulin-covered box at the bottom of the cart.

There the stranger sat himself down. 'Thankee,' he said.

A peculiar smile sped over the driver's face as he shook the reins and drove on without another word.

By degrees he grew morose and sulky. He blamed the traveller for accepting his hospitable offer.

The stranger, who was muffled to the chin in a thick pea-jacket, made a vain attempt to converse with the driver, but finding him both unwilling and witless, he turned his attention to his more pleasant thoughts. His suntanned face beamed at the thought of the meeting with his wife soon to come about, he chuckled audibly as he imagined her surprised delight, and he rubbed his hands for the twentieth time when the full subtlety of his little joke in not letting her know the day of his return was again forced upon him.

The full moon flooded the fields with light, making them appear even colder than in reality they were; a very slight fall of snow and a sharp frost had clothed the trees and hedges in a shimmering glory of sparkling white. Not a sound was in the air save the buzz of the cart's wheels, the steady beat of the hoofs, and an occasional shuddering snort from the mare. The cold was severe, at times compelling both men to beat their arms upon their bodies to restore the running of their blood.

Maybe it was the intense silence, maybe the lonely hour of the night, that oppressed the spirits; but there slowly crept over the traveller, who until now had been in so genial a humour, a stern sobriety, a vague presage of impending disaster, an unreasonable mistrust of his former jollity, so that he sat dumb and perplexed on his seat in the cart, watching the sharp-drawn shadows of the trees upon the white road flit silently by, eyeing with stealthy suspicion the burly, bowed body of the driver, and the while ardently desiring the eager arms of his wife.

The traveller got upon his feet in the cart and peered over the driver's shoulder. He could see, in the hollow ahead, the first outlying cottage of the village, and the blood surged up in his body as one by one the well-remembered landmarks of home came into view.

His heart yearned for the shelter of his house, for the kiss of the loved woman: he reminded himself of the mate of his little craft, who knew no friend in the world to give him welcome.

The driver looked back over his shoulder at the stranger, and muttered huskily, 'That be Barrowmere yonder.'

The stranger paid him no heed; at the same moment the notion had come into his head that he would get down from the cart and travel the remainder of the journey on foot; he had no mind that his surly companion should witness his meeting with his wife. So he tapped him on the shoulder. The man turned sulkily; he was bidden pull up, and obeyed with sullen tardiness. The seaman leaped out at the back, tossed a coin to the man, who pocketed it with a nod of thanks and drove on again; the peculiar smile reappeared as he muttered to something between the ears of the old mare.

'I do hope, now, he finds it easy.'

And the man of the sea was trudging slowly along the country lane towards his home; he was rejoiced to be free from his unfriendly companion; his good spirits began to return to him; when, on a sudden, the piteous, wailing howl of a dog struck upon his ears – terror seized upon him for a moment, so that he gasped for breath and trembled as he walked. Bitterly he cursed the land; he vowed he would carry his wife away to the sea and never touch England again.

With almost unwilling footsteps, he approached the bend in the road where his cottage would come into view; every tiny twig in the hedgerows was its own self in glass, not a cloud obscured the living heavens, only the pitiless, cold stare of the moon upon all and the silence of death. It ate into the heart of the man as he walked; he feared greatly, though he knew not why nor what manner of thing he feared. With bated breath, he turned the corner; there lay his home, peaceful under the white moonlight; but his surprise was great at seeing the cart he had journeyed in at a standstill before the little rustic gate. The man, apparently, had entered the house, for the horse was standing with hanging head, its reins tied to the gate-post, awaiting its driver. He walked quietly towards the house, with that strange misgiving at his heart. When he reached it, he feared to enter. He looked into the cart; the box he had used as a seat had gone. He made a weak attempt to laugh his fears down, but failed miserably.

The windows facing the roadway were in pitch darkness; no sign was there that life was within. The seaman crept with muffled footsteps to the back of the house, and there rose into the night again the desolate howling of a dog. He leant over the rough wooden rail and called softly. The dog – his dog – whined joyously, straining at its chain to welcome its master.

He leapt over the low fence; the idea crossed his mind that he was using his own house like a thief in the night. He paused for a moment, perplexed at the sudden beam of light which had dazzled his eyes. He glanced up to discover whence it came; the curtains had been drawn across one of the windows, but had not met, thus leaving a narrow space through which the bright rays of light were streaming out upon the night from within – it was the window of his bedroom.

With fitful breath he crept over to the dog, and fondled it for a while, but still keeping his eyes fixed upon that lonely beam of light. The dog licked its master's hand in unrestrained joy at his return.

And there came into the man's mind a fervent desire to look in through that window. He struggled with himself to restrain the impulse, and to knock boldly at the door, but his wild forebodings and fears of unknown evil conquered him. He looked round for some means by which he might reach the window.

A large tree grew a few yards from the house, a bough of which jetted out towards the window; he remembered that, when he had lain awake on summer nights gone by, he had heard it tapping against the pane. With reluctant steps, he crawled to the tree, clasped a projecting knot, and began to climb the weather-worn trunk. With much labour he scrambled on till at last he reached the bough that ran out towards the house. His hands were numb with the frost and cold. Slowly he crept on, trembling and panting. One last painful effort, and he lay on the branch, with his face toward the window, the light beaming out into his blue eyes.

Gradually he grew accustomed to the glare; he saw plainly into the room.

He saw the bed shrouded in a white sheet; he saw the mother of his wife, kneeling at its head, bend over and gently lift the sheet; he saw the still, pallid face of his dead wife; he saw the driver of the cart pass across the rift between the curtains, carrying the coffin on which he had sat in his joyous ride to his home. A rush of blood blinded his eyes and sang in his ears; he clawed madly at the bough of the tree with his stiff fingers. As he swung in the air, his breath shook him, his teeth chattered and bit into his tongue. He heard with strange distinctness the whispering voices of the night, the stealthy movements in the little room; he saw all things as he stared.

Gradually his clutching fingers relaxed; the whole firmament seemed to reel. In his struggling flight through the air his skull struck and cracked against a bossy branch; his body turned limply, and fell motionless upon the turf beneath.

The dog crawled nearer, shivering and dismayed: it licked the bloody hand of its master, then threw up its head to give tongue to a long-drawn howl of terror.

A : B : O .

I LOOKED UP OVER THE TOP OF MY BOOK AT THE PORTRAIT OF my great-grandfather and listened in astonishment to the sudden peal of the bell, which clanged and clanged in straggling decisive strokes until, like a dog gone back to his kennel, it slowed, slackened and fell silent again. A bell has an unfriendly tongue; it is a router of wits, a messenger of alarms. Even in the quiet of twilight it may resemble a sour virago's din. At a late hour, when the world is snug in night-cap and snoring is the only harmony, it is the devil's own discordancy. I looked over my book at my placid ancestor, I say, and listened on even after the sound had been stilled.

To tell the truth, I was more than inclined to pay no heed to the summons, and, secure in the kind warmth and solitude of my room, to ignore so rude a remembrancer of the world. Before I could decide either way, yet again the metal tongue clattered, as icily as a martinet. It pulled me to my feet. Then, my tranquillity, my inertia destroyed, it was useless and profitless to take no heed. I vowed vengeance. I would pounce sourly upon my visitor, thought I. I would send him back double-quick into the darkness of the night, and, if this were some timid feminine body (which God forefend), an antic and a grimace would effectually put such an one to route.

I rose, opened the door, and slid cautiously in my slippers to the bolted door. There I paused to climb up on a chair in an endeavour to spy out on the latecomer from the fanlight, to take his size, to analyse his intentions, but standing there even on tiptoe I could see not so much as the crown of a hat. I clambered down and, after a dismal rattling of chain and shooting of bolts, flung open the door.

Upon my top step (eight steps run down from the door to the garden and two more into the street) stood a little boy. A little boy with a ready tongue in his head, I perceived by the smirk at the corner of his mouth; a little boy of spirit too, for the knees of his knicker-bockers were patched. This I perceived by the light of a lamp-post which stands over against the doctor's house. Grimaces were wasted on this sturdy youngster in his red flannel neckerchief. I eyed him with pursed lips.

'Mr Pelluther?' said the little boy, his fists deep in the pockets of his jacket.

'Who asks for Mr Pelluther?' said I pedagogically.

'Me,' said the little boy.

'What does me want with Mr Pelluther at so untoward an hour, eh, my little man? What the gracious do you mean by making clang-our with my bell and waking the stars when all the world's asleep, and fetching me out of the warmth to this windy doorstep? I have a mind to pull your ear.'

Such sudden eloquence somewhat astonished the little boy. His 'boyness' seemed, I fancied, to leave him in the lurch; he was at school out of season; he retrogressed a few steps.

'Please sir, I've got a letter for Mr Pelluther, the gentleman said,' he turned his back on me, 'but as he ain't here I'll take it back.' He skipped down the step and at the bottom lustily set to whistling the *Marseillaise*.

My dignity was hurt, and a coward. 'Come, come, my little man,' I called, 'I myself am Mr Pelluther.'

'*Le jour de gloire…*' whistled the little boy.

'Give me the letter,' said I peremptorily.

'I've got to give it into the gentleman's own hands,' said the little boy.

'Come, give me the letter,' said I persuasively.

'I've got to give it into the gentleman's own hands,' said the little boy doggedly, 'and you don't see a corner of the envelope.'

'Come, my boy, here's a sixpence.'

He eyed me suspiciously. 'Chestnuts,' said he, retiring a step or two.

'See, a silver sixpence for the honest messenger,' said I.

'Honest be blowed!' said he. 'Put it on the step and go behind the door. I'll come up for the tanner and put the letter on the step. Catch a weasel?'

I wanted the letter; I trusted my boy; so I put the sixpence on the top step and retired behind the door. He was true to his word. With a wary eye and a whoop of triumph he made the exchange. He doubled his fist on the sixpence and retired into the garden. I came like a felon out of the stocks for my letter.

The letter was addressed simply 'Pelluther', in uncommon careless handwriting, so careless indeed that I hardly recognised the scholarly penmanship of my friend Dugdale. Forgetful of the messenger, who yet lingered upon my garden path, I shut the door and bustled into my study. I was reminded of his presence and of my discourtesy by a rattling shower of stones upon the panels of my door and by the sound of the *Marseillaise* startling the distant trees of the quiet square.

'Dear, dear me,' said I, perching my spectacles most unskilfully. Indeed, I was not a little perturbed by this untimely letter. For only a few hours ago I had walked and smoked with dear old Dugdale in his own pleasant garden, in his own gentle twilight. For twilight seems to soothe to sleep the flowers of my old friend's garden with gentler hands than she can have vouchsafed even to the gardens of Solomon.

I opened my letter in trepidation, only a little reassured of Dugdale's safety by the superscription written in his own handwriting. This is the burden of the letter – 'Dear Friend Pell. I am writing, in a fever. Come at once – *Antiquities!* – the lumber – a mere scrawl – Come at once, or I begin without you. R.D.'

'Antiquities' was the peak of the climax of this summons – the golden word. All else might be meaningless; as indeed it was. 'Come at once. *Antiquities!*'

I bustled into my coat and was pelting at perilous speed down my eight steps before the *Marseillaise* had ceased to echo from the adjacent houses. Isolated wayfarers no doubt imagined me to be a doctor, bent on enterprise of life or death. Truly an unvenerable appearance was mine, but Dugdale was itching to begin, and haste spelt glory.

His white house lay not a mile distant, and soon the squeal of his gate upon its hinges comforted my heart and gave my lungs pause. Dugdale himself, also, the noise brought flying down into his drive to greet me. He was without his coat. Under his arm was clumsily tucked a spade, his cheeks were flushed with excitement. Even his firm lips, children of science, were trembling, and his grey eyes, wives of the microscope, were agog behind the golden-rimmed spectacles set awry on his magnificent nose.

I squeezed his left hand and thus together we hurried up the steps. 'Have you begun?' said I.

'Just on the move when you came round the corner,' said he. 'Who would believe it, Old Roman, or Druidical, God knows.'

Excitement and panting made me totter and I was dismayed at the thought of my digestion. We hurried down the passage to his study, which was in great disorder and filled with a vexing dust, hardly reminiscent of his admirable housemaid, and with a most unpleasant mouldy odour, of damp paper I conjecture.

Dugdale seized a ragged piece of parchment which lay upon the table and pressed it into my hand. He sank back into his well-worn leather armchair, the spade resting against his knee, and energetically set to polishing his glasses.

I looked fixedly at him. He flourished his long forefinger at me fussily, shaking his head, eager for me to get on.

Rudely scrawled upon the chart was a diagram rectangular in shape with divers scrawls in red ink, and crazy figures. I drove my brains into the open, with vain threats and cudgelling; no, I could make nothing of it. A small chest or coffer upon the floor, of a curious workmanship, overflowing with dusty and stained papers and parchments, betrayed whence the chart had come.

I looked at Dugdale. 'What does it mean?' said I, a little disappointed, for many a trick of the foolish and of the fraudulent has sent me on an idle errand in search of 'antiquities'.

'My garden,' said Dugdale, sweeping his hand towards the window, then triumphantly pointing to the chart in my hand. 'I have studied it. My uncle, the antiquarian; it *is* genuine. I have had suspicions, ah! yes, every one of yours; I'm not blind. It may be anything. I dig at once. Come and help or go to the—'

He shouldered his spade, in which action he shivered a precious little porcelain cup upon a cabinet. He never so much as blinked at the calamity. He slackened not an inch his triumphant march to the door. Well, what is a five pound note in one's pocket to a sixpence discovered in a gutter?

I caught up the pick and another shovel. 'Bravo, Pelluther,' said he, and we strutted off arm and arm into the pleasant and spacious garden which lay at the back of the house. I felt proud as a drummer-boy.

In the garden Dugdale whipped out of his pocket a yard measure, and having lighted a wax candle stuck it with its own grease in a recess of the wall. After which he knelt down upon the mould with transparent sedateness and studied the chart by the candle-light, very clear and conspicuous in the darkness.

'Yew tree ten yards N. by seven E. three – semicir – um – square. It's mere A.B.C., 'pon my word.'

He darted away to the bottom of the garden. I followed in a canter by the path between the darkened roses. All was blackness except where the candle-light bleached the old bricks of Dugdale's wall and glittered upon the dewy trees. At the squat old yew tree he beckoned me. I had repeatedly beseeched him to fell the ugly thing – but he would not.

'Hold the reel,' said he, with trembling fingers offering me the yard-measure. Away he went. 'Ten yards by how much?'

'Five, I think,' said I.

'Spellicans,' said Dugdale, and bustled away to the house for the chart. His shirt-sleeves winked between the bushes. He fetched back with him the chart and another candlestick.

'Do wake up Pelluther, wake up! Oh, "seven", wake up?'

I was shivering with excitement and my teeth sounded like a skeleton swaying in the wind. He measured the yards and marked the place on the soil with his spade.

'Now then to work,' said he, and set the example by a savage slash at a pensive *Gloire de Dijon*.

Exceedingly solemn, yet gurgling with self-conscious laughter, I also began to pick and dig. The sweat was cold upon my forehead after a quarter of an hour's hard labour. I sat on the grass and panted.

'City dinners, orgies,' muttered Dugdale, slaving away like a man in search of his soul.

'No wind, thank goodness. See that flint flash? Good exercise! Centenarians and all the better for it. I am no chicken either. Phugh!

the place is black as a tiger's throat. I'll swear someone's been here before. Thumb that time! – bless the blister!'

Even in my own abject condition I had time to be amazed at his sinewy strokes and his fanatical energy. He was sexton, and I the owl! Exquisitely, suddenly, Dugdale's pick struck heavily and hollowly.

'Oh God!' said he, scrambling like a rat out of the hole. He leaned heavily on his pick and peered at me with round eyes. A great silence was over the place. I seemed to hear the metallic ring of the pick cleaving its way to the stars. Dugdale crept very cautiously and extinguished the candle with damp fingers.

'Eh, now,' whispered he, 'you and I, old boy, d'ye hear. In the hole – it's desecration, it's as glum a trade as body-snatching. Hush! who's that?'

His hand pounced on my shoulder. We craned our necks. A plaintive howl grew out of the silence and faded into the silence. A black cat leapt the fence and disappeared with a flutter of leaves.

'That black beast!' said I, gazing into the wormy hole. 'I would like to wait – and think.'

'No time,' said Dugdale, doubtfully bold. 'The hole must be filled up before dawn or Jenkinson will make enquiries. Tut, tut, what's that noise of thumping. Oh, yes, all right!' He clapped his hand on his chest, 'Now, Rattie, like mice!'

Rattie had been my nickname a very long time ago.

We set to work again; each tap of pick or shovel chased a shiver down my spine. And after great labour we excavated a metallic chest.

'Pell, you're a brick – I told you so!' said Dugdale.

We continued to gaze at our earthly spoil. One strange and inexplicable discovery we made was this: a thickly rusted iron tube ran out from the top of the chest into the earth, and thence by surmise we traced it to the trunk of the dwarfed yew tree; and, with the light of our candles eventually discovered its termination imbedded in a boss between two gnarled encrusted branches a few feet up. We were unable to drag out the chest without first disinterring the pipe.

I eyed it with perplexity.

'Come and get a saw,' said, Dugdale. 'It's strange, eh?'

He turned a mottled face to me. The air seemed to be slightly phosphorescent. Whether he had suspicions that I should force open the lid in his absence I know not. At any rate, I willingly accompanied him to the tool-house. We brought back a handsaw, Dugdale greased it plentifully with the candle, and I held the pipe while he sawed. What the purpose or use of the pipe might be I puzzled my brains in vain to discover.

'Perhaps,' said Dugdale, pausing, saw in hand, 'perhaps it's delicate merchandise, eh, and needs fresh air.'

'Perhaps it is not,' said I, unaccountably vexed at his halting speech.

He seemed to expect no different answer and again set busily to work. The pipe vibrated at his vigour, dealing me little shocks and numbing my fingers. At last the chest was free, we tapped it with our fingers. We scraped off flakes of mould and rust with our nails. I knelt and put my eye to the end of the pipe. Dugdale pushed me aside and did likewise.

I am assured that passing in his brain was a sequence of ideas exactly similar to my own. We nursed our excitement, we conceived the wildest fantasies, we brought forth litters of surmises. Perhaps just the shadow of apprehension lurked about us. Possibly a familiar spirit may have tapped our shoulders.

Then, at the same instant we both began to pull and push vigorously at the chest; but, in such a confined space (for the hole was ragged and unequal) its weight was too great for our strength.

'A rope,' said Dugdale, 'let's go together again. Two "old boys" in the plot.' He laughed hypocritically.

'Certainly,' said I, amused at his suspicions and wiles.

Again we stepped away to the tool-shed, and returned with a coil of rope. The pick being used as a lever, we were soon able to haul the chest out of its hole.

'Duty first,' said Dugdale, shovelling the loose earth into the cavity. I imitated him. And over the place of the disturbance we planted the dying rose bush, already hanging drooping leaves.

'Jenkinson's eyes are not microscopes, but he's damned inquisitive.'

Jenkinson, incidentally, was an old gentleman who lived in the house next to Dugdale. One who having no currants in his own bun must needs pick and steal his neighbour's! But he is dumb in the grave now, and out of hearing of any cavilling tongue.

Dugdale swore, but a man would be a saint or a fool who could refrain from swearing under the circumstance. Even I displayed blasphemous knowledge and was not ashamed.

Dugdale took one end and I the other side of the chest. Together we carried it with immense difficulty (for the thing was prodigously weighty) to the study. We cleared away all the furniture to the sides of the room. We placed the chest in the middle of the floor so that we might gloat upon it at our ease. With the fire-shovel, for we had neglected to bring the spade, Dugdale scraped away mould and rust and upon the top of the chest appeared three letters, initial to a word, I conjectured, which originally ran the whole width of the side, but the greater part of which had been rendered illegible by the action of the soil. 'A – B – O' were the letters.

'I have no idea,' said Dugdale peering at this barely perceptible record. 'I have no idea,' I echoed vaguely.

And would to God we had forthwith carried the chest unopened to the garden and buried it deeper than deep!

'Let us open it,' said I, after arduous examination of the inscription.

The fire flames glittered upon dear old Dugdale's glasses. He was a chilly man and at a suggestion of east wind would have a fire set blazing. The room was snug and cosy. I remember the carved figure of a Chinese god grinning at me in a very palpable manner as I handed Dugdale his chisel. (May he forgive me!) The intense silence was ominous. In a cranny at the lid of the chest he inserted the tool. He looked at me queerly; at the second jerk the steel snapped.

'Dugdale,' said I, eyeing the Chinese god, 'let's leave well alone.'

'Eh,' said he in an unfamiliar voice.

'Have nought to do with the thing.'

'What, eh?' said he sucking his finger, the nail of which he had broken in his digging. He hesitated an instant. 'We must get another chisel,' said he, laughing.

But somehow I cared for the laugh not at all. It was not the fair bleak laugh of Dugdale. He took my arm in his and for the third time we made our way to the tool-shed.

'It's fresh and sweet,' said I, sniffing the air of the garden. My eyes beseeched Dugdale.

'Ay, so it is, it is,' said he.

When he again set to work upon the chest he prised open the lid at the first effort. The scrap of broken steel rang upon the metal of the chest. A faint and unpleasant odour became perceptible. Dugdale remained in the position the sudden lift of the lid had given his body, his head bent slightly forward, over the open chest. I put one hand upon the side of the chest. My fingers touched a little cake of hard stuff. I looked into the chest. I took a step forward and looked in. Yellow cotton wool lined the leaden sides and was thrust into the interstices of the limbs of the creature which sat within. I will speak without emotion. I saw a flat malformed skull and meagre arms and shoulders clad in coarse fawn hair. I saw a face thrown back a little, bearing hideous and ungodly resemblance to the human face, its lids heavy blue and closely shut with coarse lashes and tangled eyebrows. This I saw, this the monstrous antiquity hid in the chest which Dugdale and I dug out of the garden. Only one glimpse I took at the thing, then Dugdale had replaced the lid, had sat down on the floor and was rocking to and fro with hands clasped over his knees.

I made my way to the window feeling stiff and sore with unaccustomed toil; I threw open the window and leaned far out into the scented air. The sweetness of the flowers eddied into the room. The night was very quiet. For many minutes so I stood counting a row of poplars at the far end of the garden. Then I returned to Dugdale.

'It's the end of the business,' said I. 'My gorge rises with despair of life. Swear it! my dear old Dugdale. I implore you to swear that this shall be the end of the business. We will go bury it now.'

'I swear it, Pelluther. Pell! Pell!' The bitterness of his childish cry is venomous even now. 'But hear me, old friend,' he said. 'I am too weak now. Come tomorrow at this time and we will bury it together.'

The chest stood in front of the fire. The metal was green with verdigris.

We went out of the room leaving the glittering candles to their watch, and in my presence Dugdale turned the key in the lock of the door. He walked with me to the church and there we parted company.

'A damnable thing,' said Dugdale, shaking my hand.

I wagged my head woefully.

The next day, being Wednesday, the charwomen invaded my house, as was customary upon that day, and to be free of the steam and the stench of soap I took my way to Kew. Throughout the day I wandered through the gardens striving to enjoy the luxuriance and the flowers.

In the first coolness of evening I turned my back upon the gorgeous west and made my way home again. I met the women red and flustered leaving the house.

'Has anyone called?' said I.

'The butcher, sir,' said Mrs Rodd.

'Thank you,' said I and entered my house.

Now in the twilight as I sat down at my own fireside, my surroundings recalled most vividly the scene of the night. I leaned heavily in my chair feeling faint and sick, and in so doing was much inconvenienced by some hard thing in the pocket of my jacket pressed to my side by the arm of the chair. I rummaged in my pocket and brought out the little cake of hard green substance which had been in the mouth of the chest. I suppose that my fingers had clutched it when they had come in contact with it the night before and unknowingly I had deposited it in my pocket.

Deeming it prudent to have care in the matter, I rose and locked up the stuff in my little medicine chest, which is hanged above the mantelpiece in the room which looks out upon the garden. For to analyse or examine the stuff I feared. This done, I came again to my chair and composed myself to reading.

Supper had been prepared by the women and was set upon the table for me in my study. It has been my custom since the death of my sister to dine at midday at my club.

True! I sat with the book upon my knee but all my thoughts were with Dugdale. A rectangular shape obtruded itself upon my retina and floated upon the white page. The hours dragged wearily. My head drooped and my chin tapped my chest. In fact I was dreaming, when I was awakened by a doubtful knock upon the front door. My senses were alert in an instant. The sound, just as though something were scraping the paint, was repeated.

I rose stealthily. A vague desire to flee out into the garden seized upon me.

The sound was repeated.

I went very slowly to the door. Again I climbed the chair. (I loved the little boy now.) But I could see nothing. I peeped through the keyhole but something obscured the opening upon the other side. A faint odour – unpleasant – was in the house. With desperation of terror I flung open the door. I fancied I heard the sound of panting. I fancied something brushing my arm; then I found myself staring down the hallway listening to the echo of the click of the latch of the door of the room which overlooks my garden. In this unseemly rhythm and this succession of words I write with intent. Thus my thoughts ran then; thus then I write now. Many years ago when I was a young man I was nearly burnt alive. I felt then an honest fear. This was a dim skulking horror of soul and an inhuman depravity. It is impossible for me to tell of my horrid strivings of brain. I staggered into my room; I sat down in my chair; I took my book upon my knee; I put my spectacles upon my nose; but all the time all my senses were dead save that of hearing. Distinctly I felt my ears move and twitch, with the help of some ancient muscle, I conjecture, long disused by humanity. And as I sat, my brain cried out with fear.

For ten minutes (I slowly counted each sounding 'cluck' of my clock) I sat so. At last my limbs began to quake, solitude was driving me to perilous ravines of thought. I crept with guilty tread into the garden. I climbed the fence which separates the next house from mine. This house, No. 17, was inhabited by a caretaker, a rude uncouth fellow who used for his living-room only the kitchen, and who had tied all the bells together so that he might not be disturbed. He was a cad of a man. But for companionship I cried out.

I went to the garden door keeping my eyes fixedly turned away from the window. I hammered at the garden door of the house. I hammered again. A sullen footstep resounded in the empty place and the door was cautiously opened a few inches. A scared face looked out at me through the chink.

'For God's sake,' said I, 'come and sup with me. I have a leg of good meat, my dear fellow, come and sup with me.'

The door opened wider. Curiosity took the place of apprehension. 'Say, Master, what is moving in the house?' said the fellow. 'Why is my 'ead all damp, and my 'ands a shiverin'. I tell you there's a thing gone wrong in the place. I sits with my back to the wall and somebody steps quick and quiet on the other side. Why am I sick like so? I ask yer why?'

The man almost wept.

'You silly fellow! May a sick man not pace his mansion. I will give you a five pound note to come and sit with me,' said I. 'Be neighbourly, my good fellow. I fear that a fit will overtake me. I am weak – the heat – epileptical too. Rats crowd in the walls, I often hear their tumult. Come, sup with me.'

The cad shook his villainous head sagely.

'A five pound note – two,' said I.

'I was chaffin,' said he, and returned into the house to fetch a poker.

We climbed the fence and crept like thieves towards the house. But not an inch beyond my door would the fellow come. I expostulated. He blasphemed. He stubbornly stuck to his purpose.

'I don't budge till I've "glimpsed" through that window,' said he.

I argued and entreated; I doubled my bribe; I tapped him upon the shoulder and twitted him of cowardice; I performed a pirouette about him; I entreated him to sit with me.

'I don't budge till I've glimpsed through that window.'

I fetched a little ladder from the greenhouse which stands to the left of the house, and the caretaker carried it to the window, the ledge of which is about five feet from the ground. He climbed laboriously step by step, stretching his neck so as to see into the black room beyond, while I, simply to be near him, climbed behind him.

He had got halfway and was breathing loudly when suddenly a long arm, thin as its bone, clad in tawny hair, pallid in the dim starlight, pounced across the window and dragged the curtains together – an arm thin as its bone. The fellow above me groaned, threw up his hands and tumbled headlong off the ladder, bringing me to the ground in his fall.

For a moment I lay dazed; then, lifting my head from the soil and the sweet lilies I perceived him clambering over the fence in savage hurry. I remember that the dew glistened upon his boots as he flung his heels over the fence.

Presently I was upon my feet and pelting after him, but he was a younger man, and when I reached the door at the back of his house he had already bolted and barred it. To all my prayers and knockings he paid no attention. Notwithstanding, I feel certain that he sat listening upon the other side, for I discerned a hoarse breathing like the breathing of an asthmatic.

'You have left the poker. I bring you the poker,' I bellowed, but he made no answer.

Again I climbed the fence, now determined to leave the house free for the thing to roam and to ravage, nor to return till daylight was come. I crept quietly through the haunted place. As I passed the room, I distinguished a sound – like the sound of a humming top – of incessant gabble. I ran and opened the front door and just then, as I peered out upon the street, a beggar clothed in rags shuffled past the garden gate. I leapt down the steps.

'Here, my good man,' said I speaking with difficulty for my tongue seemed stiff and glutinous.

He turned with an odd whine and shuffled towards me.

'Are you hungry?' said I. 'Have you an appetite – just a stubborn yearning for a delicate snack of prime Welsh lamb?'

The scraggy wretch nodded and gesticulated with warty hands.

'Come in, come in,' I screamed. 'You shall eat a meal, poor man. How dire is civilisation in rags – Evil fortune! Socialism! Millionaires! I'll be bound. Come in, come in.'

I was weeping with delight. He squinted at me with suspicion and again waved his hands. By these movements and by his articulate cries, I fancied the man was dumb. (He was vexed with a serious impediment in his speech, I now conjecture.) He was manifesting mistrust. He snuffled.

'No, no,' said I. 'Come in, my man and welcome. I am lonely – a Bohemian. Ancient books are musty company. Come sit and cheer me with an honest appetite. Take a glass of wine with me.'

I patted the wretch on the back. I gripped his arm. In my tragic acting, moreover, I hummed a little song to prove my indifference. He tottered upon my steps in front of me – his shoes were mended with brown paper and the noise of his footsteps was like the rustle of a lady's silk dress. I blithely followed him into the house, leaving the door wide open so that the clean night air might go through the house, so that the clatter of the railroad which lies behind the doctor's house might prove the reality of the world. I sat the beggar down in an armchair. I plied him with meat and drink. He luxuriated in the good fare, he guzzled my claret, he gnawed bones and crust like a bony beast, considering me the while, apprehensive of being reft of his meal. He snarled and he gobbled, he puffed, he mouthed and he chawed. He was a bird of prey, a cat, a wild beast, and a man. His belly was the only truth. He had chanced on heaven, and awaited the archangel's trump of banishment. Yet in the midst of his ravenous feeding, terror was netting him, too. Full of my own fear, in watching his hands shivering, and the pallor overspreading his grimy face, I took delight. Still he ate furiously, flouting his fears.

All the while I was thinking desperately of the horrid creature which was in my house. The while I sat grinning at my guest, the while I was inciting him to eat, drink, and be merry, the while I analysed each deplorable action of the rude fellow and sickened at his beastliness, the vile consciousness of that thing on its secret errand prowling within scent, never left me – that abortion – A-B-O, abortion; I knew then.

On a sudden, just as the tramp, having lifted the lamb bone, had set his teeth to gnawing at the gristly knuckle, there came to my ears the sound of breaking glass and then a rustling (no extraordinary sound), a rustling sound of a hand wandering upon the panel of a door. But the beggar had heard what speech cannot make intelligible. I felt younger on that day than I have since my childhood. I was drunken with terror.

My beggar, dropping his tumbler of wine but still clutching the lamb bone, scrambled to his feet and eyed me with pale grey pupils set in circles of white. His dirty bleached face was stained with his meal. Dirt seamed his skin. I took his hand in mine. I caught up the lamp and held it on high. The beggar and I stood in the doorway gazing into the darkness; the lamplight faintly lit the familiar passage. It gleamed on the door of the room whose window overlooks my garden. The handle of the door was silently turning. The door was opening – almost imperceptibly. The beggar's pulse throbbed furiously; my elbow was pressed against his arm. And a very thin abnormal thing – a fawn shadow – came out of the room and pattered past the beggar and me.

My jaws fell asunder, nor could I shut them so that I might speak. Tighter I clutched the beggar and we fled out together. Standing upon the topmost of the steps, we peered down the street; afar off with ponderous tread walked a policeman, playing the light of his lantern upon the windows of the houses and the doors. Presently he drew near to a lamp, to where flitted a monstrous shadow. I saw the policeman turn suddenly round about. With fluttering coat-tails he ran furiously down a little lane which leads to many bright shops.

The beggar and I spent the rest of the night upon the doorstep. Sometimes he made vain splutterings of speech and vexed gesticulations, but, generally we waited speechless and motionless as two stuffed owls.

At the first faint ray of dawn, which leapt above the doctor's house opposite, the beggar flung away my hand, hopped blindly down the steps and, pausing not to open the gate, vaulted over it and was immediately gone. I scarcely felt surprise. The green-shaded lamp which stood upon the doorstep slowly burned itself out. The sun rose gladly, the sparrows made the morning noisy as they fluttered and fought in their busy foraging. I think my round eyes vaguely watched them.

Soon after eight the postman brought me a letter. And this was the letter – 'God forgive me, friend, and help me to write sanely. A miserable curiosity has proved too strong for me. I went back to my house, now woefully strange to me. I could not sleep. Now pacing with me in my own bedroom, now wrapped in its unholy sleep, the thing as always with me. Each picture, indeed each chair, however severely I strove to discipline my thoughts, carried with it a pregnant suggestion. In the middle of the night I took my way downstairs and opened the door of my study. My books seemed to me disconsolate friends offended. The case stood as we had left it – we, you and I, when we locked the door upon the tragedy. In fear and trembling I went a little farther into the room. Two steps had I taken when I discovered that the lid no longer shut the thing from the stars, that the lid was gaping open. Oh! Pelluther, how will you credit so astounding a statement. I saw (I say it solemnly though I have to labour vigorously to drive back a horde of thoughts) I saw the wretched creature, which you and I had raised from the belly of the earth, lying upon the floor; its meagre limbs were coiled in front of the fire. Had the heat roused him from his long sleep? I know not, I dare not think. He – he, Pelluther – lay upon the hearth-rug sunken in slumber soundlessly breathing. Oh, my friend, I stand eyeing insanity, face to face. My mind is mutinous. There lay the wretched abortion:—it seems to me that this thing is like a pestilent secret sin, which lies hid, festering, weaving snares, befouling the wholesome air, but which, some day, creeps out and goes stalking midst healthy men, a leprous child of the sinner. Ay, and like a sin perhaps of yours and of mine. Pelluther! But, being heavy with such a woesome burden it becomes us alone to bear it. I left the thing there in its sleep. Its history the world shall never know. I write this to warn you of the awful terror of the event which has come upon you and me. When you come,* we will make our plans to destroy utterly this horrid memory. And if this be not our lot we must exist but to hide our discovery from

---

* I perceive that Dugdale omitted to post this letter in time to reach me on the second evening. I bitterly deplore the omission.

the eyes of the sane. If any suffer, it is you and I who must suffer. If murder can be just, the killing of this creature – neither man nor beast, this vile symbol – must be accounted to us a virtue. Fate has chosen her tools. Come, my old friend! I have sent away my servants and locked my door; and my prayer is that this thing may sleep until darkness comes down to cloak our horrid task from the eyes of the world. Science is slunk away shamefaced; religion is a withered flower. Oh, my friend, what shall I say! How shall I regain myself?'

From the slender record of this letter I leave you to deduce whatever conclusions you may. I may suppose that at some time of the second day (perhaps, while I was rambling through the green places of Kew!) Dugdale had again visited the thing and had found it awake, alert, vigilant in his room. No man spied upon my friend in those hours. (Sometimes in the quietude, I fancy I hear an odd footfall upon my threshold!)

In the brilliant sunshine I drove in a four-wheeled cab to Dugdale's house, for my limbs were weak and would hardly bear my body. I limped up the garden path and the familiar steps with the help of two sticks. The door was ajar – I entered. I found Dugdale in his study. He was sitting in the chest with a Bible resting on one of the sides.

He looked at me. '"For we are but of yesterday and know nothing because our days upon earth are a shadow." What is life, Pelluther? A vain longing for death. What is beauty? A question of degree. And sin is in the air – child of disease and death and springing-up and hatred of life. Fawn hair has beauty and as for bones; surely less for the worms. Worms! through lead? Pelluther, my dear old Pell. Through lead?'

He gazed at me like a child gazing at a bright light.

'Come!' said I, 'the air is bland and the sun is fierce and warm. Come!' I could say no more.

'But the sunlight has no meaning to me now,' said he. 'That breeder of corruption, tall here and a monstrous being, walks under my skull strangling all the other beings, puny and sapless. I have one idea, conception, vivid faintness, a fierce red horrid idea – and a phenomenon, too. You see, it is when a deep abstract belief rots into loathing, when hope is eaten away by horrors of sleep and a mad longing for sleep – mad! Yet fawn hair is not without beauty; provided, Pelluther, provided – through lead?'…

A vain idle report has been set about by the malicious. Oh, was there not reason and logical sequence in his conversation with me? I give it for demonstration's sake. I swear that he is not mad – a little eccentric (surely all clever men are eccentric), a little aged. I swear solemnly that my dear friend Dugdale was not mad. He was a just man. He wronged no one. He was a benevolent kindly gentleman and fine in intellect. Say you that he was eccentric – not mad. Tears ran down my cheeks as I looked at him.

THE RIDDLE

S O THESE SEVEN CHILDREN, ANN AND MATILDA, JAMES, WILLIAM
and Henry, Harriet and Dorothea, came to live with their grandmother. The house in which their grandmother had lived since her
childhood was built in the time of the Georges. It was not a pretty
house, but roomy, substantial, and square; and a great cedar tree
outstretched its branches almost to the windows.

When the children were come out of the cab (five sitting inside
and two beside the driver), they were shown into their grandmother's
presence. They stood in a little black group before the old lady,
seated in her bow-window. And she asked them each their names,
and repeated each name in her kind, quavering voice. Then to one
she gave a workbox, to William a jack-knife, to Dorothea a painted
ball; to each a present according to age. And she kissed all her grand-
children to the youngest.

'My dears,' she said, 'I wish to see all of you bright and gay in my
house. I am an old woman, so that I cannot romp with you; but Ann
must look to you, and Mrs Fenn too. And every morning and every
evening you must all come in to see your granny; and bring me smiling
faces, that call back to my mind my own son Harry. But all the rest of
the day, when school is done, you shall do just as you please, my dears.
And there is only one thing, just one, I would have you remember. In
the large spare bedroom that looks out on the slate roof there stands
in the corner an old oak chest; aye, older than I, my dears, a great deal
older; older than my grandmother. Play anywhere else in the house,
but not there.' She spoke kindly to them all, smiling at them; but
she was very old, and her eyes seemed to see nothing of this world.

And the seven children, though at first they were gloomy and strange, soon began to be happy and at home in the great house. There was much to interest and to amuse them there; all was new to them. Twice every day, morning and evening, they came in to see their grandmother, who every day seemed more feeble; and she spoke pleasantly to them of her mother, and her childhood, but never forgetting to visit her store of sugar-plums. And so the weeks passed by...

It was evening twilight when Henry went upstairs from the nursery by himself to look at the oak chest. He pressed his fingers into the carved fruit and flowers, and spoke to the dark-smiling heads at the corners; and then, with a glance over his shoulder, he opened the lid and looked in. But the chest concealed no treasure, neither gold nor baubles, nor was there anything to alarm the eye. The chest was empty, except that it was lined with silk of old rose, seeming darker in the dusk, and smelling sweet of potpourri. And while Henry was looking in, he heard the softened laughter and the clinking of the cups downstairs in the nursery; and out at the window he saw the day darkening. These things brought strangely to his memory his mother who in her glimmering white dress used to read to him in the dusk; and he climbed into the chest; and the lid closed gently down over him.

When the other six children were tired with their playing, they filed into their grandmother's room for her good-night and her sugar-plums. She looked out between the candles at them as if she were uncertain of something in her thoughts. The next day Ann told her grandmother that Henry was not anywhere to be found.

'Dearie me, child. Then he must be gone away for a time,' said the old lady. She paused. 'But remember, all of you, do not meddle with the oak chest.'

But Matilda could not forget her brother Henry, finding no pleasure in playing without him. So she would loiter in the house thinking where he might be. And she carried her wooden doll in her bare arms, singing under her breath all she could make up about it. And when one bright morning she peeped in on the chest, so sweet-scented and secret it seemed that she took her doll with her into it – just as Henry himself had done.

So Ann, and James, and William, Harriet and Dorothea were left at home to play together. 'Some day maybe they will come back to you, my dears,' said their grandmother, 'or maybe you will go to them. Heed my warning as best you may.'

Now Harriet and William were friends together, pretending to be sweethearts; while James and Dorothea liked wild games of hunting, and fishing, and battles.

On a silent afternoon in October, Harriet and William were talking softly together, looking out over the slate roof at the green fields, and they heard the squeak and frisking of a mouse behind them in the room. They went together and searched for the small, dark hole from whence it had come out. But finding no hole, they began to finger the carving of the chest, and to give names to the dark-smiling heads, just as Henry had done. 'I know! let's pretend you are Sleeping Beauty, Harriet,' said William, 'and I'll be the Prince that squeezes through the thorns and comes in.' Harriet looked gently and strangely at her brother but she got into the box and lay down, pretending to be fast asleep, and on tiptoe William leaned over, and seeing how big was the chest, he stepped in to kiss the Sleeping Beauty and to wake her from her quiet sleep. Slowly the carved lid turned on its noiseless hinges. And only the clatter of James and Dorothea came in sometimes to recall Ann from her book.

But their old grandmother was very feeble, and her sight dim, and her hearing extremely difficult.

Snow was falling through the still air upon the roof; and Dorothea was a fish in the oak chest, and James stood over the hole in the ice, brandishing a walking-stick for a harpoon, pretending to be an Esquimau. Dorothea's face was red, and her wild eyes sparkled through her tousled hair. And James had a crooked scratch upon his cheek. 'You must struggle, Dorothea, and then I shall swim back and drag you out. Be quick now!' He shouted with laughter as he was drawn into the open chest. And the lid closed softly and gently down as before.

Ann, left to herself, was too old to care overmuch for sugar-plums, but she would go solitary to bid her grandmother good-night; and the old lady looked wistfully at her over her spectacles. 'Well, my dear,' she said with trembling head; and she squeezed Ann's fingers between her own knuckled finger and thumb. 'What lonely old people, we two are, to be sure!' Ann kissed her grandmother's soft, loose cheek. She left the old lady sitting in her easy chair, her hands upon her knees, and her head turned sidelong towards her.

When Ann was gone to bed she used to sit reading her book by candle-light. She drew up her knees under the sheets, resting her book upon them. Her story was about fairies and gnomes, and the gently flowing moonlight of the narrative seemed to illumine the white pages, and she could hear in fancy fairy voices, so silent was the great many-roomed house, and so mellifluent were the words of the story. Presently she put out her candle, and, with a confused babel of voices close to her ear, and faint swift pictures before her eyes, she fell asleep.

And in the dead of night she rose out of her bed in dream, and with eyes wide open yet seeing nothing of reality, moved silently through the vacant house. Past the room where her grandmother was snoring in brief, heavy slumber, she stepped lightly and surely, and down the wide staircase. And Vega the far-shining stood over against the window above the slate roof. Ann walked into the strange room beneath as if she were being guided by the hand towards the oak chest. There, just as if she were dreaming it was her bed, she laid herself down in the old rose silk, in the fragrant place. But it was so dark in the room that the movement of the lid was indistinguishable.

Through the long day, the grandmother sat in her bow-window. Her lips were pursed, and she looked with dim, inquisitive scrutiny upon the street where people passed to and fro, and vehicles rolled by. At evening she climbed the stair and stood in the doorway of the large spare bedroom. The ascent had shortened her breath. Her magnifying spectacles rested upon her nose. Leaning her hand on the doorpost she peered in towards the glimmering square of window in the quiet gloom. But she could not see far, because her sight was dim and the light of day feeble. Nor could she detect the faint fragrance as of autumnal leaves. But in her mind was a tangled skein of memories – laughter and tears, and children long ago become old-fashioned, and the advent of friends, and last farewells. And gossiping fitfully, inarticulately, with herself, the old lady went down again to her window-seat.

OUT OF THE DEEP

THE STEELY LIGHT OF DAYBREAK, INCREASING IN VOLUME AND intensity as the east grew larger with the day, showed clearly at length that the prodigious yet elegant Arabian bed was empty. What might tenderly have cradled the slumbers of some exquisite Fair of romance now contained no human occupant at all. The whole immense room – its air dry and thin as if burnt – was quiet as a sepulchre.

To the right of the bed towered a vast and heavily carved wardrobe. To the left, a lofty fireplace of stone flanked by its grinning frigid dogs. A few cumbrous and obscure oil paintings hung on the walls. And, like the draperies of a proscenium, the fringed and valanced damask curtains on either side the two high windows, poured down their motionless cataract of crimson.

They had been left undrawn over night, and yet gave the scene a slight theatricality, a theatricality which the painted nymphs disporting themselves on the ceiling scarcely helped to dispel.

Not that these coy and ogling faces suggested any vestige of chagrin at the absence of the young man who for some weeks past had shared the long nights with them. They merely smiled on. For, after all, Jimmie's restless head upon the pillow had never really been in harmony with his pompous inanimate surroundings – the thin high nose, like the beak of a small ship, between the fast-sealed lids and narrow cheekbones, the narrow bird-like brow, the shell of the ear slightly pointed. If, inspired by the distant music of the spheres, the painted creatures had with this daybreak broken into song, it would certainly not have been to the tune of 'Oh Where, and Oh Where

Is My Little Dog Gone?' There was even less likelihood of Jimmie's voice now taking up their strains from out of the distance.

And yet, to judge from appearances, the tongue within that head might have been that of an extremely vivacious talker – even though, apart from Mrs Thripps, its talk these last few days had been for the most part with himself.

Indeed, as one of his friends had remarked: 'Don't you believe it. Jimmie has pots and pots to say, though he don't say it. That's what makes him such a dam good loser.' Whether or not; if Jimmie *had* been in the habit of conversing with himself, he must have had odd company at times.

Night after night he had lain there, flat on his back, his hands crossed on his breast – a pose that never failed to amuse him. A smooth eminence in the dark, rich quilt about sixty inches from his chin indicated to his attentive eye the points of his toes. The hours had been heavy, the hours had been long – still there are only twelve or so of utter darkness in the most tedious of nights, and matins tinkles at length. Excepting the last of them – a night, which was now apparently for ever over – he had occupied this majestic bed for about six weeks, though on no single occasion could he have confessed to being really at home in it.

He had chosen it, not from any characteristic whim or caprice, and certainly not because it dominated the room in which his Uncle Timothy himself used to sleep, yes, and for forty years on end, only at last to expire in it. He had chosen it because, when its Venetian blinds were pulled high up under the fringed cornice, it was as light as a London April sky could make it; and because – well, just one single glance in from the high narrow doorway upstairs had convinced him that the attic in which he was wont to sleep as a small boy was simply out of the question. A black heavy flood of rage swept over him at sight of it – he had never before positively realised the abominations of that early past. To a waif and stray any kind of shelter is, of course, a godsend, but even though this huge sumptuous barrack of a house had been left to him (or, rather, abandoned to him) by his Uncle Timothy's relict, Aunt Charlotte, Jimmie could not – even at his loosest – have been described as homeless.

Friendless rather – but that of his own deliberate choice. Not so very long ago, in fact, he had made a clean sweep of every single living being, male or female, to whom the term friend could, with some little elasticity, be applied. A little official affair, to put it politely, eased their exit. And then, this vacant hostel. The house, in fact (occupied only by a caretaker in the service of his aunt's lawyers) had been his for the asking at any time during the last two or three years. But he had steadily delayed taking possession of it until there was practically no alternative.

Circumstances accustom even a young man to a good many inconveniences. Still it would have been a little too quixotic to sleep in the street, even though his Uncle Timothy's house, as mere 'property', was little better than a white and unpleasing elephant. He could not sell it, that is, not *en masse*. It was more than dubious if he was legally entitled to make away with its contents.

But, quite apart from an extreme aversion to your Uncle Timothy's valuables in themselves, you cannot eat, even if you can subsist on, articles of *virtu*. Sir Richard Grenville – a hero for whom Jimmie had every respect – may have been accustomed to chewing up his wine-glass after swigging off its contents. But this must have been on the spur of an impulse, hardly in obedience to the instinct of self-preservation. Jimmie would have much preferred to balance a chair at the foot of his Uncle's Arabian bed and salute the smiling lips of the painted nymphs on the ceiling. Though even that experiment would probably have a rather gritty flavour. Still, possession is nine points of the law, and necessity is the deadly enemy of convention. Jimmie was unconscious of the faintest scruples on that score.

His scruples, indeed, were in another direction. Only a few days ago – the day, in fact, before his first indulgence in the queer experience of pulling the bell – he had sallied out with his Aunt Charlotte's black leather dressing bag positively bulging with a pair of Bow candlesticks, an illuminated missal, mutely exquisite, with its blues and golds and crimsons, and a tiny old silver-gilt bijouterie box. He was a young man of absurdly impulsive aversions, and the dealer to whom he carried this further consignment of loot was one of them.

After a rapid and contemptuous examination, this gentleman spread out his palms, shrugged his shoulders, and suggested a sum that would have caused even a more phlegmatic connoisseur than his customer's Uncle Timothy to turn in his grave.

And Jimmie replied, nicely slurring his r's, 'Really Mr So-and-so, it is impossible. No doubt the things have an artificial value, but not for me. I must ask you to oblige me by giving me only half the sum you have kindly mentioned. Rather than accept *your* figure, you know, I would—well, perhaps it would be impolite to tell you what I would prefer to do. *Dies irae, dies illa,* and so on.'

The dealer flushed, though he had been apparently content to leave it at that. He was not the man to be easily insulted by a good customer. And Jimmie's depredations were methodical. With the fastidiousness of an expert he selected from the rare and costly contents of the house only what was light and portable and became inconspicuous by its absence. The supply, he realised, though without any perceptible animation, however recklessly it might be squandered, would easily last out his lifetime.

Certainly *not*. After having once made up his mind to accept his Uncle Timothy's posthumous hospitality, the real difficulty was unlikely to be a conscientious one. It was the attempt merely to accustom himself to the house – the hated house – that grew more and more arduous. It falsified his hope that, like other experiences, this one would prove only the more piquant for being so precarious. Days and moments quickly flying – just his one funny old charwoman, Mrs Thripps, himself, and the Past.

After pausing awhile under the dingy and dusty portico, Jimmie had entered into his inheritance on the last afternoon in March. The wind was fallen; the day was beginning to narrow; a chill crystal light hung over the unshuttered staircase. By sheer force of a forgotten habit he at once ascended to the attic in which he had slept as a child.

Pausing on the threshold, he looked in, conscious not so much of the few familiar sticks of furniture – the trucklebed, the worn strip of Brussels carpet, the chipped blue-banded ewer and basin, the framed illuminated texts on the walls – as of a perfect hive of abhorrent memories.

That high cupboard in the corner from which certain bodiless shapes had been wont to issue and stoop at him cowering out of his dreams; the crab-patterned paper that came alive as you stared; the window cold with menacing stars; the mouseholes, the rusty grate – trumpet of every wind that blows – these objects at once lustily shouted at him in their own original tongues.

Quite apart from themselves, they reminded him of incidents and experiences which at the time could scarcely have been so nauseous as they now seemed in retrospect. He found himself suffocatingly resentful even of what must have been kindly intentions. He remembered how his Aunt Charlotte used to read to him – with her puffy cheeks, plump ringed hands, and the moving orbs of her eyes showing under her spectacles.

He wasn't exactly accusing the past. Even in his first breeches he was never what could be called a nice little boy. He had never ordered himself lowly and reverently to any of his betters – at least in their absence. Nevertheless, what stirred in his bosom as he gazed in on this discarded scene was certainly not remorse.

He remembered how gingerly and with what peculiar breathings, his Uncle Timothy used to lift his microscope out of its wooden case; and how, after the necessary manipulation of the instrument, he himself would be bidden mount a footstool and fix his dazzled eye on the slides of sluggish or darting horrors of minute magnified 'life'. And how, after a steady um-aw-ing drawl of inapprehensible instruction, his uncle would suddenly flick out a huge silk pocket handkerchief as a signal that little tongue-tied nervous boys were themselves nothing but miserable sluggish or darting reptiles, and that his nephew was the most deplorable kind of little boy.

Jimmie remembered, too, once asking the loose bow-shaped old gentleman in his chair if he might himself twist the wheel; and his Uncle Timothy had replied in a loud ringing voice, and almost as if he were addressing a public meeting: 'Um, ah, my boy, I say No to that!' He said No to most things, and just like that, if he vouchsafed speech at all.

And then there was Church on Sundays; and his hoop on week-days in the Crescent; and days when, with nothing to do, little Jimmie had been wont to sit watching the cold silvery rain on the window, the body he was in slowly congealing the while into a species of rancid suet pudding. Mornings too, when his Aunt Charlotte would talk nasally to him about Christianity; or when he was allowed to help his uncle and a tall, scared parlourmaid dust and re-arrange the contents of a cabinet or bureau. The smell of the air, the check duster, the odious *objets d'art* and the ageing old man snorting and looking like a superannuated Silenus beside the neat and frightened parlourmaid – it was a curious thing; though Death with his louring grin had beckoned him off: there he was – alive as ever.

And when amid these ruminations, Jimmie's eyes had at last fixed themselves on the frayed, dangling cord that hung from the ceiling over the trucklebed, it was because he had already explored all that the name Soames had stood for. Soames the butler – a black-clothed, tub-bellied, pompous man that might have been his Uncle Timothy's impoverished first cousin or illegitimate step-brother: Soames: Soames.

Soames used frequently to wring Jimmie's then protuberant ears. Soames sneaked habitually; and with a sort of gloating piety on his drooping face, was invariably present at the subsequent castigation. Soames had been wont to pile up his plate with lumps of fat that even Destiny had never intended should consort with any single leg of mutton or even sirloin of beef – jelly-like, rapidly cooling *nuggets* of fat. And Soames invariably brought him cold rice pudding when there was hot ginger roll.

Jimmie remembered the lines that drooped down from his pale long nose. The sleek set of his whiskers as he stood there in his coat-tails reflected in the glass of the sideboard, carving the Sunday joint.

But that slack green bell-cord! – his very first glimpse of it had set waggling *scores* of peculiar remembrances. First, and not so very peculiarly, perhaps, it recalled an occasion when, as he stood before his Aunt's footstool to bid her Good-night, her aggrieved pupils had visibly swum down from beneath their lids out of a nap, to fix themselves and look at him at last as if neither he nor she, either in this or in any other world, had ever so much as seen one another before. Perhaps his own face, if not so puffy, appeared that evening to be unusually pasty and pallid – with those dark rings which even to this day added vivacity and lustre to his extremely clear eyes. And his Aunt Charlotte had asked him why he was such a cowardly boy and so wickedly frightened of the dark.

'You know very well your dear Uncle will not permit gas in the attic, so there's no use asking for it. You have nothing on your conscience, I trust? You have not been talking to the servants?'

Infallible liar, he had shaken his head. And his Aunt Charlotte in return wagged hers at him.

'It's no good staring in that rebellious, sullen way at me. I have told you repeatedly that if you are really in need of anything, just ring the bell for Soames. A good little boy with nothing on his conscience *knows* that God watches over him. I hope you are at least trying to be a good little boy. There is a limit even to your Uncle's forbearance.'

It was perfectly true. Even bad little boys might be 'watched over' in the dead of night, and as for his Uncle Timothy's forbearance, he had discovered the limitations of that fairly early in life.

Well, it was a pity, he smiled to himself, that his Aunt Charlotte could not be present to see his Uncle Timothy's bedroom on that first celebration of their prodigal nephew's return. Jimmie's first foray had been to range the house from attic to cellar (where he had paused to rest) for candlesticks. And that night something like six dozen of the 'best wax' watched over his heavy and galvanic slumbers in the Arabian bed. Aunt Charlotte, now rather more accustomed to the dark even than Jimmie himself, would have opened her eyes at *that*.

Gamblers are naturally superstitious folk, he supposed; but that was the queerest feature of the whole thing. He had not then been conscious of even the slightest apprehension or speculation. It was far rather a kind of ribaldry than any sort of foreboding that had lit up positive constellations of candles as if for a Prince's – as if for a princely Cardinal's – lying-in-state.

It had taken a devil of a time too. His Uncle Timothy's port was not the less potent for a long spell of obscure mellowing, and the hand that held the taper had been a shaky one. Yet it had proved an amusing process too. Almost childish. Jimmie hadn't laughed like that for years. Certainly until then he had been unconscious of the feeblest squeamish inkling of anything – apart from old remembrances – peculiar in the house. And yet – well, no doubt even the first absurd impulsive experiment that followed *had* shaken him up.

Its result would have been less unexpected if he hadn't made a point and almost a duty of continually patrolling the horrible old vacant London mansion. Hardly a day had lately passed – and there was nothing better to do – but it found him on his rounds. He was not waiting for anything (except for the hour, maybe, when he would have to wait no more). Nevertheless, faithful as the sentinel on Elsinore's hoary ramparts, he would find himself day after day treading almost catlike on from room to room, surveying his paradoxical inheritance, jotting down a list in a nice order of the next 'sacrifices', grimacing at the Ming divinities, and pirouetting an occasional long nose at the portraits on the walls.

He had sometimes had a few words – animated ones, too – with Mrs Thripps, and perhaps if he could have persuaded himself to talk 'sensibly', and not to gesticulate, not to laugh himself so easily into a fit of coughing, she would have proved better company. She was amazingly honest and punctual and quiet; and why to heaven a woman with such excellent qualities should customarily wear so scared a gleam in her still, colourless eyes, and be so idiotically timid and nervous in his company, he could not imagine.

She was being paid handsome wages anyhow; and, naturally, he was aware of no rooted objection to other people helping themselves; at least if they managed it as skilfully as he did himself. But Mrs Thripps, it seemed, had never been able in any sense at all to help herself. She was simply a crape-bonneted 'motherly' creature, if not excessively intelligent, if a little slow in seeing 'points'. It was, indeed, her alarm when he asked her if she had happened to notice any young man about the house that had irritated him – though, of course, it was hardly fair not to explain what had given rise to the question. That was perfectly simple. It was like this—

For years – for centuries, in fact – Jimmie had been, except in certain unusual circumstances, an exceedingly bad sleeper. He still hated sleeping in the dark. But a multitude of candles at various degrees of exhaustion make rather lively company when you are sick of your Uncle Timothy's cellar. And even the best of vintage wines may prove an ineffectual soporific. His, too, was a wretchedly active mind.

Even as a boy he had thought a good deal about his uncle and aunt, and Soames, and the house, and the Rev Mr Grayson, and spectres, and schoolmasters, and painted nymphs, and running away to sea, and curios, and dead silence, and his early childhood. And though, since then, other enigmas had engaged his attention, this purely automatic and tiresome activity of mind still persisted.

On his oath he had been in some respects and in secret rather a goody-goody little boy; though his piety had been rather the off-spring of fear than of love. Had he not been expelled from Mellish's almost solely for that reason? What on earth was the good of repeatedly thrashing a boy when you positively knew that he had lied merely from terror of your roaring voice and horrible white face?

But there it was; if there had been someone to talk to, he would not have talked so much to himself. He would not have lain awake thinking, night after night, like a rat in a trap. Thinking was like a fountain. Once it gets going at a certain pressure, well, it is almost impossible to turn it off. And, my hat! what odd things come up with the water!

On the particular night in question, in spite of the candles and the mice and the moon, he badly wanted company. In a moment of pining yet listless jocosity, then, he had merely taken his Aunt Charlotte's advice. True, the sumptuous, crimson, pleated silk bell-pull, dangling like a serpent with a huge tassel for skull over his Uncle Timothy's pillow, was a more formidable instrument than the yard or two of frayed green cord in the attic. Yet they shared the same purpose. Many a time must his Uncle Timothy have stretched up a large loose hand in that direction when in need of Soames's nocturnal ministrations. And now, alas, both master and man were long since gone the way of all flesh. You couldn't, it appeared, pull bells in your coffin.

But Jimmie was not as yet in his coffin, and as soon as his fingers slipped down from the smooth pull, the problem, in the abstract, as it were, began to fascinate him. With cold froggy hands crossed over his beautiful puce-patterned pyjamas, he lay staring at the crimson tassel till he had actually seen the hidden fangs flickeringly jet out at him.

The effort, then, must have needed some little courage. It *might* almost have needed a tinge of inspiration. It was in no sense intended as a challenge. He would, in fact, rather remain alone than chance summoning – well, *any* (once animate) relic of the distant past. But obviously the most practical way of proving – if only to yourself – that you can be content with your own reconnaissances in the very dead of night, was to demonstrate to that self that, even if you should ask for it, assistance would not be forthcoming.

He had been as fantastic as that. At the prolonged, pulsating, faint, distant tintinnabulation he had fallen back on to his pillow with an absurd little quicket of laughter, like that of a naughty boy up to mischief. But instant sobriety followed. Poor sleepers should endeavour to compose themselves. Tampering with empty space, stirring up echoes in pitch-black pits of darkness is scarcely sedative. And then, as he lay striving with extraordinary fervour not to listen, but to concentrate his mind on the wardrobe, and to keep his eyes from the door, that door must gently have opened.

It must have opened, and as noiselessly closed again. For a more or less decent-looking young man, seemingly not a day older than himself, was now apparent in the room. It might almost be said that he had insinuated himself into the room. But well-trained domestics are accustomed to move their limbs and bodies with a becoming unobtrusiveness. There was also that familiar slight inclination of the apologetic in this young man's pose, as he stood there solitary in his black, in that terrific blaze of candle-light. And for a sheer solid minute the occupant of the Arabian bed had really stopped thinking.

When indeed you positively press your face, so to speak, against the crystalline window of your eyes, your mind is apt to become a perfect vacuum. And Jimmie's first rapid and instinctive 'Who the devil...?' had remained inaudible.

In the course of the next few days Jimmie was to become familiar (at least in memory) with the looks of this new young butler or valet. But first impressions are usually the vividest. The dark blue-grey eyes, the high nose, the scarcely perceptible smile, the slight stoop of the shoulders – there was no doubt of it. There was just a flavour, a flicker, there, of resemblance to himself. Not that he himself could ever have cut as respectful and respectable a figure as that. And the smile! – the fellow seemed to be ruminating over a thousand dubious, long-interred secrets, secrets such as one may be a little cautious of digging up even to share with one's self.

His face turned sidelong on his pillow, and through air as visibly transparent as a sheet of glass, Jimmie had steadily regarded this strange bell-answerer; and the bell-answerer had never so much as stirred his frigid glittering eyes in response. The silence that hung between them produced eventually a peculiar effect on Jimmie. Menials as a general rule should be less emphatic personally. Their unobtrusiveness should surely not emphasise their immanence. It had been Jimmie who was the first to withdraw his eyes, only once more to find them settling as if spellbound on those of his visitor.

Yet, after all, there was nothing to take offence at in the young man's countenance or attitude. He did not seem even to be thinking-back at the bell-puller; but merely to be awaiting instructions. Yet Jimmie's heart at once rapidly began to beat again beneath his icy hands. And at last he made a perfectly idiotic response.

Wagging his head on his pillow, he turned abruptly away. 'It was only to tell you that I shall need nothing more tonight,' he had said.

Good heavens. The fatuity of it! He wanted, thirsted for, scores upon scores of things. Aladdin's was the cupidity of a simpleton by comparison. Time, and the past, for instance, and the ability to breathe again as easily as if it were natural – as natural as the pro-cesses of digestion. Why, if you were intent only on a little innocent companionship, one or two of those nymphs up there would be far more amusing company than Mrs Thripps. If, that is, apart from yearning to their harps and viols, they could have been persuaded to scrub and sweep. Jimmie wanted no other kind of help. There is a beauty that is but skin-deep.

Altogether it had been a far from satisfactory experience. Jimmie was nettled. His mincing tones echoed on in his mind. They must have suggested that he was unaccustomed to menservants and bell-pulls and opulent surroundings. And the fellow had instantly taken him at his word. A solemn little rather agreeable and unservile inclination of the not unfriendly head – and he was gone.

And there was Jimmie, absolutely exhausted, coughing his lungs out, and entirely incapable of concluding whether the new butler was a creature of actuality or of dream. Well, well, well: that was nothing new. That's just how things do take one in one's weak moments, in the dead of night. Nevertheless, the experience had apparently proved sedative. He had slept like an infant.

The morning found him vivacious with curiosity. He had paused to make only an exceedingly negligent toilet before beginning his usual wanderings about the house. Calm cold daylight reflection may dismiss almost any nocturnal experience as a dream, if, at any rate, one's temperature in the night hours is habitually above the norm. But Jimmie could not, or would not, absolutely make up his mind. So clear a picture had his visitant imprinted on his memory that he even found himself (just like a specialist sounding a patient in search of the secret ravages of phthisis) – he had even found himself stealthily tapping over the basement walls – as if in search of a concealed pantry! A foolish proceeding if one has not the least desire in the world to attract the attention of one's neighbours.

Having at length satisfied himself in a rather confused fashion that whatever understudy of Soames might share the house with him in the small hours, he must be a butler of the migratory order, Jimmie then began experimenting with the bells. Mounted on a kitchen chair, cornice brush in hand, he had been surprised by Mrs Thripps, in her quiet boots, as he stood gently knocking one by one the full eighteen of the long, greened, crooked jingle row which hung open-mouthed above the immense dresser.

She had caught him in the act, and Jimmie had once more exercised his customary glib presence of mind.

'They ought to be hung in a scale, you know. Oughtn't they, Mrs Thripps? Then we could have "Home, Sweet Home!" and a hunting up and a hunting down, grandsires and treble bobs, and a grand maximus, even on week days. And if we were in danger of any kind of fire – which *you* will never be, we could ring them backwards. *Couldn't* we, Mrs Thripps? Not that there's much quality in them – no medieval monkish tone or timbre in *them*. They're a bit mouldy, too, and one can't tell t'other from which. Not like St Faiths's! One would recognise that old clanker in one's shroud, wouldn't one, Mrs Thripps? Has it ever occurred to you that the first campanologist's real intention was not so much to call the congregation, as to summon – well – what the congregation's after?'

'Yes, sir,' Mrs Thripps had agreed, her watery grey eyes fixed largely on the elevated young man. 'But it don't matter which of them you ring; I'll answer *hany* – at least while I'm in the house. I don't think, sir, you rest your mind enough. My own boy, now; *he's* in the Navy...'

But with one graceful flourish Jimmie had run his long-handled brush clean east to west along the clanging row. 'You mustn't,' he shouted, 'you shouldn't. Once aboard the lugger, they are free! It's you *mothers*...' He gently shook his peculiar wand at the flat-looking little old woman. 'No, Mrs Thripps; what I'm after is he who is here, *here! Couchant, perdu, laired,* in these same subterranean vaults when you and I are snug in our nightcaps. A most nice-spoken young man! *Not* in the Navy, Mrs Thripps!' And before the old lady had had time to seize any one of these seductive threads of conversation, Jimmie had flashed his usual brilliant smile or grimace at her, and soon afterwards sallied out of the house to purchase a further gross or two of candles.

Gently and furtively pushing across the counter half a sovereign – not as a douceur, but merely as from friend to friend – he had similarly smiled back at the secretive-looking old assistant in the staid West End family-grocer's.

'No, I didn't suppose you *could* remember me. One alters. One ages. One deals elsewhere. But anyhow, a Happy New Year to you – if the next ever comes, you know.'

'You see, sir,' the straight-aproned old man had retorted with equal confidentiality, 'it is not so much the alterations. They are what you might call un-cir-cum-ventible, sir. It's the stream, sir. Behind the counter here, we are like rocks in it. But even if I can't for the moment put a thought to your face – though it's already stirring in me in a manner of speaking, I shall in the future, sir. You may rely upon that. And the same, sir, to you; and many *of* them, I'm sure.'

Somehow or other Jimmie's vanity had been mollified by this pleasing little ceremoniousness; and that even before he had smiled yet once again at the saffron young lady in the Pay Box.

'The truth is, my dear,' he had assured himself, as he once more ascended into the dingy porch, 'the truth *is* when once you begin to tamper, you won't know where you are. You won't, really.'

And that night he had lain soberly on, in a peculiar state of physical quiescence and self-satisfaction, his dark bright eyes wandering from nymph to nymph, his hands folded over his breast under the bedclothes, his heart persisting in its usual habits. Nevertheless, the fountain of his thoughts had continued softly to plash on its worn basin. With ears a-cock, he had frankly enjoyed inhaling the parched, spent, brilliant air.

And when his fingers had at last manifested the faintest possible itch to experiment once more with the bell-pull, he had slipped out of bed, and hastily searching through a little privy case of his uncle's bedside books, had presently slipped back again, armed with a fat little copy of *The Mysteries of Paris,* in its original French.

The next day a horrible lassitude descended upon him. For the better part of an hour he had stood staring out of the drawing-room window into the London street. At last, with a yawn that was almost a groan, and with an absurdly disproportionate effort, he turned himself about. Heavily hung the gilded chandeliers in the long vista of the room; heavily gloomed the gilded furniture. Scarcely distinguishable in the obscurity of the further wall stood watching him from a mirror what might have appeared to be the shadowy reflection of himself. With a still, yet extreme aversion he kept his eyes fixed on this distant nonentity, hardly realising his own fantastic resolve that if he did catch the least, faint independent movement there, he would give Soames Junior a caustic piece of his mind…

He must have been abominably fast asleep for hours when, a night or two afterwards, he had suddenly awakened, sweat streaming along his body, his mouth stretched to a long narrow O, and his right hand clutching the bell-rope, as might a drowning man at a straw.

The room was adrowse with light. All was still. The flitting horrors between dream and wake in his mind were already thinning into air. Through their transparency he looked out once more on the substantial, the familiar. His breath came heavily, like puffs of wind over a stormy sea, and yet a profound peace and tranquillity was swathing him in. The relaxed mouth was now faintly smiling. Not a sound, not the feeblest, distant unintended tinkling was trembling up from the abyss. And for a moment or two the young man refrained even from turning his head at the soundless opening and closing of the door.

He lay fully conscious that he was not alone; that quiet eyes had him steadily in regard. But, like rats, his wits were beginning to busy themselves again. Sheer relief from the terrors of sleep, shame of his extremity and weakness, a festering sense of humiliation – yes, he must save his face at all costs. He must put this preposterous spying valet in his place. Oddly enough, too, out of the deeps a peculiar little vision of recollection had inexplicably obtruded itself into consciousness. It would be a witticism of the first water.

'They are dreadfully out of season, you know,' he began murmuring affectedly into the hush, 'dreadfully. But what I'm really pining for is a bunch of primroses... A primrose by the river's brim... *must* be a little conservative.' His voice was once more trailing off into a maudlin drowsiness. With an effort he roused himself, and now with an extremely sharp twist of his head, he turned to confront his visitor.

But the room was already vacant, the door ajar, and Jimmie's lids were on the point of closing again, sliding down over his tired eyes like leaden shutters which no power on earth could hinder or restrain, when at the faintest far whisper of sound they swept back suddenly – and almost incredibly wide – to drink in all they could of the spectacle of a small odd-looking child who at that moment had embodied herself in the doorway.

She seemed to have not the least intention of returning the compliment. Her whole gaze, from out of her fair flaxen-pigtailed face, was fixed on the coarse blue-banded kitchen bowl which she was carrying with extreme care and caution in her two narrow hands. The idiots down below had evidently filled it too full of water, for the pale wide-petalled flowers and thick crinkled leaves it contained were floating buoyantly nid-nod to and fro as she moved – pushing on each slippered foot in turn in front of the other, her whole mind concentrated on her task.

A plain child, but extraordinarily fair, as fair as the primroses themselves in the congregation of candle-light that motionlessly flooded the room – a narrow-chested long-chinned little creature who had evidently outgrown her strength. Jimmie was well accustomed to take things as they come; and his brief sojourn in his uncle's house in his present state of health had already enlarged the confines of the term 'thing'. Anyhow, she was a relief from the valet.

He found himself, then, watching this new visitor without the least trace of astonishment or even of surprise. And as his dark eyes coursed over the child, he simply couldn't decide whether she most closely 'took after' Soames Junior or Mrs Thripps. All he could positively assure himself of was just the look, 'the family likeness'. And that in itself was a queerish coincidence, since whatever your views might be regarding Soames Junior, Mrs Thripps was real enough – as real, at any rate, as her scrubbing-brush and her wholesome evil-smelling soap.

As a matter of fact, Jimmie was taking a very tight hold of himself. His mind might fancifully be compared to a quiet green swarming valley between steep rock-bound hills in which a violent battle was proceeding – standards and horsemen and smoke and terror and violence – but no sound.

Deep down somewhere he really wanted to be 'nice' to the child. She meant no ill; she was a demure faraway harmless-looking creature. Ages ago... On the other hand he wished to heaven they would leave him alone. They were pestering him. He knew perfectly well how far he was gone, and bitterly resented this renewed interference. And if there was one thing he detested, it was being made to look silly – 'I hope you are trying to be a good little boy?... You have not been talking to the servants?' That kind of thing.

It was, therefore, with mixed feelings and with a tinge of shame-facedness that he heard his own sneering, toneless voice insinuate itself into the silence; 'And what, missikins, can I do for you?...

What, you will understand; not *How?*' The sneer had degenerated into a snarl.

The child at this had not perceptibly faltered. Her face had seemed to lengthen a little, but that might have been due solely to her efforts to deliver her bowl without spilling its contents. Indeed she actually succeeded in so doing, almost before Jimmie had time to withdraw abruptly from the little gilt-railed table on which she deposited the clumsy pot. Frock, pigtail, red hands – she seemed to be as 'real' a fellow creature as you might wish to see. But Jimmie stared quizzically on. Unfortunately primroses have no scent, so that he could not call on his nose to bear witness to his eyes. And the congested conflict in the green valley was still proceeding.

The child had paused. Her hands hung down now as if they were accustomed to service; and her pale blue eyes were fixed on his face in that exasperating manner which suggests that the owner of them is otherwise engaged. Not that she was looking *through* him. Even the sharpest of his 'female friends' had never been able to boast of that little accomplishment. She was looking into him; and as if he occupied time rather than space. Or was she, sneered that weary inward voice again, was she merely waiting for a tip?

'Look here,' said Jimmie, dexterously raising himself to his elbow on the immense lace-fringed pillow, 'it's all very well; you have managed things quite admirably, considering your age and the season, and so on. But I didn't ask for primroses, I asked for violets. That's a very old trick – very old trick.'

For one further instant, dark and fair, crafty and simpleton face communed, each with each. But the smile on the one had fainted into a profound childlike contemplation. And then, so swift and imperceptible had been his visitant's envanishment out of the room, that the very space she had occupied seemed to remain for a while outlined in the air – a nebulous shell of vacancy. She must, apparently, have glided *backwards* through the doorway, for Jimmie had assuredly not been conscious of the remotest glimpse of her pigtail from behind.

Instantly on that, the stony hillside within had resounded with a furious clangour – cries and shouts and screamings – and Jimmie, his face bloodless with rage, his eyes almost blind with it, had leapt out of the great bed as if in murderous pursuit. There must, however, have been an unusual degree or so of fever in his veins that night, so swift was his reaction. For the moment he was on his feet an almost unendurable self-pity had swept into possession of him. To take a poor devil as literally as that! To catch him off his guard; not to give him the mere fleck of an opportunity to get his balance, to explain, to answer back! Curse the primroses.

But there was no time to lose.

With one hand clutching his pyjamas, the other carrying the bowl, he poked forward out of the flare of the room into the cold lightlessness of the wide stone staircase.

'Look here,' he called down in a low argumentative voice, 'look here, You! You can cheat and you can cheat, but to half strangle a fellow in his sleep, and then send him up the snuffling caretaker's daughter – No, No... Next time, you old makebelieve, we'd prefer company a little more – a little more *congenial.*'

He swayed slightly, grimacing vacantly into the darkness, and listening to his speech as dimly as might a somnambulist to the distant roar of falling water. And then, poor benighted creature, Jimmie tried to spit, but his lips and tongue were dry, and that particular insult was spared him.

He had stooped laboriously, had put down the earthenware bowl on the Persian mat at the head of the staircase, and was self-congratulatorily re-welcoming himself into the scene of still lustre he had dared for that protracted minute to abandon, when he heard as if from beneath and behind him a kind of lolloping disquietude and the sound as of a clumsy-clawed, but persistent animal pushing its uncustomary awkward way up the soap-polished marble staircase.

It was to be tit for tat, then. The miserable ménage had let loose its menagerie. That. They were going to experiment with the mouse-cupboard-and-keyhole trickery of his childhood. Jimmie was violently shivering; his very toes were clinging to the mat on which he stood.

Swaying a little, and casting at the same time a strained whitened glance round the room in which every object rested in the light as if so it had rested from all eternity, he stood mutely and ghastly listening.

Even a large bedroom, five times the size of a small boy's attic, affords little scope for a fugitive, and shutting your eyes, darkening your outward face, is no escape. It had been a silly boast, he agreed – that challenge, that 'dare' on the staircase; the boast of an idiot. For the 'congenial company' that had now managed to hoof and scrabble its way up the slippery marble staircase was already on the threshold.

All was utterly silent now. There was no obvious manifestation of danger. What was peering steadily in upon him out of the obscurity beyond the door, was merely a blurred whitish beast-like shape with still, passive, almost stagnant eyes in its immense fixed face. A perfectly ludicrous object – on paper. Yet a creature so nauseous to soul and body, and with so obscene a greed in its motionless piglike grin that with one vertiginous swirl Jimmie's candles had swept up in his hand like a lateral race of streaming planets into outer darkness.

If his wet groping fingers had not then encountered one of the carved pedestals of his uncle's bedstead, Jimmie would have fallen; Jimmie would have found, in fact, the thing's physical level.

*

Try as he might, he had never in the days that followed made quite clear in his mind why for the third time he had not made a desperate plunging clutch at the bell-rope. The thing *must* have been Soames Junior's emissary, even if the bird-faced scullery maid with the primroses had not also been one of the 'staff'.

That he had desisted simply in case she should herself have answered his summons and so have encountered the spurious animal as she mounted the dark staircase seemed literally too 'good' to be true. Not only was Jimmie no sentimentalist, but that particular kind of goodness, even in a state of mind perfectly calm and collected, was not one of his pleasanter characteristics.

Yet facts are facts – even comforting ones. And unless his memory was utterly untrustworthy, he had somehow – somehow contrived to regain his physical balance. Candelabrum in hand, he had actually, indeed, at last emerged from the room, and stooped his dark head over the balusters in search of what unaccountably had *not* awaited his nearer acquaintance. And he had – he must have – flung the substantial little blue-banded slop-basin, primroses and all, clean straight down in the direction of any kind of sentient target that happened to be in its way.

'You must understand, Mrs Thripps,' he had afterwards solemnly explained, 'I don't care to be disturbed, and particularly at night. All litter should, of course, be immediately cleared away. That's merely as things go in a well-regulated household, as, in fact, they *do* go. And I see you have replaced the one or two little specimens I was looking over out of the cabinet on the staircase. Pretty things, too; though you hadn't the advantage of being in the service of their late owner – my uncle. As I was. Of course, too, breakages cannot be avoided. There, I assure you, you are absolutely free. Moth and rust, Mrs Thripps. No; all that I was merely enquiring about at the moment is that particular pot. There was an accident last night – primroses and so on. And one might have expected, one might almost have sworn, Mrs Thripps, that at least a shard or two, as the Psalmist says, would have been pretty conspicuous even if the water *had* completely dried away. Not that I heard the smash, mind. I don't go so far as that. Nor am I making any insinuations *whatever.* You are the best of good creatures, you are indeed – and it's no good looking at me like Patience on a monument; because at present life is real and life is earnest. All I mean is that if one for a single moment ceases to guide one's conduct on reasonable lines – well, one comes a perfectly indescribable cropper, Mrs Thripps. Like the pot.'

Mrs Thripps's grey untidy head had remained oddly stuck out from her body throughout this harangue. 'No, sir,' she repeated once more. 'High and low I've searched the house down, and there isn't a shadder of what you might be referring to, not a shadder. And once more, I ask you, sir; let me call in Dr Stokes. He's a very nice gentle-man; and one as keeps what should be kept as close to himself as it being his duty he sees right and proper to do. Chasing and racketing of yourself up and down these runs of naked stairs – in the dead of night – is no proper place for you, sir, in *your* state. And I don't like to take the responsibility. It's first the candles, then the bells, and then the kitching, and then the bason; I know what I'm talking about, sir, having lost two, and one at sea.'

'And suppose, my dear,' Jimmie had almost as brilliantly as ever smiled; 'suppose we are all of us "at sea". What then?'

'Why then, sir,' Mrs Thripps had courageously retorted, 'I'd as lief be at the bottom of it. There's been as much worry and trouble and making two ends meet in *my* life not to make the getting out of it what you'd stand on no ceremony for. I say it with all decent respect for what's respectful and proper, sir; but there isn't a morning

I step down those area steps but my heart's in my mouth for fear there won't be anything in the house but what can't answer back. It's been a struggle to keep on, sir; and you as generous a gentleman as need be, if only you'd remain warm and natural in your bed when once there.'

A little inward trickle of laughter had entertained Jimmie as he watched the shapeless patient old mouth utter these last few words.

'That's just it, Mrs Thripps,' he had replied softly. 'You've done for me far more effectively than anyone I care to remember in my insignificant little lifetime. You have indeed.' Jimmie had even touched the hand bent like the claw of a bird around the broomhandle. 'In fact, you know – and I'm bound to confess it as gratefully as need be – they are *all* of them doing for me as fast as they can. I don't complain, not the least little bit in the world. All that I might be asking is, How the devil – to put it politely – how the goodness gracious is one to tell which is which? In my particular case, it seems to be the miller that sets the wind: not, of course, that he's got any particular grain to grind. Not even wild oats, you funny old mother of a youthful mariner. No, no, no. Even the fact that there wasn't perhaps any pot after all, you will understand, doesn't positively prove that neither could there have been any primroses. And before next January's four months old we shall be at the end of yet another April. At least—' and a sort of almost bluish pallor had spread like a shadow over his face – 'at least you will be. All of which is only to say, dear Madam, as Beaconsfield remarked to Old Vic, that I am thanking you *now*.'

At which Mrs Thripps immediately fell upon her knees on her housemaid's pad and plunged her hands into her zinc pail – only instantly after to sit back on her heels, skinny hands on canvas apron. 'All I says, sir, is, We go as we go; and a nicer gentleman, taking things on the surface, I never worked for. But one don't want to move too much in the Public Heye, sir. Of all the houses below stairs I've worked for and all alone in I don't want to charnst on a more private in a manner of speaking than this. All that I was saying, sir, and I wouldn't to none but you, is the life's getting on my nerves. When that door there closes after me, and every day drawing out steady as you can see without so much as glancing at the clock – I say, to myself, Well, better that pore young gentleman alone up there at night, cough and all, than *me*. I wouldn't sleep in this house, sir, not if you was to offer me a plateful of sovereigns... Unless, sir, you *wanted* me.'

On reflection Jimmie decided that he had cut almost a gallant figure as he had retorted gaily – yet with extraordinary sobriety: 'You shall have a whole dishful before I'm done, Mrs Thripps – with a big scoop in it for the gravy. But on my oath, I assure you there's absolutely nothing or nobody in this old barn of a museum except you and me. Nobody, unless, of course, you will understand, one happens to pull the bell. And that we're not likely to do in broad daylight. Are we, Mrs Thripps?' Upon which he had hastily caught up his aunt's handbag and had emerged into a daylight a good deal bleaker if not broader than he could gratefully stomach.

For a while Jimmie had let well alone. Indeed, if it had been a mere matter of choice, he would far rather have engaged in a friendly and jocular conversation of this description with his old charwoman than in the endless monologues in which he found himself submerged on other occasions. One later afternoon, for instance, at half-past three by his watch, sitting there by a small fire in the large muffled drawing room, he at length came definitely to the conclusion that some kind of finality should be reached in his relations with the Night Staff in his Uncle Timothy's.

It was pretty certain that *his* visit would soon be drawing to a close. Staying out at night until he was almost too exhausted to climb down to the pavement from his hansom – the first April silver of dawn warning the stark and empty chimney-pots – had proved a dull and tedious alternative. The mere spectator of gaiety, he concluded, as he stared at the immense picture of the Colosseum on his Uncle Timothy's wall, may have as boring a time as must the slaves who cleaned out the cages of the lions that ate the Christians. And snapping out insults at former old cronies who couldn't help their faces being as tiresome as a whitewashed pigsty had soon grown wearisome.

Jimmie, of course, was accustomed to taking no interest in things which did not interest him; but quite respectable people could manage that equally well. What fretted him almost beyond endurance was an increasing inability to keep his attention fixed on what was really *there*, what at least all such respectable people, one might suppose, would unanimously agree was there.

A moment's fixture of the eyes – and he would find himself steadily, steadily listening, now in a creeping dread that somewhere, down below, there was a good deal that needed an almost constant attention, and now in sudden alarm that, after all, there was absolutely nothing. Again and again in recollection he had hung over the unlighted staircase listening in an extremity of foreboding for the outbreak of a rabbit-like childish squeal of terror which would have proved – well, *what* would it have proved? My God, what a world! you can prove nothing.

The fact that he was all but certain that any such intolerably helpless squeal never *had* wailed up to him out of its pit of blackness could be only a partial consolation. He hadn't meant to be a beast. It was only his facetious little way. And you would have to be something pretty piggish in pigs to betray a child – however insubstantial – into the nausea and vertigo he had experienced in the presence of that unspeakable abortion. The whole thing had become a fatuous obsession. If, it appeared, you only remained solitary and secluded enough, and let your mind wander on in its own sweet way, the problem was almost bound to become, if not your one and only, at least your chief concern. Unless you were preternaturally busy and preoccupied, you simply couldn't live on and on in a haunted house without being occasionally reminded of its ghosts.

To dismiss the matter as pure illusion – the spectral picturing of life's fitful fever – might be all very well; that is if you had the blood of a fish. But who on earth had ever found the world the pleasanter and sweeter a place to bid good-bye to simply because it was obviously 'substantial', whatever *that* might mean? Simply because it did nothing you wanted it to do unless you paid for it pretty handsomely; or unless you accepted what it proffered with as open a hospitality as Jimmie had bestowed on his pilgrims of the night. Not that he much wanted – however pressing the invitation – to wander off out of his body into a better world, or, for that matter, into a worse.

Upstairs under the roof years ago Jimmie as a small boy would rather have died of terror than meddle with the cord above his bed-rail – simply because he knew that Soames Senior was at the other end of it. He had hated Soames; he had merely feared the nothings of his night hours. But, suppose Soames had been a different kind of butler. There must be almost as many kinds as there are human beings. Suppose his Uncle Timothy and Aunt Charlotte had chosen theirs a little less idiosyncratically; what then?

Well, anyhow, in a sense, he was not sorry life had been a little exciting these last few weeks. How odd that what all but jellied your soul in your body at night or in a dream, might merely amuse you like a shilling shocker in the safety of day. The safety of day – at the very cadence of the words in his mind, as he sat there in his aunt's 'salon', his limbs huddled over Mrs Thripps's fire, Jimmie's eyes had fixed themselves again. Again he was listening. Was it that, if you saw 'in your mind' *any* distant room or place, that place must actually at the moment contain you – some self, some 'astral body'? If so, wouldn't, of course, you *hear* yourself moving about in it?

There was a slight whining wind in the street outside the rainy window that afternoon, and once more the bright idea crossed Jimmie's mind that he should steal upstairs before it was dark, mount up onto the Arabian bed and just cut the bell-pull – once for all. But would that necessarily dismiss the Staff? Necessarily? His eye wandered to the discreet S of yet another bell-pull – that which graced the wall beneath the expansive white marble chimney-piece.

He hesitated. There was no doubt his mind was now hopelessly jaundiced against all bell-ropes – whether they failed to summon one to church or persisted in summoning one to a six-foot hole in a cemetery. His Uncle Timothy lay in a mausoleum. On the other hand he was properly convinced that a gentleman is as a gentleman does, and that it was really 'up to you' to treat *all* bell-answerers with decent courtesy. No matter who, when, where. A universal rule like that is a sheer godsend. If they didn't answer, well, you couldn't help yourself. Or rather, you would have to.

This shivering was merely physical. When a fellow is so thin that he can almost hear his ribs grind one against the other when he stoops to pick up a poker, such symptoms must be expected. There was still an hour or two of daylight – even though clouds admitted only a greyish light upon the world, and his Uncle Timothy's house was by nature friendly to gloom. That house at this moment seemed to hang domed upon his shoulders like an immense imponderable shell. The flames in the chimney whispered, fluttered, hovered, like fitfully playing, once-happy birds.

Supposing if, even against his better judgement, he leaned forward now in his chair and – what was infinitely more conventional and in a sense more proper than summoning unforeseen entities to one's bedside – supposing he gave just one discreet little tug at that small porcelain knob; what would he ask for? He need ask nothing. He could act. Yes, if he could be perfectly sure that some monstrous porcine caco-demon akin to the shapes of childish nightmare would come hoofing up out of the deeps at his behest – well, he would chance it. He would have it out with the brute. It was still day.

It was still day. But, maybe, the ear of pleasanter visitors might catch the muffled tinkle? In the young man's mind there was now no vestige of jocularity. In an instant's lightness of heart he had once thought of purchasing from the stiff-aproned old assistant at his Aunt Charlotte's family grocer's, a thumping big box of chocolates. Why, just that one small bowl in *famille rose* up there could be bartered for the prettiest little necklet of seed pearls. She had done her best – with her skimpy shoulders, skimpier pigtail and soda-reddened hands. Pigtail! But no; you might pull real bells: to pull dubiously genuine pigtails seemed now a feeble jest. The old Jimmie of that kind of facetiousness was a thing of the past.

Apart from pigs and tweeny-maids, what other peculiar emanations might in the future respond to his summonings, Jimmie's exhausted imagination could only faintly prefigure. For a few minutes a modern St Anthony sat there in solitude in the vast half-blinded London drawing-room; while shapes and images and apparitions of memory and fantasy sprang into thin being and passed away in his mind. No, no.

'Do to the Book; quench the candles;
Ring the bell. *Amen, Amen.*'

– he was done with all that. Maledictions and anathemas; they only
tangled the hank.

So when at last – his meagre stooping body mutely played on by
the flamelight – he jerked round his dark narrow head to glance at
the distant mirror, it must have been on the mere after-image, so to
speak, of the once quite substantial-looking tweeny-maid that his
exhausted eyes thirstily fixed themselves.

She was there – over there, where Soames Junior had more than
once taken up his obsequious station. She was smiling – if the dusk
of the room could be trusted that far; and not through, but really *at*
Jimmie. She was fairer than ever, fairer than the flaxenest of nymphs
on his uncle's ceiling, fairer than the saffronest of young ladies in the
respectablest of family grocers, fairer even than—

Jimmie hung on this simple vision as did Dives on the spectacle
of Lazarus in bliss. At once, of course, after his very first sigh of
relief and welcome, he had turned back on his lips a glib little speech
suggesting forgiveness – Let auld acquaintance be forgot; that kind
of thing. He was too tired even to be clever now. And the oddest of
convictions had at once come into his mind – seemed almost to fill
his body even – that she was waiting for something else. Yes, she was
smiling as if in hope. She was waiting to be told to go. Jimmie was
no father. He didn't want to be considerate to the raw little creature,
to cling to her company for but a few minutes longer, with a view to
returns in kind. No, nothing of all that. 'Oh, me God; my God!' a voice
groaned within him, but not at any unprecedented jag or stab of pain.

The child was still waiting. Quite quietly there – as if a shadow,
as if a secret and obscure ray of light. And it seemed to Jimmie that

in its patient face hung veil upon veil of uncountable faces of the past – in paint, stone, actuality, dream – that he had glanced at or brooded on in the enormous history of his life. That he may have coveted, too. And as well as his rebellious features could and would, he smiled back at her.

'I understand, my dear,' he drew back his dry lips to explain. 'Perfectly. And it was courtesy itself of you to look in when I didn't ring. I *didn't*. I absolutely put my tongue out at the grinning old knob... But no more of that. One mustn't talk for talking's sake. Else, why all those old Trappists... though none of 'em such a bag-of-bones as me, I bet. But without jesting, you know...'

Once more a distant voice within spoke in Jimmie's ear. 'It's important'; it said. 'You really must hold your tongue – until, well, it holds itself.' But Jimmie's face continued to smile.

And then suddenly, every vestige of amusement abandoned it. He stared baldly, almost emptily at the faint inmate of his solitude. 'All that I have to say,' he muttered, 'is just this: – I have Mrs Thripps. I haven't absolutely cut the wire. I wish to be alone. But if I ring, I'm not *asking*, do you see? In time I may be able to know what I want. But what is important now is that no more than that accursed Pig were your primroses 'real', my dear. You see things *must* be real. And now, I suppose,' he had begun shivering again, 'you must go to – you must go. But listen! listen! We part friends!'

The coals in the grate, with a scarcely audible shuffling, recomposed themselves to their consuming.

When there hasn't been anything there, nothing can be said to have vanished from the place where it has not been. Still, Jimmie had felt infinitely colder and immeasurably lonelier when his mouth had thus fallen to silence; and he was so empty and completely exhausted that his one apprehension had been lest he should be unable to ascend the staircase to get to bed. There was no doubt of it: his ultimatum had been instantly effective. The whole house was now preternaturally empty. It was needless even to listen to prove that. So absolute was its pervasive quietude that when at last he gathered his bones together in the effort to rise, to judge from the withering colour of the cinders and ashes in the fireplace, he must have been for some hours asleep; and daybreak must be near.

He managed the feat at last, gathered up the tartan travelling shawl that had tented in his scarecrow knees, and lit the only candle in its crystal stick in his Aunt Charlotte's drawing-room. And it was an almost quixotically peaceful though forebodeful Jimmie who, step by step, the fountain of his thoughts completely stilled, his night-mind as clear and sparkling as a cavern bedangled with stalagmites and stalactites, climbed laboriously on and up, from wide shallow marble stair to stair.

He paused in the corridor above. But the nymphs within – Muses, Graces, Fates, what not – piped in vain their mute decoy. His Uncle Timothy's Arabian bed in vain summoned him to its downy embraces. At the wide-open door he brandished his guttering candle in a last smiling gesture of farewell: and held on.

That is why when, next morning, out of a sounding slanting shower of rain Mrs Thripps admitted herself into the house at the area door, she found the young man, still in his clothes, lying very fast asleep indeed on the truckle-bed in the attic. His hands were not only crossed but convulsively clenched in that position on his breast. And it appeared from certain distressing indications that he must have experienced a severe struggle to refrain from a wild blind tug at the looped-up length of knotted whip-cord over his head.

As a matter of fact it did not occur to the littered old charwoman's mind to speculate whether or not Jimmie had actually made such a last attempt. Or whether he had been content merely to wait on a Soames who might, perhaps, like all good servants, come when he was wanted rather than when he was called. All her own small knowledge of Soameses, though not without comfort, had been acquired at second-hand.

Nor did Mrs Thripps waste time in surmising how Jimmie could ever have persuaded himself to loop up the cord like that out of his reach, unless he had first become abysmally ill-content with his small, primitive, and belated knowledge of campanology.

She merely looked at what was left of him; her old face almost comically transfixed in its appearance of pity, horror, astonishment, and curiosity.

SEATON'S AUNT

I HAD HEARD RUMOURS OF SEATON'S AUNT LONG BEFORE I ACTU-
ally encountered her. Seaton, in the hush of confidence, or at any
little show of toleration on our part, would remark, 'My aunt', or
'My old aunt, you know', as if his relative might be a kind of cement
to an *entente cordiale*.

He had an unusual quantity of pocket-money; or, at any rate, it
was bestowed on him in unusually large amounts; and he spent it
freely, though none of us would have described him as an 'awfully
generous chap'. 'Hullo, Seaton,' we would say, 'the old Begum?' At
the beginning of term, too, he used to bring back surprising and
exotic dainties in a box with a trick padlock that accompanied him
from his first appearance at Gummidge's in a billycock hat to the
rather abrupt conclusion of his schooldays.

From a boy's point of view he looked distastefully foreign with
his yellowish skin, slow chocolate-coloured eyes, and lean weak
figure. Merely for his looks he was treated by most of us true-blue
Englishmen with condescension, hostility, or contempt. We used
to call him 'Pongo', but without any much better excuse for the
nickname than his skin. He was, that is, in one sense of the term
what he assuredly was not in the other sense, a sport.

Seaton and I, as I may say, were never in any sense intimate
at school; our orbits only intersected in class. I kept deliberately
aloof from him. I felt vaguely he was a sneak, and remained quite
unmollified by advances on his side, which, in a boy's barbarous
fashion, unless it suited me to be magnanimous, I haughtily
ignored.

We were both of us quick-footed, and at Prisoner's Base used occasionally to hide together. And so I best remember Seaton – his narrow watchful face in the dusk of a summer evening; his peculiar crouch, and his inarticulate whisperings and mumblings. Otherwise he played all games slackly and limply; used to stand and feed at his locker with a crony or two until his 'tuck' gave out; or waste his money on some outlandish fancy or other. He bought, for instance, a silver bangle, which he wore above his left elbow, until some of the fellows showed their masterly contempt of the practice by dropping it nearly red-hot down his neck.

It needed, therefore, a rather peculiar taste, and a rather rare kind of schoolboy courage and indifference to criticism, to be much associated with him. And I had neither the taste nor, probably, the courage. Nonetheless, he did make advances, and on one memorable occasion went to the length of bestowing on me a whole pot of some outlandish mulberry-coloured jelly that had been duplicated in his term's supplies. In the exuberance of my gratitude I promised to spend the next half-term holiday with him at his aunt's house.

I had clean forgotten my promise when, two or three days before the holiday, he came up and triumphantly reminded me of it.

'Well, to tell you the honest truth, Seaton, old chap—' I began graciously: but he cut me short.

'My aunt expects you,' he said; 'she is very glad you are coming. She's sure to be quite decent to *you*, Withers.'

I looked at him in sheer astonishment; the emphasis was so uncalled for. It seemed to suggest an aunt not hitherto hinted at, and a friendly feeling on Seaton's side that was far more disconcerting than welcome.

★

We reached his aunt's house partly by train, partly by a lift in an empty farm-cart, and partly by walking. It was a whole-day holiday, and we were to sleep the night; he lent me extraordinary night-gear, I remember. The village street was unusually wide, and was fed from a green by two converging roads, with an inn, and a high green sign at the corner. About a hundred yards down the street was a chemist's shop – a Mr Tanner's. We descended the two steps into his dusky and odorous interior to buy, I remember, some rat poison. A little beyond the chemist's was the forge. You then walked along a very narrow path, under a fairly high wall, nodding here and there with weeds and tufts of grass, and so came to the iron garden-gates, and saw the high flat house behind its huge sycamore. A coachhouse stood on the left of the house, and on the right a gate led into a kind of rambling orchard. The lawn lay away over to the left again, and at the bottom (for the whole garden sloped gently to a sluggish and rushy pondlike stream) was a meadow.

We arrived at noon, and entered the gates out of the hot dust beneath the glitter of the dark-curtained windows. Seaton led me at once through the little garden-gate to show me his tadpole pond, swarming with what (being myself not in the least interested in low life) seemed to me the most horrible creatures – of all shapes, consistencies, and sizes, but with which Seaton was obviously on the most intimate of terms. I can see his absorbed face now as, squatting on his heels he fished the slimy things out in his sallow palms. Wearying at last of these pets, we loitered about awhile in an aimless fashion. Seaton seemed to be listening, or at any rate waiting, for something to happen or for someone to come. But nothing did happen and no one came.

That was just like Seaton. Anyhow, the first view I got of his aunt was when, at the summons of a distant gong, we turned from the garden, very hungry and thirsty, to go in to luncheon. We were approaching the house, when Seaton suddenly came to a standstill. Indeed, I have always had the impression that he plucked at my sleeve. Something, at least, seemed to catch me back, as it were, as he cried, 'Look out, there she is!'

She was standing at an upper window which opened wide on a hinge, and at first sight she looked an excessively tall and overwhelming figure. This, however, was mainly because the window reached all but to the floor of her bedroom. She was in reality rather an undersized woman, in spite of her long face and big head. She must have stood, I think, unusually still, with eyes fixed on us, though this impression may be due to Seaton's sudden warning and to my consciousness of the cautious and subdued air that had fallen on him at sight of her. I know that without the least reason in the world I felt a kind of guiltiness, as if I had been 'caught'. There was a silvery star pattern sprinkled on her black silk dress, and even from the ground I could see the immense coils of her hair and the rings on her left hand which was held fingering the small jet buttons of her bodice. She watched our united advance without stirring, until, imperceptibly, her eyes raised and lost themselves in the distance, so that it was out of an assumed reverie that she appeared suddenly to awaken to our presence beneath her when we drew close to the house.

'So this is your friend, Mr Smithers, I suppose?' she said, bobbing to me.

'Withers, aunt,' said Seaton.

'It's much the same,' she said, with eyes fixed on me. 'Come in, Mr Withers, and bring him along with you.'

She continued to gaze at me – at least, I think she did so. I know that the fixity of her scrutiny and her ironical 'Mr' made me feel peculiarly uncomfortable. Nonetheless she was extremely kind and attentive to me, though, no doubt, her kindness and attention showed up more vividly against her complete neglect of Seaton. Only one remark that I have any recollection of she made to him: 'When I look on my nephew, Mr Smithers, I realise that dust we are, and dust shall become. You are hot, dirty, and incorrigible, Arthur.'

She sat at the head of the table, Seaton at the foot, and I, before a wide waste of damask tablecloth, between them. It was an old and rather close dining-room, with windows thrown wide to the green garden and a wonderful cascade of fading roses. Miss Seaton's great chair faced this window, so that its rose-reflected light shone full on her yellowish face, and on just such chocolate eyes as my schoolfellow's, except that hers were more than half-covered by unusually long and heavy lids.

There she sat, steadily eating, with those sluggish eyes fixed for the most part on my face; above them stood the deep-lined fork between her eyebrows; and above that the wide expanse of a remarkable brow beneath its strange steep bank of hair. The lunch was copious, and consisted, I remember, of all such dishes as are generally considered too rich and too good for the schoolboy digestion – lobster mayonnaise, cold game sausages, an immense veal and ham pie farced with eggs, truffles, and numberless delicious flavours; besides kickshaws, creams and sweetmeats. We even had a wine, a half-glass of old darkish sherry each.

Miss Seaton enjoyed and indulged an enormous appetite. Her example and a natural schoolboy voracity soon overcame my nervousness of her, even to the extent of allowing me to enjoy to the best of my bent so rare a spread. Seaton was singularly modest; the greater part of his meal consisted of almonds and raisins, which he nibbled surreptitiously and as if he found difficulty in swallowing them.

I don't mean that Miss Seaton 'conversed' with me. She merely scattered trenchant remarks and now and then twinkled a baited question over my head. But her face was like a dense and involved accompaniment to her talk. She presently dropped the 'Mr', to my intense relief, and called me now Withers, or Wither, now Smithers, and even once towards the close of the meal distinctly Johnson, though how on earth my name suggested it, or whose face mine had reanimated in memory, I cannot conceive.

'And is Arthur a good boy at school, Mr Wither?' was one of her many questions. 'Does he please his masters? Is he first in his class? What does the reverend Dr Gummidge think of him, eh?'

I knew she was jeering at him, but her face was adamant against the least flicker of sarcasm or facetiousness. I gazed fixedly at a blushing crescent of lobster.

'I think you're eighth, aren't you, Seaton?'

Seaton moved his small pupils towards his aunt. But she continued to gaze with a kind of concentrated detachment at me.

'Arthur will never make a brilliant scholar, I fear,' she said, lifting a dexterously burdened fork to her wide mouth…

After luncheon she preceded me up to my bedroom. It was a jolly little bedroom, with a brass fender and rugs and a polished floor, on which it was possible, I afterwards found, to play 'snow-shoes'. Over the washstand was a little black-framed water-colour drawing, depicting a large eye with an extremely fishlike intensity in the spark of light on the dark pupil; and in 'illuminated' lettering beneath was printed very minutely, 'Thou God Seest ME', followed by a long looped monogram, 'S.S.', in the corner. The other pictures were all of the sea; brigs on blue water; a schooner overtopping chalk cliffs; a rocky island of prodigious steepness, with two tiny sailors dragging a monstrous boat up a shelf of beach.

'This is the room, Withers, my poor dear brother William died in when a boy. Admire the view!'

I looked out of the window across the tree-tops. It was a day hot with sunshine over the green fields, and the cattle were standing swishing their tails in the shallow water. But the view at the moment was no doubt made more vividly impressive by the apprehension that she would presently enquire after my luggage, and I had brought not even a toothbrush. I need have had no fear. Hers was not that highly civilised type of mind that is stuffed with sharp, material details. Nor could her ample presence be described as in the least motherly.

'I would never consent to question a schoolfellow behind my nephew's back,' she said, standing in the middle of the room, 'but tell me, Smithers, why is Arthur so unpopular? You, I understand, are his only close friend.' She stood in a dazzle of sun, and out of it her eyes regarded me with such leaden penetration beneath their thick lids that I doubt if my face concealed the least thought from her. 'But there, there,' she added very suavely, stooping her head a little, 'don't trouble to answer me. I never extort an answer. Boys are queer fish. Brains might perhaps have suggested his washing his hands before luncheon; but – not my choice, Smithers. God forbid! And now, perhaps, you would like to go into the garden again. I cannot actually see from here, but I should not be surprised if Arthur is now skulking behind that hedge.'

He was. I saw his head come out and take a rapid glance at the windows.

'Join him, Mr Smithers; we shall meet again, I hope, at the tea-table. The afternoon I spend in retirement.'

Whether or not, Seaton and I had not been long engaged with the aid of two green switches in riding round and round a lumbering old grey horse we found in the meadow, before a rather bunched-up figure appeared, walking along the field-path on the other side of the water, with a magenta parasol studiously lowered in our direction throughout her slow progress, as if that were the magnetic needle and we the fixed Pole. Seaton at once lost all nerve and interest. At the next lurch of the old mare's heels he toppled over into the grass, and I slid off the sleek broad back to join him where he stood, rubbing his shoulder and sourly watching the rather pompous figure till it was out of sight.

'Was that your aunt, Seaton?' I enquired; but not till then.

He nodded.

'Why didn't she take any notice of us, then?'

'She never does.'

'Why not?'

'Oh, she knows all right, without; that's the dam awful part of it.' Seaton was one of the very few fellows at Gummidge's who had the ostentation to use bad language. He had suffered for it too. But it wasn't, I think, bravado. I believe he really felt certain things more intensely than most of the other fellows, and they were generally things that fortunate and average people do not feel at all – the peculiar quality, for instance, of the British schoolboy's imagination.

'I tell you, Withers,' he went on moodily, slinking across the meadow with his hands covered up in his pockets, 'she sees everything. And what she doesn't see she knows without.'

'But how?' I said, not because I was much interested, but because the afternoon was so hot and tiresome and purposeless, and it seemed more of a bore to remain silent. Seaton turned gloomily and spoke in a very low voice.

'Don't appear to be talking of her, if you wouldn't mind. It's – because she's in league with the Devil.' He nodded his head and stooped to pick up a round flat pebble. 'I tell you,' he said, still stooping, 'you fellows don't realise what it is. I know I'm a bit close and all that. But so would you be if you had that old hag listening to every thought you think.'

I looked at him, then turned and surveyed one by one the windows of the house.

'Where's your *pater*?' I said awkwardly.

'Dead, ages and ages ago, and my mother too. She's not my aunt even by rights.'

'What is she, then?'

'I mean she's not my mother's sister, because my grandmother married twice; and she's one of the first lot. I don't know what you call her, but anyhow she's not my real aunt.'

'She gives you plenty of pocket-money.'

Seaton looked steadfastly at me out of his flat eyes. 'She can't give me what's mine. When I come of age half of the whole lot will be mine; and what's more' – he turned his back on the house – 'I'll make her hand over every blessed shilling of it.'

I put my hands in my pockets and stared at Seaton; 'Is it much?'

He nodded.

'Who told you?' He got suddenly very angry, a darkish red came into his cheeks, his eyes glistened, but he made no answer, and we loitered listlessly about the garden until it was time for tea…

Seaton's aunt was wearing an extraordinary kind of lace jacket when we sidled sheepishly into the drawing-room together. She greeted me with a heavy and protracted smile, and bade me bring a chair close to the little table.

'I hope Arthur has made you feel at home,' she said as she handed me my cup in her crooked hand. 'He don't talk much to me; but then

I'm an old woman. You must come again, Wither, and draw him out of his shell. You old snail!' She wagged her head at Seaton, who sat munching cake and watching her intently.

'And we must correspond, perhaps.' She nearly shut her eyes at me. 'You must write and tell me everything behind the creature's back.' I confess I found her rather disquieting company. The evening drew on. Lamps were brought in by a man with a nondescript face and very quiet footsteps. Seaton was told to bring out the chess-men. And we played a game, she and I, with her big chin thrust over the board at every move as she gloated over the pieces and occasionally croaked 'Check!' – after which she would sit back inscrutably staring at me. But the game was never finished. She simply hemmed me in with a gathering cloud of pieces that held me impotent, and yet one and all refused to administer to my poor flustered old king a merciful *coup de grâce*.

'There,' she said, as the clock struck ten – 'a drawn game, Withers. We are very evenly matched. A very creditable defence, Withers. You know your room. There's supper on a tray in the dining-room. Don't let the creature over-eat himself. The gong will sound three-quarters of an hour *before* a punctual breakfast.' She held out her cheek to Seaton, and he kissed it with obvious perfunctoriness. With me she shook hands.

'An excellent game,' she said cordially, 'but my memory is poor, and' – she swept the pieces helter-skelter into the box – 'the result will never be known.' She raised her great head far back. 'Eh?'

It was a kind of challenge, and I could only murmur: 'Oh I was absolutely in a hole, you know!' when she burst out laughing and waved us both out of the room.

Seaton and I stood and ate our supper, with one candlestick to light us, in a corner of the dining-room. 'Well, and how would you

like it?' he said very softly, after cautiously poking his head round
the doorway.

'Like what?'

'Being spied on – every blessed thing you do and think?'

'I shouldn't like it at all,' I said, 'if she does.'

'And yet you let her smash you up at chess!'

'I didn't let her!' I said indignantly.

'Well, you funked it, then.'

'And I didn't funk it either,' I said; 'she's so jolly clever with her
knights.' Seaton stared at the candle. 'Knights,' he said slowly. 'You
wait, that's all.' And we went upstairs to bed.

I had not been long in bed, I think, when I was cautiously awakened by a touch on my shoulder. And there was Seaton's face in the
candle-light – and his eyes looking into mine.

'What's up?' I said, lurching on to my elbow.

'*Ssh!* Don't scurry,' he whispered. 'She'll hear. I'm sorry for
waking you, but I didn't think you'd be asleep so soon.'

'Why, what's the time, then?' Seaton wore, what was then rather
unusual, a night-suit, and he hauled his big silver watch out of the
pocket in his jacket.

'It's a quarter to twelve. I never get to sleep before twelve – not
here.'

'What do you do, then?'

'Oh, I read: and listen.'

'Listen?'

Seaton stared into his candle-flame as if he were listening even
then. 'You can't guess what it is. All you read in ghost stories, that's
all rot. You can't see much, Withers, but you know all the same.'

'Know what?'

'Why, that they're there.'

'Who's there?' I asked fretfully, glancing at the door.

'Why, in the house. It swarms with 'em. Just you stand still and listen outside my bedroom door in the middle of the night. I have, dozens of times; they're all over the place.'

'Look here, Seaton,' I said, 'you asked me to come here, and I didn't mind chucking up a leave just to oblige you and because I'd promised; but don't get talking a lot of rot, that's all, or you'll know the difference when we get back.'

'Don't fret,' he said coldly, turning away. 'I shan't be at school long. And what's more, you're here now, and there isn't anybody else to talk to. I'll chance the other.'

'Look here, Seaton,' I said, 'you may think you're going to scare me with a lot of stuff about voices and all that. But I'll just thank you to clear out; and you may please yourself about pottering about all night.'

He made no answer; he was standing by the dressing-table looking across his candle into the looking-glass; he turned and stared slowly round the walls.

'Even this room's nothing more than a coffin. I suppose she told you – "It's all exactly the same as when my brother William died" – trust her for that! And good luck to him, say I. Look at that.' He raised his candle close to the little water-colour I have mentioned. 'There's hundreds of eyes like that in this house; and even if God does see you, He takes precious good care you don't see Him. And it's just the same with them. I tell you what, Withers, I'm getting sick of all this. I shan't stand it much longer.'

The house was silent within and without, and even in the yellowish radiance of the candle a faint silver showed through the open window on my blind. I slipped off the bedclothes, wide awake, and sat irresolute on the bedside.

'I know you're only guying me,' I said angrily, 'but why is the house full of – what you say? Why do you hear – what you *do* hear? Tell me that, you silly fool!'

Seaton sat down on a chair and rested his candlestick on his knee. He blinked at me calmly. 'She brings them,' he said, with lifted eyebrows.

'Who? Your aunt?'

He nodded.

'How?'

'I told you,' he answered pettishly. 'She's in league. You don't know. She as good as killed my mother; I know that. But it's not only her by a long chalk. She just sucks you dry. I know. And that's what she'll do for me; because I'm like her – like my mother, I mean. She simply hates to see me alive. I wouldn't be like that old she-wolf for a million pounds. And so' – he broke off, with a comprehensive wave of his candlestick – 'they're always here. Ah, my boy, wait till she's dead! She'll hear something then, I can tell you. It's all very well now, but wait till then! I wouldn't be in her shoes when she has to clear out – for something. Don't you go and believe I care for ghosts, or whatever you like to call them. We're all in the same box. We're all under her thumb.'

He was looking almost nonchalantly at the ceiling at the moment, when I saw his face change, saw his eyes suddenly drop like shot birds and fix themselves on the cranny of the door he had left just ajar. Even from where I sat I could see his cheek change colour; it went greenish. He crouched without stirring, like an animal. And I, scarcely daring to breathe, sat with creeping skin, sourly watching him. His hands relaxed, and he gave a kind of sigh.

'Was *that* one?' I whispered, with a timid show of jauntiness. He looked round, opened his mouth, and nodded. 'What?' I said. He jerked his thumb with meaningful eyes, and I knew that he meant that his aunt had been there listening at our door cranny.

'Look here, Seaton,' I said once more, wriggling to my feet. 'You may think I'm a jolly noodle; just as you please. But your aunt has been civil to me and all that, and I don't believe a word you say about her, that's all, and never did. Every fellow's a bit off his pluck at night, and you may think it a fine sport to try your rubbish on me. I heard your aunt come upstairs before I fell asleep. And I'll bet you a level tanner she's in bed now. What's more, you can keep your blessed ghosts to yourself. It's a guilty conscience, I should think.'

Seaton looked at me intently, without answering for a moment. 'I'm not a liar, Withers; but I'm not going to quarrel either. You're the only chap I care a button for; or, at any rate, you're the only chap that's ever come here; and it's something to tell a fellow what you feel. I don't care a fig for fifty thousand ghosts, although I swear on my solemn oath that I know they're here. But she' – he turned deliberately – 'you laid a tanner she's in bed, Withers; well, I know different. She's never in bed much of the night, and I'll prove it, too, just to show you I'm not such a nolly as you think I am. Come on!'

'Come on where?'

'Why, to see.'

I hesitated. He opened a large cupboard and took out a small dark dressing-gown and a kind of shawl-jacket. He threw the jacket on the bed and put on the gown. His dusky face was colourless, and I could see by the way he fumbled at the sleeves he was shivering. But it was no good showing the white feather now. So I threw the tasselled shawl over my shoulders and, leaving our candle brightly burning on the chair, we went out together and stood in the corridor.

'Now then, listen!' Seaton whispered.

We stood leaning over the staircase. It was like leaning over a well, so still and chill the air was all around us. But presently, as I suppose happens in most old houses, began to echo and answer in my ears a medley of infinite small stirrings and whisperings. Now out of the distance an old timber would relax its fibres, or a scurry die away behind the perishing wainscot. But amid and behind such sounds as these I seemed to begin to be conscious, as it were, of the lightest of footfalls, sounds as faint as the vanishing remembrance of voices in a dream. Seaton was all in obscurity except his face; out of that his eyes gleamed darkly, watching me.

'You'd hear, too, in time, my fine soldier,' he muttered. 'Come on!'

He descended the stairs, slipping his lean fingers lightly along the balusters. He turned to the right at the loop, and I followed him barefooted along a thickly carpeted corridor. At the end stood a door ajar. And from here we very stealthily and in complete blackness ascended five narrow stairs. Seaton, with immense caution, slowly pushed open a door, and we stood together, looking into a great pool of duskiness, out of which, lit by the feeble clearness of a night-light, rose a vast bed. A heap of clothes lay on the floor; beside them two slippers dozed, with noses each to each, a foot or two apart. Somewhere a little clock ticked huskily. There was a close smell; lavender and eau de Cologne, mingled with the fragrance of ancient sachets, soap, and drugs. Yet it was a scent even more peculiarly compounded than that.

And the bed! I stared warily in; it was mounded gigantically, and it was empty.

Seaton turned a vague pale face, all shadows: 'What did I say?' he muttered. 'Who's – who's the fool now, I say? How are we going to get back without meeting her, I say? Answer me that! Oh, I wish to God you hadn't come here, Withers.'

He stood audibly shivering in his skimpy gown, and could hardly speak for his teeth chattering. And very distinctly, in the hush that followed his whisper, I heard approaching a faint unhurried voluminous rustle. Seaton clutched my arm, dragged me to the right across the room to a large cupboard, and drew the door close to on us. And, presently, as with bursting lungs I peeped out into the long, low, curtained bedroom, waddled in that wonderful great head and body. I can see her now, all patched and lined with shadow, her tied-up hair (she must have had enormous quantities of it for so old a woman), her heavy lids above those flat, slow, vigilant eyes. She just passed across my ken in the vague dusk; but the bed was out of sight.

We waited on and on, listening to the clock's muffled ticking. Not the ghost of a sound rose up from the great bed. Either she lay archly listening or slept a sleep serener than an infant's. And when, it seemed, we had been hours in hiding and were cramped, chilled, and half-suffocated, we crept out on all fours, with terror knocking at our ribs, and so down the five narrow stairs and back to the little candle-lit blue-and-gold bedroom.

Once there, Seaton gave in. He sat livid on a chair with closed eyes.

'Here,' I said, shaking his arm, 'I'm going to bed; I've had enough of this foolery; I'm going to bed.' His lips quivered, but he made no answer. I poured out some water into my basin and, with that cold pictured azure eye fixed on us, be-spattered Seaton's sallow face and forehead and dabbled his hair. He presently sighed and opened fish-like eyes.

'Come on!' I said, 'Don't get shamming, there's a good chap. Get on my back, if you like, and I'll carry you into your bedroom.'

He waved me away and stood up. So, with my candle in one hand, I took him under the arm and walked him along according to his direction down the corridor. His was a much dingier room than mine, and littered with boxes, paper, cages, and clothes. I huddled him into bed and turned to go. And suddenly, I can hardly explain it now, a kind of cold and deadly terror swept over me. I almost ran out of the room, with eyes fixed rigidly in front of me, blew out my candle, and buried my head under the bedclothes.

When I awoke, roused not by a gong, but by a long-continued tapping at my door, sunlight was raying in on cornice and bedpost, and birds were singing in the garden. I got up, ashamed of the night's folly, dressed quickly, and went downstairs. The breakfast room was sweet with flowers and fruit and honey. Seaton's aunt was standing in the garden beside the open French window, feeding a great flutter of birds. I watched her for a moment, unseen. Her face was set in a deep reverie beneath the shadow of a big loose sun-hat. It was deeply lined, crooked, and, in a way I can't describe, fixedly vacant and strange. I coughed politely, and she turned with a prodigious smiling grimace to ask how I had slept. And in that mysterious fashion by which we learn each other's secret thoughts without a syllable said, I knew that she had followed every word and movement of the night before, and was triumphing over my affected innocence and ridiculing my friendly and too easy advances.

We returned to school, Seaton and I, lavishly laden, and by rail all the way. I made no reference to the obscure talk we had had, and resolutely refused to meet his eyes or to take up the hints he let fall. I was relieved – and yet I was sorry – to be going back, and strode on as fast as I could from the station, with Seaton almost trotting at my heels. But he insisted on buying more fruit and sweets – my share of which I accepted with a very bad grace. It was uncomfortably like a bribe; and, after all, I had no quarrel with his rum old aunt, and hadn't really believed half the stuff he had told me.

I saw as little of him as I could after that. He never referred to our visit or resumed his confidences, though in class I would sometimes catch his eye fixed on mine, full of a mute understanding, which I easily affected not to understand. He left Gummidge's, as I have said, rather abruptly, though I never heard of anything to his discredit. And I did not see him or have any news of him again till by chance we met one summer afternoon in the Strand.

He was dressed rather oddly in a coat too large for him and a bright silky tie. But we instantly recognised one another under the awning of a cheap jeweller's shop. He immediately attached himself to me and dragged me off, not too cheerfully, to lunch with him at an Italian restaurant nearby. He chattered about our old school, which he remembered only with dislike and disgust; told me cold-bloodedly of the disastrous fate of one or two of the older fellows who had been among his chief tormentors; insisted on an expensive wine and the whole gamut of the foreign menu; and finally informed me, with a good deal of niggling, that he had come up to town to buy an engagement-ring.

And of course: 'How is your aunt?' I enquired at last.

He seemed to have been awaiting the question. It fell like a stone into a deep pool, so many expressions flitted across his long, sad, sallow, un-English face.

'She's aged a good deal,' he said softly, and broke off.

'She's been very decent,' he continued presently after, and paused again. 'In a way.' He eyed me fleetingly. 'I dare say you heard that – she – that is, that we – had lost a good deal of money.'

'No,' I said.

'Oh, yes!' said Seaton, and paused again.

And somehow, poor fellow, I knew in the clink and clatter of glass and voices that he had lied to me; that he did not possess, and never had possessed, a penny beyond what his aunt had squandered on his too ample allowance of pocket-money.

'And the ghosts?' I enquired quizzically.

He grew instantly solemn, and, though it may have been my fancy, slightly yellowed. But 'You are making game of me, Withers,' was all he said.

He asked for my address, and I rather reluctantly gave him my card.

'Look here, Withers,' he said, as we stood together in the sunlight on the kerb, saying good-bye, 'here I am, and – and it's all very well. I'm not perhaps as fanciful as I was. But you are practically the only friend I have on earth – except Alice... And there – to make a clean breast of it, I'm not sure that my aunt cares much about my getting married. She doesn't say so, of course. You know her well enough for that.' He looked sidelong at the rattling gaudy traffic.

'What I was going to say is this: Would you mind coming down? You needn't stay the night unless you please, though, of course, you know you would be awfully welcome. But I should like you to meet my – to meet Alice; and then, perhaps, you might tell me your honest opinion of – of the other too.'

I vaguely demurred. He pressed me. And we parted with a half promise that I would come. He waved his ball-topped cane at me and ran off in his long jacket after a bus.

A letter arrived soon after, in his small weak handwriting, giving me full particulars regarding route and trains. And without the least curiosity, even perhaps with some little annoyance that chance should have thrown us together again, I accepted his invitation and arrived one hazy midday at his out-of-the-way station to find him sitting on a low seat under a clump of 'double' hollyhocks, awaiting me.

He looked preoccupied and singularly listless; but seemed, none-theless, to be pleased to see me.

We walked up the village street, past the little dingy apothecary's and the empty forge, and, as on my first visit, skirted the house together, and, instead of entering by the front door, made our way down the green path into the garden at the back. A pale haze of cloud muffled the sun; the garden lay in a grey shimmer – its old trees, its snap-dragoned faintly glittering walls. But now there was an air of slovenliness where before all had been neat and methodical. In a patch of shallowly dug soil stood a worn-down spade leaning against a tree. There was an old decayed wheelbarrow. The roses had run to leaf and briar; the fruit-trees were unpruned. The goddess of neglect had made it her secret resort.

'You ain't much of a gardener, Seaton,' I said at last, with a sigh of relief.

'I think, do you know, I like it best like this,' said Seaton. 'We haven't any man now, of course. Can't afford it.' He stood staring at his little dark oblong of freshly turned earth. 'And it always seems to me,' he went on ruminatingly, 'that, after all, we are all nothing better than interlopers on the earth, disfiguring and staining wherever we go. It may sound shocking blasphemy to say so; but then it's different here, you see. We are further away.'

'To tell you the truth, Seaton, I *don't* quite see,' I said; 'but it isn't a new philosophy, is it? Anyhow, it's a precious beastly one.'

'It's only what I think,' he replied, with all his odd old stubborn meekness. 'And one thinks as one *is*.'

We wandered on together, talking little, and still with that expression of uneasy vigilance on Seaton's face. He pulled out his watch as we stood gazing idly over the green meadows and the dark motion-less bulrushes.

'I think, perhaps, it's nearly time for lunch,' he said. 'Would you like to come in?'

We turned and walked slowly towards the house, across whose windows I confess my own eyes, too, went restlessly meandering in search of its rather disconcerting inmate. There was a pathetic look of bedraggledness, of want of means and care, rust and overgrowth and faded paint. Seaton's aunt, a little to my relief, did not share our meal. So he carved the cold meat, and dispatched a heaped-up plate by an elderly servant for his aunt's private consumption. We talked little and in half-suppressed tones, and sipped some Madeira which Seaton after listening for a moment or two fetched out of the great mahogany sideboard.

I played him a dull and effortless game of chess, yawning between the moves he himself made almost at haphazard, and with attention elsewhere engaged. Towards five o'clock came the sound of a distant ring, and Seaton jumped up, overturning the board, and so ended a game that else might have fatuously continued to this day. He effusively excused himself, and after some little while returned with a slim, dark, pale-faced girl of about nineteen, in a white gown and hat, to whom I was presented with some little nervousness as his 'dear old friend and schoolfellow'.

We talked on in the golden afternoon light, still, as it seemed to me, and even in spite of our efforts to be lively and gay, in a half-suppressed, lacklustre fashion. We all seemed, if it were not my fancy, to be expectant, to be almost anxiously awaiting an arrival, the appearance of someone whose image filled our collective consciousness. Seaton talked least of all, and in a restless interjectory way, as he continually fidgeted from chair to chair. At last he proposed a stroll in the garden before the sun should have quite gone down.

Alice walked between us. Her hair and eyes were conspicuously dark against the whiteness of her gown. She carried herself not ungracefully, and yet with peculiarly little movement of her arms and body, and answered us both without turning her head. There was a curious provocative reserve in that impassive melancholy face. It seemed to be haunted by some tragic influence of which she herself was unaware.

And yet somehow I knew – I believe we all knew – that this walk, this discussion of their future plans was a futility. I had nothing to base such scepticism on, except only a vague sense of oppression, a foreboding consciousness of some inert invincible power in the background, to whom optimistic plans and love-making and youth are as chaff and thistledown. We came back, silent, in the last light. Seaton's aunt was there – under an old brass lamp. Her hair was as barbarously massed and curled as ever. Her eyelids, I think, hung even a little heavier in age over their slow-moving, inscrutable pupils. We filed in softly out of the evening, and I made my bow.

'In this short interval, Mr Withers,' she remarked amiably, 'you have put off youth, put on the man. Dear me, how sad it is to see the young days vanishing! Sit down. My nephew tells me you met by chance – or act of Providence, shall we call it? – and in my beloved Strand! You, I understand, are to be best man – yes, best man! Or am I divulging secrets?' She surveyed Arthur and Alice with overwhelming graciousness. They sat apart on two low chairs and smiled in return.

'And Arthur – how do you think Arthur is looking?'

'I think he looks very much in need of a change,' I said.

'A change! Indeed?' She all but shut her eyes at me and with an exaggerated sentimentality shook her head. 'My dear Mr Withers! Are we not *all* in need of a change in this fleeting, fleeting world?' She mused over the remark like a connoisseur. 'And you,' she continued, turning abruptly to Alice, 'I hope you pointed out to Mr Withers all my pretty bits?'

'We only walked round the garden,' the girl replied; then, glancing at Seaton, added almost inaudibly, 'it's a very beautiful evening.'

'*Is* it?' said the old lady, starting up violently. 'Then on this very beautiful evening we will go in to supper. Mr Withers, your arm; Arthur, bring your bride.'

We were a queer quartet, I thought to myself, as I solemnly led the way into the faded, chilly dining-room, with this indefinable old creature leaning wooingly on my arm – the large flat bracelet on the yellow-laced wrist. She fumed a little, breathing heavily, but as if with an effort of the mind rather than of the body; for she had grown much stouter and yet little more proportionate. And to talk into that great white face, so close to mine, was a queer experience in the dim light of the corridor, and even in the twinkling crystal of the candles. She was naïve – appallingly naïve; she was crafty and challenging; she was even arch; and all these in the brief, rather puffy passage from one room to the other, with these two tongue-tied children bringing up the rear. The meal was tremendous. I have never seen such a monstrous salad. But the dishes were greasy and over-spiced, and were indifferently cooked. One thing only was quite unchanged – my hostess's appetite was as Gargantuan as ever. The heavy silver candelabra that lighted us stood before her high-backed chair. Seaton sat a little removed, his plate almost in darkness.

And throughout this prodigious meal his aunt talked, mainly to me, mainly *at* him, but with an occasional satirical sally at Alice and muttered explosions of reprimand to the servant. She had aged, and yet, if it be not nonsense to say so, seemed no older. I suppose to the Pyramids a decade is but as the rustling down of a handful of dust. And she reminded me of some such unshakeable prehistoricism. She certainly was an amazing talker – rapid, egregious, with a delivery that was perfectly overwhelming. As for Seaton – her flashes of silence were for him. On her enormous volubility would suddenly fall a hush: acid sarcasm would be left implied; and she would sit softly moving her great head, with eyes fixed full in a dreamy smile; but with her whole attention, one could see, slowly, joyously absorbing his mute discomfiture.

She confided in us her views on a theme vaguely occupying at the moment, I suppose, all our minds. 'We have barbarous institutions, and so must put up, I suppose, with a never-ending procession of fools – of fools *ad infinitum*. Marriage, Mr Withers, was instituted in the privacy of a garden; *sub rosa*, as it were. Civilisation flaunts it in the glare of day. The dull marry the poor; the rich the effete; and so our New Jerusalem is peopled with naturals, plain and coloured, at either end. I detest folly; I detest still more (if I must be frank, dear Arthur) mere cleverness. Mankind has simply become a tailless host of uninstinctive animals. We should never have taken to Evolution, Mr Withers. "Natural Selection!" – little gods and fishes! – the deaf for the dumb. We should have used our brains – intellectual pride, the ecclesiastics call it. And by brains I mean – what do I mean, Alice? – I mean, my dear child,' and she laid two gross fingers on Alice's narrow sleeve, 'I mean courage. Consider it, Arthur. I read that the scientific world is once more beginning to be afraid of spiritual agencies. Spiritual agencies that tap, and actually float, bless their hearts! I think just one more of those mulberries – thank you.

'They talk about "blind Love",' she ran on derisively as she helped herself, her eyes roving over the dish, 'but why blind? I think, Mr Withers, from weeping over its rickets. After all, it is we plain women that triumph, is it not so – beyond the mockery of time. Alice, now! Fleeting, fleeting is youth, my child. What's that you were confiding to your plate, Arthur? Satirical boy. He laughs at his old aunt: nay, but thou didst laugh. He detests all sentiment. He whispers the most acid asides. Come, my love, we will leave these cynics; we will go and commiserate with each other on our sex. The choice of two evils, Mr Smithers!' I opened the door, and she swept out as if borne on a torrent of unintelligible indignation; and Arthur and I were left in the clear four-flamed light alone.

For a while we sat in silence. He shook his head at my cigarette-case, and I lit a cigarette. Presently he fidgeted in his chair and poked his head forward into the light. He paused to rise, and shut again the shut door.

'How long will you be?' he asked me.

I laughed.

'Oh, it's not that!' he said, in some confusion. 'Of course, I like to be with her. But it's not that. The truth is, Withers, I don't care about leaving her too long with my aunt.'

I hesitated. He looked at me questioningly.

'Look here, Seaton,' I said, 'you know well enough that I don't want to interfere in your affairs, or to offer advice where it is not wanted. But don't you think perhaps you may not treat your aunt quite in the right way? As one gets old, you know, a little give and take. I have an old godmother, or something of the kind. She's a bit queer, too… A little allowance; it does no harm. But hang it all, I'm no preacher.'

He sat down with his hands in his pockets and still with his eyes fixed almost incredulously on mine. 'How?' he said.

'Well, my dear fellow, if I'm any judge – mind, I don't say that I am – but I can't help thinking she thinks you don't care for her; and perhaps takes your silence for – for bad temper. She has been very decent to you, hasn't she?

'"Decent"? My God!' said Seaton.

I smoked on in silence; but he continued to look at me with that peculiar concentration I remembered of old.

'I don't think, perhaps, Withers,' he began presently, 'I don't think you quite understand. Perhaps you are not quite our kind. You always did, just like the other fellows, guy me at school. You laughed at me that night you came to stay here – about the voices and all that. But I don't mind being laughed at – because I know.'

'Know what?' It was the same old system of dull question and evasive answer.

'I mean I know that what we see and hear is only the smallest fraction of what is. I know she lives quite out of this. She *talks* to you; but it's all make-believe. It's all a "parlour game". She's not really with you; only pitting her outside wits against yours and enjoying the fooling. She's living on inside on what you're rotten without. That's what it is – a cannibal feast. She's a spider. It doesn't much matter what you call it. It means the same kind of thing. I tell you, Withers, she hates me; and you can scarcely dream what that hatred means. I used to think I had an inkling of the reason. It's oceans deeper than that. It just lies behind: herself against myself. Why, after all, how much do we really understand of anything? We don't even know our own histories, and not a tenth, not a tenth of the reasons. What has life been to me? – nothing but a trap. And when one sets oneself free for a while, it only begins again. I thought you might understand; but you are on a different level: that's all.'

'What on earth are you talking about?' I said contemptuously, in spite of myself.

'I mean what I say,' he said gutturally. 'All this outside's only make-believe – but there! what's the good of talking? So far as this is concerned I'm as good as done. You wait.'

Seaton blew out three of the candles and, leaving the vacant room in semi-darkness, we groped our way along the corridor to the drawing-room. There a full moon stood shining in at the long garden windows. Alice sat stooping at the door, with her hands clasped in her lap, looking out, alone.

'Where is she?' Seaton asked in a low tone.

She looked up; and their eyes met in a glance of instantaneous understanding, and the door immediately afterwards opened behind us.

'*Such* a moon!' said a voice, that once heard, remained unforgettably on the ear. 'A night for lovers, Mr Withers, if ever there was one. Get a shawl, my dear Arthur, and take Alice for a little promenade. I dare say we old cronies will manage to keep awake. Hasten, hasten, Romeo! My poor, poor Alice, how laggard a lover!'

Seaton returned with a shawl. They drifted out into the moonlight. My companion gazed after them till they were out of hearing, turned to me gravely, and suddenly twisted her white face into such a convulsion of contemptuous amusement that I could only stare blankly in reply.

'Dear innocent children!' she said, with inimitable unctuousness. 'Well, well, Mr Withers, we poor seasoned old creatures must move with the times. Do you sing?'

I scouted the idea.

'Then you must listen to my playing. Chess' – she clasped her forehead with both cramped hands – 'chess is now completely beyond my poor wits.'

She sat down at the piano and ran her fingers in a flourish over the keys. 'What shall it be? How shall we capture them, those passionate hearts? That first fine careless rapture? Poetry itself.' She gazed softly into the garden a moment, and presently, with a shake of her body, began to play the opening bars of Beethoven's 'Moonlight' Sonata.

The piano was old and woolly. She played without music. The lamp-light was rather dim. The moonbeams from the window lay across the keys. Her head was in shadow. And whether it was simply due to her personality or to some really occult skill in her playing I cannot say; I only know that she gravely and deliberately set herself to satirise the beautiful music. It brooded on the air, disillusioned, charged with mockery and bitterness. I stood at the window; far down the path I could see the white figure glimmering in that pool of colourless light. A few faint stars shone, and still that amazing woman behind me dragged out of the unwilling keys her wonderful grotesquerie of youth and love and beauty. It came to an end. I knew the player was watching me. 'Please, please, go on!' I murmured, without turning. '*Please* go on playing, Miss Seaton.'

No answer was returned to this honeyed sarcasm, but I realised in some vague fashion that I was being acutely scrutinised, when suddenly there followed a procession of quiet, plaintive chords which broke at last softly into the hymn, 'A Few More Years Shall Roll'.

I confess it held me spellbound. There is a wistful, strained plangent pathos in the tune; but beneath those masterly old hands it cried softly and bitterly the solitude and desperate estrangement of the world. Arthur and his lady-love vanished from my thoughts. No one could put into so hackneyed an old hymn tune such an appeal who had never known the meaning of the words. Their meaning, anyhow, isn't commonplace.

I turned a fraction of an inch to glance at the musician. She was leaning forward a little over the keys, so that at the approach of my silent scrutiny she had but to turn her face into the thin flood of moonlight for every feature to become distinctly visible. And so, with the tune abruptly terminated, we steadfastly regarded one another; and she broke into a prolonged chuckle of laughter.

'Not quite so seasoned as I supposed, Mr Withers. I see you are a real lover of music. To me it is too painful. It evokes too much thought...'

I could scarcely see her little glittering eyes under their penthouse lids.

'And now,' she broke off crisply, 'tell me, as a man of the world, what do you think of my new niece?'

I was not a man of the world, nor was I much flattered in my stiff and dullish way of looking at things by being called one; and I could answer her without the least hesitation.

'I don't think, Miss Seaton, I'm much of a judge of character. She's very charming.'

'A brunette?'

'I think I prefer dark women.'

'And why? Consider, Mr Withers; dark hair, dark eyes, dark cloud, dark night, dark vision, dark death, dark grave, dark DARK!'

Perhaps the climax would have rather thrilled Seaton, but I was too thick-skinned. 'I don't know much about all that,' I answered rather pompously. 'Broad daylight's difficult enough for most of us.'

'Ah,' she said, with a sly inward burst of satirical laughter.

'And I suppose,' I went on, perhaps a little nettled, 'it isn't the actual darkness one admires, it's the contrast of the skin, and the colour of the eyes, and – and their shining. Just as,' I went blundering on, too late to turn back, 'just as you only see the stars in the dark. It would be a long day without any evening. As for death and the grave, I don't suppose we shall much notice that.' Arthur and his sweetheart were slowly returning along the dewy path. 'I believe in making the best of things.'

'How very interesting!' came the smooth answer. 'I see you are a philosopher, Mr Withers. H'm! "As for death and the grave, I don't

suppose we shall much notice that." Very interesting... And I'm sure,'
she added in a particularly suave voice, 'I profoundly hope so.' She
rose slowly from her stool. 'You will take pity on me again, I hope.
You and I would get on famously – kindred spirits – elective affini-
ties. And, of course, now that my nephew's going to leave me, now
that his affections are centred on another, I shall be a very lonely old
woman... Shall I not, Arthur?'

Seaton blinked stupidly. 'I didn't hear what you said, Aunt.'

'I was telling our old friend, Arthur, that when you are gone I
shall be a very lonely old woman.'

'Oh, I don't think so;' he said in a strange voice.

'He means, Mr Withers, he means, my dear child,' she said,
sweeping her eyes over Alice, 'he means that I shall have memory for
company – heavenly memory – the ghosts of other days. Sentimental
boy! And did you enjoy our music, Alice? Did I really stir that youthful
heart?... O. O, O,' continued the horrible old creature, 'you billers
and cooers, I have been listening to such flatteries, such confessions!
Beware, beware, Arthur, there's many a slip.' She rolled her little eyes
at me, she shrugged her shoulders at Alice, and gazed an instant
stonily into her nephew's face.

I held out my hand. 'Good night, good night!' she cried. 'He that
fights and runs away. Ah, good night, Mr Withers; come again soon!'
She thrust out her cheek at Alice, and we all three filed slowly out
of the room.

Black shadow darkened the porch and half the spreading sycamore. We walked without speaking up the dusty village street. Here
and there a crimson window glowed. At the fork of the high-road I
said good-bye. But I had taken hardly more than a dozen paces when
a sudden impulse seized me.

'Seaton!' I called.

He turned in the cool stealth of the moonlight.

'You have my address; if by any chance, you know, you should care to spend a week or two in town between this and the – the Day, we should be delighted to see you.'

'Thank you, Withers, thank you,' he said in a low voice.

'I dare say' – I waved my stick gallantly at Alice – 'I dare say you will be doing some shopping; we could all meet,' I added, laughing.

'Thank you, thank you, Withers – immensely,' he repeated.

And so we parted.

But they were out of the jog-trot of my prosaic life. And being of a stolid and incurious nature, I left Seaton and his marriage, and even his aunt, to themselves in my memory, and scarcely gave a thought to them until one day I was walking up the Strand again, and passed the flashing gloaming of the second-rate jeweller's shop where I had accidentally encountered my old schoolfellow in the summer. It was one of those stagnant autumnal days after a night of rain. I cannot say why, but a vivid recollection returned to my mind of our meeting and of how suppressed Seaton had seemed, and of how vainly he had endeavoured to appear assured and eager. He must be married by now, and had doubtless returned from his honeymoon. And I had clean forgotten my manners, had sent not a word of congratulation, nor – as I might very well have done and as I knew he would have been pleased at my doing – even the ghost of a wedding present. It was just as of old.

On the other hand, I pleaded with myself, I had had no invitation. I paused at the corner of Trafalgar Square, and at the bidding of one of those caprices that seize occasionally on even an unimaginative mind, I found myself pelting after a green bus, and actually bound on a visit I had not in the least intended or foreseen.

The colours of autumn were over the village when I arrived. A beautiful late afternoon sunlight bathed thatch and meadow. But it was close and hot. A child, two dogs, a very old woman with a heavy basket I encountered. One or two incurious tradesmen looked idly up as I passed by. It was all so rural and remote, my whimsical impulse had so much flagged, that for a while I hesitated to venture under the shadow of the sycamore-tree to enquire after the happy pair. Indeed I first passed by the faint-blue gates and continued my walk under the high, green and tufted wall. Hollyhocks had attained their topmost bud and seeded in the little cottage gardens beyond; the Michaelmas daisies were in flower; a sweet warm aromatic smell of fading leaves was in the air. Beyond the cottages lay a field where cattle were grazing, and beyond that I came to a little churchyard. Then the road wound on, pathless and houseless, among gorse and bracken. I turned impatiently and walked quickly back to the house and rang the bell.

The rather colourless elderly woman who answered my enquiry informed me that Miss Seaton was at home, as if only taciturnity forbade her adding, 'But she doesn't want to see *you*.'

'Might I, do you think, have Mr Arthur's address?' I said.

She looked at me with quiet astonishment, as if waiting for an explanation. Not the faintest of smiles came into her thin face.

'I will tell Miss Seaton,' she said after a pause. 'Please walk in.'

She showed me into the dingy undusted drawing-room, filled with evening sunshine and with the green-dyed light that penetrated the leaves overhanging the long French windows. I sat down and waited on and on, occasionally aware of a creaking footfall overhead. At last the door opened a little, and the great face I had once known peered round at me. For it was enormously changed; mainly, I think, because the aged eyes had rather suddenly failed, and so a kind of stillness and darkness lay over its calm and wrinkled pallor.

'Who is it?' she asked.

I explained myself and told her the occasion of my visit.

She came in, shut the door carefully after her, and, though the fumbling was scarcely perceptible, groped her way to a chair. She had on an old dressing-gown, like a cassock, of a patterned cinnamon colour.

'What is it you want?' she said, seating herself and lifting her blank face to mine.

'Might I just have Arthur's address?' I said deferentially, 'I am so sorry to have disturbed you.'

'H'm. You have come to see my nephew?'

'Not necessarily to see him, only to hear how he is, and, of course, Mrs Seaton, too. I am afraid my silence must have appeared...'

'He hasn't noticed your silence,' croaked the old voice out of the great mask; 'besides, there isn't any Mrs Seaton.'

'Ah, then,' I answered, after a momentary pause, 'I have not seemed so black as I painted myself! And how is Miss Outram?'

'She's gone into Yorkshire,' answered Seaton's aunt.

'And Arthur too?'

She did not reply, but simply sat blinking at me with lifted chin, as if listening, but certainly not for what I might have to say. I began to feel rather at a loss.

'You were no close friend of my nephew's, Mr Smithers?' she said presently.

'No,' I answered, welcoming the cue, 'and yet, do you know, Miss Seaton, he is one of the very few of my old schoolfellows I have come across in the last few years, and I suppose as one gets older one begins to value old associations...' My voice seemed to trail off into a vacuum. 'I thought Miss Outram', I hastily began again, 'a particularly charming girl. I hope they are both quite well.'

Still the old face solemnly blinked at me in silence.

'You must find it very lonely, Miss Seaton, with Arthur away?'

'I was never lonely in my life,' she said sourly. 'I don't look to flesh and blood for my company. When you've got to be my age, Mr Smithers (which God forbid), you'll find life a very different affair from what you seem to think it is now. You won't seek company then, I'll be bound. It's thrust on you.' Her face edged round into the clear green light, and her eyes groped, as it were, over my vacant, disconcerted face. 'I dare say, now,' she said, composing her mouth, 'I dare say my nephew told you a good many tarra-diddles in his time. Oh, yes, a good many, eh? He was always a liar. What, now, did he say of me? Tell me, now.' She leant forward as far as she could, trembling, with an ingratiating smile.

'I think he is rather superstitious,' I said coldly, 'but, honestly, I have a very poor memory, Miss Seaton.'

'Why?' she said. 'I haven't.'

'The engagement hasn't been broken off, I hope.'

'Well, between you and me,' she said, shrinking up and with an immensely confidential grimace, 'it has.'

'I'm sure I'm very sorry to hear it. And where is Arthur?'

'Eh?'

'Where is Arthur?'

We faced each other mutely among the dead old bygone furniture. Past all my analysis was that large, flat, grey, cryptic countenance. And then, suddenly, our eyes for the first time really met. In some indescribable way out of that thick-lidded obscurity a far, small something stooped and looked out at me for a mere instant of time that seemed of almost intolerable protraction. Involuntarily I blinked and shook my head. She muttered something with great rapidity, but quite inarticulately; rose and hobbled to the door. I thought I heard, mingled in broken mutterings, something about tea.

'Please, please, don't trouble,' I began, but could say no more, for the door was already shut between us. I stood and looked out on the long-neglected garden. I could just see the bright weedy green-ness of Seaton's tadpole pond. I wandered about the room. Dusk began to gather, the last birds in that dense shadowiness of trees had ceased to sing. And not a sound was to be heard in the house. I waited on and on, vainly speculating. I even attempted to ring the bell; but the wire was broken, and only jangled loosely at my efforts.

I hesitated, unwilling to call or to venture out, and yet more unwilling to linger on, waiting for a tea that promised to be an exceedingly comfortless supper. And as darkness drew down, a feel-ing of the utmost unease and disquietude came over me. All my talks with Seaton returned on me with a suddenly enriched meaning. I recalled again his face as we had stood hanging over the staircase, listening in the small hours to the inexplicable stirrings of the night. There were no candles in the room; every minute the autumnal dark-ness deepened. I cautiously opened the door and listened, and with some little dismay withdrew, for I was uncertain of my way out. I even tried the garden, but was confronted under a veritable thicket of foliage by a padlocked gate. It would be a little too ignominious to be caught scaling a friend's garden fence!

Cautiously returning into the still and musty drawing-room, I took out my watch, and gave the incredible old woman ten minutes in which to reappear. And when that tedious ten minutes had ticked by I could scarcely distinguish its hands. I determined to wait no longer, drew open the door and, trusting to my sense of direction, groped my way through the corridor that I vaguely remembered led to the front of the house.

I mounted three or four stairs and, lifting a heavy curtain, found myself facing the starry fanlight of the porch. From here I glanced into the gloom of the dining-room. My fingers were on the latch of the outer door when I heard a faint stirring in the darkness above the hall. I looked up and became conscious of, rather than saw, the huddled old figure looking down on me.

There was an immense hushed pause. Then, 'Arthur, Arthur,' whispered an inexpressibly peevish rasping voice, 'is that you? Is that you, Arthur?'

I can scarcely say why, but the question horribly startled me. No conceivable answer occurred to me. With head craned back, hand clenched on my umbrella, I continued to stare up into the gloom, in this fatuous confrontation.

'Oh, oh,' the voice croaked. 'It is *you*, is it? *That* disgusting man!... Go away out. Go away out.'

At this dismissal, I wrenched open the door and, rudely slamming it behind me, ran out into the garden, under the gigantic old sycamore, and so out at the open gate.

I found myself half up the village street before I stopped running. The local butcher was sitting in his shop reading a piece of newspaper by the light of a small oil-lamp. I crossed the road and enquired the way to the station. And after he had with minute and needless care directed me, I asked casually if Mr Arthur Seaton still lived with his aunt at the big house just beyond the village. He poked his head in at the little parlour door.

'Here's a gentleman enquiring after young Mr Seaton, Millie,' he said. 'He's dead, ain't he?'

'Why, yes, bless you,' replied a cheerful voice from within. 'Dead and buried these three months or more – young Mr Seaton. And just before he was to be married, don't you remember, Bob?'

I saw a fair young woman's face peer over the muslin of the little door at me.

'Thank you,' I replied, 'then I go straight on?'

'That's it, sir; past the pond, bear up the hill a bit to the left, and then there's the station lights before your eyes.'

We looked intelligently into each other's faces in the beam of the smoky lamp. But not one of the many questions in my mind could I put into words.

And again I paused irresolutely a few paces further on. It was not, I fancy, merely a foolish apprehension of what the raw-boned butcher might 'think' that prevented my going back to see if I could find Seaton's grave in the benighted churchyard. There was precious little use in pottering about in the muddy dark merely to discover where he was buried. And yet I felt a little uneasy. My rather horrible thought was that, so far as I was concerned – one of his extremely few friends – he had never been much better than 'buried' in my mind.

WINTER

*All the other gifts appertinent to man, as the malice of
this age shapes them, are not worth a gooseberry...*

ANY EVENT IN THIS WORLD – ANY HUMAN BEING FOR THAT
matter – that seems to wear even the faintest cast or warp
of strangeness, is apt to leave a disproportionately sharp impression on one's senses. So at least it appears to me. The experience
lives on secretly in the memory, and you can never tell what trivial
reminder may not at some pregnant moment bring it back – bring
it back as fresh and living and green as ever. That, at any rate, is
my experience.

Life's mere ordinary day-by-day – its thoughts, talk, doings –
wither and die away out of the mind like leaves from a tree. Year
after year a similar crop recurs: and that goes too. It is mere débris;
it perishes. But these other anomalies survive, even through the cold
of age – forsaken nests, everlasting clumps of mistletoe.

Not that they either are necessarily of any use. For all we
know they may be no less alien and parasitic than those flat and
spotted fungi that rise in a night on time-soiled birch trees. But
such is their power to haunt us. Why else, indeed, should the
recollection of that few moments' confrontation with one who, I
suppose, must have been some sort of a 'fellow-creature' remain so
sharp and vivid?

There was nothing much unusual in the circumstances. I must
have so met, faced, passed by thousands of human beings: many of

them in almost as unfrequented places. Without effort I can recall not one. But this one! At the first unexpected premonitory gloom of winter; at sight of any desolate stretch of snow; at sound at dusk of the pebble-like tattling of a robin; at call, too, of a certain kind of dream I have – any such reminder instantly catches me up, transports me back. The old peculiar disquietude possesses me. I am once more an unhappy refugee. It is a distasteful experience.

But such things are difficult to describe – to share. Date, year are, at any rate, of no account; if only for the reason that what impresses us most in life is independent of time. One can in memory indeed live over again events in one's life even twenty years or more gone by, with the same fever of shame, anxiety, unrest. Mere time is nothing.

Nor is now the actual motive of my journey of any consequence. At the moment I was in no particular trouble. No burden lay on my mind – nothing, I mean, heavier than that of being the kind of self one is – a fret common enough in these late days. And though my immediate surroundings were unfamiliar, they were not unusual or unwelcome, since, like others who would not profess to be morbid, I can never pass unvisited either a church of any age or its yard.

Even if I have but a few minutes to spare I cannot resist hastening in to ponder awhile on its old glass and brasses, its stones, shrines, and monuments. Sir Tompkins This, Lord Mount Everest That – one reads with a curious amusement the ingenuous bygones of their blood and state. I have sometimes laughed out. And queer the echo sounds in a barrel roof. And perhaps an old skimpy verger looks at you, round a pillar. Like a bat.

In sober fact this human pomposity of ours shows a little more amiably against any protracted background of time – even a mere two centuries of it. There is an almost saturnine vanity in the sepulchral – 'scutcheons, pedigrees, polished alabaster cherubim and what not. You see it there – like a scarcely legible scribbling on the wall. – Well, on this occasion it was not any such sacred interior I was exploring, but a mere half-acre of gravestones huddling under their tower, in the bare glare of a winter's day.

It was an afternoon in January. For hours I had been trudging against a bitter winter wind awhirl with snow. Fatigue had set in – that leaden fatigue when the body seems to have shrunken; while yet the bones keep up a kind of galvanic action like the limbs of a machine. Thought itself – that capricious deposit – had ceased for the time being. I was like the half-dried mummy of a man, pressing on with bent head along an all but obliterated track.

Then, as if at a signal, I looked up; to find that the snow had ceased to fall: that only a few last, and as if forgotten, flakes were still floating earthwards to their rest in the pallid light of the declining sun.

With this breaking of the clouds a profounder silence had fallen upon the dome-shaped summit of the hill on which I stood. And at its point of vantage I came to a standstill awhile, surveying beneath me under the blueing vacancy of the sky, amidst the white-sheeted fields, a squat church tower, its gargoyles stooping open-mouthed – scarcely less open-mouthed than the frosted bells within. The low mounded wall that encircled the place was but just perceptible, humped with its snow. Its yews stood like gigantic umbrellas clotted with swansdown; its cypresses like torches, fringed, crested, and tufted with ash.

No sound broke the frozen hush as I entered the lych-gate; not a figure of man or beast moved across that far-stretching savannah of new-fallen snow. You could have detected the passage of a fly. Dazzling light and gem-clear coloured shadow played in hollow and ripple. I was treading a virgin wilderness, but one long since settled and densely colonised.

In surroundings like these – in any vast vacant quiet – the senses play uncommonly queer tricks with their possessor. The very air, cold and ethereal and soon to be darkened, seemed to be astir with sounds and shapes on the edge of complete revelation. Such are our fancies. A curious insecure felicity took possession of me. Yet on the face of it the welcome of a winter churchyard is cold enough; and the fare scanty!

The graves were old: many of them recorded only with what nefarious pertinacity time labours and the rain gnaws. Others befrosted growths had now patterned over, and their tale was done. But for the rest – some had texts: 'I am a Worm, and no Man'; 'In Rama was there a Voice heard: Lamentation and Weeping'; 'He knoweth the Way that I take'. And a few still bore their bits of doggerel:

> Stranger, a light I pray!
> Not that I pine for day:
> Only one beam of light –
> To show me Night!

That struck me as a naïve appeal to a visitor not as yet in search of a roof 'for when the slow dark hours begin', and almost blinded for the time being by the dazzle of the sunlight striking down on these abodes around him!

I smiled to myself and went on. Dusk, as a matter of fact, is *my* mind's natural illumination. How many of us, I wonder, 'think' in anything worthy of being called a noonday of consciousness? Not many: it's all in a mirk, without arrangement or prescience. And as for dreaming – well, here were sleepers enough. I loafed on – cold and vacant.

A few paces further I came to a stand again, before a large oval stone, encircled with a blunt loop of marble myrtle leaves embellishing the words:

> He shall give His angels charge over thee,
> To keep thee in all thy ways.

This stone was clasped by two grotesque marble hands, as if he who held it knelt even now behind it in hiding. Facing north, its lower surface was thickly swathed with snow. I scraped it off with my hands:

> I was afraid,
> Death stilled my fears:
> In sorrow I went,
> Death dried my tears:
> Solitary too,
> Death came. And I
> Shall no more want
> For company.

So, so: the cold alone was nipping raw, and I confess its neighbour's philosophy pleased me better: i.e., it's better to be anything animate than a dead lion; even though that lion be a Corporal Pym:

> This quiet mound beneath
> Lies Corporal Pym.
> He had no fear of death;
> Nor Death of him.

Or even if the anything animate be nothing better than a Logge:

Here lies Thomas Logge – a Rascally Dogge;
A poor useless creature – by choice as by nature;
Who never served God – for kindness or Rod;
Who, for pleasure or penny, – never did any
Work in his life – but to marry a Wife,
And live aye in strife:
And all this he says – at the end of his days
Lest some fine canting pen
Should be at him again.

Canting pens had had small opportunity in this hillside acre: and
the gentry of the surrounding parts, like those of most parts,
had preferred to lie inside under cover – where no doubt Mr
Jacob Todd had prepared for many of them a far faster and less
starry lodging:

Here be the ashes of Jacob Todd,
Sexton now in the land of Nod.
Digging he lived, and digging died,
Pick, mattock, spade, and nought beside.
Here oft at evening he would sit
Tired with his toil, and proud of it;
Watching the pretty Robins flit.
Now slumbers he as deep as they
He bedded for ye Judgement Day.

Mr Todd's successor, it seemed, had entrusted him with a little
protégée, who for a few years – not quite nine – had been known
as Alice Cass:

My mother bore me:
My father rejoiced in me:
The good priest blest me:
All people loved me:
But Death coveted me:
And free'd this body
Of its youthful soul.

For youthful company she had another Alice. A much smaller parcel
of bones this – though in sheer date upwards of eighty years her
senior:

Here lyeth our infant, Alice Rodd;
    She were so small,
    Scarce aught at all,
But a mere breath of Sweetness sent from God.

Sore we did weepe; our heartes on sorrow set.
    Till on our knees
    God sent us ease:
And now we weepe no more than we forget.

Tudor roses had been carved around the edge of her stone – vigorously and delicately too, for a rustic mason. Every petal held
its frozen store. I wandered on, restlessly enough, now that my
journey was almost at an end, stooping to read at random; here
an old broken wooden cross leaning crookedly over its one legible
word 'Beloved'; here the great, flat, seventeenth-century vault of
Abraham Devoyage, 'who was of France, and now, please God,
is of Paradise'; and not far distant from him some Spanish exile,

though what had brought such a wayfarer to these outlandish parts, heaven alone could tell:

> Laid in this English ground
> A Spaniard slumbers sound.
> Well might the tender weep
> To think how he doth sleep –
> Strangers on either hand –
> So far from his own land.
> O! when the last Trump blow,
> May Christ ordain that so
> This friendless one arise
> Under his native skies.
> How bleak to wake, how dread a doom,
> To cry his sins so far from home!

And then Ann Poverty's stone a pace or two beyond him:

> Stranger, here lies
>   Ann Poverty;
> Such was her name
>   And such was she.
> May Jesu pity
>   Poverty.

A meagre memorial, and a rather shrill appeal somehow in that vacancy. Indeed I must confess that this snowy waste, these magpie stones, the zebra-like effect of the thin snow-stripings on the dark tower beneath a leaden winter sky suggested an influence curiously pagan in effect. Church sentiments were far more alien in this scene of nature than beneath a roof. And after all, Nature herself instils into us mortals, I suppose, little but endurance, patience, resignation; despair – or fear. That she can be entrancing proves nothing.

On the contrary, the rarer kinds of natural loveliness – enormous forests of flowering chestnuts, their league-long broken chasms sonorous with cataracts and foaming with wild flowers; precipitous green steeps – quartz, samphire, cormorant – plunging a thousand fathoms into dark gulfs of emerald ocean – such memories hint far rather at the inhuman divinities. This place, too, was scarcely one that happy souls would choose to haunt. And yet, here was I… in a Christian burial ground.

But then, of course, one's condition of spirit and body must be taken into account. I was exhausted, and my mind like a vacant house with the door open – so vacant by now that I found I had read over and over the first two or three lines of Asrafel (or was it Israfel?) Holt's blackened inscription without understanding a single word; and then, suddenly, two dark eyes in a long cadaverous face pierced out at me as if from the very fabric of his stone:

> Here is buried a Miser:
> Had he been wiser,
> He would not have gone bare
> Where Heaven's garmented are.
> He'd have spent him a penny
> To buy a Wax Taper;
> And of Water a sprinkle
> To quiet a poor Sleeper.
> He'd have cried on his soul,
> 'O my Soul, moth & rust! –
> What treasure shall profit thee

When thou art dust?'
'*Mene, Tekel, Upharsin!*'
God grant, in those Scales,
His Mercy avail us
When all Earth's else fails!

'… Departed this life May the First 1700'. Two long centuries dead, seraphic Israfel! Was time nothing to him either?

'Now withered is the Garland on the…' the fragment of old rhyme chased its tail awhile in the back of my mind, and then was gone.

And I must be going. Winter twilight is brief. Frost was already glittering along the crisping surface of the snow. A crescent moon showed silvery in the sun's last red. I made her a distant obeisance. But the rather dismal sound of the money I rattled in my pocket served only to scare the day's last robin off. *She* – she paid me no heed.

Here was the same old unanswerable question confronting the traveller. 'I have no Tongue,' cried one from his corner, 'and Ye no Ears.' And this, even though nearby lay Isaac Meek, who in certain features seems easily to have made up for these deficiencies:

Hook-nosed was I; loose-lipped. Greed fixed its gaze
In my young eyes ere they knew brass from gold.
Doomed to the blazing market-place my days,
A sweating chafferer of the bought, and sold.
Frowned on and spat at, flattered and decried,
One only thing man asked of me – my price.
I lived, detested; and forsaken, died,
Scorned by the Virtuous and the jest of Vice.
And now behold, you Christians, my true worth!
Step close: I have inherited the Earth.

I turned to go – wearied a little even of the unwearying. Epitaphs in any case are only 'marginal' reading. There is rarely anything unusual or original in such sentiments as theirs. Up to that moment (apart from the increasing cold) this episode – this experience – had been merely that of a visitor ordinarily curious, vulgarly intrusive, perhaps, and one accustomed to potter about among the antiquated and forgotten.

No: what followed came without premonition or warning. I had been stooping, for the last time, my body now dwarfed by the proximity of the dark stone tower. I had been reading all that there was to be read about yet another forgotten stranger; and so rapidly had the now north-east wind curdled the air that I had been compelled to scrape off the rime from the lettering with numb finger-tips. I had stooped (I say) to read:

> O passer-by, beware!
> Is the day fair? –
> Yet unto evening shall the day spin on
> And soon thy sun be gone;
> Then darkness come,
> And this, a narrow home.
> Not that I bid thee fear:
> Only, when thou at last lie here,
> Bethink thee, there shall surely be
>> Thy Self for company.

And with its last word a peculiar heat coursed through my body. Consciousness seemed suddenly to concentrate itself (like the tentacles of an anemone closing over a morsel of strange food), and I realised that I was no longer alone. But – and of this I am certain – there was no symptom of positive *fear* in the experience. Intense awareness, a peculiar physical, ominous absorption, possibly foreboding; but not actual fear.

I say this because what impressed me most in the figure that I now saw standing amid that sheet of whiteness – three or four grave-mounds distant on these sparse northern skirts of the churchyard – what struck me instantly was the conviction that to him I myself was truly such an object. Not exactly of fear; but of unconcealed horror. It is not, perhaps, a pleasing thing to have to record. My appearance there – dark clothes, dark hair, wearied eyes, ageing face, a skin maybe somewhat cadaverous at that moment with fasting and the cold – all this (just what my body and self looked like, I mean) cannot have been much more repellent than that of scores and scores of men of my class and means and kind.

I was merely, that is, like one of the 'Elder Ladies or Children' who were bidden (by Mr Nash's Rules of the Pump Room in Bath in 1709) to be contented 'with a second bench... as being past, or not come to, Perfection'.

Nonetheless, there was no doubt of it. The fixed open gaze answering mine suggested that of a child confronted with a fascinating but repulsive reptile. Yet so strangely and arrestingly beautiful was that face, beautiful with the strangeness I mean of the dream-like, with its almost colourless eyes and honey-coloured skin, that unless the experience of it had been thus sharply impressed, no human being could have noticed the emotion depicted upon its features.

There was not the faintest faltering in the steady eyes – fixed, too, as if this crystal graveyard air were a dense medium for a sight unused to it. And so intent on them was I myself that, though I noticed the slight trembling of the hand that held what (on reflection) appeared to resemble the forked twig which 'diviners' of water use in their mysteries, I can give no account of this stranger's dress except that it was richly yet dimly coloured.

As I say, my own dark shape was now standing under the frowning stonework of the tower. With an effort one of its gargoyles could have spilt heaven's dews upon my head, had not those dews been frozen. And the voice that fell on my ear – as if from within rather than from without – echoed cold and solemnly against its parti-coloured stone:

'Which is the way?'

Realising more sharply with every tardy moment that this being, in human likeness, was not of my kind, nor of my reality; standing there in the cold and snow, winter nightfall now beginning to lour above the sterile landscape; I could merely shake a shivering head.

'Which is yours?' sang the tranquil and high yet gentle voice.

'There!' I cried, pointing with my finger to the pent-roofed gate which led out on to the human road. The astonishment and dread in the strange face seemed to deepen as I looked.

'But I would gladly...' I began, turning an instant towards the gloomy snow clouds that were again gathering in the north – 'I would gladly...' But the sentence remained unfinished, for when I once more brought my eyes back to this confronter, he was gone.

I agree I was very tired; and never have I seen a more sepulchral twilight than that which now overspread this desolate descent of hill. Yet, strange though it may appear, I knew then and know now that this confrontation was no illusion of the senses. There are hours in life, I suppose, when we are weaker than we know; when a kind of stagnancy spreads over the mind and heart that is merely a masking of what is gathering beneath the surface. Whether or not, as I stood looking back for an instant before pushing on through the old weathered lych-gate, an emotion of intense remorse, misery, terror – I know not – swept over me. My eyes seemed to lose for that moment their power to see aright. The whole scene was distorted, awry.

THE GREEN ROOM

ONLY MR ELLIOTT'S CHOICER CUSTOMERS WERE IN HIS OWN due season let into his little secret – namely, that at the far end of his shop – beyond, that is, the little table on which he kept his account books, his penny bottle of ink, and his rusty pen, there was an annexe. He first allowed his victims to ripen; and preferred even to see their names installed in the pages of his fat, dumpy ledger before he decided that they were really worthy of this little privilege.

Alan, at any rate, though a young man of ample leisure and moderate means, had been browsing and pottering about on and off in the shop for weeks before he even so much as suspected there *was* a hidden door. He must, in his innocence, have spent pounds and pounds on volumes selected from the vulgar shelves before his own initiation.

This was on a morning in March. Mr Elliott was tying up a parcel for him. Having no scissors handy he was burning off the ends of the string with a lighted match. And as if its small flame had snapped at the same moment both the string and the last strands of formality between them, he glanced up almost roguishly at the young man through his large round spectacles with the remark: 'P'r'aps, sir, you would like to take a look at the books in the parlour?' And a birdlike jerk of his round bald head indicated where the parlour was to be found.

Alan had merely looked at him for a moment or two out of his blue eyes with his usual pensive vacancy. 'I didn't know there *was* another room,' he said at last. 'But then, I suppose it wouldn't have occurred to me to think there might be. I fancied these books were all the books you had.' He glanced over the dingy hugger-mugger of second-hand literature that filled the shelves and littered the floor – a mass that would have twenty-fold justified the satiety of a Solomon.

'Oh, dear me, no, sir!' said Mr Elliott, with the pleasantest confidentiality. 'All this is chiefly riff-raff. But I don't mention it except to those gentlemen who are old clients, in a manner of speaking. What's in there is all in the printed catalogue and I can always get what's asked for. Apart from that, there's some who – well, at any rate, I *don't,* sir. But if by any chance you should care to take a look round at any time, you would, I'm sure, be very welcome. This is an oldish house, as you may have noticed, sir, and out there is the oldest parts of it. We call it the parlour – Mrs Elliott and me; we got it from the parties that were here before we came. Take a look now, sir, if you please; it's a nice little place.'

Mr Elliott drew aside. Books – and particularly old books – tend to be dusty company. This may account for the fact that few antiquarian booksellers are of Falstaffian proportions. They are more usually lean, ruminative, dryish spectators of life. The gnawing of the worm in the tome is among the more melancholy of nature's lullabies; and the fluctuations in price of 'firsts' and of 'mint states' must incline any temperament, if not towards cynicism, at least towards the philosophical. Herodotus tells of a race of pygmies whose only diet was the odour of roses; and though morocco leather is sweeter than roses, it is even less fattening.

Mr Elliott, however, flourished on it. He was a rotund little man with a silver watch-chain from which a gold locket dangled, and he had uncommonly small feet. He might have been a ballet-master. 'You make your way up those four stairs, sir,' he went on, as he ushered his customer beneath the curtain, 'turn left down the passage, and the door's on the right. It's quiet in there, but that's no harm done. No hurry, sir.'

★

So Alan proceeded on his way. The drugget on the passage floor showed little trace of wear. The low panelled walls had been white-washed. He came at last to the flowered china handle of the door beyond the turn of the passage, then stood for a moment lost in surprise. But it was the trim cobbled garden beyond the square window on his right that took his glance rather than the room itself. Yellow crocuses, laden with saffron pollen, stood wide agape in the black mould, and the greening buds of a bush of lilac were tapping softly against the glass. And above was a sky of the gentlest silken blue; wonderfully still.

He turned and looked about him. The paint on wainscot and cornice must once have been of a bright apple green. It had faded now. A gate-leg table was in the far corner beyond the small-paned window; and on his left, with three shallow steps up to it, was another door. And the shelves were lined from floor to ceiling with the liter-ary treasures which Mr Elliott kept solely for his elect. So quiet was the room that even the flitting of a clothes-moth might be audible, though the brightness of noonday now filled it to the brim. For the three poplars beyond the lilac bush were still almost as bare as the frosts of winter had made them.

In spite of the flooding March light, in spite of this demure sprightliness after the gloom and disorder of the shop he had left behind him, Alan – as in his languid fashion he turned his head from side to side – became conscious first and foremost of the *age* of Mr Elliott's pretty parlour. The paint was only a sort of 'Let's pretend'. The space between its walls seemed, indeed, to be as much a res-ervoir of time as of light. The panelled ceiling, for example, was cracked and slightly discoloured; so were the green shutter-cases to the windows; while the small and beautiful chimneypiece – its carved marble lintel depicting a Cupid with pan pipes dancing before a smiling goddess under a weeping willow – enshrined a grate that at this moment contained nothing, not even the ashes of a burnt-out fire. Its bars were rusty, and there were signs of damp in the moulded plaster above it.

A gentle breeze was now brisking the tops of the poplar trees, but no murmur of it reached Alan where he stood. With his parcel tucked under his arm, he edged round softly from shelf to shelf, and even after so cursory an examination as this – and it was one of Mr Elliott's principles to mark all his books in plain figures – he realised that his means were much too moderate for his appetite. He came to a standstill, a little at a loss. What was he to do next? He stifled a yawn. Then, abstracting a charming copy of *Hesperides*, by that 'Human and divine' poet, Robert Herrick, he seated himself idly on the edge of the table and began to turn over its leaves. They soon became vocal:

> Aske me, why I do not sing
> To the tension of the string.
> As I did, not long ago,
> When my numbers full did flow?
> Griefe (ay me!) hath struck my Lute,
> And my tongue – at one time – mute.

His eye strayed on, and he read slowly – muttering the words to himself as he did so – 'The Departure of the Good *Daemon*':

> What can I do in Poetry,
> Now the good Spirit's gone from me?
> Why nothing now, but lonely sit,
> And over-read what have I writ.

Alan's indolence was even more extreme; he was at this moment merely over-reading what he had *read* – and what he had read again and again and again. For the eye may be obedient while the master of the mind sits distrait and aloof. His wits had gone wool-gathering. He paused, then made yet another attempt to fix his attention on the sense of this simple quatrain. But in vain. For in a moment or two his light, clear eyes had once more withdrawn themselves from the printed page and were once more, but now more intently, exploring the small green room in which he sat.

And as he did so – though nothing of the bright external scene around him showed any change – out of some daydream, it seemed, of which until then he had been unaware, there had appeared to him from the world of fantasy the image of a face.

No known or remembered face – a phantom face, as alien and inscrutable as are the apparitions that occasionally visit the mind in sleep. This in itself was not a very unusual experience. Alan was a young man of an imaginative temperament, and possessed that inward eye which is often, though not unfailingly, the bliss of solitude. And yet there was a difference. This homeless image was at once so real in effect, so clear, and yet so unexpected. Even the faint shadowy colours of the features were discernible – the eyes dark and profound, the hair drawn back over the rather narrow temples of the oval head; a longish, quiet, intent face, veiled with reverie and a sort of vigilant sorrowfulness, and yet possessing little of what at first sight might be called beauty – or what at least is usually accepted as beauty.

So many and fleeting, of course, are the pictures that float into consciousness at the decoy of a certain kind of poetry that one hardly heeds them as they pass and fade. But this, surely, was no after-image of one of Herrick's earthly yet ethereal Electras or Antheas or Dianemes, vanishing like the rainbows in a fountain's falling waters.

There are degrees of realisation. And, whatever 'good Spirit' this shadowy visitant may have represented, and whatever its origin, it had struck *some* 'observer' in Alan's mind mute indeed, and had left him curiously disquieted. It was as if in full sight of a small fishing smack peacefully becalmed beneath the noonday blue, the spars and hulk of some such phantom as the *Flying Dutchman* had suddenly appeared upon the smooth sea green; though this perhaps was hardly a flattering account of it. Anyhow, it had come, and now it was gone – except out of memory – as similar images do come and go.

Mere figment of a daydream, then, though this vision must have been, Alan found himself vacantly searching the room as if for positive corroboration of it, or at least for some kind of evidence that would explain it away. Faces are but faces, of course, whether real or imaginary, and whether they appear in the daytime or the dark, but there is at times a dweller behind the eye that looks out, though only now and again, from that small window. And *this* looker-out – unlike most – seemed to be innocent of any attempt at concealment. 'Here am I… And you?' *That* had seemed to be the mute question it was asking; though with no appearance of needing an answer; and, well, Alan distrusted feminine influences. He had once or twice in his brief career loved not wisely but too idealistically, and for the time being he much preferred first editions. Besides, he disliked mixing things up – and how annoying to be first slightly elated and then chilled by a mere fancy!

The sun in his diurnal round was now casting a direct beam of light from between the poplars through one of the little panes of glass in Mr Elliott's parlour. It limned a clear-cut shadow-pattern on the fading paint of the frame and on the floor beneath. Alan watched it and was at the same time listening – as if positively in hope of detecting that shadow's indetectable motion!

In the spell of this reverie, time seemed to have become of an almost material density. The past hung like cobwebs in the air. He turned his head abruptly; he was beginning to feel a little uneasy. And his eyes now fixed themselves on the narrow panelled door above the three stairs on the other side of the room. When consciousness is thus unusually alert it is more easily deceived by fancies. And yet so profound was the quiet around him it seemed improbable that the faint sound he had heard as of silk very lightly brushing against some material obstacle was imaginary. Was there a listener behind that door? Or was there not? If so, it must be one as intent as himself, but far more secret.

For a full minute, and as steadily as a cat crouching over a mouse's hole – though there wasn't the least trace of the predatory on his mild fair features, he scrutinised the key in the lock. He breathed again; and then with finger in book to keep his place tiptoed across the room and gently – by a mere finger's breadth – opened the door. Another moment and he had pushed it wider. Nothing there. Exactly as he had expected, of course, and yet – why at the same moment was he both disappointed and relieved?

He had exposed a narrow staircase – unstained, uncarpeted. Less than a dozen steep steps up was another door – a shut door, with yet another pretty flowered china handle and china finger-plates to it. A rather unusual staircase, too, he realised, since, unless one or other of its two doors were open, it must continually be in darkness. But you never know what oddity is going to present itself next in an old rambling house. How many human beings, he speculated, as he scanned this steep and narrow vacancy, must in the two or three centuries gone by have ascended and descended that narrow ladder – as abrupt as that of Jacob's dream? They had come, disguised in the changing fashions of their time; they had gone, leaving apparently not a wrack behind.

Well, that was that. This March morning might be speciously bright and sunny, but in spite of its sunshine it was cold. Books, too, may cheer the mind, but even when used as fuel they are apt to fail to warm the body, and rust on an empty grate diminishes any illusion of heat its bars might otherwise convey. Alan sighed, suddenly aware that something which had promised to be at least an arresting little experience had failed him. The phantasmal face so vividly seen, and even watched for a moment, had already become a little blurred in memory. And now there was a good deal more disappointment in his mind than relief. He felt like someone who has been cheated at a game he never intended to play. A particularly inappropriate simile, nonetheless, for he hadn't the smallest notion what the stakes had been, or, for that matter, what the game. He took up his hat and walking-stick, and still almost on tiptoe, and after quietly but firmly shutting both doors behind him, went back into the shop.

'I think I will take *this,* please,' he said almost apologetically to the old bookseller, who with his hands under his black coat-tails was now surveying the busy world from his own doorstep.

'Certainly, sir.' Mr Elliott wheeled about and accepted the volume with that sprightly turn of his podgy wrist with which he always welcomed a book that was about to leave him for ever. 'Ah, the *Hesperides,* sir. I'll put the three into one parcel. A nice tall clean copy, I see. It came, if memory serves me right, from the library of Colonel Anstey, sir, who purchased the Talbot letters – and at a very reasonable price, too. Now if I had a *first* in this condition!…'

Alan dutifully smiled. 'I found it in the parlour,' he said. 'What a charming little room – and garden too; I had no idea the house was so old. Who lived in it before you did? I suppose it wasn't always a bookshop?'

He tried in vain to speak naturally and not as if he had plums in his mouth.

'Lived here before me, now?' the bookseller repeated ruminatively. 'Well, sir, there was first, of course, my immediate predecessor. *He* came before me; and *we* took over his stock. Something of a disappointment, too, when I came to go through with it.'

'And before *him*?' Alan persisted.

'Before him, sir? I fancy this was what might be called a *private* house. You could see if you looked round a bit how it has been converted. It was a doctor's, I understand – a Dr Marchmont's. And what we call the parlour, sir, from which you have just emerged, was always, I take it, a sort of book room. Leastways some of the books there now were there then – with the book-plate and all. You see, the Mr Brown who came before me and who, as I say, converted the house, *he* bought the doctor's library. Not merely medical and professional works neither. There was some choice stuff besides; and a few moderate specimens of what is known in the trade as the curious, sir. Not that I go out of my way for it, myself.'

Alan paused in the doorway, parcel in hand.

'A bachelor, I suppose?'

'The doctor, sir, or Mr Brown?'

'The doctor.'

'Well, now, that I couldn't rightly say,' replied Mr Elliott cheerfully. 'Let us hope *not*. They tell me, sir, it makes things seem more homely-like to have a female about the house. And' – he raised his voice a little – 'I'll warrant that Mrs Elliott, sir, if she were here to say so, would bear me out.' Mrs Elliott, in fact, a pasty-looking old woman, with a mouth like a cod's and a large marketing basket on her arm, was at this moment emerging out from behind a curtained

doorway. Possibly her husband had caught a glimpse of her reflection in his spectacles. She came on with a beetle-like deliberation.

'What's that you were saying about me, Mr Elliott?' she said.

'This gentleman was inquiring, my love, if Dr Marchmont-as-was
lived in a state of single blessedness or if there was a lady in the case.'

Mrs Elliott fixed a slow, flat look on her husband, and then on
Alan.

'There was a sister or niece or something, so they say. But I never
knew anything about them, and don't want to,' she declared. And
Alan, a little chilled by her demeanour, left the shop.

Not that that one fish-like glance of Mrs Elliott's censorious eye
had by any means freed his fancy of what had passed. In the days
that followed he could never for an instant be sure when or where
the face that reverie had somehow conjured up out of the recesses
of his mind on his first visit to the old bookseller's parlour was not
about to reappear. And it chose the oddest of moments. Even when
his attention was definitely fixed on other things it would waft itself
into his consciousness again – and always with the same serene yet
vivid, naïve yet serious question in the eyes – a question surely that
only life itself could answer, and that not always with a like candour
or generosity. Alan was an obstinate young man in spite of appearances. But to have the rudiments of an imagination is one thing, to
be at the beck and call of every passing fancy is quite another. He
was not, he reassured himself, as silly as all that. He held out for
days together; and then when he had been left for twenty-four hours
wholly at peace – he suddenly succumbed.

A westering sun was sharply gilding its windows when he once
more made his way into Mr Elliott's parlour. It was empty. And
almost at the same instant he realised how anxious he had been that
this *should* be so, and how insipid a bait as such the little room now

proved to be. He hadn't expected that. And yet – not exactly insipid; its flavour had definitely soured. He wished he had never come; he tried to make up his mind to go. Ill at ease, angry with himself, and as if in open defiance of some inward mentor, he took down at random a fusty old quarto from its shelf and seating himself on a chair by the table, he began, or rather attempted, to read.

Instead, with downcast eyes shelled in by the palm of his hand, and leaning gently on his elbow in an attitude not unlike that of the slippered and pensive Keats in the portrait, he found himself listening again. He did more than listen. Every nerve in his body was stretched taut. And time ebbed away. At this tension his mind began to wander off again into a dreamlike vacuum of its own, when, 'What was that?' a voice within whispered at him. A curious thrill ebbed through his body. It was as though unseen fingers had tugged at a wire – with no bell at the end of it. For this was no sound he had heard – no stir of the air. And yet in effect it so nearly resembled one that it might have been only the sigh of the blast of the east wind at the window. He waited a minute, then, with a slight shiver, glanced up covertly but steadily through his fingers.

He was shocked – by what he saw – yet not astonished. It seemed as if his whole body had become empty and yet remained as inert and heavy as lead. He was no longer alone. The figure that stood before him in the darker corner there, and only a few paces away, was no less sharply visible and even more actual in effect than the objects around her. One hand, from a loose sleeve, resting on the edge of the door to the staircase, she stood looking at him, her right foot with its high-heeled shoe poised delicately on the lowest of the three steps. With head twisted back sidelong over her narrow shoulder, her eyes were fixed on this earthly visitor to her haunts – as he sat, hand to forehead, drawn up stiff and chill at the table. She was watching

Alan. And the face, though with even fewer claims to be beautiful, and none to be better than knowing and wide awake, was without any question the face he had shared with Herrick's *Hesperides*.

A peculiar vacancy – like a cold mist up from the sea – seemed to have spread over his mind, and yet he was alert to his very finger-tips. Had she seen he had seen her? He couldn't tell. It was as cold in the tiny room as if the windows were wide open and the garden beyond them full of snow. The late afternoon light, though bleakly clear, was already thinning away, and, victim of this silly decoy, he was a prisoner who in order to regain his freedom must pass *her* way out. He stirred in his chair, his eyes now fixed again on the book beneath them.

And then at last, as if with confidence restored, he withdrew his hand from his face, lifted his head, and affecting a boldness he far from felt, deliberately confronted his visitor. At this the expression on her features – her whole attitude – changed too. She had only at this moment seen that he had seen her, then? The arm dropped languidly to her side. Her listless body turned a little, her shoulders slightly lifted themselves, and a faint provocative smile came into her face, while the dark jaded eyes resting on his own remained half mocking, half deprecatory – almost as if the two of them, he and she, were old cronies who had met again after a long absence from one another, with ancient secrets awaiting discreet discussion. With a desperate effort Alan managed to refrain from making any answering signal of recognition. He stared back with a face as blank as a turnip. How he knew with such complete assurance that his visitor was not of this world he never attempted to explain to himself. Real! She was at least as real as a clearly lit reflection of anything seen in a looking-glass, and in *effect* on his mind was more positive than the very chair on which he was sitting and the table beneath his elbow to which that chair was drawn up. For this was a reality of the soul, and not of the senses. Indeed, he himself might be the ghost and she the dominating pervasive actuality.

But even if he had been able to speak he had no words with which to express himself. He was shuddering with cold and had suddenly become horribly fatigued and exhausted. He wanted to 'get out' of all this and yet knew not only that this phantasm must have been lying in wait for him, but that sooner or later she would compel him to find out what she wanted of him, that she meant to be satisfied. Her face continued to change in expression even while he watched her. Its assurance seemed to intensify. The head stooped forward a little; the narrow, pallid, slanting eyelids momentarily closed; and then, with a gesture not merely of arm or shoulder but of her whole body, she once more fixed him with a gaze more intense, more challenging, more crammed with meaning than he had supposed possible in any human eye. It was as if some small wicket gate into the glooms of Purgatory had suddenly become thronged with bright-lit faces.

Until this moment they had been merely eyeing one another while time's sluggish moments ebbed away. They had been merely 'looking at' one another. Now there had entered those glazed dark fixed blue eyes the very self within. It stayed there gazing out at him transfixed – the pleading, tormented, dangerous spirit within that intangible husk. And then the crisis was over. With a slow dragging movement of his head Alan had at last succeeded in breaking the spell – he had turned away. A miserable disquietude and self-repulsion possessed him. He felt sick, body and soul. He had but one thought – to free himself once and for all from this unwarranted ordeal. Why should *he* have been singled out? What hint of any kind of 'encouragement' had he been responsible for? Or was this ghostly encounter an experi- ence that had been shared by other visitors to the old bookseller's sanctum – maybe less squeamish than himself? His chilled, bloodless fingers clenched on the open page of the book beneath them. He strove in vain to master himself, to fight the thing out. It was as if an icy hand had him in its grip, daring him to stir.

The evening wind had died with the fading day. The three poplars, every budded double-curved twig outlined against the glassy grey of the west, stood motionless. Daylight, even dusk, was all very well, but supposing this presence, as the dark drew on, ventured a little nearer? And suddenly his alarms – as much now of the body as of the mind – were over. She had been interrupted.

A footstep had sounded in the corridor. Alan started to his feet. The handle of the door had turned in the old brass lock; he watched it. With a jerk he twisted his head on his shoulders. He was alone. Yet again the interrupter had rattled impatiently with the door handle. Alan at last managed to respond to the summons. But even as he grasped the handle on his own side of it, the door was pushed open against him and a long-bearded face peered through.

'Pardon,' said this stranger, 'I didn't realise you had locked yourself in.'

In the thin evening twilight that was now their only illumination Alan found himself blushing like a schoolgirl.

'But I hadn't,' he stammered. 'Of course not. The catch must have jammed. I came in here myself only a few minutes ago.'

The long face with its rather watery blue-grey eyes placidly continued to survey him in the dusk. 'And yet, you know,' its owner drawled, with a soupçon of incredulity, 'I should have guessed myself that I have been poking about in our patron's shop out there for at least the best part of half an hour. But that, of course, is one of the charms of lit-er-a-ture. You haven't chanced, I suppose, on a copy of the *Vulgar Errors* – Sir Thomas Browne?'

Alan shook his head. 'The B's, I think, are in that corner,' he replied, 'alphabetical. But I didn't notice the *Errors*.'

Nor did he stay to help his fellow-customer find the volume. He hurried out, and this time he had no spoil to present to the old book-seller in recognition of the rent due for his occupation of the parlour.

A whole week went by, its last few days the battleground of a con-tinuous conflict of mind. He hadn't, he assured himself with the utmost conviction, the faintest desire in the world to set eyes again on – on what he *had* set eyes on. That was certain. It had been the oddest of shocks to what he had thought about things, to what had gone before, and, yes, to his vanity. Besides, the more he occupied himself with and pondered over his peculiar little experience the more probable it seemed that it and she and everything connected with her had been nothing but a cheat of the senses, a triumph of self-deception – a pure illusion, induced by the quiet, the solitude, the stirrings of springtime at the window, the feeling of age in the room, the romantic associations – and last, to the Herrick!

All this served very well in the middle of the morning or at two o'clock in the afternoon. But a chance waft of the year's first waxen hyacinths, the onset of evening, a glimpse of the waning moon – at any such oblique reminder of what had happened, these pretty arguments fell flat as a house of cards. Illusion! Then why had everything else in his life become by comparison so empty of interest and himself at a loose end? The thought of Mr Elliott's bookshop at such moments was like an hypnotic lure. Cheat himself as he might, he knew it was only cheating. Distrust the fowler as he might, he knew what nets he was in. How gross a folly to be at the mercy of one vehement coupling of glances. If only it had been that other face! And yet, supposing he were wrong about all this; supposing this phantasm really was in need of help, couldn't rest, had come back for something – there *were* things one might want to come back for – and even for something which he alone could give?

What wonder this restless conflict of mind reacted on his body and broke his sleep? Naturally a little invalidish in his appetite, Alan now suffered the pangs of a violent attack of indigestion. And at last he could endure himself no longer. On the following Tuesday he once more pushed open the outer door of Mr Elliott's bookshop, with its jangling bell, and entered, hot and breathless, from out of the pouring rain.

'There was a book I caught sight of,' he panted out to the old gentleman as he came in, 'when I was here last, you know. In the other room. I won't keep you a minute.'

At this, the bookseller's bland eye fixed itself an instant on the fair flushed face, almost as if he too could a tale unfold.

'Let me take your umbrella, sir,' he entreated. 'Sopping! A real downpour. But very welcome to the farmers, I'll be bound – if for once in a while they'd only *say* so. No hurry whatever, sir.'

Downpour indeed it was. As Alan entered the parlour the cold, sullen gush of rain on the young lilac buds and cobblestones of the little yard in the dreary leaden light at the window resounded steadily on. He had set out in the belief that his one desire was to prove that his 'ghost' was no ghost at all, that he had been the victim of a pure hallucination. Yet throughout his journey, with only his umbrella for company, he had been conscious of a thrill of excitement and expectation. And now that he had closed the door behind him, and had shut himself in, the faded little room in this obscurity at once began to influence his mind in much the same fashion as the livid gloom of an approaching thunderstorm affects the scenery of the hills and valleys over which it broods.

And this, it soon seemed, was to be his sole reward! His excitement fizzled out. With every passing moment his heart fell lower. He had gone away filled with a stark irrational hatred of the poor, restless, phantasmal creature who had intruded on his solitude. He had come back only to realise not only that she herself had been his lodestone, but that, even though any particular spot may undoubtedly be 'haunted', it by no means follows that its ghost is always at home. Everything about him seemed to have changed a little. Or was the change only in himself? In this damp air the room smelt of dry-rot and mouldering leather. Even the pretty grate looked thicklier scurfed with rust. And the books on the shelves had now taken to themselves the leaden livery of the weather. 'Look not too closely on us,' they seemed to cry. 'What are we all but memorials of the dead? And we too are swiftly journeying towards the dust.'

The prospect from the window was even more desolating. Nonetheless Alan continued to stare stupidly out of it. By the time he had turned away again he had become certain – though how he couldn't tell – that he need have no apprehension whatever of intangible company today. Mr Elliott's 'parlour' was emptier than he supposed a room could be. It seemed as if by sheer aversion for its late inmate he had exorcised it, and, irrational creature that he was, a stab of regret followed.

He turned to go. He gave a last look round – and paused. Was it that the skies had lightened a little or had he really failed to notice at his entry that the door at which his visitor had appeared was a few inches open? He stepped across softly and glanced up the staircase. Only vacancy there too. But that door was also ajar. The two faint daylights from above and below mingled midway. For a moment or two he hesitated. The next he had stolen swiftly and furtively up the staircase and had looked in.

This room was not only empty but abandoned. It was naked of any stick of furniture and almost of any trace of human occupation. Yet with its shallow bow window, low ceiling, and morning sun it must once in its heyday have blossomed like the rose. The flowered paper on its walls was dingy now; a few darker squares and oblongs alone showed where pictures had once hung. The brass gas bracket was green with verdigris, and a jutting rod was the only evidence of the canopy where once a bed had been.

But even vacancy may convey a sense of age and tell its tale. Alan was looking into the past. Indeed, the stale remnant of some once pervasive perfume still hung in the musty atmosphere of the room, though its sole refuse consisted of a few dust-grimed books in a corner and – on a curved white narrow shelf that winged the minute fireplace – a rusty hairpin.

Alan stooped, and very gingerly, with gloved finger and thumb, turned the books over – a blistered green-bound *Enoch Arden,* a small thick copy of *The Mysteries of Paris,* Dante Gabriel Rossetti's *House of Life,* a *Nightingale Valley,* a few damp, fly-blown shockers, some of them in French and paper-bound; and last, a square black American cloth-bound exercise book with E.F. cut out with a clumsy penknife at one of the top corners. The cockled cloth was slightly greened.

He raised the cover with the extreme tips of his fingers, stooped forward a little, and found himself in the window-light scanning with peculiar intensity the vanishing lineaments of a faded photograph – the photograph of a young woman in clothes somehow made the more old-fashioned in appearance by the ravages of time and light on the discoloured cardboard. He knew this face; and yet not *this* face. For days past it had not been out of his mind for more than a few hours together. But while his first impression had been that of the vivid likeness of the one to the other, what next showed clearest were the differences between them. Differences that stirred his heart into a sudden tumult.

The hair in the photograph was dressed in pretty much the same fashion – drawn up and back from the narrow temples across the widening head. The lips were, possibly, not so full; certainly not so dark. And though the cheek even of this much younger face was a little sunken, these faded eyes – a fading only of the paper depicting them and not of age – looked out at him without the faintest trace of boldness or effrontery. They were, it is true, fixed profoundly on his own. But they showed no interest in him, little awareness, no speculation – only a remote settled melancholy. What strange surmises, the young man reflected, must the professional photographer at times indulge in when from beneath his ink-black inquisitorial velvet cowl he peers into his camera at a face as careless of human curiosity as this had been. The young woman in the photograph had made, if any, a more feeble attempt to conceal her secret sorrows than a pall to conceal its bier or a broken sepulchre its bones.

At a breath the young man's aversion had died away. A shame-stricken compassion of which he had never dreamed himself capable had swept over him in its stead. He gazed on for a minute or two at the photograph – this withering memento which not even the removing men seemed to have considered worth flinging into a dustbin; then he opened the book at random – towards the middle of it – and leaning into the light at the window read these lines:

> My midnight lamp burns dim with shame,
>   In Heaven the moon is low;
> Sweet sharer of its secret flame,
>   Arise, and go!

Haste, for dawn's envious gaping grave
Bids thee not linger here;
Though gone is all I am, and have –
Thy ghost once absent, dear.

He read them over again, then glanced stealthily up and out. They were a voice from the dead. It was as if he had trespassed into the echoing cold of a vault. And as he looked about him he suddenly realised that at any moment he might be interrupted, caught – prying. With a swift glance over his shoulder he pushed the photograph back into the old exercise book, and tucking this under his arm beneath his coat, tiptoed down the unlighted stairs into the parlour.

It had been a bold venture – at least for Alan. For, of all things in this world he disliked, he disliked by far the most being caught out in any little breach of the conventions. Suppose that old, cod-like Mrs Elliott had caught him exploring this abandoned bedroom? After listening yet again for any rumour either of herself or of her husband, he drew out from the lowest shelf near by two old sheep-skin folios, seated himself in full view of the door that led into the shop, and having hidden the exercise book well within cover of these antiquated tomes he began to turn over its pages. The trick took him back to his early schooldays – the sun, the heat, the drone of bees at the window, a settling wayward fly, the tick of the clock on the wall, and the penny 'blood' half concealed in his arithmetic book. He smiled to himself. Wasn't he being kept in now? And how very odd he should be minding so little what, only an hour before, he had foreseen he would be minding so much. How do ghosts *show* that you needn't expect them? Not even in their chosen haunts?

The book he was now examining was not exactly a penny 'blood'. In spite of appearances it must have cost at least sixpence. The once black ink on its pages had faded, and mildew dappled the leaves. The handwriting was irregular, with protracted loops. And what was written in the book consisted of verses, interlarded with occasional passages in prose, and a day or a date here and there, and all set down apparently just as it had taken the writer's fancy. And since many of the verses were heavily corrected and some of them interlined, Alan concluded – without any very unusual acumen! – that they were home made. Moreover, on evidence as flimsy as this, he had instantly surmised who this E.F. was, and that here was not only her book but a book of her own authorship. So completely, too, had his antipathy to the writer of it now vanished out of memory, so swiftly had the youthful, tragic face in the photograph secreted itself in his sentiments, that he found himself reading these scribbled 'effusions' with a mind all but bereft of its critical faculties. And of these the young man had hitherto rather boasted himself.

Still, poetry, good or bad, depends for its very life on the hospitable reader, as tinder awaits the spark. After that, what else matters? The flame leaps, the bosom glows! And as Alan read on he never for an instant doubted that here, however faultily expressed, was what the specialist is apt to call 'a transcript of life'. He knew of old – how remotely of old it now seemed – what feminine wiles are capable of; but here, surely, was the truth of self to self. He had greedily and yet with real horror looked forward to his reappearance here, as if Mr Elliott's little parlour was the positive abode of the Evil One. And yet now that he was actually pecking about beneath the very meshes of his nets, he was drinking in these call-notes as if they were cascading down upon him out of the heavens from the throat of Shelley's skylark itself. For what is Time to the artifices of Eros? Had he not (with Chaucer's help) once fallen head over ears in love with the faithless Criseyde? He drank in what he had begun to read as if his mind were a wilderness thirsty for rain, though the pall of cloud that darkened the window behind him was supplying it in full volume. He was elated and at the same time dejected at the thought that he was perhaps the very first human creature, apart from the fountain head, to sip of these secret waters.

And he had not read very far before he realised that its contents referred to an actual experience as well as to one of the imagination. He realised too that the earlier poems had been written at rather long intervals; and, though he doubted very much if they were first attempts, that their technique tended to improve as they went on – at least, that of the first twenty poems or so. With a small ivory pocket paper-knife which he always carried about with him he was now delicately separating page 12 from page 13, and he continued to read at random:

> There was sweet water once,
> Where in my childhood I
> Watched for the happy innocent nonce
> Day's solemn clouds float by.
>
> O age blur not that glass;
> Kind Heaven still shed thy rain;
> Even now sighs shake me as I pass
> Those gentle haunts again.

He turned over the page:

> Lullay, my heart, and find thy peace
>   Where thine old solitary pastures lie;
> Their light, their dews need never cease,
>   Nor sunbeams from on high.

Lullay, and happy dream, nor roam,
    Wild though the hills may shine,
Once there, thou soon would'st long for home,
    As I for mine!

and then:

Do you see; O, do you see? –
    Speak – and some inward self that accent knows,
    Bidding the orient East its rose disclose –
And daybreak wake in me.

Do you hear? O, do you hear? –
    This heart whose pulse like menacing night-bird cries?
    Dark, utter dark, my loved, is in these eyes
When gaunt good-bye draws near.

and then, after a few more pages:

'There is a garden in her face':
My face! Woe's me were *that* my all! –
Nay, but my *self,* though thine its grace,
Thy fountain is, thy peach-bloomed wall.

Come soon that twilight dusky hour,
When thou thyself shalt enter in
And take thy fill of every flower,
Since thine they have always been.

No rue? No myrrh? No nightshade? Oh,
Tremble not, spirit! All is well.
For Love's is that lovely garden; and so,
There only pleasures dwell.

Turning over the limp fusty leaves, one by one, he browsed on:

> When you are gone, and I'm alone,
> From every object that I see
> Its secret source of life is flown:
> All things look cold and strange to me.
>
> Even what I use – my rings, my gloves,
> My parasol, the clothes I wear –
> 'Once she was happy; now she loves!
> Once young,' they cry, 'now carked with care!'
>
> I wake and watch when the moon is here –
> A shadow tracks me on. And I –
> Darker than any shadow –
> fear Her fabulous inconstancy.
>
> That sphinx, the Future, marks its prey;
> I who was ardent, sanguine, free,
> Starve now in fleshly cell all day –
> And yours the rusting key.

and then:

> Your maddening face befools my eyes,
>   Your hand – I wake to feel –
> Lost in deep midnight's black surmise –
>   Its touch my veins congeal.
>
> What peace for me in star or moon?
>   What solace in nightingale!
> They tell me of the lost and gone –
>   And dawn completes the tale.

A note in pencil – the point of which must have broken in use – followed at the foot of the page:

All this means all but *nothing* of what was in my mind when I began to write it. *Dawn!!* I look at it, read it – it is like a saucer of milk in a cage full of asps. I didn't *know* one's mind could dwell only on one thought, one face, one longing, on and on without any respite, and yet remain sane. I didn't even know – until when? – it was possible to be happy, unendurably happy, and yet as miserable and as hopeless as a devil in hell. It is as if I were sharing my own body with a self I hate and fear and shake in terror at, and yet am powerless to be rid of. Well, never mind. If I *can* go on, that's my business. They mouth and talk and stare and sneer at me. What do I care! The very leaves of the trees whisper against me, and last night came thunder. I see my haunted face in every stone. And what cares *he*! Why should he? Would I, if I were a man? I sit here alone in the evening – waiting. My heart is a quicksand biding its time to swallow me up. Yet it isn't even that I question now whether he ever loved me or not – I only thirst and thirst for him to come. One look, a word, and I am at peace again. At peace! And yet I wonder sometimes, if I – if it is even *conceivable* that I still love him. Does steel *love* the magnet? Surely that moon which shone last night with her haggard glare in both our faces *abhors* the earth from which, poor wretch, she parted to perish and yet from which she can never, never, never utterly break away? Never, never, never. O God, how tired I am! – knowing as I do – as if my life were all being lived over again – that only worse lies in wait for me, that the more I feel the less I am able to please him. I *see* myself dragging on and on – and that other sinister mocking one within rises up and looks at me – 'What? And shall I never come into my own!'

Alan had found some little difficulty in deciphering the faint, blurred, pencilled handwriting – he decided to come back to this page again, then turned it over and read on:

> Your hate I see, and can endure, nay, *must* –
> Endure the stark denial of your love;
> It is your *silence,* like a cankering rust,
> That I am perishing of.
>
> What reck you of the blinded hours I spend
> Crouched on my knees beside a shrouded bed?
> Grief even for the loveliest has an end;
> No end in one whose soul it is lies dead.
>
> I watch the aged who've dared the cold slow ice
> That creeps from limb to limb, from sense to sense,
> Yet never dreamed this also is the price
> Which youth must pay for a perjured innocence.
>
> Yours that fond lingering lesson. Be content!
> Not one sole moment of its course I rue.
> The all I had was little. Now it's spent.
> Spit on the empty purse: 'tis naught to you.

And then these *Lines on Ophelia:*

She found an exit from her life;
She to an earthly green-room sped
Where parched-up souls distraught with strife
Sleep and are comforted.

Hamlet! I know that dream-drugged eye,
That self-coiled melancholic mien!
Hers was a happy fate – to die:
Mine – her foul Might-have-been.

and then:

Tomorrow waits me at my gate,
While all my yesterdays swarm near;
And one mouth whines, Too late, too late:
And one is dumb with fear.

Was this the all that life could give
Me – who from cradle hungered on.
Body and soul aflame, to *live* –
Giving my all – and then be gone?

O sun in heaven, to don that shroud,
When April's cuckoo thrilled the air!
Light thou no more the fields I loved.
Be only winter there!

and then:

Have *done* with moaning, idiot heart;
If it so be that Love has wings
I with my shears will find an art
To still his flutterings.

> Wrench off that bandage too will I,
> And show the imp he is blind indeed;
> Hot irons will prove my mastery;
> He shall not weep, but bleed.

> And when he is dead, and cold as stone,
> Then in his Mother's book I'll con
> The lesson none need learn alone,
> And, callous as she, play on.

He raised his eyes. The heavy rain had ebbed into a drifting drizzle; the day had darkened. He stared vacantly for a moment or two out of the rain-drenched window, and then, turning back a few of the damp cockled leaves, once more resumed his reading:

> And when at last I journey where
> All thought of you I must resign,
> Will the least memory of me be fair,
> Or will you even my ghost malign?

> I plead for nothing. Nay, Time's tooth –
> That frets the very soul away –
> May prove at last your slanders *truth*,
> And me the Slut you say.

There followed a series of unintelligible scrawls. It was as if the writer had been practising a signature in various kinds of more or less affected handwritings: 'Esther de Bourgh, Esther de Bourgh, Esther De Bourgh, E. de Bourgh, E de B, E de B, E. de Ice Bourgh, Esther de la Ice Bourgh, Esther de Borgia, Esther Césarina de Borgia,

Esther de Bauch, Esther de Bausch, E. de Bosh.' And then, this
unfinished scrap:

> Why cheat the heart with old deceits? –
> Love – was it *love* in thine
> Could leave me thus grown sick of sweets
> And...

The words sounded on – forlornly and even a little self-pityingly –
in Alan's mind. Sick of sweets, sick of sweets. He had had enough
for today. He shut the book, lifted his head, and with a shuddering
yawn and a heavy frown on his young face, once more stared out
of the window.

This E.F., whoever she was, had often sat in this room, alert,
elated, drinking in its rosily reflected morning sunshine from that
wall, happy in being merely herself, young, alone, and alive. He
could even watch in fancy that intense lowered face as she stitched
steadily on, lost in a passionate reverie, while she listened to as
dismal a downpour as that which had but lately ceased on the moss-
grown cobbles under the window. 'It's only one's inmost *self* that
matters,' she had scribbled at the end of one of her rhymes. And
then – how long afterwards? – the days, empty of everything but
that horror and dryness of the heart, when desire had corrupted
and hope was gone, and every hour of solitude must have seemed
to be lying in wait only to prove the waste, the bleakness, the
desolation to which the soul within can come. No doubt in time
they would learn even a bookworm to be a worm. 'That is one
of the charms of lit-er-a-ture', as the bland, bearded, supercilious
gentleman had expressed it. But he wouldn't have sentimentalised
about it.

Oddly enough, it hadn't yet occurred to Alan to speculate what kind of human being it was to whom so many of these poems had been addressed, and to whom seemingly every one of them had clearer or vaguer reference. There are ghosts for whom spectre is the better word. In this, the gloomiest hour of an English spring, he glanced again at the door he had shut behind him in positive hope that it might yet open once more – that he was not so utterly alone as he seemed. Sick: sick: surely, surely a few years of life could not have wreaked such horrifying changes in any human face and spirit as that!

But the least promising method apparently of evoking a visitant from another world is to wait on to welcome it. Better, perhaps, postpone any little experiment of this kind until after the veils of nightfall have descended. Not that he had failed to notice how overwhelming is the evidence that when once you have gone from this world you have gone for ever. Still, even if he *had* been merely the victim of an illusion, it would have been something just to smile or to nod in a common friendly human fashion, to lift up the dingy little black exercise book in his hand, merely to show that its owner had not confided in him in vain.

He was an absurdly timid creature – tongue-tied when he wanted most to express himself. And yet, if only… His glance strayed from door to book again. It was curious that the reading of poems like these should yet have proved a sort of solace. They had triumphed even over the miserable setting destiny had bestowed on them. Surely lit-er-a-ture without any vestige of merit in it couldn't do that. A veil of daydream drew over the fair and rather effeminate face. And yet the young man was no longer merely brooding; he was beginning to make plans. And he was making them without any help from the source from which it might have been expected.

Seeming *revenants*, of course, in this busy world are not of much account. They make indelible impressions if they do chance to visit one, though it is imprudent, perhaps, to share them with the sceptic. Nonetheless at this moment he was finding it almost impossible to recall the face not of the photograph but of his phantasm. And though there was nothing in the earlier poems he had read to suggest that they could not have been the work of the former, was it conceivable that they could ever have been the work of – that other one? But why not! To judge from some quite famous poets' faces their owners would have flourished at least as successfully in the pork-butchering line. Herrick himself – well, he was not exactly ethereal in appearance. But what need for these ridiculous unanswerable questions? Whoever E.F. had been, and whatever the authorship of the poems, he himself could at least claim now to be their only re-begetter.

At this thought a thrill of excitement had run through Alan's veins. Surely the next best thing to publishing a first volume of verse of one's own – and that he had now decided never to attempt – is to publish someone else's. He had seen worse stuff than this in print, and on hand-made paper, too. Why shouldn't he turn editor? How could one tell for certain that it is impossible to comfort – or, for that matter, to soothe the vanity of – some poor soul simply because it has happened to set out on the last long journey a few years before oneself? Mere initials are little short of anonymity, and even kindred spirits may be all the kinder if kept at the safe distance which anonymity ensures. But what about the old bookseller? An Englishman's shop is his castle, and this battered old exercise book, Alan assumed, must fully as much as any other volume on the shelves around him be the legal property of the current tenant of the house. Or possibly the ground-landlord's? He determined to take Mr Elliott into his confidence – but very discreetly.

With this decision, he got up – dismayed to discover that it was now a full half-hour after closing time. Nonetheless he found the old bookseller sitting at his table and apparently lost to the cares of business beneath a wire-protected gas bracket now used for an electric bulb. The outer door was still wide open, and the sullen clouds of the last of evening seemed to have descended even more louringly over the rain-soaked streets. A solitary dog lopped by the shrouded entrance. Not a sound pierced the monotony of the drizzle.

'I wonder,' Alan began, keeping the inflexions of his voice well in check, 'I wonder if you have ever noticed *this* particular book? It is in manuscript... Verse.'

'Verse, sir?' said the bookseller, fumbling in a tight waistcoat pocket for the silver case of his second pair of spectacles. 'Well, now, verse – in manuscript. *That* doesn't sound as if it's likely to be of much value, though finds there have been, I grant you. Poems and sermons – we are fairly glutted out with them nowadays; still, there was this Omar Khayyám fuss, sir, so you never know.'

He adjusted his spectacles and opened the book where the book opened itself. Alan stooped over the old man's shoulder and read with him:

> Once in kind arms, alas, you held me close;
> Sweet to its sepals was the unfolding rose.
> Why, then – though wind-blown, hither, thither,
> I languish still, rot on, and wither
> Yet *live*, God only knows.

A queer, intent, an almost hunted expression drew over Mr Elliott's greyish face as he read on.

'Now I wonder,' he said at last, firmly laying the book down again and turning an eye as guileless as an infant's to meet Alan's scrutiny,

'I wonder now who could have written that? Not that I flatter myself to be much of a judge. I leave that to my customers, sir.'

'There is an E.F. cut out on the cover,' said Alan, 'and' – the words came with difficulty – 'there is a photograph inside. But then, I suppose,' he added hastily, automatically putting out his hand for the book and withdrawing it again, 'I suppose just a loose photograph doesn't prove anything. Not at least to whom it belonged – the book, I mean.'

'No, sir,' said the bookseller, as if he thoroughly enjoyed little problems of this nature; 'in a manner of speaking I suppose it don't.' But he made no attempt to find the photograph, and a rather prolonged pause followed.

'It's quiet in that room in there,' Alan managed to remark at last. 'Extraordinarily quiet. You haven't yourself, I suppose, ever noticed the book before?'

Mr Elliott removed both pairs of spectacles from the bridge of his nose. 'Quiet is the word, sir,' he replied, in a voice suiting the occasion. 'And it's quieter yet in the two upper rooms above it. Especially of a winter's evening. Mrs Elliott and me don't use that part of the house much, though there is a good bit of lumber stowed away in the nearest of 'em. We can't sell more than a fraction of the books we get, sir, so we store what's over up there for the pulpers. I doubt if I have even so much as seen the inside of the other room these six months past. As a matter of fact' – he pursed his mouth and nodded – 'what with servant-girls and the like, and not everybody being as commonsensical as most, we don't mention it much.'

The bookseller's absent eye was now fixed on the rain-soaked street, and Alan waited, leaving his 'What?' unsaid.

'You see, sir, the lady that lived with Dr Marchmont here – his niece, or ward, or whatever it may be – well, they say she came to what they call an untimely end. A love affair. But there, for the matter of that you can't open your evening newspaper without finding more of such things than you get in a spring season's fiction. Strychnine, sir – that was the way of it; and it isn't exactly the poison I myself should choose for the purpose. It erects up the body like an arch, sir. So.' With a gesture of his small, square hand Mr Elliott pictured the effect in the air. 'Dr Marchmont hadn't much of a practice by that time, I understand; but I expect he came to a pretty sudden standstill when he saw *that* on the bed. A tall man, sir, with a sharp nose.'

Alan refrained from looking at the bookseller. His eyes stayed fixed on the doorway which led out into the world beyond, and they did not stir. But he had seen the tall dark man with the sharp nose as clearly as if he had met him face to face, and was conscious of a repulsion far more deadly than the mere features would seem to warrant. And yet; *why* should he have come to a 'standstill' quite like that if…? But the bookseller had opened the fusty, mildewed book at another page. He sniffed, then having rather pernicketily adjusted his spectacles, read over yet another of the poems:

> *Esther!* came whisper from my bed.
> *Answer me, Esther – are you there?*
> 'Twas waking self to self that's dead
> Called on the empty stair.
>
> Stir not that pit; she is lost and gone
> A Jew decoyed her to her doom.
> Sullenly knolls her passing bell
> Mocking me in the gloom.

The old man gingerly turned the leaf, and read on:

Last evening, as I sat alone –
Thimble on finger, needle and thread –
Light dimming as the dusk drew on,
   I dreamed that I was dead.

Like wildering timeless plains of snow
Which bitter winds to ice congeal
The world stretched far as sight could go
   'Neath skies as hard as steel.

Lost in that nought of night I stood
And watched my body – brain and breast
In dreadful anguish – in the mould
   Grope to'rd its final rest.

Its craving dreams of sense dropped down
Like crumbling maggots in the sod:
Spectral, I stood; all longing gone,
   Exiled from hope and God.

And you I loved, who once loved me,
And shook with pangs this mortal frame,
Were sunk to such an infamy
   That when I called your name,

Its knell so racked that sentient clay
That my lost spirit lurking near,
Wailed, liked the damned, and fled away –
   And woke me, stark with *Fear*.

He pondered a moment, turned back the leaf again, and holding the book open with his dumpy forefinger, 'A *Jew*, now,' he muttered to himself, 'I never heard any mention of a Jew. But what, if you follow me,' he added, tapping on the open page with his spectacles, 'what I feel about such things as these is that they're not so much what may be called mournful as *morbid*, sir. They rankle. I don't say, mind you, there isn't a ring of truth in them – but it's so *put*, if you follow me, as to make it worse. Why, if all our little mistakes were dealt with in such a vengeful spirit as this – as *this*, where would any of us be? And death... Say things out, sir, by all means. But what things? It isn't human nature. And what's more,' he finished pensively, 'I haven't noticed that the stuff *sells* much the better for it.'

Alan had listened but had not paid much attention to these moralisings. 'You mean,' he said, 'that you think the book *did* actually belong to the lady who lived here, and that – that it was she herself who wrote the poems? But then, you see, it's E.F. on the cover, and I thought you said the name was Marchmont?'

'Yes, sir, Marchmont. Between you and me, there *was* a Mrs, I understand; but she went away. And who this young woman was I don't rightly know. Not much good, I fancy. At least—' He emptily eyed again the blurred lettering of the poem. 'But there, sir,' he went on with decision, 'there's no need that I can see to worry about that. The whole thing's a good many years gone, and what consequence is it now? You'd be astonished how few of my customers really care who wrote a book so long as wrote it was. Which is not to suggest that if we get someone – someone with a name, I mean – to lay out the full story of the young woman as a sort of foreword, there might not be money in it. There *might* be. It doesn't much signify nowadays what you say about the dead, not legally, I mean. And especially these poets, sir. It all goes in under "biography". Besides, a suicide's a suicide all the world over. On the other hand' – and he glanced over his shoulder – 'I rather fancy Mrs E. wouldn't care to be mixed up in the affair. What she reads she never much approves of, though that's the kind of reading she likes best. The ladies can be so very scrupulous.'

Alan had not seen the old bookseller in quite so bright a light as this before.

'What I was wondering, Mr Elliott,' he replied in tones so frigid they suggested he was at least twenty years older than he appeared to be, 'is whether you would have any objection to my sending the book myself to the printers. It's merely an idea. One can't tell. It could do no harm. Perhaps who*ever* it was who wrote the poems may have hoped some day to get them printed – you never know. It would be at my expense, of course. I shouldn't dream of taking a penny piece and I would rather there were no introduction – by *anyone*. There need be no name or address on the title-page, need there? But this is, of course, only if you see no objection?'

Mr Elliott had once more lifted by an inch or two the back cover of the exercise book, as if possibly in search of the photograph. He found only this pencilled scrawl:

Well, well, well! squeaked the kitten to the cat;
Mousie refuses to play any more! so that's the end of that!

He shut up the book and rested his small plump hand on it.

'I suppose, sir,' he inquired discreetly, 'there *isn't* any risk of any infringement of copyright? I mean,' he added, twisting round his unspectacled face a little in Alan's direction, 'there isn't likely to be anybody who would *recognise* what's in here? I am not, of course, referring to the photograph, but a book, even nowadays, may be what you may call *too* true-spoken – when it's new, I mean. And it's not so much Mrs E. I have in mind now as the police' – he whispered the word – 'the *police*.'

Alan returned his blurred glance without flinching.

'Oh, no…' he said. 'Besides, I should merely put E.F. on the title-page and say it had been printed privately. I am quite prepared to take the risk.'

The cold tones of the young man seemed to have a little daunted the old bookseller.

'Very well, sir. I will have just a word with a young lawyer friend of mine, and if that's all right, why, sir, you are welcome.'

'And the books could be sold from here?'

'Sold? Why, yes, sir – they'll have plenty of respectable company, at any rate.'

But if Alan had guilelessly supposed that the mere signing of a cheque for £33 10s. in settlement of a local printer's account would finally exile a ghost that now haunted his mind far more persistently than it could ever have haunted Mr Elliott's green parlour, he soon discovered his mistake. He had kept the photograph, but had long since given up any attempt to find his way through the maze in which he found himself. Why, why, should he concern himself with what an ill-starred life had done to that young face? If the heart, if the very soul is haunted by a ghost, need one heed the frigid dictates of the mind? Infatuated young man, he was in servitude to one who had left the world years before he was born, and had left it, it seemed, only the sweeter by her exit. He was sick for love of one who was once alive but was now dead, and – why should he deny it? Mrs E. wouldn't! – damned.

Still, except by way of correspondence he avoided Mr Elliott and his parlour for weeks, until, in fact, the poems were finally in print, until their neat grey deckled paper covers had been stitched on, and the copies were ready for a clamorous public! So it was early one morning in the month of June before he once more found himself in the old bookseller's quiet annexe. The bush of lilac, stirred by the warm, languid breeze at the window, was shaking free its faded once-fragrant tassels of bloom and tapering heart-shaped leaves from the last dews of night. The young poplars stood like gold-green torches against the blue of the sky. A thrush was singing somewhere out of sight. It was a scene worthy of Arcady.

Alan had trailed through life without any positive need to call on any latent energy he might possess. And now that he had seen through the press his first essay in publishing a reaction had set in. A cloud of despondency shadowed his young features as he stared out through the glass of the window. Through the weeks gone by he had been assuring himself that it was no more than an act of mere decency to get the poems into print. A vicarious thirty pounds or so, just to quiet his conscience. What reward was even thinkable? And yet but a few nights before he had found himself sitting up in bed in the dark of the small hours just as if there had come a tap upon the panel of his door or a voice had summoned him out of dream. He had sat up, leaning against his bed-rail, exhausted by his few hours' broken sleep. And in the vacancy of his mind had appeared yet again in silhouette against the dark the living presentment of the young face in the photograph. Merely the image of a face floating there, with waxen downcast lids, the features passive as those of a death-mask – as unembodied an object as the after-image of a flower. There was no speculation in the downcast eyes, and in that lovely, longed-for face; no, nothing whatever for *him* – and it had faded out as a mirage of green-fronded palm trees and water fades in the lifeless sands of the desert.

He hadn't any desire to sleep again that night. Dreams might come; and wakeful questions pestered him. How old was she when the first of the poems was written? How old when no more came, and she herself had gone on – gone on? That barren awful road of disillusionment, satiety, self-disdain. Had she even when young and untroubled ever been happy? Was what she had written even true? How far are poems *true*? What had really happened? What had been left out? You can't even tell – yourself – what goes on in the silent places of your mind when you have swallowed, so to speak, the dreadful *outside* things of life. What, for example, had *Measure for Measure* to do with the author of *Venus and Adonis,* and what *Don Juan* with Byron as a child? One thing, young women of his own day didn't take their little affairs like that. They kept life in focus. But that ghost! The ravages, the paint, the insidiousness, the very clothes!

Coming to that, then, who the devil had he been taking such pains over? The question kept hammering at his mind day after day; it was still unanswered, showed no promise of an answer. And the Arcadian scene beyond the windows suddenly became an irony and a jeer. The unseen bird itself sang on in vulgar mockery: 'Come *off* of it! Come off of it! Come off of it! Dolt, dolt, dolt!'

He turned away out of the brightness of the light, and fixed his eyes on the bulky brown-paper package that contained the printed volumes. It was useless to stay here any longer. He would open the package, but merely to take a look at a copy and assure himself that no ingenuity of the printer had restored any little aberration of spelling or punctuation which he himself had corrected three times in the proofs. He knew the poems – or some of them – by heart now.

With extreme reluctance he had tried one or two of them on a literary friend: 'An anonymous thing, you know, I came across it in an old book.'

The friend had been polite rather than enthusiastic. After, cigarette between fingers, idly listening to a few stanzas, he had smiled and asked Alan if he had ever read a volume entitled *Poems of Currer, Ellis, and Acton Bell.*

'Well, there you are! A disciple of Acton's, dear boy, if you ask *me.* Stuff as common as blackberries.'

And Alan had welcomed the verdict. He didn't want to share the poems with anybody. If nobody bought them and nobody cared, what matter? All the better. And he wasn't being sentimental about them now either. He didn't care if they had any literary value or not. He had entrusted himself with them, and that was the end of the matter. What was Hecuba to him, or he to Hecuba? What?

And what did it signify that he had less right to the things even than Mrs Elliott – who fortunately was never likely to stake out any claim? The moral ashbins old women can be, he thought bitterly. Simply because this forlorn young creature of the exercise book had been forced at last to make her exit from the world under the tragic but hardly triumphant arch of her own body this old woman had put her hand over her mouth and looked 'volumes' at that poor old hen-pecked husband of hers even at mention of her name. Suicides, of course, are a nuisance in any house. But all those years gone by! And what did they *know* the poor thing had done to merit their insults? *He* neither knew nor cared, yet for some obscure reason steadily wasted at least five minutes in untying the thick knotted cord of the parcel instead of chopping it up with his pocket-knife in the indignant fashion which he had admired when he visited the printers.

The chastest little pile of copies was disclosed at last in their grey-blue covers and with their enrichingly rough edges. The hand-made paper had been an afterthought. A further cheque was due to the printer, but Alan begrudged not a farthing. He had even incited them to be expensive. He believed in turning things out nicely – even himself. He and his pretty volumes were 'a pair'!

Having opened the parcel, having neatly folded up its prodigal wrappings of brown paper, and thrown away the padding and hanked the string, there was nothing further to do. He sat back in Mr Elliott's old Windsor chair, leaning his chin on his knuckles. He was waiting, though he didn't confess it to himself. What he did confess to himself was that he was sick of it all. Age and life's usage may obscure, cover up, fret away a fellow-creature at least as irrevocably as six feet of common clay.

When, then, he raised his eyes at some remote inward summons he was already a little hardened in hostility. He was looking clean across the gaily lit room at its other occupant standing there in precisely the same attitude – the high-heeled shoe coquettishly arched on the lowest of the three steps, the ridiculous flaunting hat, the eyes aslant beneath the darkened lids casting back on him their glitter from over a clumsy blur that was perfectly distinct on the cheekbone in the vivid light of this June morning. And even this one instant's glimpse clarified and crystallised all his old horror and hatred. He knew that she had seen the tender first fruits on the table. He knew that he had surprised a gleam of triumph in her snakish features, and he knew that she no more cared for that past self and its literary exercises than she cared for his silly greenhorn tribute to them. What then was she after?

The darkening, glittering, spectral eyes were once more communicating with him with immense rapidity, and yet were actually conveying about as empty or as mindless a message as eyes can. If half-extinguished fires in a dark room can be said to look coy, these did. But a coyness practised in a face less raddled and ravaged by time than by circumstance is not an engaging quality. 'Arch!' My God, 'arch' was the word!

Alan was shivering. How about the ravages that life's privy paw had made in his *own* fastidious consciousness? Had his own heart been a shade more faithful would the horror which he knew was now distorting his rather girlish features and looking out of his pale blue eyes have been quite so poisonously bitter?

Fortunately his back was turned to the window, and he could in part conceal his face with his hand before this visitor had had time to be fully aware what that face was saying. She had stirred. Her head was trembling slightly on her shoulders. Every tinily exquisite plume in the mauve ostrich feathers on her drooping hat trembled as if in sympathy. Her ringed fingers slipped down from the door to her narrow hip; her painted eyelids narrowed, as if she were about to speak to him. But at this moment there came a sudden flurry of wind in the lilac tree at the window, ravelling its dried-up flowers and silky leaves. She stooped, peered; and then, with a sharp, practised, feline, seductive nod, as bold as grass-green paint, she was gone. An instant or two, and in the last of that dying gust, the door above at the top of the narrow staircase, as if in a sudden access of bravado, violently slammed: 'Touch me, tap at me, force me, if you dare!'

The impact shook the walls and rattled the windows of the room beneath. It jarred on the listener's nerves with the force of an imprecation. As abrupt a silence followed. Nauseated and slightly giddy he got up from his chair, resting his fingers automatically on the guileless pile of books, took up his hat, glanced vacantly at the gilded Piccadilly maker's name on the silk lining, and turned to go. As he did so, a woeful, shuddering fit of remorse swept over him, like a parched-up blast of the sirocco over the sands of a desert. He shot a hasty strangulated look up the narrow empty staircase as he passed by. Then, 'O God,' he groaned to himself, 'I wish – I *pray* – you poor thing, you could only be a little more at peace – whoever, wherever you are – whatever I am.'

And then he was with the old bookseller again, and the worldly-wise old man was eyeing him as ingenuously as ever over his steel-rimmed glasses.

'He isn't looking quite himself,' he was thinking. 'Bless me, sir,' he said aloud, 'sit down and rest a bit. You must have been overdoing it. You look quite het up.'

Alan feebly shook his head. His cheek was almost as colourless as the paper on which the poems had been printed; small beads of sweat lined his upper lip and damped his hair. He opened his mouth to reassure the old bookseller, but before he could utter a word they were both of them caught up and staring starkly at one another – like conspirators caught in the act. Their eyes met in glassy surmise. A low, sustained, sullen rumble had come sounding out to them from the remoter parts of the shop which Alan had but a moment before left finally behind him. The whole house shuddered as if at the menace of an earthquake.

'Bless my soul, sir!' cried the old bookseller. 'What in merciful heaven was that!'

He hurried out, and the next instant stood in the entry of his parlour peering in through a dense fog of dust that now obscured the light of the morning. It silted softly down, revealing the innocent cause of the commotion. No irreparable calamity. It was merely that a patch of the old cracked plaster ceiling had fallen in, and a mass of rubble and plaster was now piled up, inches high, on the gate-leg table and the chair beside it, while the narrow laths of the ceiling above them, a few of which were splintered, lay exposed like the bones of a skeleton. A thick film of dust had settled over everything, intensifying with its grey veil the habitual hush of the charming little room. And almost at one and the same moment the old bookseller began to speculate first, what damages he might have been called upon to pay if his young customer had not in the nick of time vacated that chair, and next, that though perhaps his own little stock of the rare and the curious would be little the worse for the disaster, Alan's venture might be very much so. Indeed, the few that were visible of the little pile of books – but that morning come virgin and speckless from the hands of the binders – were bruised and scattered. And as Mr Elliott eyed them, his conscience smote him: 'Softly now, softly,' he muttered to himself, 'or we shall have Mrs E. down on this in pretty nearly no time!'

But Mrs E. had not heard. No footfall sounded above; nothing stirred; all remained as it might be expected to remain. And Alan, who meanwhile had stayed motionless in the outer shop, at this moment joined the old bookseller, and looked in on the ruins.

'Well, there, sir,' Mr Elliott solemnly assured him, 'all I can say is, it's a mercy you had come out of it. And by no more than a hair's-breadth!'

But Alan made no answer. His mind was a void. He was listening again – and so intently that it might be supposed the faintest stirrings even on the uttermost outskirts of the unseen might reach his ear. It was too late now – and in any case it hadn't occurred to him – to add to the title-page of his volume that well-worn legend: 'The heart knoweth his own bitterness; and a stranger doth not intermeddle with his joy.' But it might at least have served for his own brief *apologia*. He had meant well – it would have suggested. You never can tell.

As they stood there, then, a brief silence had fallen on the ravaged room. And then a husky, querulous, censorious voice had broken out behind the pair of them: 'Mr E., where are you?'

ALL HALLOWS

'And because time in itself... can receive no alteration, the hallowing... must consist in the shape or countenance which we put upon the affaires that are incident in these days.'

RICHARD HOOKER

I T WAS ABOUT HALF-PAST THREE ON AN AUGUST AFTERNOON when I found myself for the first time looking down upon All Hallows. And at glimpse of it, fatigue and vexation passed away. I stood 'at gaze', as the old phrase goes – like the two children of Israel sent in to spy out the Promised Land. How often the imagined transcends the real. Not so All Hallows. Having at last reached the end of my journey – flies, dust, heat, wind – having at last come limping out upon the green sea-bluff beneath which lay its walls – I confess the actuality excelled my feeble dreams of it.

What most astonished me, perhaps, was the sense not so much of its age, its austerity, or even its solitude, but its air of abandonment. It lay couched there as if in hiding in its narrow sea-bay. Not a sound was in the air; not a jackdaw clapped its wings among its turrets. No other roof, not even a chimney, was in sight; only the dark-blue arch of the sky; the narrow snowline of the ebbing tide; and that gaunt coast fading away into the haze of a west over which were already gathering the veils of sunset.

We had met, then, at an appropriate hour and season. And yet – I wonder. For it was certainly not the 'beauty' of All Hallows, lulled as if into a dream in this serenity of air and heavens, which was to leave the sharpest impression upon me. And what kind of first showing would it have made, I speculated, if an autumnal gale had been shrilling and trumpeting across its narrow bay – clots of wind-borne spume floating among its dusky pinnacles – and the roar of the sea echoing against its walls. Imagine it frozen stark in winter, icy hoar-frost edging its every boss, moulding, finial, crocket, cusp!

Indeed, are there not works of man, legacies of a half-forgotten past, scattered across this human world of ours from China to Peru, which seem to daunt the imagination with their incomprehensibility? Incomprehensible, I mean, in the sense that the passion that inspired and conceived them is incomprehensible. Viewed in the light of the passing day, they might be the monuments of a race of demi-gods. And yet, if we could but free ourselves from our timidities, and follies, we might realise that even we ourselves have an obligation to leave behind us similar memorials – testaments to the creative and faithful genius not so much of the individual as of Humanity itself.

However that may be, it was my own personal fortune to see All Hallows for the first time in the heat of the Dog Days, after a journey which could hardly be justified except by its end. At this moment of the afternoon the great church almost cheated one into the belief that it was possessed of a life of its own. It lay, as I say, couched in its natural hollow, basking under the dark dome of the heavens like some half-fossilised monster that might at any moment stir and awaken out of the swoon to which the wand of the enchanter had committed it. And with every inch of the sun's descending journey it changed its appearance.

That is the charm of such things. Man himself, says the philosopher, is the sport of change. His life and the life around him are but the flotsam of a perpetual flux. Yet, haunted by ideals, egged on by

impossibilities, he builds his vision of the changeless; and time diversi-
fies it with its colours and its 'effects' at leisure. It was drawing near
to harvest now; the summer was nearly over; the corn would soon be
in stook; the season of silence had come, not even the robins had yet
begun to practise their autumnal lament. I should have come earlier.

The distance was of little account. But nine flinty hills in seven
miles is certainly hard commons. To plod (the occupant of a cloud
of dust) up one steep incline and so see another; to plod up that and
so see a third; to surmount that and, half-choked, half-roasted, to
see (as if in unbelievable mirage) a fourth – and always stone walls,
discoloured grass, no flower but ragged ragwort, whited fleabane,
moody nettle, and the exquisite stubborn bindweed with its almond-
burdened censers, and always the glitter and dazzle of the sun – well,
the experience grows irksome. And then that endless flint erection
with which some jealous Lord of the Manor had barricaded his ver-
durous estate! A fly-infested mile of the company of that wall was
tantamount to making one's way into the infernal regions – with
Tantalus for fellow-pilgrim. And when a solitary and empty dung-cart
had lumbered by, lifting the dumb dust out of the road in swirling
clouds into the heat-quivering air, I had all but wept aloud.

No, I shall not easily forget that walk – or the conclusion of
it – when footsore, all but dead beat – dust all over me, cheeks, lips,
eyelids, in my hair, dust in drifts even between my naked body and
my clothes – I stretched my aching limbs on the turf under the strag-
gle of trees which crowned the bluff of that last hill, still blessedly
green and verdant, and feasted my eyes on the cathedral beneath me.
How odd Memory is – in her sorting arrangements. How perverse
her pigeon-holes.

It had reminded me of a drizzling evening many years ago. I had
stayed a moment to listen to an old Salvation Army officer preaching

at a street corner. The sopped and squalid houses echoed with his harangue. His penitents' drum resembled the block of an executioner. His goatish beard wagged at every word he uttered. 'My brothers and sisters,' he was saying 'the very instant our fleshly bodies are born they begin to perish; the moment the Lord has put them together, time begins to take them to pieces again. *Now* at this very instant if you listen close, you can hear the nibblings and frettings of the moth and rust within – the worm that never dies. It's the same with human causes and creeds and institutions – just the same. O, then, for that Strand of Beauty where all that is mortal shall be shed away and we shall appear in the likeness and verisimilitude of what in sober and awful truth we are!'

The light striking out of an oil-and-colourman's shop at the street corner lay across his cheek and beard and glassed his eye. The soaked circle of humanity in which he was gesticulating stood staring and motionless – the lassies, the probationers, the melancholy idlers. I had had enough. I went away. But is is odd that so utterly inappropriate a recollection should have edged back into my mind at this moment. There was, as I have said, not a living soul in sight. Only a few sea-birds – oyster-catchers maybe – were jangling on the distant beach.

It was now a quarter to four by my watch, and the usual pensive 'lin-lan-lone' from the belfry beneath me would soon no doubt be ringing to evensong. But if at that moment a triple bob-major had suddenly clanged its alarm over sea and shore I couldn't have stirred a finger's breadth. Scanty though the shade afforded by the wind-shorn tuft of trees under which I lay might be – I was ineffably at peace.

No bell, as a matter of fact, loosed its tongue that stagnant half-hour. Unless then the walls beneath me already concealed a few such chance visitors as myself, All Hallows would be empty. A cathedral not only without a close but without a congregation – yet another

romantic charm. The Deanery and the residences of its clergy, my
old guidebook had long since informed me, were a full mile or more
away. I determined in due time, first to make sure of an entry, and
then having quenched my thirst, to bathe.

How inhuman any extremity – hunger, fatigue, pain, desire –
makes us poor humans. Thirst and drouth so haunted my mind that
again and again as I glanced towards it I supped up in one long draught
that complete blue sea. But meanwhile, too, my eyes had been steadily
exploring and searching out this monument of the bygone centuries
beneath me.

The headland faced approximately due west. The windows of the
Lady Chapel therefore lay immediately beneath me, their fourteenth-
century glass showing flatly dark amid their traceries. Above it,
the shallow V-shaped, leaden-ribbed roof of the chancel converged
towards the unfinished tower, then broke away at right angles – for
the cathedral was cruciform. Walls so ancient and so sparsely adorned
and decorated could not but be inhospitable in effect. Their stone
was of a bleached bone-grey; a grey that nonetheless seemed to be
as immaterial as flame – or incandescent ash. They were substantial
enough, however, to cast a marvellously lucent shadow, of a blue no
less vivid but paler than that of the sea, on the shelving sward beneath
them. And that shadow was steadily shifting as I watched. But even
if the complete edifice had vanished into the void, the scene would
still have been of an incredible loveliness. The colours in air and sky
on this dangerous coast seemed to shed a peculiar unreality even on
the rocks of its own outworks.

So, from my vantage place on the hill that dominates it, I continued for a while to watch All Hallows; to spy upon it; and no less
intently than a sentry who, not quite trusting his own eyes, has seen
a dubious shape approaching him in the dusk. It may sound absurd,

but I felt that at any moment I too might surprise All Hallows in the act of revealing what in very truth it looked like – and *was,* when, I mean, no human witness was there to share its solitude.

Those gigantic statues, for example, which flanked the base of the unfinished tower, an intense bluish-white in the sunlight and a bluish-purple in shadow – images of angels and of saints, as I had learned of old from my guidebook. Only six of them at most could be visible, of course, from where I sat. And yet I found myself counting them again and yet again, as if doubting my own arithmetic. For my first impression had been that seven were in view – though the figure furthest from me at the western angle showed little more than a jutting fragment of stone which might perhaps be only part and parcel of the fabric itself.

But then the lights even of day may be deceitful, and fantasy plays strange tricks with one's eyes. With exercise, nonetheless, the mind is enabled to detect minute details which the unaided eye is incapable of particularising. Given the imagination, man himself indeed may some day be able to distinguish what shapes are walking during our own terrestrial midnight amid the black shadows of the craters in the noonday of the moon. At any rate, I could trace at last frets of carving, minute weather marks, crookednesses, incrustations, repairings, that had before passed unnoticed. These walls, indeed, like human faces, were maps and charts of their own long past.

In the midst of this prolonged scrutiny, the hypnotic air, the heat, must suddenly have overcome me. I fell asleep up there in my grove's scanty shade; and remained asleep, too, long enough (as time is measured by the clocks of sleep) to dream an immense panoramic dream. On waking, I could recall only the faintest vestiges of it, and found that the hand of my watch had crept on but a few minutes in the interval. It was eight minutes past four.

I scrambled up – numbed and inert – with that peculiar sense of panic which sometimes follows an uneasy sleep. What folly to have been frittering time away within sight of my goal at an hour when no doubt the cathedral would soon be closed to visitors, and abandoned for the night to its own secret ruminations. I hastened down the steep rounded incline of the hill, and having skirted under the sunlit expanse of the walls, came presently to the south door, only to discover that my forebodings had been justified, and that it was already barred and bolted. The discovery seemed to increase my fatigue fourfold. How foolish it is to obey mere caprices. What a straw is a man!

I glanced up into the beautiful shell of masonry above my head. Shapes and figures in stone it showed in plenty – symbols of an imagination that had flamed and faded, leaving this signature for sole witness – but not a living bird or butterfly. There was but one faint chance left of making an entry. Hunted now, rather than the hunter, I hastened out again into the full blazing flood of sunshine – and once more came within sight of the sea; a sea so near at last that I could hear its enormous sallies and murmurings. Indeed I had not realised until that moment how closely the great western doors of the cathedral abutted on the beach.

It was as if its hospitality had been deliberately designed, not for a people to whom the faith of which it was the shrine had become a weariness and a commonplace, but for the solace of pilgrims from over the ocean. I could see them tumbling into their cockleboats out of their great hollow ships – sails idle, anchors down; see them leaping ashore and straggling up across the sands to these all-welcoming portals – 'Parthians and Medes and Elamites; dwellers in Mesopotamia and in the parts of Egypt about Cyrene; strangers of Rome, Jews and Proselytes – we do hear them speak in our own tongue the wonderful works of God.'

And so at last I found my way into All Hallows – entering by a rounded dwarfish side-door with zigzag mouldings. There hung for corbel to its dripstone a curious leering face, with its forked tongue out, to give me welcome. And an appropriate one, too, for the figure I made!

But once beneath that prodigious roof-tree, I forgot myself and everything that was mine. The hush, the coolness, the unfathomable twilight drifted in on my small human consciousness. Not even the ocean itself is able so completely to receive one into its solacing bosom. Except for the windows over my head, filtering with their stained glass the last western radiance of the sun, there was but little visible colour in those great spaces, and a severe economy of decoration. The stone piers carried their round arches with an almost intimidating impassivity.

By deliberate design, too, or by some illusion of perspective, the whole floor of the building appeared steadily to ascend towards the east, where a dark, wooden multitudinously figured rood-screen shut off the choir and the high altar from the nave. I seemed to have exchanged one universal actuality for another: the burning world of nature for this oasis of quiet. Here, the wings of the imagination need never rest in their flight out of the wilderness into the unknown.

Thus resting, I must again have fallen asleep. And so swiftly can even the merest freshet of sleep affect the mind, that when my eyes opened, I was completely at a loss.

Where was I? What demon of what romantic chasm had swept my poor drowsy body into this immense haunt? The din and clamour of an horrific dream whose fainting rumour was still in my ear, became suddenly stilled. Then at one and the same moment, a sense of utter dismay at earthly surroundings no longer serene and peaceful, but grim and forbidding, flooded my mind, and I became aware that I was no longer alone. Twenty or thirty paces away, and a little this side of the rood-screen, an old man was standing.

To judge from the black and purple velvet and tassel-tagged gown he wore, he was a verger. He had not yet realised, it seemed, that a visitor shared his solitude. And yet he was listening. His head was craned forward and leaned sideways on his rusty shoulders. As I steadily watched him, he raised his eyes, and with a peculiar stealthy deliberation scanned the complete upper regions of the northern transept. Not the faintest rumour of any sound that may have attracted his attention reached me where I sat. Perhaps a wild bird had made its entry through a broken pane of glass and with its cry had at the same moment awakened me and caught his attention. Or maybe the old man was waiting for some fellow-occupant to join him from above.

I continued to watch him. Even at this distance, the silvery twilight cast by the clerestory windows was sufficient to show me, though vaguely, his face: the high sloping nose, the lean cheekbones and protruding chin. He continued so long in the same position that I at last determined to break in on his reverie.

At sound of my footsteps his head sunk cautiously back upon his shoulders; and he turned; and then motionlessly surveyed me as I drew near. He resembled one of those old men whom Rembrandt delighted in drawing: the knotted hands, the black drooping eyebrows, the wide thin-lipped ecclesiastical mouth, the intent cavernous dark eyes beneath the heavy folds of their lids. White as a miller with dust, hot and draggled, I was hardly the kind of visitor that any self-respecting custodian would warmly welcome, but he greeted me nonetheless with every mark of courtesy.

I apologised for the lateness of my arrival, and explained it as best I could. 'Until I caught sight of you,' I concluded lamely, 'I hadn't ventured very far in: otherwise I might have found myself a prisoner for the night. It must be dark in here when there is no moon.'

The old man smiled – but wryly. 'As a matter of fact, sir,' he replied, 'the cathedral is closed to visitors at four – at such times, that is, when there is no afternoon service. Services are not as frequent as they were. But visitors are rare too. In winter, in particular, you notice the gloom – as you say, sir. Not that I ever spend the night here: though I am usually last to leave. There's the risk of fire to be thought of and… I think I should have detected your presence here, sir. One becomes accustomed after many years.'

There was the usual trace of official pedantry in his voice, but it was more pleasing than otherwise. Nor did he show any wish to be rid of me. He continued his survey, although his eye was a little absent and his attention seemed to be divided.

'I thought perhaps I might be able to find a room for the night and really explore the cathedral tomorrow morning. It has been a tiring journey; I come from B—'

'Ah, from B—; it *is* a fatiguing journey, sir, taken on foot. I used to walk in there to see a sick daughter of mine. Carriage parties occasionally make their way here, but not so much as once. We are too far out of the hurly-burly to be much intruded on. Not that them who come to make their worship here are intruders. Far from it. But most that come are mere sightseers. And the fewer of them, I say, in the circumstances, the better.'

Something in what I had said or in my appearance seemed to have reassured him. 'Well, I cannot claim to be a regular churchgoer,' I said. 'I am myself a mere sightseer. And yet – even to sit here for a few minutes is to be reconciled.'

'Ah, reconciled, sir—' the old man repeated, turning away. 'I can well imagine it after that journey on such a day as this. But to live here is another matter.'

'I was thinking of that,' I replied in a foolish attempt to retrieve the position. 'It must, as you say, be desolate enough in the winter – for two-thirds of the year, indeed.'

'We have our storms, sir – the bad with the good,' he agreed, 'and our position is specially prolific of what they call sea-fog. It comes driving in from the sea for days and nights together – gale and mist, so that you can scarcely see your open hand in front of your eyes even in broad daylight. And the noise of it, sir, sweeping across overhead in that wooliness of mist, if you take me, is most peculiar. It's shocking to a stranger. No, sir, we are left pretty much to ourselves when the fine-weather birds are flown… You'd be astonished at the power of the winds here. There was a mason – a local man too – not above two or three years ago was blown clean off the roof from under the tower – tossed up in the air like an empty sack. But' – and the old man at last allowed his eyes to stray upwards to the roof again – 'but there's not much doing now.' He seemed to be pondering. 'Nothing open.'

'I mustn't detain you,' I said, 'but you were saying that services are infrequent now. Why is that? When one thinks of—' But tact restrained me.

'Pray don't think of keeping me, sir. It's a part of my duties. But from a remark you let fall I was supposing you may have seen something that appeared, I understand, not many months ago in the newspapers. We lost our dean – Dean Pomfrey – last November. To all intents and purposes, I mean; and his office has not yet been filled. Between you and me, sir, there's a hitch – though I should wish it to go no further. They are greedy monsters – those newspapers: no respect, no discretion, no decency, in my view. And they copy each other like cats in a chorus.

'We have never wanted to be a notoriety here, sir: and not of late of all times. We must face our own troubles. You'd be astonished how callous the mere sightseer can be. And not only them from over the water whom our particular troubles cannot concern – but far worse – parties as English as you or me. They ask you questions you wouldn't believe possible in a civilised country. Not that they care what becomes of us – not one iota, sir. We talk of them masked-up Inquisitors in olden times, but there's many a human being in our own would enjoy seeing a fellow-creature on the rack if he could get the opportunity. It's a heartless age, sir.'

This was queerish talk in the circumstances: and after all myself was of the glorious company of the sightseers. I held my peace. And the old man, as if to make amends, asked me if I would care to see any particular part of the building. 'The light is smalling,' he explained, 'but still if we keep to the ground level there'll be a few minutes to spare; and we shall not be interrupted if we go quietly on our way.'

For the moment the reference eluded me: I could only thank him for the suggestion and once more beg him not to put himself to any inconvenience. I explained, too, that though I had no personal acquaintance with Dr Pomfrey, I had read of his illness in the newspapers. 'Isn't he,' I added a little dubiously, 'the author of *The Church and the Folk*? If so, he must be an exceedingly learned and delightful man.'

'Ay, sir.' The old verger put up a hand towards me. 'You may well say it: a saint if ever there was one. But it's worse than "illness", sir – it's oblivion. And, thank God, the newspapers didn't get hold of more than a bare outline.'

He dropped his voice. 'This way, if you please'; and he led me off gently down the aisle, once more coming to a standstill beneath the roof of the tower. 'What I mean, sir, is that there's very few left in this world who have any place in their minds for a sacred confidence – no reverence, sir. They would as lief All Hallows and all it stands for were swept away tomorrow, demolished to the dust. And that gives me the greatest caution with whom I speak. But sharing one's troubles is sometimes a relief. If it weren't so, why do those Catholics have their wooden boxes all built for the purpose? What else, I ask you, is the meaning of their fasts and penances?

'You see, sir, I am myself, and have been for upwards of twelve years now, the dean's verger. In the sight of no respecter of persons – of offices and dignities, that is, I take it – I might claim to be even an elder brother. And our dean, sir, was a man who was all things to all men. No pride of place, no vauntingness, none of your apron-and-gaiter high-and-mightiness whatsoever, sir. And then that! And to come on us without warning; or at least without warning as could be taken as *such*.' I followed his eyes into the darkening stony spaces above us; a light like tarnished silver lay over the soundless vaultings. But so, of course, dusk, either of evening or daybreak, would affect the ancient stones. Nothing moved there.

'You must understand, sir,' the old man was continuing, 'the procession for divine service proceeds from the vestry over yonder out through those wrought-iron gates and so under the rood-screen and into the chancel there. Visitors are admitted on showing a card or a word to the verger in charge; but not otherwise. If you stand a pace or two to the right, you will catch a glimpse of the altar-screen – fourteenth-century work, Bishop Robert de Beaufort – and a unique example of the age. But what I was saying is that when we proceed for the services *out* of here *into* there, it has always been our custom to keep pretty close together; more seemly and decent, sir, than straggling in like so many sheep.

'Besides, sir, aren't we at such times in the manner of an *array,* "marching as to war", if you take me: it's a lesson in objects. The third verger leading: then the choristers, boys and men, though sadly depleted; then the minor canons; then any other dignitaries who may happen to be present, with the canon in residence; then myself, sir, followed by the dean.

'There hadn't been much amiss up to then, and on that afternoon, I can vouch – and I've repeated it *ad naushum* – there was not a single stranger out in this beyond here, sir – nave or transepts. Not within view, that is: one can't be expected to see through four feet of Norman stone. Well, sir, we had gone on our way, and I had actually turned about as usual to bow Dr Pomfrey into his stall, when I found to my consternation, to my consternation, I say, he wasn't there! It alarmed me, sir, and as you might well believe if you knew the full circumstances.

'Not that I lost my presence of mind. My first duty was to see all things to be in order and nothing unseemly to occur. My feelings were another matter. The old gentleman had left the vestry with us: that I knew: I had myself robed 'im as usual, and he in his own manner, smiling with his "Well, Jones, another day gone; another day gone." He was always an anxious gentleman for *time,* sir. How we spend it and all.

'As I say, then, he was behind me when we swepp out of the gates. I saw him coming on out of the tail of my eye – we grow accustomed to it, to see with the whole of the eye, I mean. And then – not a vestige; and me – well, sir, nonplussed, as you may imagine. I gave a look and sign at Canon Ockham, and the service proceeded as usual, while I hurried back to the vestry thinking the poor gentleman must have been taken suddenly ill. And yet, sir, I was not surprised to find the vestry vacant, and him not there. I had been expecting matters to come to what you might call a head.

'As best I could I held my tongue, and a fortunate thing it was that Canon Ockham was then in residence and not Canon Leigh Shougar, though perhaps I am not the one to say it. No, sir, our beloved dean – as pious and unworldly a gentleman as ever graced the Church – was gone for ever. He was not to appear in our midst again. He had been' – and the old man with elevated eyebrows and long lean mouth nearly whispered the words into my ear – 'he had been absconded – abducted, sir.'

'Abducted!' I murmured.

The old man closed his eyes, and with trembling lids added, 'He was found, sir, late that night up there in what they call the Trophy Room – sitting in a corner there, weeping. A child. Not a word of what had persuaded him to go or misled him there, not a word of sorrow or sadness, thank God. He didn't know us, sir – didn't know *me*. Just simple; harmless; memory all gone. Simple, sir.'

It was foolish to be whispering together like this beneath these enormous spaces with not so much as a clothes-moth for sign of life within view. But I even lowered my voice still further: 'Were there no premonitory symptoms? Had he been failing for long?'

The spectacle of grief in any human face is afflicting, but in a face as aged and resigned as this old man's – I turned away in remorse the moment the question was out of my lips; emotion is a human solvent and a sort of friendliness had sprung up between us.

'If you will just follow me,' he whispered, 'there's a little place where I make my ablutions that might be of service, sir. We would converse there in better comfort. I am sometimes reminded of those words in Ecclesiastes: "And a bird of the air shall tell of the matter."

There is not much in our poor human affairs, sir, that was not known to the writer of *that* book.'

He turned and led the way with surprising celerity, gliding along in his thin-soled, square-toed, clerical springside boots; and came to a pause outside a nail-studded door. He opened it with a huge key, and admitted me into a recess under the central tower. We mounted a spiral stone staircase and passed along a corridor hardly more than two feet wide and so dark that now and again I thrust out my finger-tips in search of his black velveted gown to make sure of my guide.

This corridor at length conducted us into a little room whose only illumination I gathered was that of the ebbing dusk from within the cathedral. The old man with trembling rheumatic fingers lit a candle, and thrusting its stick into the middle of an old oak table, pushed open yet another thick oaken door. 'You will find a basin and a towel in there, sir, if you will be so kind.'

I entered. A print of the Crucifixion was tin-tacked to the panelled wall, and beneath it stood a tin basin and jug on a stand. Never was water sweeter. I laved my face and hands and drank deep; my throat like a parched river-course after a drought. What appeared to be a tarnished censer lay in one corner of the room; a pair of seven-branched candlesticks shared a recess with a mouse-trap and a book. My eyes passed wearily yet gratefully from one to another of these mute discarded objects while I stood drying my hands.

When I returned, the old man was standing motionless before the spike-barred grill of the window, peering out and down.

'You asked me, sir,' he said, turning his lank waxen face into the feeble rays of the candle, 'you asked me, sir, a question which, if I understood you aright, was this: Was there anything that had occurred *previous* that would explain what I have been telling you?

Well, sir, it's a long story, and one best restricted to them perhaps that have the goodwill of things at heart. All Hallows, I might say, sir, is my second home. I have been here, boy and man, for close on fifty-five years – have seen four bishops pass away and have served under no less than five several deans, Dr Pomfrey, poor gentleman, being the last of the five.

'If such a word could be excused, sir, it's no exaggeration to say that Canon Leigh Shougar is a greenhorn by comparison; which may in part be why he has never quite hit it off, as they say, with Canon Ockham. Or even with Archdeacon Trafford, though he's another kind of gentleman altogether. And *he* is at present abroad. He had what they call a breakdown in health, sir.

'Now in my humble opinion, what was required was not only wisdom and knowledge but simple common sense. In the circum-stances I am about to mention, it serves no purpose for any of us to be talking too much; to be for ever sitting at a table with shut doors and finger on lip, and discussing what to most intents and purposes would hardly be called evidence at all, sir. What is the use of argu-fying, splitting hairs, objurgating about trifles, when matters are sweeping rapidly on from bad to worse. I say it with all due respect and not, I hope, thrusting myself into what doesn't concern me: Dr Pomfrey might be with us now in his own self and reason if only common caution had been observed.

'But now that the poor gentleman is gone beyond all that, there is no hope of action or agreement left, none whatsoever. They meet and they meet, and they have now one expert now another down from London, and even from the continent. And I don't say they are not knowledgeable gentlemen either, nor a pride to their profession. But why not tell *all*? Why keep back the very secret of what we know? That's what I am asking. And, what's the answer? Why simply that what they don't want to believe, what runs counter to their hopes and wishes and credibilities – and comfort – in this world, that's what they keep out of sight as long as decency permits.

'Canon Leigh Shougar *knows*, sir, what I know. And how, I ask, is he going to get to grips with it at this late day if he refuses to acknowledge that such things are what every fragment of evidence goes to prove that they are. It's *we*, sir, and not the rest of the heedless world outside, who in the long and the short of it are responsible. And what I say is: no power or principality here or hereunder can take possession of a place while those inside have faith enough to keep them out. But once let that falter – the seas are in. And when I say no power, sir, I mean – with all deference – even Satan himself.' The lean lank face had set at the word like a wax mask. The black eyes beneath the heavy lids were fixed on mine with an acute intensity and – though more inscrutable things haunted them – with an unfaltering courage. So dense a hush hung about us that the very stones of the walls seemed to be of silence solidified. It is curious what a refreshment of spirit a mere tin basinful of water may be. I stood leaning against the edge of the table so that the candle-light still rested on my companion.

'What is *wrong* here?' I asked him baldly.

He seemed not to have expected so direct an inquiry. 'Wrong, sir? Why, if I might make so bold,' he replied with a wan, faraway smile and gently drawing his hand down one of the velvet lapels of his gown, 'if I might make so bold, sir, I take it that you have come as a direct answer to prayer.'

His voice faltered. 'I am an old man now, and nearly at the end of my tether. You must realise, if you please, that I can't get any help that I can understand. I am not doubting that the gentlemen I have mentioned have only the salvation of the cathedral at heart – the cause, sir; and a graver responsibility yet. But they refuse to see how close to the edge of things we are: and how we are drifting.

'Take mere situation. So far as my knowledge tells me, there is no sacred edifice in the whole kingdom – of a piece, that is, with All Hallows not only in mere size and age but in what I might call sanctity and tradition – that is so open – open, I mean, sir, to attack of this peculiar and terrifying nature.'

'Terrifying?'

'*Terrifying,* sir; though I hold fast to what wits my Maker has bestowed on me. Where else, may I ask, would you expect the powers of darkness to congregate in open besiegement than in this narrow valley? First, the sea out there. Are you aware, sir, that ever since living remembrance flood-tide has been gnawing and mumbling its way into this bay to the extent of three or four feet *per annum*? Forty inches, and forty inches, and forty inches corroding on and on: Watch it, sir, man and boy as I have these sixty years past and then make a century of it. Not to mention positive leaps and bounds.

'And now, think a moment of the floods and gales that fall upon us autumn and winter through and even in spring, when this valley is liker paradise to young eyes than any place on earth. They make the roads from the nearest towns well-nigh impassable; which means that for some months of the year we are to all intents and purposes clean cut off from the rest of the world – as the Schindels out there are from the mainland. Are you aware, sir, I continue, that as we stand now we are above a mile from traces of the nearest human habitation, and them merely the relics of a burnt-out old farmstead? I warrant that if (and which God forbid) you had been shut up here during the coming night, and it was a near thing but what you weren't – I warrant you might have shouted yourself dumb out of the nearest window if window you could reach – and not a human soul to heed or help you.'

I shifted my hands on the table. It was tedious to be asking questions that received only such vague and evasive replies: and it is always a little disconcerting in the presence of a stranger to be spoken to so close, and with such positiveness.

'Well', I smiled, 'I hope I should not have disgraced my nerves to such an extreme as that. As a small boy, one of my particular fancies was to spend a night in a pulpit. There's a cushion, you know!'

The old man's solemn glance never swerved from my eyes. 'But I take it, sir,' he said, 'if you had ventured to give out a text up there in the dark hours, your jocular young mind would not have been prepared for any kind of a congregation?'

'You mean,' I said a little sharply, 'that the place is haunted?' The absurd notion flitted across my mind of some wandering tribe of gipsies chancing on a refuge so ample and isolated as this, and taking up its quarters in its secret parts. The old church must be honeycombed with corridors and passages and chambers pretty much like the one in which we were now concealed: and what does 'cartholic' imply but an infinite hospitality within prescribed limits? But the old man had taken me at my word.

'I mean, sir,' he said firmly, shutting his eyes, 'that there are devilish agencies at work here.' He raised his hand. 'Don't, I entreat you, dismiss what I am saying as the wanderings of a foolish old man.' He drew a little nearer. 'I have heard them with these ears; I have seen them with these eyes; though whether they have any positive substance, sir, is beyond my small knowledge to declare. But what indeed might we expect their substance to *be*? First: "I take it," says the Book, "to be such as no man can by learning define, nor by wisdom search out." Is that so? Then I go by the Book. And next: what does the same Word or very near it (I speak of the Apocrypha) say of their *purpose*? It says – and correct me if I go astray – "Devils are creatures made by God, and *that for vengeance*."

'So far, so good, sir. We stop when we can go no further. Vengeance. But of their power, of what they can *do*, I can give you definite evidences. It would be a byword if once the rumour was spread abroad. And if it is *not* so, why, I ask, does every expert that comes here leave us in haste and in dismay? They go off with their tails between their legs. They see, they grope in, but they don't believe. They *invent* reasons. And they *hasten* to leave us!' His face shook with the emphasis he laid upon the word. 'Why? Why, because the experience is beyond their knowledge, sir.' He drew back breathless and, as I could see, profoundly moved.

'But surely,' I said, 'every old building is bound in time to show symptoms of decay. Half the cathedrals in England, half its churches, even, of any age, have been "restored" – and in many cases with ghastly results. This new grouting and so on. Why, only the other day... All I mean is, why should you suppose mere wear and tear should be caused by any other agency than—'

The old man turned away. 'I must apologise,' he interrupted me with his inimitable admixture of modesty and dignity. 'I am a poor mouth at explanations, sir. Decay – stress – strain – settling – dissolution: I have heard those words bandied from lip to lip like a game at cup and ball. They fill me with nausea. Why, I am speaking not of dissolution, sir, but of *repairs, restorations*. Not decay, *strengthening*. Not a corroding loss, an awful *progress*. I could show you places – and chiefly obscured from direct view and difficult of a close examination, sir, where stones lately as rotten as pumice and as fretted as a sponge have been replaced by others fresh-quarried – and nothing of their kind within twenty miles.

'There are spots where massive blocks a yard or more square

have been *pushed* into place by sheer force. All Hallows is safer at this moment than it has been for three hundred years. They meant well – them who came to see, full of talk and fine language, and went dumb away. I grant you they meant well. I allow that. They hummed and they hawed. They smirked this and they shrugged that. But at heart, sir, they were cowed – horrified: all at a loss. Their very faces showed it. But if you ask me for what purpose such doings are afoot – I have no answer; none.

'But now, supposing you yourself, sir, were one of them, with *your* repute at stake, and you were called in to look at a house which the owners of it and them who had it in trust were disturbed by its being re-edificated and restored by some agency unknown to them. Supposing that! *Why*,' and he rapped with his knuckles on the table, 'being human and *not one of us* mightn't you be going away too with mouth shut, because you didn't want to get talked about to your disadvantage? And wouldn't you at last dismiss the whole thing as a foolish delusion, in the belief that living in out-of-the-way parts like these cuts a man off from the world, breeds maggots in the mind?

'I assure you, sir, they don't – not even Canon Ockham himself to the full – they don't believe even me. And yet, when they have their meetings of the Chapter they talk and wrangle round and round about nothing else. I can bear the other without a murmur. What God sends, I say, we humans deserve. We have laid ourselves open to it. But when you buttress up blindness and wickedness with downright folly, why then, sir, I sometimes fear for my own reason.'

He set his shoulders as square as his aged frame would permit, and with fingers clutching the lapels beneath his chin, he stood gazing out into the darkness through that narrow inward window.

'Ah, sir,' he began again, 'I have not spent sixty years in this solitary place without paying heed to my own small wandering thoughts and instincts. Look at your newspapers, sir. What they call the Great War is over – and he'd be a brave man who would take an oath before heaven that *that* was only of human designing – and yet what do we see around us? Nothing but strife and juggleries and hatred and contempt and discord wherever you look. I am no scholar, sir, but so far as my knowledge and experience carry me, we human beings are living today merely from hand to mouth. We learn today what ought to have been done yesterday, and yet are at a loss to know what's to be done tomorrow.

'And the Church, sir. God forbid I should push my way into what does not concern me; and if you had told me half an hour gone by that you were a regular churchman, I shouldn't be pouring out all this to you now. It wouldn't be seemly. But being not so gives me confidence. By merely listening you can help me, sir; though you can't help *us*. Centuries ago – and in my humble judgement, rightly – we broke away from the parent stem and rooted ourselves in our own soil. But, right or wrong, doesn't that of itself, I ask you, make us all the more open to attack from him who never wearies in going to and fro in the world seeking whom he may devour?

'I am not wishing you to take sides. But a gentleman doesn't scoff; you don't find him jeering at what he doesn't rightly understand. He keeps his own counsel, sir. And that's where, as I say, Canon Leigh Shougar sets me doubting. He refuses to make allowances; though up there in London things may look different. He gets his company there; and then for him the whole kallyidoscope changes, if you take me.'

The old man scanned me an instant as if inquiring within himself whether, after all, I too might not be one of the outcasts. 'You see, sir,' he went on dejectedly, 'I can bear what may be to come. I can, if need be, live on through what few years may yet remain to

me and keep going, as they say. But only if I can be assured that my
own inmost senses are not cheating and misleading me. Tell me the
worst, and you will have done an old man a service he can never
repay. Tell me, on the other hand, that I am merely groping along
in a network of devilish *delusion*, sir – well, in that case I hope to be
with my master, with Dr Pomfrey, as soon as possible. We were all
children once; and now there's nothing worse in this world for him
to come into, in a manner of speaking.

'Oh, sir, I sometimes wonder if what we call childhood and
growing up isn't a copy of the fate of our ancient forefathers. In the
beginning of time there were Fallen Angels, we are told; but even
if it weren't there in Holy Writ, we might have learnt it of our own
fears and misgivings. I sometimes find myself looking at a young
child with little short of awe, sir, knowing that within its mind is a
scene of peace and paradise of which we older folk have no notion,
and which will fade away out of it, as life wears on, like the mere
tabernacling of a dream.'

There was no trace of unction in his speech, though the phraseol-
ogy might suggest it, and he smiled at me as if in reassurance. 'You
see, sir – if I have any true notion of the matter – then I say, heaven
is dealing very gently with Dr Pomfrey. He has gone back, and, I take
it, his soul is elsewhere and at rest.'

He had come a pace or two nearer, and the candle-light now cast
grotesque shadows in the hollows of his brows and cheekbones, sil-
vering his long scanty hair. The eyes, dimming with age, were fixed on
mine as if in incommunicable entreaty. I was at a loss to answer him.

He dropped his hands to his sides. 'The fact is,' he looked cautiously about him, 'what I am now being so bold as to suggest,
though it's a familiar enough experience to me, may put you in actual
physical danger. But then, duty's duty, and a deed of kindness from

stranger to stranger quite another matter. You seem to have come, if I may say so, in the nick of time; that was all. On the other hand, we can leave the building at once if you are so minded. In any case we must be gone well before dark sets in; even mere human beings are best not disturbed at any night-work they may be after. The dark brings recklessness: conscience cannot see as clear in the dark. Besides, I once delayed too long myself. There is not much of day left even now, though I see by the almanac there should be a slip of moon tonight – unless the sky is over-clouded. All that I'm meaning is that our all-in-all, so to speak, is the calm untrammelled evidence of the outer senses, sir. And there comes a time when – well, when one hesitates to trust one's own.'

I have read somewhere that it is only its setting – the shape, the line, the fold, the angle of the lid and so on – that gives its finer shades of meaning and significance to the human eye. Looking into his, even in that narrow and melancholy light, was like pondering over a grey, salt, desolate pool – such as sometimes neighbours the sea on a flat and dangerous coast.

Perhaps if I had been a little less credulous, or less exhausted, I should by now have begun to doubt this old creature's sanity. And yet, surely, at even the faintest contact with the insane, a sentinel in the mind sends up flares and warnings; the very landscape changes; there is a sense of insecurity. If, too, the characters inscribed by age and experience on a man's face can be evidence of goodness and simplicity, then my companion was safe enough. To trust in his sagacity was another matter.

But then, there was All Hallows itself to take into account. That first glimpse from my green headland of its louring yet lovely walls had been strangely moving. There are buildings (almost as though they were once copies of originals now half-forgotten in the human mind) that have a singular influence on the imagination. Even now in this remote candlelit room, immured between its massive stones, the vast edifice seemed to be gently and furtively fretting its impression on my mind.

I glanced again at the old man: he had turned aside as if to leave me, unbiased, to my own decision. How would a lifetime spent between these sombre walls have affected *me*, I wondered? Surely it would be an act of mere decency to indulge their worn-out hermit! He had appealed to me. If I were ten times more reluctant to follow him, I could hardly refuse. Not at any rate without risking a retreat as humiliating as that of the architectural experts he had referred to – with my tail between my legs.

'I only wish I could hope to be of any real help.'

He turned about; his expression changed, as if at the coming of a light. 'Why, then, sir, let us be gone at once. You are with me, sir: that was all I hoped and asked. And now there's no time to waste.'

He tilted his head to listen a moment – with that large, flat, shell-like ear of his which age alone seems to produce. 'Matches and candle, sir,' he had lowered his voice to a whisper, 'but – though we mustn't lose each other; you and me, I mean – *not*, I think, a naked light. What I would suggest, if you have no objection, is your kindly grasping my gown. There is a kind of streamer here, you see – as if made for the purpose. There will be a good deal of up-and-downing, but I know the building blindfold and as you might say inch by inch. And now that the bell-ringers have given up ringing it is more in my charge than ever.'

He stood back and looked at me with folded hands, a whimsical childlike smile on his aged face. 'I sometimes think to myself I'm like the sentry, sir, in that play by William Shakespeare. I saw it, sir, years ago, on my only visit to London – when I was a boy. If ever there were a villain for all his fine talk and all, commend me to that ghost. I see him yet.'

Whisper though it was, a sort of chirrup had come into his voice, like that of a cricket in a baker's shop. I took tight hold of the velveted tag of his gown. He opened the door, pressed the box of safety matches into my hand, himself grasped the candlestick and then blew out the light. We were instantly marooned in an impenetrable darkness. 'Now, sir, if you would kindly remove your walking shoes,' he muttered close in my ear, 'we should proceed with less noise. I shan't hurry you. And please to tug at the streamer if you need attention. In a few minutes the blackness will be less intense.'

As I stooped down to loose my shoelaces I heard my heart thumping merrily away. It had been listening to our conversation apparently! I slung my shoes round my neck – as I had often done as a boy when going paddling – and we set out on our expedition.

I have endured too often the nightmare of being lost and abandoned in the stony bowels of some strange and prodigious building to take such an adventure lightly. I clung, I confess, desperately tight to my lifeline and we groped steadily onward – my guide ever and again turning back to mutter warning or encouragement in my ear.

Now I found myself steadily ascending; and then in a while, feeling my way down flights of hollowly worn stone steps, and anon brushing along a gallery or corkscrewing up a newel staircase so narrow that my shoulders all but touched the walls on either side. In spite of the sepulchral chill in these bowels of the cathedral, I was soon suffocatingly hot, and the effort to see became intolerably fatiguing. Once, to recover our breath we paused opposite a slit in the thickness of the masonry, at which to breathe the tepid sweetness of the outer air. It was faint with the scent of wild flowers and cool of the sea. And presently after, at a barred window, high overhead, I caught a glimpse of the night's first stars.

We then turned inward once more, ascending yet another spiral staircase. And now the intense darkness had thinned a little, the groined roof above us becoming faintly discernible. A fresher air softly fanned my cheek; and then trembling fingers groped over my breast, and, cold and bony, clutched my own.

'Dead still here, sir, if you please.' So close sounded the whispered syllables the voice might have been a messenger's within my own consciousness. 'Dead still, here. There's a drop of some sixty or seventy feet a few paces on.'

I peered out across the abyss, conscious, as it seemed, of the huge super-incumbent weight of the noble fretted roof only a small space now immediately above our heads. As we approached the edge of this stony precipice, the gloom paled a little, and I guessed that we must be standing in some coign of the southern transept, for what light the evening skies now afforded was clearer towards the right. On the other hand, it seemed the northern windows opposite us were most of them boarded up, or obscured in some fashion. Gazing out, I could detect scaffolding poles – like knitting needles – thrust out from the walls and a balloon-like spread of canvas above them. For the moment my ear was haunted by what appeared to be the droning of an immense insect. But this presently ceased. I fancy it was internal only.

'You will understand, sir,' breathed the old man close beside me – and we still stood, grotesquely enough, hand in hand – 'the scaffolding over there has been in position a good many months now. It was put up when the last gentleman came down from London to inspect the fabric. And there it's been left ever since. Now, sir! – though I implore you to be cautious.'

I hardly needed the warning. With one hand clutching my box of matches, the fingers of the other interlaced with my companion's, I strained every sense. And yet I could detect not the faintest stir or murmur under that wide-spreading roof. Only a hush as profound as that which must reign in the Royal Chamber of the pyramid of Cheops faintly swirled in the labyrinths of my ear.

How long we stayed in this position I cannot say; but minutes sometimes seem like hours. And then, suddenly, without the slightest warning, I became aware of a peculiar and incessant vibration. It is impossible to give a name to it. It suggested the remote whirring of an enormous millstone, or that – though without definite pulsation – of revolving wings, or even the spinning of an immense top.

In spite of his age, my companion apparently had ears as acute as mine. He had clutched me tighter a full ten seconds before I myself became aware of this disturbance of the air. He pressed closer. 'Do you see that, sir?'

I gazed and gazed, and saw nothing. Indeed even in what I had seemed to *hear* I might have been deceived. Nothing is more treacherous in certain circumstances – except possibly the eye – than the ear. It magnifies, distorts, and may even invent. As instantaneously as I had become aware of it, the murmur had ceased. And then – though I cannot be certain – it seemed the dingy and voluminous spread of canvas over there had perceptibly trembled, as if a huge cautious hand had been thrust out to draw it aside. No time was given me to make sure. The old man had hastily withdrawn me into the opening of the wall through which we had issued; and we made no pause in our retreat until we had come again to the narrow slit of window which I have spoken of and could refresh ourselves with a less stagnant air. We stood here resting awhile.

'Well, sir?' he inquired at last, in the same flat muffled tones.

'Do you ever pass along here alone?' I whispered.

'Oh, yes, sir. I make it a habit to be the last to leave – and often the first to come; but I am usually gone by this hour.'

I looked close at the dim face in profile against that narrow oblong of night. 'It is so difficult to be sure of oneself,' I said. 'Have you ever actually *encountered* anything – near at hand, I mean?'

'I keep a sharp lookout, sir. Maybe they don't think me of enough importance to molest – the last rat, as they say.'

'But *have* you?' – I might myself have been communicating with the phantasmal *genius loci* of All Hallows – our muffled voices; this intense caution and secret listening; the slight breathlessness, as if at any instant one's heart were ready for flight: 'But *have* you?'

'Well yes, sir,' he said. 'And in this very gallery. They nearly had me, sir. But by good fortune there's a recess a little further on – stored up with some old fragments of carving, from the original building, sixth-century, so it's said: stone-capitals, heads and hands, and suchlike. I had had my warning, and managed to leap in there and conceal myself. But only just in time. Indeed, sir, I confess I was in such a condition of terror and horror I turned my back.'

'You mean you heard, but didn't look? And – something came?'

'Yes, sir, I seemed to be reduced to no bigger than a child, huddled up there in that corner. There was a sound like clanging metal – but I don't think it was metal. It drew near at a furious speed, then passed me, making a filthy gust of wind. For some instants I couldn't breathe; the air was gone.'

'And no other sound?'

'No other, sir, except out of the distance a noise like the sounding of a stupendous kind of gibberish. A calling; or so it seemed – no human sound. The air shook with it. You see, sir, I myself wasn't of any consequence, I take it – unless a mere obstruction in the way.

But – I have heard it said somewhere that the rarity of these happenings is only because it's a pain and torment and not any sort of pleasure for such beings, such apparitions, sir, good or bad, to visit our outward world. That's what I have heard said; though I can go no further.

'The time I'm telling you of was in the early winter – November. There was a dense sea-fog over the valley, I remember. It eddied through that opening there into the candle-light like flowing milk. I never light up now: and, if I may be forgiven the boast, sir, I seem to have almost forgotten how to be afraid. After all, in any walk of life a man can only do his best, and if there weren't such opposition and hindrances in high places I should have nothing to complain of. What is anybody's life, sir (come past the gaiety of youth), but marking time... Did you hear anything *then,* sir?'

His gentle monotonous mumbling ceased and we listened together. But every ancient edifice has voices and soundings of its own: there was nothing audible that I could put a name to, only what seemed to be a faint perpetual stir or whirr of grinding such as (to one's over-stimulated senses) the stablest stones set one on top of the other with an ever slightly varying weight and stress might be likely to make perceptible in a world of matter. A world which, after all, they say, is itself in unimaginably rapid rotation, and under the tyranny of time.

'No, I hear nothing,' I answered: 'but please don't think I am doubting what you say. Far from it. You must remember I am a stranger, and that therefore the influence of the place cannot but be less apparent to me. And you have no help in this now?'

'No, sir. Not now. But even at the best of times we had small company hereabouts, and no money. Not for any substantial outlay, I mean. And not even the boldest suggests making what's called a public appeal. It's a strange thing to me, sir, but whenever the newspapers get hold of anything, they turn it into a byword and a sham. Yet how can they help themselves? – with no beliefs to guide them and nothing to stay their mouths except about what for sheer human decency's sake they daren't talk about. But then, who am I to complain? And now, sir,' he continued with a sigh of utter weariness, 'if you are sufficiently rested, would you perhaps follow me on to the roof? It is the last visit I make – though by rights perhaps I should take in what there is of the tower. But I'm too old now for that – clambering and climbing over naked beams; and the ladders are not so safe as they were.'

We had not far to go. The old man drew open a squat heavily ironed door at the head of a flight of wooden steps. It was latched but not bolted, and admitted us at once to the leaden roof of the building and to the immense amphitheatre of evening. The last faint hues of sunset were fading in the west; and silver-bright Spica shared with the tilted crescent of the moon the serene lagoon-like expanse of sky above the sea. Even at this height, the air was audibly stirred with the low lullaby of the tide.

The staircase by which we had come out was surmounted by a flat penthouse roof about seven feet high. We edged softly along, then paused once more; to find ourselves now all but *tête-à-tête* with the gigantic figures that stood sentinel at the base of the buttresses to the unfinished tower.

The tower was so far unfinished, indeed, as to wear the appearance of the ruinous; besides which, what appeared to be scars and stains as if of fire were detectable on some of its stones, reminding me of the legend which years before I had chanced upon, that this stretch of coast had more than once been visited centuries ago by pillaging Norsemen.

The night was unfathomably clear and still. On our left rose the conical bluff of the headland crowned with the solitary grove of trees beneath which I had taken refuge from the blinding sunshine that very afternoon. Its grasses were now hoary with faintest moonlight. Far to the right stretched the flat cold plain of the Atlantic – that enormous darkened looking-glass of space; only a distant lightship ever and again stealthily signalling to us with a lean phosphoric finger from its outermost reaches.

The mere sense of that abysm of space – its waste powdered with the stars of the Milky Way; the mere presence of the stony leviathan on whose back we two humans now stood, dwarfed into insignificance beside these gesturing images of stone, were enough of themselves to excite the imagination. And – whether matter-of-fact or pure delusion – this old verger's insinuations that the cathedral was now menaced by some inconceivable danger and assault had set my nerves on edge. My feet were numb as the lead they stood upon; while the tips of my fingers tingled as if a powerful electric discharge were coursing through my body.

We moved gently on – the spare shape of the old man a few steps ahead, peering cautiously to right and left of him as we advanced. Once with a hasty gesture, he drew me back and fixed his eyes for a full minute on a figure – at two removes – which was silhouetted at that moment against the starry emptiness: a forbidding thing enough, viewed in this vague luminosity, which seemed in spite of the unmoving stare that I fixed on it to be perceptibly stirring on its windworn pedestal.

But no; 'All's well!' the old man had mutely signalled to me, and we pushed on. Slowly and cautiously; indeed I had time to notice in passing that this particular figure held stretched in its right hand a bent bow, and was crowned with a high weather-worn stone coronet.

One and all were frigid company. At last we completed our circuit of the tower, had come back to the place we had set out from, and stood eyeing one another like two conspirators in the clear dusk. Maybe there was a tinge of incredulity on my face.

'No, sir,' murmured the old man, 'I expected no other. The night is uncommonly quiet. I've noticed that before. They seem to leave us at peace on nights of quiet. We must turn in again and be getting home.'

Until that moment I had thought no more of where I was to sleep or to get food, nor had even realised how famished with hunger I was. Nevertheless, the notion of fumbling down again out of the open air into the narrow inward blackness of the walls from which we had just issued was singularly uninviting. Across these wide, flat stretches of roof there was at least space for flight, and there were recesses for concealment. To gain a moment's respite, I inquired if I should have much difficulty in getting a bed in the village. And as I had hoped, the old man himself offered me hospitality.

I thanked him; but still hesitated to follow, for at that moment I was trying to discover what peculiar effect of dusk and darkness a moment before had deceived me into the belief that some small animal – a dog, a spaniel I should have guessed – had suddenly and surreptitiously taken cover behind the stone buttress nearby. But that apparently had been a mere illusion. The creature, whatever it might be, was no barker at any rate. Nothing stirred now; and my companion seemed to have noticed nothing amiss.

'You were saying,' I pressed him, 'that when repairs – restorations – of the building were in contemplation, even the experts were perplexed by what they discovered? What did they actually say?'

'Say, sir!' Our voices sounded as small and meaningless up here as those of grasshoppers in a noonday meadow. 'Examine that balustrade which you are leaning against at this minute. Look at that gnawing and fretting – that furrowing above the lead. All that is honest wear and tear – constant weathering of the mere elements, sir – rain and wind and snow and frost. That's honest *nature*-work, sir. But now compare it, if you please, with this St Mark here; and remember, sir, these images were intended to be part and parcel of the fabric as you might say, sentries on a castle – symbols, you understand.'

I stooped close under the huge grey creature of stone until my eyes were scarcely more than six inches from its pedestal. And, unless the moon deceived me, I confess I could find not the slightest trace of fret or friction. Far from it. The stone had been grotesquely decorated in low relief with a gaping crocodile – a two-headed crocodile; and the angles, knubs and undulations of the creature were cut as sharp as with a knife in cheese. I drew back.

'Now cast your glance upwards, sir. Is that what you would call a saintly shape and gesture?'

What appeared to represent an eagle was perched on the image's lifted wrist – an eagle resembling a vulture. The head beneath it was poised at an angle of defiance – its ears abnormally erected on the skull; the lean right forearm extended with pointing forefinger as if in derision. Its stony gaze was fixed upon the stars; its whole aspect was hostile, sinister and intimidating. I drew aside. The faintest puff of milk-warm air from over the sea stirred on my cheek.

'Ay, sir, and so with one or two of the rest of them,' the old man commented, as he watched me, 'there are other wills than the Almighty's.'

At this, the pent-up excitement within me broke bounds. This nebulous insinuatory talk! – I all but lost my temper. 'I can't, for the life of me, understand what you are saying,' I exclaimed in a voice that astonished me with its shrill volume of sound in that intense lofty quiet. 'One doesn't *repair* in order to destroy.'

The old man met me without flinching. 'No, sir? Say you so? And why not? Are there not two kinds of change in this world? – a building-up and a breaking-down? To give strength and endurance for evil or misguided purposes, would that be power wasted, if such was your aim? Why, sir, isn't that true even of the human mind and heart? We here are on the outskirts, I grant, but where would you expect the enemy to show himself unless in the outer defences? An institution may be beyond saving, sir: it may be being restored for a worse destruction. And a hundred trumpeting voices would make no difference when the faith and life within is tottering to its fall.'

Somehow, this muddle of metaphors reassured me. Obviously the old man's wits had worn a little thin: he was the victim of an intelligible but monstrous hallucination.

'And yet you are taking it for granted,' I expostulated, 'that, if what you say is true, a stranger could be of the slightest help. A visitor – mind you – who hasn't been inside the doors of a church, except in search of what is old and obsolete, for years.'

The old man laid a trembling hand upon my sleeve. The folly of it – with my shoes hanging like ludicrous millstones round my neck!

'If you please, sir,' he pleaded, 'have a little patience with me. I'm preaching at nobody. I'm not even hinting that them outside the fold circumstantially speaking aren't of the flock. All in good time, sir; the Almighty's time. Maybe – with all due respect – it's from them within we have most to fear. And indeed, sir, believe an old man: I could never express the gratitude I feel. You have given me the occasion to unbosom myself, to make a clean breast, as they say. All Hallows is my earthly home, and – well, there, let us say no more. You couldn't *help me* – except only by your presence here. God alone knows who can!'

At that instant, a dull enormous rumble reverberated from within the building – as if a huge boulder or block of stone had been shifted or dislodged in the fabric; a peculiar grinding nerve-wracking sound. And for the fraction of a second the flags on which we stood seemed to tremble beneath our feet.

The fingers tightened on my arm. 'Come, sir; keep close; we must be gone at once' the quavering old voice whispered; 'we have stayed too long.'

But we emerged into the night at last without mishap. The little western door, above which the grinning head had welcomed me on my arrival, admitted us to *terra firma* again, and we made our way up a deep sandy track, bordered by clumps of hemp agrimony and fennel and hemlock, with viper's bugloss and sea-poppy blooming in the gentle dusk of night at our feet. We turned when we reached the summit of this sandy incline and looked back. All Hallows, vague and enormous, lay beneath us in its hollow, resembling some natural prehistoric outcrop of that sea-worn rock-bound coast; but strangely human and saturnine.

The air was mild as milk – a pool of faintest sweetnesses – gorse, bracken, heather; and not a rumour disturbed its calm, except only the furtive and stertorous sighings of the tide. But far out to sea and beneath the horizon summer lightnings were now in idle play – flickering into the sky like the unfolding of a signal, planet to planet – then gone. That alone, and perhaps too this feeble moonlight glinting on the ancient glass, may have accounted for the faint vitreous glare that seemed ever and again to glitter across the windows of the northern transept far beneath us. And yet how easily deceived is the imagination. This old man's talk still echoing in my ear, I could have vowed this was no reflection but the glow of some light shining fitfully from within outwards.

We paused together beside a flowering bush of fuchsia at the wicket-gate leading into his small square of country garden. 'You'll forgive me, sir, for mentioning it; but I make it a rule as far as possible to leave all my troubles and misgivings outside when I come home. My daughter is a widow, and not long in that sad condition, so I keep as happy a face as I can on things. And yet: well, sir, I wonder at times if – if a personal sacrifice isn't incumbent on them that have their object most at heart. I'd go out myself very willingly, sir, I can assure you, if there was any certainty in my mind that it would serve the cause. It would be little to me if—' He made no attempt to complete the sentence.

On my way to bed, that night, the old man led me in on tiptoe to show me his grandson. His daughter watched me intently as I stooped over the child's cot – with that bird-like solicitude which all mothers show in the presence of a stranger.

Her small son was of that fairness which almost suggests the unreal. He had flung back his bedclothes – as if innocence in this world needed no covering or defence – and lay at ease, the dews of sleep on lip, cheek, and forehead. He was breathing so quietly that not the least movement of shoulder or narrow breast was perceptible.

'The lovely thing!' I muttered, staring at him. 'Where is he now, I wonder?' His mother lifted her face and smiled at me with a drowsy ecstatic happiness, then sighed.

And from out of the distance, there came the first prolonged whisper of a wind from over the sea. It was eleven by my watch, the storm after the long heat of the day seemed to be drifting inland; but All Hallows apparently, had forgotten to wind its clock.

A RECLUSE

WHICH OF THE WORLD'S WISEACRES, I WONDER, WAS responsible for the aphorism that 'the best things in life are to be found at its edges'? It is too vague, of course. So much depends on what you mean by the 'best' and the 'edges'. And in any case most of us prefer the central. It has been explored; it is safe; you know where you are; it has been amply, copiously corroborated. But, 'Amusing? Well, hardly. Quite so!' as my friend Mr Bloom would have said. But then, Mr Bloom has now ventured over the 'borderline'. He is, I imagine, interested in edges no longer.

I have been reminded of him again – as if there were any need of it! – by an advertisement in *The Times*. It announces that his house, which he had himself renamed Montrésor, is for sale by auction – 'This singularly charming freehold Residential Property... in all about thirty-eight acres... the Matured Pleasure Grounds of unusual Beauty'. I don't deny it. But was it quite discreet to describe the house as *imposing*? A pair of slippers in my possession prompts this query. But how to answer it? It is important in such matters to be clear and precise, and, alas, all that I can say about Mr Bloom can be only vague and inconclusive. As, indeed, in some respects *he* was.

It was an afternoon towards the end of May – a Thursday. I had been to see a friend who, after a long illness, seemed now to be creeping back into the world again. We sat and talked for a while. Smiling, whispering, he lay propped up upon his pillows, gaunt and deathly, his eyes fixed on the green branches beyond his window, and that bleak hungry look on his face one knows so well. But when we fell silent, and his nurse looked covertly round the door and nodded her head at me, I rose with an almost indecent readiness, clasped his cold, damp, bony hand in mine, and said good-bye. 'You *look* miles better,' I assured him again and again.

It is a relief to leave a sick room – to breathe freely again after that fumy and stagnant atmosphere. The medicine bottles, the stuffiness, the hush, the dulcet optimism, the *gauche* self-consciousness. I even found myself softly whistling as I climbed back into my cosy two-seater again. A lime-tree bower her garage was: the flickering leafy evening sunshine gilded the dust on her bonnet. I released the brake; she leapt to life.

And what wonder? Flora and her nymphs might at any moment turn the corner of this sequestered country road. I felt adventurous. It would be miserably unenterprising to go back by the way I had come. I would just chance my way home.

Early evening is, with daybreak, May's most seductive hour; and how entrancing is any scene on earth after even a fleeting glance into the valley of shadows – the sun-striped, looping, wild-flowered lanes, the buttercup hollows, the parsleyed nooks and dusky coppices, the amorous birds and butterflies. But nothing lovely can long endure. The sickly fragrance of the hawthorns hinted at that. Drowsy, lush, tepid, inexhaustible – an English evening.

And as I bowled idly on, I overtook a horseman. So far as I can see he has nothing whatever to do with what came after – no more, at most, than my poor thin-nosed, gasping friend. I put him in only because he put himself in. And in an odd way too. For at first sight (and at a distance) I had mistaken the creature for a bird – a large, strange, ungainly bird. It was the cardboard box he was carrying accounted for that.

Many shades lighter than his clothes and his horse, it lay on his back cornerwise, suspended about his neck with a piece of cord. As he trotted along he bumped in the saddle, and his box bumped too. Meanwhile, odd mechanical creature, he beat time to these bumpings on his animal's shoulder-blade with the little leafy switch poised between his fingers. I glanced up into his face as I passed him – a greyish, hairy, indefinite face, like a miller's. To mistake a cardboard box for a bird! He amused me. I burst out laughing; never dreaming but that he was gone for ever.

Two or three miles further on, after passing a huddle of tumbledown cottages and a duck-pond, I caught my first glimpse of Mr Bloom's house – of Montrésor. And I defy anybody with eyes in his head to pass that house unheeded. The mere quiet diffident looks of it brought me instantly to a standstill. 'Imposing'!

And as I sat on, looking in on it through its high wrought-iron gates, I heard presently the hollow thump of a horse's hoofs in the muffling dust behind me. Even before I glanced over my shoulder, I knew what I should see – my man on horseback. These narrow lanes – he must have taken a short cut.

> There rode a Miller on a horse,
> A jake on a jackass could do no worse –
> *With a Hey, and a Hey, lollie, lo!*
>
> Meal on his chops and his whiskers too –
> The devil sowed tares, where the tare-crop grew –
> *With a Hey, and a Hey, lollie, lo!*

Up he bumped, down he bumped, and his leafy switch kept time. When he drew level, I twisted my head and yelled up at him a question about the house. He never so much as paused. He merely lowered that indiscriminately hairy face of his a few inches nearer me, opened his mouth, and flung up his hand with the switch. Perhaps the poor fellow was dumb; his raw-boned horse had coughed, as if in sympathy. But, dumb or not, his gesture had clearly intimated – though with unnecessary emphasis – that Montrésor wasn't worth asking questions about, that I had better 'move on'. And, naturally, it increased my interest. I watched him out of sight. Why, as I say, I have mentioned him I scarcely know, except that for an instant there he was, at those gates – Mr Bloom's – gates from which Mr Bloom himself was so soon to depart. When he was completely gone and the dust of him had settled, I turned to enjoy another look at the house – a protracted look too.

To all appearance it was vacant; but if so, it could not have been vacant long. The drive was sadly in need of weeding; though the lawns had been recently mown. High-grown forest trees towered round about it, overtopping its roof – chiefly chestnuts, their massive lower branches drooping so close to the turf they almost brushed its surface. They were festooned from crown to root with branching candelabra-like spikes of blossom. Now it was daylight; but imagine them on a still, pitch-black night, their every twig upholding a tiny, phosphoric cluster of tapers!

Not that Montrésor (or rather what of its façade was in view) was an old or even in itself a very beautiful house. It must have been built about 1750 and at second sight was merely of pleasing proportions. And then one looked again, and it looked back – with a furtive reticence as if it were withholding itself from any direct scrutiny behind its widespread blossoming chestnut trees. 'We could if we would,' said its windows, as do certain human faces; though no doubt the queer gesture and the queerer looks of my cardboard-boxed gentleman on horseback accounted for something of its effect.

A thin haze of cloud had spread over the sky, paling its blue. The sun had set. And a diffused light hung over walls and roof. It suited the house – as powder may suit a pale face. Even nature appeared to be condoning these artifices – the hollow lawns, the honeyed azaleas.

How absurd are one's little hesitations. All this while I had been debating whether to approach nearer on foot or to drive boldly in. I chose the second alternative, with the faint notion in my mind perhaps that it would ensure me, if necessary, a speedier retreat. But then, premonitions are apt to display themselves a little clearer in retrospect! Anyhow, if I had *walked* up to the house, that night would not have been spent with Mr Bloom. But no, the house looked harmless enough, and untenanted. I pushed open the gates and, gliding gently in under the spreading chestnut trees towards the entrance, again came to a standstill.

A wide, low, *porte-cochère,* supported by slender stone columns, sheltered the beautiful doorway. The metalwork of its fanlight, like that of the gates, was adorned with the device of a pelican feeding her young. The owner's crest, no doubt. But in spite of the simplicity of the porch, it was not in keeping, and may have been a later addition to the house. Its hollow echoings stilled, I sat on in the car, idly surveying the scene around me, and almost without conscious thought of it. What state of mind can be more serene – or more active?

No notice whatever seemed to have been taken of my intrusion. Silence, silence remained. Indeed, in spite of the abundant cover around me, there was curiously little bird-song – only a far-away thrush calling faintly, 'Ahoy! ahoy! ahoy! Come to tea! Come to tea!' And after all it was the merry month of May, and still early. But near at hand, not even a wren shrilled. So presently I got out of the car, and mooned off to the end of the shallow, stone-vased terrace, stepping deliberately from tuft to tuft of grass and moss. Only a dense shrubbery beyond: yew, ilex, holly; a dampish winding walk. But on this – the western aspect of the house – there showed faded blinds to the windows, and curtains too – bleached by numberless sunsets, but still rich and pleasant in colour.

What few live things may have spied out the intruder had instantly withdrawn. I sighed, and turned away. The forsaken pierces quicker to the heart than by way of the mind. My green-winged car looked oddly out of place – even a little homesick – under the porch. She was as grey with dust as were my odd horseman's whiskers. I had come to the conclusion – quite wrongly – that for the time being, at least, the place *was* unoccupied; though possibly at any moment caretaker or housekeeper might appear.

Indeed, my foot was actually on the step of the car, when, as if at a definite summons, I turned my head and discovered not only that the door was now open, but that a figure – Mr Bloom's – was standing a pace or so beyond the threshold, his regard steadily fixed on me. Mr Bloom – a memorable figure. He must have been well over six feet in height, but he carried his heavy head and heavy shoulders with a pronounced stoop. He was both stout and fat, and yet his clothes now hung loosely upon him, as if made to old measurements – a wide, black morning-coat and waistcoat, and brown cloth trousers. I noticed in particular his elegant boots. They were adorned with what I had supposed was an obsolete device – imitation laces. A well-cut pair of boots, nonetheless, by a good maker. His head was bald on the crown above a fine lofty forehead – but it wore a superfluity of side hair, and his face was bushily bearded. With chin drawn up a little, he was surveying me from under very powerful magnifying spectacles, his left hand resting on the inside handle of the door.

He had taken me so much by surprise that for the moment I was speechless. We merely looked at one another; he, with a more easily justifiable intentness than I. He seemed, as the saying goes, to be

sizing me up; to be fitting me in; and it was *his* voice that at length
set the porch echoing again – a voice, as might have been inferred
from the look of him, sonorous but muffled, as if his beard interfered
with its resonance.

'I see you are interested in the appearance of my house,' he was
saying.

The greeting was courteous enough; and yet extraordinarily
impersonal. I made the lamest apologies, adding some trivial comment on the picturesqueness of the scene, and the general 'evening
effects'. But of this I am certain; the one thing uppermost in my
mind, even at this stage in our brief acquaintance, was the desire
not to continue it. Mr Bloom had somehow exhausted my interest in
his house. I wanted to shake him off, to go away. He was an empty-
looking man in spite of his domed brow. If his house had suggested
vacancy, so did he; and yet – I wonder.

Far from countenancing this inclination, however, he was inviting
me not to leave him. He was welcoming the interloper. With a slow
comprehensive glance to left and right, he actually stepped out at last
under the porch, and – with a peculiar tentative gesture – thrust out
a well-kept, fleshy hand in my direction, as if with the intention of
putting me entirely at my ease. He then stood solemnly scrutinising
my tiny car, which, with him as solitary passenger, would appear
more like a perambulator!

At a loss for any alternative, I withdrew a pace or so, and took
another long look at the façade – the blank windows, their red-brick
mouldings, the peeping chimney-stacks, the quiet, serene sufficiency
of it all. There was, I remember, a sorry little array of half-made,
abandoned martins' nests plastered up under the narrow jutting of
the roof. But this craning attitude was fatiguing, and I turned and
looked back at Mr Bloom.

Mr Bloom apparently had not stirred. Thus inert, he resembled the provincial statue of some forgotten Victorian notability – his feet set close together in those neat, polished, indoor boots, his fat fingers on his watch-chain. And now he seemed to be smiling at me out of his bluish-grey, rather prominent eyes, from under those thick distorting glasses. He was suggesting that I should come in, an invitation innocent of warmth, but more pressing than the mere words implied. To a mouse the wreathing odour of toasted cheese – before the actual trap comes into sight – must be similar in effect. There was a suppressed eagerness in the eyes behind those glasses. They had rolled a little in their sockets. And yet, even so, why should I have distrusted him? It would be monstrous to take this world solely on its face value. I was on the point of blurting out a churlish refusal when he stepped back and pushed the door open. The glimpse within decided me.

For the hall beyond that hospitable gape was peculiarly attractive. Not very lofty, but of admirable proportions, it was panelled in light wood, the carving on its cornice and pilasters tinged in here and there with gilt. From its roof hung three chandeliers of greenish-grey glass – entrancing things, resembling that mysterious exquisite ice that comes from Waterford. The evening light swam softly in through the uncurtained windows as if upon the stillness of a dream.

Empty, it would have been a fascinating room; but just now it was grotesquely packed with old furniture – beautiful, costly things in themselves, but, in this hugger-mugger, robbed of all elegance and grace. Only the narrowest alley-way had been left unoccupied – an alley-way hardly wide enough to enable a human being to come and go without positively mounting up off the floor, as in the Land-and-Water game beloved of children. It might have been some antique furniture dealer's interior, prepared for 'a moonlight flit'. Mr Bloom smiled at the air of surprise which must have been evident in my face.

'Here today,' he murmured, as if he were there and then preparing to be off – 'and gone tomorrow.'

But having thus enticed me in under his roof, he rapidly motioned me on, not even turning his head to see if I were following him. For so cumbersome a man he was agile, and at the dusky twist of the corridor I found him already awaiting me, his hand on an inner door. 'This is the library,' he informed me, with a suavity that suggested that I was some wealthy visitor to whom he wished to dispose of the property. 'One moment,' he added hurriedly, 'I think I neglected to shut the outer door.'

A library is often in effect little better than a mausoleum. But on a sunny morning this room must have looked as jocund as some 'beauty's' boudoir. It was evening now. Dimmed old Persian rugs lay on the floor; there was a large writing-table. The immense armchairs were covered with vermilion morocco leather, and the walls, apart from a few engravings and mezzotints, were lined with exquisitely bound books, and jade and geranium and primrose-yellow were apparently Mr Bloom's favourite colours. On one side many of the books had been removed and lay stacked up in portable bundles beneath the shelves on which they had stood. Opposite these was a lofty chimneypiece surmounted by mouldings in plaster – some pagan scene. And once again the self-sacrificing pelican showed in the midmost panel – still engaged in feeding her young.

I was looking out of the long windows when Mr Bloom reappeared. He still seemed to be smiling in his non-committal fashion and treated me to yet another slow scrutiny; the most conspicuous feature of his person, apart from his spectacles, being at such moments the spade-guinea that dangled from his watch-chain. Brown trousers, my friend, I was thinking to myself, why brown? And why not wear clothes that fit?

'You are a lover of books?' he was murmuring, in that flat, muffled voice of his; and we were soon conversing amiably enough on the diversions of literature. He led me steadily from shelf to shelf; but for the time being he was only making conversation. He was definitely detaining me, and staved off every opportunity I attempted to seize of extricating myself from his company. At last I bluntly held out my hand, and in spite of his protestations – so insistent that he began stuttering – I made my way out of the room.

Daylight was failing now, and the spectacle of that hoard of furniture in the gloaming was oddly depressing. Mr Bloom had followed me out, cooing, as he came on, his apologies and regrets that I could spare him no more time – 'The upper rooms... the garden... my china.' I persisted, nevertheless, and myself opened the outer door. And there in the twilight, with as disconsolate an appearance as a cocker spaniel that has wearied of waiting for its mistress, sat my car.

I had actually taken my seat in it – having omitted to shake hands with Mr Bloom – when I noticed not only that in a moment of absent-mindedness I must have locked the gears but that the Yale gear-key which usually lay in the little recess to the left of the dashboard was missing. Accidents of this kind may be absurdly disconcerting. I searched my pockets; leapt out and searched them again; and not only in vain, but without the faintest recollection in my mind of having even touched the key. It was a ridiculous, a mortifying situation. With eyes fixed, in an effort to recall my every movement, I gazed out over the wide green turf beneath the motionless chestnut trees, and then at last turned again, and looked at Mr Bloom.

With plump hands held loosely and helplessly a little in front of him, and head on one side, he was watching my efforts with an almost paternal concern.

'I have mislaid the key,' I almost shouted at him, as if he were hard of hearing.

'Is it anything of importance? Can I get you anything? Water? A little grease?'

That one word, grease, was accompanied with so ridiculous a trill that I lost patience.

'It's the gear-key,' I snapped at him. 'She's fixed, immovable, useless! I wish to heaven I…' I stopped aimlessly, fretfully searching the porch and the turf beyond it. Mr Bloom watched me with the solicitude of a mother. 'I ought to have been home an hour ago,' I stuttered over my shoulder.

'Most vexatious! Dear me! I am distressed. But my memory too… A Slough of Despond. Do you think by any chance, Mr Dash, you can have put the key into your *pocket*?'

I stared at him. The suggestion was little short of imbecile; and yet he had evidently had the sagacity to look for my name on my licence! 'What is the nearest town?' I all but shouted.

'The nearest,' he echoed; 'ah, the nearest! Now, let me see! The nearest *town* – garage, of course. A nice question. Come in again. We must get a map; yes, a map, don't you think? That will be our best course; an excellent plan.'

I thrust my hand into the leather pocket of the car, and produced my own. But only the eyes of an owl could have read its lettering in that light, and somehow it did not occur to me in this tranquil dusky scene to switch on the lamps. There was no alternative. I followed Mr Bloom into the house again, and on into his study. He lit a couple of candles and we sat down together at the writing-table and examined the map. It was the closest I ever got to him.

The position was ludicrous. Montrésor was a good four miles from the nearest village of any size and seven from the nearest railway station – and that on a branch line. And here was this recluse peppering me with futile advice and offers of assistance, and yet obviously beaming with satisfaction at the dilemma I was in. There was not even a servant in the house to take a telegram to the village – if a telegram had been of the slightest use. I hastily folded up my map – folded it up wrong, of course – and sat glooming. He was breathing a little rapidly after this exercise of intelligence.

'But why be disturbed?' he entreated me. 'Why? A misadventure; but of no importance. Indeed not. You will give me the pleasure of being my guest for the night – nothing but a happiness, I assure you. Say no more. It won't incommode me in the slightest degree. This old house… A most unfortunate accident. They should make larger, heavier keys. Ridiculous! But then I am no mechanic.'

He stooped round at me – the loose, copious creature – and was almost flirtatious. 'Frankly, my dear young sir, I cannot regret an accident that promises me more of your company. We bookish people, you understand.'

I protested, stood up, and once more began searching my pockets! His head jerked back into its habitual posture.

'Ah! I see what is in your mind. Think nothing of it. Yes, yes, yes. Comforts, convenience curtailed, I agree. But my good housekeeper always prepares a meal sufficient for two – mere habit, Mr Dash, almost animal habit. And besides – why not? I will forage for myself. A meal miscellaneous, perhaps, but not unsatisfying.' He beamed. 'Why not take a look at the garden meanwhile before it is dark?' The tones had fallen still flatter, the face had become impassive.

I was cornered. It was useless to protest – it would have been atrociously uncivil. He himself thrust open the windows for me. Fuming within, I stumped out on to the terrace while he went off to 'forage'. I saw in fancy those thick spectacles eyeing the broken meats in the great larder. What was wrong with the man? What made him so extortionately substantial, and yet in effect, so elusive and unreal? What indeed constitutes the *reality* of any fellow creature? The some-thing, the someone within, surely; not the mere physical frame.

In Mr Bloom's company that physical frame seemed to be mainly a kind of stalking horse. If so, the fowler was exquisitely intent on not alarming his prey. Those honeyed decoy-notes. But then, what conceivably could he want with *me*? Whom had he been waiting for, skulking there at some convenient window? Why was he alone in this great house? Only Mr Bloom could answer these questions: and owing to some odd scruple of manners or what-not, I couldn't put them to him. Ridiculous!

My mind by this time had wearied of these vexations and had begun to follow my eyes. I was looking southward – a clear lustre as of glass was in the heavens. It had been a calm but almost colourless sunset, and westward the evening star floated like a morsel of silver in a dove-grey fleece of cloud drawn gently across the fading blue of the horizon. The countryside lay duskily purple and saturnine, and about a hundred yards away in this direction was a wide stretch of water – dead-white under the sky – a lake that must have been thronged with wild-fowl; yet not so much as a peewit crying.

In front of me the garden was densely walled in with trees, and an exceedingly skilful topiarian had been at work on the nearer yews. Year after year he must have been clipping his birds and arches and vast mushrooms and even an obelisk. They were now in their freshest green. Mr Bloom's servants cannot have forsaken him in a batch. They were gone, though. Not a light showed in the dusk; no movement; no sound except out of the far distance, presently, the faint hypnotic *churring* of a night-jar. It is the bird of woody solitude. Well, there would be something of a moon that night, I knew. She would charm out the owls, and should at least ensure me a lullaby. But why this distaste, this sense of inward disquietude?

And suddenly I wheeled about at the sound, as I thought, of a footstep. But no; I was alone. Mr Bloom must still be busy foraging in his back-quarters or his cellarage. And yet – is it credible? – once more in a last forlorn hope I began to search my pockets for the missing key! But this time Mr Bloom interrupted the operation. He came out sleeking his hands together in front of him and looking as amiably hospitable as a churchwarden at a parochial soirée. He led me in, volubly explaining the while that since he had been alone in the house he had all but given up the use of the upper rooms. 'As a matter of fact, I am preparing to leave,' he told me, 'as soon as it is – convenient. Meanwhile I camp on the ground-floor. There is many a novelty in the ordinary routine of life, Mr Dash, that we seldom enjoy. It amused my secretary, this system of picnicking, poor fellow – at least for a while.'

He came to a standstill on the threshold of the room into which he was leading me. A cluster of candles burned on the long oak table set out for our evening meal, but otherwise the room – larger than the study, and containing, apart from its cabinets of china and old ivory, almost as many books – was thickly curtained, and in gloom.

'I must explain,' he was saying, and he laid the four fingers of his left hand very gently on my shoulder, 'that my secretary has left me. He has left me for good. He is dead.' With owl-like solemnity he scrutinised the blank face I turned on him, as if he were expectant of sympathy. But I had none to give. You cannot even feign sympathy without *some* preparation.

Mr Bloom glanced over his shoulder into the corridor behind us. 'He has been a great loss,' he added. 'I miss him. On the other hand,' he added more cheerfully, 'we mustn't allow our personal feelings to interfere with the enjoyment of what I am afraid even at best is a lamentably modest little meal.'

Again Mr Bloom was showing himself incapable of facing facts. It was by no means a modest little meal. Our cold *bouillon* was followed by a pair of spring chickens, the white sauce on their delicate breasts adorned in a chaste design with fragments of cucumber, truffle and mushroom – hapless birds that seemed to have been fattened on cowslips and honeysuckle buds. There was an asparagus salad, so cold to the tongue as to suggest ice; and neighbouring it were old silver dishes of meringues and an amber-coloured wine jelly, thickly clotted with cream. After the sherry champagne was our only wine; and it was solely owing to my abstemiousness that we failed to finish the second bottle.

Between mouthfuls Mr Bloom indulged in general conversation – of the exclamatory order. It covered a pretty wide autobiographical field. He told me of his boyhood in Montrésor. The estate had been in his family for close on two centuries. For some years he had shared it with the last of his three sisters – all now dead.

'She's there!' he exclaimed, pointing an instant with uplifted fork at a portrait that hung to the right of the chimneypiece. 'And that's my mother.' I glanced up at Miss Bloom; but she was looking in the other direction, and our real and painted eyes did not meet. It seemed incredible that these two could ever have been children, have played together, giggled, quarrelled, made it up. Even if I could imagine the extinguished lady in the portrait as a little girl, no feat of fancy could convert Mr Bloom into a small boy – a sufferable one, I mean.

By the time I had given up the attempt, and, having abandoned the jelly, we had set to work on some Camembert cheese, Mr Bloom's remarks about his secretary had become almost aggrieved.

'He was of indispensable use to me in my literary work,' he insisted as he chawed rapidly on, 'modest enough in itself – I won't trouble you with that – only an obscure byway of interest. Indis*pen*sable. We differed in our views, of course: no human beings ever see perfectly eye to eye on such a topic... In a word, the occult. But he had an unusual *flair* of which he himself, you will hardly believe it, until he came to me, was completely ignorant.' He laid his left hand on the table. 'I am not denying that for one moment. We succeeded in attaining the most curious and interesting results from our little experiments. I could astonish you.'

I tried in vain to welcome the suggestion; but the light even of only six candles is a little stupefying when one has to gaze through them at one's host, and Mr Bloom was sitting up immediately opposite to me on the other side of the table.

'My own personal view,' he explained, 'is that his ill-health was in no way due to these investigations. It was, I assure you, against my wish that he should continue them even on his own account. Flatly, two heads, two wills, two cautions even, are better than one in such matters. Dr Ponsonby – I should explain that Dr Ponsonby is my medical adviser; he attended my poor sister in her last illness – Dr Ponsonby, unfortunately, lives at some little distance, but he did not hesitate to sacrifice all the time he could spare. On the other hand, as far as I can gather, he was not in the least surprised that when the end came, it came suddenly. My secretary, Mr Dash, was found dead in his bed – that is, in his bedroom. Speaking for myself, I should—' back went his head again, and once more his slightly bolting eyes gazed out at me like polished agates across the silvery lustre of the candle-light – 'speaking for myself,' his voice had muffled itself almost into the inarticulate beneath his beard, 'I should prefer to go quickly when I have to go at all.'

The white plump hand replenished his glass with champagne. 'Not that I intend to imply that I have any immediate desire for that. While as for you, my dear young sir,' he added almost merrily, 'having enjoyed only a morsel of my experience in this world, you must desire that consummation even less.'

'You mean, to die, Mr Bloom?' I put it to him. His chin lowered itself into his collar again; the eyelids descended over his eyes.

'Precisely. Though it is as well to remember there is more than one way of dying. There is first the body to be taken into account; and there is next – what remains: though nowadays, of course – well, I leave it to you.'

Mr Bloom was a peculiar conversationalist. Like an astute letter-writer he ignored questions in which he was not interested, or which he had no wish to answer; and with the agility of a chimpanzee in its native wilds would swing off from a topic not to his liking to another that up to that point had not even been hinted at. Quite early in our extravagantly *tête-à-tête* meal I began to suspect that the secret of his welcome to a visitor who had involuntarily descended on him from out of the blue, was an insensate desire to hear himself talk. His vanity was elephantine. Events proved this surmise to be true only in part. But in the meantime it became pretty evident why Mr Bloom should be in want of company; I mean of ordinary human company, though he seemed to have wearied of his secretary's some little time before that secretary had been summoned away.

'You will agree, my dear sir, that to see eye to eye with an invalid for any protracted period is a severe strain. Illness breeds fancies, not all of them considerate. Not a happy youth, *ever*: introspective – an "introvert" in the cant term of our time. But still meaning well; and, oh yes, endeavouring not to give way when – when in company. My sister never really liked him, either. Not at all. But then, she was the prey of conventions that are yet for some, perhaps, a safeguard. We shared the same interests, of course – he and I. Our arrangement was based on that. He had his own views, but was at times, oh yes' – he filled his glass again – 'exceedingly obstinate about them. He had little *staying* power. He began to fumble, to hesitate, to question, to fluster himself – and me, too, for that matter – at the very moment perhaps when we were arriving at an excessively interesting juncture.

'You know the general process, of course?' He had glanced up over his food at me, but not in order to listen to any answer I might have given. 'It is this' – and he forthwith embarked on a long and tedious discourse concerning the sweet uses of the planchette, of automatic writing, table-rapping, the hidden slate, ectoplasm, and all the other – to me rather disagreeable – paraphernalia of the spiritualistic *séance*. Nothing I could say or do, not even unconcealed and deliberate yawning, had the least effect upon Mr Bloom's fluency. 'Lung trouble' appeared to have been the primary cause of his secretary's final resignation. But if the unfortunate young man had night after night been submitted to the experience that I was now enduring, exasperation and boredom alone would have accounted for it. How on earth indeed, I asked myself, could he have endured Mr Bloom so long.

I ceased to listen. The cascade of talk suddenly came to an end. Mr Bloom laid his hands on either side of his dessert plate and once more fixed me in silence under his glasses. 'You, yourself, have possibly dabbled a little in my hobby?' he enquired.

I had indeed. In my young days my family had possessed an elderly female friend – a Miss Algood. She had been one of my mother's bridesmaids, and it was an unwritten law in our household that all possible consideration and affection should be shown to her in all circumstances. She, poor soul, had come down in the world – until indeed she had come down at last to one small room on the top floor in lodgings in Westbourne Park. She was gaunt, loquacious, and affectionate; and she had a consuming interest in the other world. I hear her now: 'On the other side, my dear Charles.' 'Another plane, Charles.' 'When I myself pass over.' It is curious; she was absolutely fearless and quixotically independent.

For old sake's sake, and I am afraid for very little else, I used to go to tea with her occasionally. And we would sit together, the heat welling up out of the sun-struck street outside her window; and she would bring out the hateful little round Victorian table, and the wine-glass and the cardboard alphabet; and we would ask questions of the unseen, the mischievous and the half-crazy concerning the unknowable; and she would become flushed and excited, her lean hands trembling, while she urged me now to empty my mind, and now, to concentrate! And though I can honestly say I never deliberately tampered with that execrable little wine-glass in its wanderings over the varnished table; and though she herself never, so far as I could detect, deliberately cooked the messages it spelt out for us; we enjoyed astonishing revelations. Revelations such as an intelligent monkey or parrot might invent – yet which by any practical test proved utterly valueless.

These 'spiritistic' answers to our cross-examination were at the same time so unintelligibly intelligent, and yet so useless and futile, that I had been cured once and for all of the faintest interest in 'the other side' – thus disclosed, I mean. If anything, in fact, the experience had even a little tarnished the side Mr Bloom now shared with me.

For this reason alone his first mention of the subject had almost completely taken away my appetite for his chicken, his jelly and his champagne. After all, that 'other side's' border-line from which, according to the poet, no traveller returns, must be a good many miles longer even than the wall of China, and not *all* its gates can lead to plains of peace or paradise or even of mere human endurableness.

I explained at last to Mr Bloom that my interest in spiritualism was of the tepidest variety. Alas, his prominent stone-blue eyes – lit up as they were by this concentrated candle-light – incited me to be more emphatic than I intended. I told him I detested the whole subject. 'I am convinced,' I assured him, 'that if the messages, communications, whatever you like to call them, that you get that way are anything else than the babblings and mumblings of sub-consciousness – a deadly dubious term, in itself – then they are probably the work of something or somebody even more "sub" than that.'

Convinced! I knew, of course, practically nothing at first hand about the subject – Miss Algood, poor soul, was only the fussiest and flimsiest of amateurs – but ignorance, with a glimmer of intuition, perhaps gives one assurance. 'Whatever I have heard,' I told him flatly, 'from *that* source – of the future, I mean, which awaits us when we get out of this body of ours, Mr Bloom, fills me with nothing but regret that this life is not the end of everything. I don't say that you get *no*where, even by that route, and I don't say that you mayn't get further some day than you intend, but,' I stupidly blustered on, 'my own personal opinion is that the whole business, so conducted, is a silly and dangerous waste of time.'

His eyes never wavered, he lowered his head by not so much as the fraction of an inch, and then, as if in an aside, his lips hardly stirring, he ejaculated 'Quite so, but not exactly *no*where, it may be'.

And then, as I sat looking at him – it is difficult to put it into words – his face 'went out' so to speak; it became a face (not only abandoned but) forsaken, vacant, and as if uncurtained too, bleak and mute as a window. The unspeculating eyes remained open, one inert hand lay on the table beside his plate, but he, Mr Bloom, was gone. And for perhaps two minutes I myself sat on there, in the still clear candle-light of that festal board, in a solitude I do not covet to experience again. Yet – as I realised even then – Mr Bloom had succeeded in this miserable manoeuvre merely by a trick. The next instant his bluish eyes became occupied, his face took life, and he once again looked out at me with a leer of triumph, an almost coquettish vanity, though he blinked a little as if the light offended him, and as if he were trying to conceal the fact that he had not much appreciated the scene or state which he had come *from*.

He gave me no time to reflect on this piece of buffoonery. 'So, so,' he was informing me, 'shutters up or shutters down, we are what we are; and all that you have been saying, my dear Mr Dash, amuses me. Extraordinary! Most amusing! Illuminating! Quite so! Quite so! Capital! You tell me that you know nothing about the subject. Precisely. And that it is silly and dangerous. Ah, yes! And why not? Dangerous! Well, one word in your ear. Here, my dear sir, we are in the very thick of it; a positive hotbed. But if there is one course I should avoid,' his eyes withdrew themselves, and the thick glasses blazed into the candle-light once more, 'it would be that of taking any personal steps to initiate you into – into our mysteries. No; I shall leave matters completely to themselves.'

He had scarcely raised his voice; his expression had never wavered; he continued to smile at me; only his thick fingers trembled a little on the tablecloth. But he was grey with rage. It seemed even that the scalp of his head had a little raised the hair on its either side, so intense was his resentment.

'A happy state – ignorance, Mr Dash. That of our first parents.'

And then, like a fool, I flared up and mentioned Miss Algood. He listened, steadily smiling.

'I see. A superannuated novice, a would-be professional medium,' he insinuated at last with a shrug of his great heavy shoulders. 'You pay your money and you take your choice. Pooh! Banal!'

I hotly defended my well-meaning sentimental old friend.

'Ah, indeed, a retired governess! An – an old maid!' and once more his insolence nearly mastered him. 'Have no fear, Mr Dash, she is not on *my* visiting list. There are deeps, and vasty deeps.'

With that he thrust out a hand and snatched up the chicken bone that lay on my plate.

'Come out there!' he called baldly. 'Here, *you!*' His head dipped out of sight as he stooped; and a yellowish dog – with a white-gleaming sidelong eye – of which up to the present I had seen or heard no sign, came skulking out from under a chair in the corner of the room to enjoy its evening meal. For awhile only the crunching of teeth on bones broke the silence.

'Greedy, you! You glutton!' Mr Bloom was cajoling him. 'Aye, but where's Steve? An animal's intelligence, Mr Dash' – his voice floated up to me from under the other side of the table – 'is situated in his belly. And even when one climbs up to human prejudices one usually detects as primitive a source.'

For an instant I could make no reply to this pleasantry. He took advantage of the pause to present me with a smile, and at the same moment filled a little tulip-shaped glass for me with green Chartreuse.

'There, there: I refuse to disagree,' he was saying. 'Your company has been very welcome to me; and – well, one should never embark on one's little private preserves without encouragement. My own in particular meet with very scant courtesy usually. That animal could tell a tale.' The crunching continued. 'Couldn't yer, you old rascal? Where's Steve; where's Steve? Now get along back!' The scrunching ceased. The yellowish dog retreated into its corner.

'And now, Mr Dash,' declared Mr Bloom, 'if you have sufficiently refreshed yourself, let us leave these remains. These last few months I have detested being encumbered with servants in the house. A foreign element. They are further away from us, I assure you, in all that really matters, than that rascal, Chunks, there in the corner. Eh, you old devil?' he called at his pet, 'Ain't it so? Now, let me see,' he took out his watch, a gold half-hunter, its engraving almost worn away with long service – 'nine o'clock; h'm; h'm; h'm! Just nine! We have a long evening before us. Believe me, I am exceedingly grateful for your company, and regret that – but there, I see you have already condoned an old man's foibles.'

There was something curiously aimless, even pathetic in the tone of that last remark. He had eaten with excellent appetite, and had accounted for at least four-fifths of our champagne. But he rose from the table looking more dejected than I should have supposed possible, and shuffled away in his slippers, as if the last ten minutes had added years to his age.

He was leading the way with one of the candlesticks in his hand, but, to avoid their guttering, I suppose, had blown out two of its candles. A dusky moonlight loomed beyond the long hinged windows of his study. The faint earthy odour of spring and night saturated the air, for one of them was open. He paused at sight of it, glancing about him.

'If there is an animal I cannot endure,' he muttered over his shoulder at me, 'it is the cat – the feline cat. They have a history; they retreat into the past; we meet them in far other circumstances. Yes, yes.'

He had closed and bolted the window, drawn shutters and curtains, while he was speaking.

'And now, bless my soul, Mr Dash, how about your room – a room for you? I ought to have thought of that before: bachelor habits. Now where shall we be – put?' With feet close together he stood looking at me. 'My secretary's, now? Would that meet the case? He was a creature for comfort. But one has fancies, reluctances, perhaps. As I say, the upper rooms are all bare, dismantled, though we *might* together put up a camp-bed and – and water in the bathroom. I myself sleep in here.'

He stepped across and drew aside a curtain hung between the bookcases. But there was not light enough to see beyond it.

'The room I propose is also on this floor, so we should not, if need be, be far apart. Eh? What think we? Well, now, come this way.'

He paused. Once more he led me out, and stopped at the third door of the corridor on the left-hand side. So long was *this* pause, one might have supposed he was waiting for permission to enter. I followed him in. It was a lofty room – a bed and sitting-room combined, and its curtains and upholstery were of a pale purple. Its window was shut, the air stuffy and faintly sweet. The bed was in the further corner to the left of the window; and there again the dusky moonlight showed.

I stood looking at the mute inanimate things around me in that blending of the two faint lights. No doubt if I had been ignorant that the owner, or rather user, of the room had made his last exit thence, I should have noticed nothing unusual in its stillness, its vacant calm. And yet, well, I had left a friend only that afternoon still a little breathless after his scramble up the nearer bank of the Jordan. And now – this was the last place on earth – these four walls, these colours, this bookcase, that table, that window – which Mr Bloom's secretary had set eyes on before setting out, not to return.

My host watched me. He would, I think, have shut and pulled the curtains over these windows too, if I had given him the opportunity.

'How's that, then? You think, you will be – but there, I hesitate to press the matter... In fact, Mr Dash, this is the only room I *can* offer you.'

I mumbled my thanks and assured him not very graciously that I should be comfortable.

'Capital!' cried Mr Bloom. 'Eureka! My only apprehension – well, you know how touchy, how sensitive people can be. Why, my dear Mr Dash, in a world as superannuated as ours is every other mouthful of air we breathe must have been *some*body's last. I leave you reconciled, then. You will find me in the study, and I can promise you that one little theme shall not intrude on us again. The bee may buzz, but Mr Bloom will keep his bonnet on! The *fourth* door on the right – after turning to your *right* down the corridor. Ah! I am leaving you no light.'

He lit the twin wax candles on his late secretary's dressing-table, and withdrew.

I myself stood for awhile gazing stupidly out of the window. In spite of his extraordinary fluency, Mr Bloom, I realised, was a secretive old man. I had realised all along of course that it was not my beautiful eyes he was after; nor even my mere company. The old creature – admirable mask though his outward appearance might be – was on edge. He was detesting his solitude, though until recently, at any rate, it had been the one aim of his life. It had even occurred to me that he was not much missing his secretary. Quite the reverse. He had spoken of him with contempt, but not exactly with the contempt one feels for the completely gone and worsted. Two things appeared to have remained unforgiven in Mr Bloom's mind indeed: some acute disagreement between them, and the fact that Mr Champneys had left him without due notice – unless inefficient lungs constitute due notice.

I took one of the candles and glanced at the books. They were chiefly of fiction and a little poetry, but there was one on mosses, one on English birds, and a little medical handbook in green cloth.

There was also a complete row of manuscript books with pigskin backs labelled *Proceedings*. I turned to the writing-table. Little there of interest – a stopped clock, a dried-up inkwell, a tarnished silver cup, and one or two more books: *The Sentimental Journey*, a *Thomas à Kempis*, bound in limp maroon leather. I opened the *Thomas à Kempis* and read the spidery inscription on the fly-leaf: 'To darling Sidney, with love from Mother. F.C.' It startled me, as if I had been caught spying. 'Life surely should never come quite to this,' some secret sentimental voice within piped out of the void. I shut the book up.

The drawer beneath contained only envelopes and letter paper – *Montrésor*, in large pale-blue letters on a 'Silurian' background – and a black book, its cover stamped with the word *Diary:* and on the fly-leaf, 'S.S. Champneys'. I glanced up, then turned to the last entry – dated only a few months before – just a few scribbled words: 'Not me, at any rate: not *me*. But even if I could get away for—' the ink was smudged and had left its ghost on the blank page opposite it. A mere scrap of handwriting and that poor hasty smudge of ink – they resembled an incantation. Mr Bloom's secretary seemed also to be intent on sharing his secrets with me. I shut up that book too, and turned away. I washed my hands in S.S.C.'s basin, and – with my fingers – did my hair in his glass. I even caught myself beginning to undress – sheer reluctance, I suppose, to go back and face another cataract of verbiage.

To my astonishment a log fire was handsomely burning in the grate when at length I returned to the study, and Mr Bloom, having drawn up two of his voluminous vermilion armchairs in front of it, was now deeply and amply encased in one of them. He had taken off his spectacles, and appeared to be asleep. But his eyes opened at my footstep. He had been merely 'resting' perhaps.

'I hope,' was his greeting, 'you found everything needful, Mr Dash? In the circumstances...'

He called this up at me as if I were deaf or at a distance, but his tone subsided again. 'There's just one little matter we missed, eh? – night attire! Not that you wouldn't find a complete trousseau to choose from in the wardrobe. My secretary, in fact, was inclined to the foppish. No blame; no blame; fine feathers, Mr Dash.'

It is, thank heaven, an unusual experience to be compelled to spend an evening as the guest of a stranger one distrusts. It was not only that Mr Bloom's manner was obviously a mask but even the occasional stupidity of his remarks seemed to be an affectation – and one of an astute and deliberate kind. And yet Montrésor – in itself it was a house of unusual serenity and charm. Its urbane eighteenth-century reticence showed in every panel and moulding. One fell in love with it at first sight, as with an open, smiling face. And then – a look in the eyes! It reeked of the dubious and distasteful. But how can one produce definite evidence for such sensations as these? They lie outside the tests even of Science – as do a good many other things that refuse to conform with the norm of human evidence.

Mr Bloom's company at a dinner-party or a *conversazione*, shall we say, might have proved refreshingly droll. He did his best to make himself amusing. He had read widely – and in out-of-the-way books, too; and he had an unusual range of interests. We discussed music and art – and he brought out portfolio after portfolio of drawings and etchings to illustrate some absurd theory he had of the one, and played a scrap or two of Debussy's and of Ravel's *Gaspard de la Nuit* to prove some far-fetched little theory of his own about the other. We talked of Chance and Dreams and Disease and Heredity, edged on to Woman, and skated rapidly away. He dismissed life as 'an episode in disconcerting surroundings', and scuttled off from a detraction of St Francis of Assisi to the problem of pain.

'Mr Dash, we *fear* pain too much – and the giving of it. The very mention of the word stifles us. And how un-Christian!'

The look he peeked down at me at this was proof enough that he was intent only on leading me on and drawing me out. But I was becoming a little more cautious, and mumbled that that kind of philosophy best begins at home.

'Aye, indeed! A retort, a retort. With Charity on the other side of the hearth in a mob-cap and carpet slippers, I suppose? I see the dear creature: I see her! Still, you will agree, even *you* will agree that once, Mr Dash, the head has lost its way in the heart, one's brain-pan might as well be a basin of soap-bubbles. A man of feeling, by all means – but just a trace, a *soupçon* of rationality, well, it serves! Eh?'

A few minutes afterwards, in the midst of a discourse on the progress of human thought, he suddenly enquired if I cared for the game of backgammon.

'And why not? Or draughts? Or *solitaire,* Mr Dash? – a grossly underestimated amusement.'

But all this badinage, these high spirits were clearly an elaborate disguise, and a none too complimentary one at that. He was 'keeping it up' to keep *me* up; and maybe, to keep himself up. Much of it was automatic – mere mental antics. Like a Thibetan praying-wheel, his mind went round and round. And his attention was divided. One at least of those long, fleshy, hairy ears was cocked in another direction. And at last the question that had been on my tongue throughout most of the evening popped out almost inadvertently. I asked if he was expecting a visitor. At the moment his round black back was turned on me; he was rummaging in a corner cupboard for glasses to accompany the decanter of whisky he had produced; his head turned slyly on his heavy shoulders.

'A visitor? You astonish me. Here? Now? As if, my dear Mr Dash, this rural retreat were Bloomsbury or Mayfair. You amuse me. Callers! Thank heaven, not so. You came, you saw, but you did not *expect* a welcome. The unworthy tenant of Montrésor took you by surprise. Confess it! So be it. And why not? What if you yourself were my looked-for visitor? What then? There are surmises, intuitions, forebodings – to give a pleasant tinge to the word. Yes, yes, I agree. I was on the watch; patiently, *patiently*. In due time your charming little car appears at my gate. You pause: I say to myself, Here he is. Company at last; discussion; pow-wow; even controversy perhaps. Why not? We are sharing the same hemisphere. Plain as a pikestaff. I foresaw your decision as may the shepherd in contemplation of a red sunrise foresee the deluge. I step downstairs; and here we are!'

My reply came a little more warmly than I intended. I assured Mr Bloom that if it had not been for the loss of my key, I shouldn't have stayed five minutes. 'I prefer *not* to be expected in a strange house.' It was unutterably *gauche*.

He chuckled; he shrugged his shoulders; he was vastly amused. 'Ah, but are we not forgetting that such little misadventures are merely part and parcel of the general plan? The end-shaping process, as the poet puts it?'

'What general plan?'

'Mr Dash, when you fire out your enquiries at me like bullets out of the muzzle of a gun, I am positively disconcerted, I can scarcely keep my wits together. Pray let us no longer treat each other like witnesses in the witness-box, or even' – a cat-like smile crept into his face – 'like prisoners in the dock. Have a little whisky? Pure malt;

a tot? It may be whimsical, but for me one of the few exasperating things about my poor secretary, Mr Champneys, was his aversion to "alcohol". His own word! £300 a year – Mr Dash. No less. And everything "found". No expenses except tobacco, shockers – his own word again – pyjamas, tooth-powder and petrol – a motor-bicycle, in fact, soon *hors de combat*. And "alcohol", if you please! The libel! These specialists! Soda water or Apollinaris?'

In sheer chagrin I drank the stuff, and rose to turn in. Not a bit of it! With covert glances at his watch, Mr Bloom kept me there by hook and by crook until it was long past midnight, and try as he might to conceal it, the disquietude that had peeped out earlier in the evening became more and more obvious. The only effect of this restlessness on his talk, however, was to increase its volume and incoherence. If Mr Bloom had been play-acting, and had been cast for his own character, his improvisations could not have been more masterly. He made no pretence now of listening to my own small part in this display; and when he did, it was only in order to attend to some other business he had in mind. Ever and again, as if to emphasise his point, he would haul himself up out of his deep-bottomed chair, and edge off towards the door – with the pretence perhaps of looking for a book. He would pause there for but an instant – and the bumbling muffled voice would yet again take up the strain. Once, however, he came to a dead stop, raised his hand and openly stood listening.

'A nightingale certainly; if not two,' he murmured *sotto voce,* 'but tell me, Mr Dash,' he called softly out across the room, 'was I deceived into thinking I heard a distant knocking? In a house as large as this; articles of some value perhaps; we read even of violence. You never can tell.'

I enquired with clumsy irony if there would be anything remarkable in a knocking. 'Don't your friends ever volunteer even a rap or two on their own account? I should have supposed it would be the least they could offer.'

'A signal; m'm; a rap or two,' he echoed me blandly. 'Why that?'

'From "the other side"?'

'Eh? Eh?' he suddenly broke off, his cheek whitening; the sole cause of his dismay being merely a scratching at the door-panel, announcing that his faithful pet had so much wearied of solitude in the dining-room that he had come seeking even his master's company. But Mr Bloom did not open the door.

'Be off!' he called at the panel. 'Away, sir! To your mat! That dog, Mr Dash, is more than human – or shall we say, less than human?' The words were jovial enough, but the lips that uttered them trembled beneath his beard.

I had had enough, and this time had my way. He accompanied me to the door of the study but not further, and held out his hand.

'If by any chance,' he scarcely more than murmured, 'you should want anything in the night, you will remember, of course, where to find me; I am in there.' He pointed. 'On the other hand,' he laid his hand again on my arm, deprecatingly, almost as if with shy affection – 'I am an exceedingly poor sleeper. And occasionally I find a brief amble round proves a sedative. Follow me up? At any alarm, eh? I should welcome it. But tonight I expect – nothing.'

He drew-to the door behind him. 'Have you ever tried my own particular little remedy for insomnia? Cold air? And perhaps a hard biscuit, to humour the digestion. But *fol, lol,* a young man – no: the machine comparatively new! My housekeeper returns at six: breakfast, I hope, at eight-thirty. A most punctual woman; a treasure. But then, servants; I detest the whole race of them. Good-night; good-night. And none of those *Proceedings,* I warn you!'

But even now I had not completely shaken him off. He hastened after me, puffing as he came, and clutched at my coat sleeve.

'What I was meaning, Mr Dash, is that I have never attempted to make converts – a fruit, let me tell you, that from being at first incredibly raw and unwholesome, rapidly goes rotten. Besides, my secretary had very little talent for marshalling facts. That's why I mentioned the *Proceedings*. A turn for *writing*, maybe, but no method. Just that. And now, of course, you *must* go. Our evening is at an end. But who knows? Of course. Never matter. What must come, comes.'

At last I was free, though a hoarse whisper presently pursued me down the corridor. 'No need for caution, Mr Dash, should you need me. No infants, no invalids; sleep well.'

Having put my candlestick on the table, shut the door of Mr Champneys's bedroom, and very cautiously locked it, I sat down on the bed to think things over. Easier said than done. The one thing in my mind was relief at finding myself alone again, and of extreme distaste (as I wound my watch) at the recollection of how many hours still remained before dawn. I opened the window and looked out. My room was at the back of the house, then; and over yonder must lie the lake, ebon-black under the stars. I listened for the water-birds, but not a sound. Mr Bloom's nightingales, too, if not creatures of his imagination, had ceased to lament. A ground mist wreathed the boles of the chestnut trees, soundlessly lapping their lowermost boughs.

I drew in. The draught had set my candles guttering. Almost automatically I opened one of the long drawers in Mr Champneys's chest. It was crammed with his linen. Had he no relatives, then, I wondered, or had Mr Bloom succeeded to his property? Such gay pyjamas would grace an Arabian prince; of palest blue silk with 'S.S.C.' in beautiful scarlet lettering. It was needlessly fastidious perhaps, but I left them undisturbed.

There were a few photographs above the chimneypiece; but photographs of the relatives and friends of a deceased stranger are not exhilarating company. Mr Champneys himself being dead, they seemed to be tinged with the same eclipse. One of them was a snapshot of a tall, dark, young man, in tennis clothes. He was smiling; he had a longish nose; a tennis racket was under his arm; and a tiny strip of maroon and yellow ribbon had been glued to the glass of the frame. Another Champneys, a brother, perhaps. I stood there, idly gazing at it for minutes together, as if in search of inspiration.

No talker has ever more completely exhausted me than Mr Bloom. Even while I was still deep in contemplation of the photograph I was seized suddenly with a series of yawns almost painful in their extremity. I turned away. My one longing was for the bathroom. But no – Mr Bloom had failed to show me the way there, and any attempt to find it for myself might involve me in more talk. It is embarrassing to meet anyone after farewells have been said – and *that* one? – no. Half-dressed, and having hunted in vain for a second box of matches, I lay down on the bed, drew its purple quilt over me – after all, Mr Bloom's secretary had not died in it! – and blew out my candle.

I must have at once fallen asleep – a heavy and, seemingly, dreamless sleep. And now, as if in a moment I was awake again – completely wide awake, as if at an inward signal. Night had gone; the creeping grey of dawn was at the window, its colder, mist-burdened airs filled the room. I lay awhile inert, sharply scrutinising my surroundings, realising precisely where I was and at the same time that something was radically and inexplicably wrong with them. What?

It is difficult to suggest; but it was as if a certain aspect – the *character* of the room, its walls, angles, patterns, furniture, had been peculiarly intensified. Whatever was naturally grotesque in it was now more grotesque – and less real. Matter seldom advertises the precariousness imputed to it by the physicist. But now, every object around me seemed to be proclaiming its impermanence, the danger, so to speak, it was in. With a conviction that thrilled me like an unexpected touch of ice, I suddenly realised that this is how Mr Champneys's room would appear to anyone who had become for some reason or another intensely afraid. It may sound wildly preposterous, but there it is. I myself was *not* afraid – there was as yet nothing to be afraid of; and yet everything I saw seemed to be dependent on that most untrustworthy but vivid condition of consciousness. Once let my mind, so to speak, accept the evidences of my senses, then I should be as helpless as the victim of a drug or of the wildest nightmare. I sat there, stiff and cold, eyeing the door.

And then I heard the sound of voices: the faint, hollow, incoherent sound that voices make at a distance in a large house. At that, I confess, a deadly chill came over me. I stepped soundlessly on to the floor, looked about me but in vain in the half-light for the coat I had been wearing the previous night, and slipped on instead a pair of Mr Champneys's slippers and the floral silk dressing gown that hung on the door-hook. In these, I was not exactly myself, but at any rate ready for action. It took me half a minute to unlock the door; caution is snail-slow. I was shivering a little, but that may have been due to the cold May morning. The voices were more distinct now; one of them, I fancied, was Mr Bloom's. But there was a curious similarity between them; so much so that I may have been playing eavesdropper to Mr Bloom talking to himself. The sound was filtering down from an upper room; the corridor beneath, and now in its perspective stretching out before me in the pallor of dawn, being as still as a drop-scene in a theatre, the footlights out.

I listened, but could detect no words. And then the talking ceased. There came a sort of thump at the *other* end of the house, and then, overhead, the sound as of someone retreating towards me – heavily, unaccustomedly, but at a pretty good pace. Inaction is unnerving; and yet I hesitated, detesting the thought of meeting Mr Bloom again (and especially if he had company). But that little risk had to be taken; there was no help for it. I tiptoed along the corridor and looked into his study.

The curtain at the further end of the room was drawn a little aside. A deep-piled Turkey carpet covered the floor. I crossed it, soundlessly, and looked in. The light here was duskier than in my own room, and at first, after one comprehensive glance, I saw nothing unusual except that near at hand and beside a chair on which a black morning-coat had been flung, was a small bed, half-covered by a travelling rug; and standing beside it, a familiar pair of boots. Unmistakable, ludicrous, excellent boots! Empty as only boots can be, they squatted there side by side, like creatures by no means mute, yet speechless. And towards the foot of the bed, on a little round table drawn up beside it, lay the miscellaneous contents, obviously, of Mr Bloom's pockets. The old gold watch and the spade guinea, a note-case, a pocket-book, a pencil-case, a scrap of carved stained ivory, an antique silver toothpick, a couple of telegram envelopes, a bunch of keys, a heap of loose money – I see them all, but I see even more distinctly – and it was actually hob-nobbing with the spade-guinea – a Yale key. Why Mr Bloom emptied his pockets at night, I cannot guess – a mere habit perhaps. To that habit nonetheless I owe, perhaps, the brevity of my acquaintance with him.

There is, I suppose, no limit to human stupidity. Never until this moment had it occurred to me that Mr Bloom himself might have been responsible for the loss of my key, that he had in fact purloined it. I stole nearer, and examined his. Yale keys at a casual glance are almost as like one another as leaves on a tree. Was this mine? I was uncertain. I must risk it. And it baffles me why I should have been so fastidious about it. Mr Bloom had not been fastidious. The distant footsteps seemed now to be dully thumping down a remote flight of wooden stairs, and it was unmistakably *his* voice that I heard faintly booming as if in querulous protestation, and with all its manlier resonance and its gusto gone.

'Yes, yes: coming, coming!' and the footsteps stumped on.

Well, I had no wish to meddle in any assignation. I had long since suspected that Mr Bloom's activities may have proved responsible for guests even more undesirable than myself, even though, unlike myself, they may, perhaps, have been of a purely subjective order. Like attracts like, I assume, in *any* sphere. Still raw prejudices such as mine were not exactly a fair test of his peculiar methods of spiritistic investigation. More generous critics might merely surmise that he had only pressed on a little further than most. That is all: a pioneer.

What – as I turned round – I was not prepared for was the spectacle of Mr Bloom's bed. When I entered the room, I am certain there had been nothing unusual about that, except that it had not been slept in. True, the light had meanwhile increased a little, but not much. No, the bed had then been empty.

Not so now. The lower part of it was all but entirely flat, the white coverlid having been drawn almost as neat and close from side to side of it as the carapace of a billiard table. But on the pillow – the grey-flecked brown beard protruding over the turned-down sheet – now showed what appeared to be the head and face of Mr Bloom. With chin jerked up, I watched that face steadily, transfixedly. It was a flawless facsimile, waxen, motionless; but it was not a real face and head. It was an hallucination. How induced is quite another matter. No spirit of life, no livingness had ever stirred those soap-like, stagnant features. It was a travesty utterly devoid – whatever its intention – of the faintest hint of humour. It was merely a mask, a lifelike mask (past even the dexterity of a Chinese artist to rival), and – though I hardly know why – it was inconceivably shocking.

My objections to indiscriminate spiritualism the evening before may have been hasty and shallow. They seemed now to have been grotesquely inadequate. This house was not haunted, it was infested. Catspaw, poor young Mr Champneys may have been, but he had indeed helped with the chestnuts. A horrible weariness swept over me. Without another glance at the bed, I made my way as rapidly as possible to the door – and broke into a run.

Still thickly muffled with her last journey's dust – except for the fingerprints I afterwards noticed on her bonnet – and just as I had left her the previous evening, my car stood awaiting me in the innocent blue of dawn beneath the porch. So must Tobias have welcomed his angel. My heart literally stood still as I inserted the key – but all was well. The first faint purring of the engine was accompanied by the sound of a window being flung open. It was above and behind me, and beyond the porch. I turned my head, and detected a vague grey-ish figure standing a little within cover of the hollies and ilexes – a short man, about twenty or thirty yards away, not looking at me. But he too may have been pure illusion, pure hallucination. When I had blinked and looked again he was gone. There was no sunshine yet; the garden was as still as a mechanical panorama, but the hubbub, the gabbling was increasing overhead.

In an instant I had shot out from under the porch, and dignity forgotten, was on my way helter-skelter round the semicircular drive. But to my utter confusion the gates at this end of it were heavily padlocked. I all but stripped the gears in my haste to retreat, but succeeded nonetheless; and then, without so much as turning my head towards the house, I drove clean across the lawn, the boughs of the blossom-burdened trees actually brushing the hood of the car as I did so. In five minutes I must have been nearly as many miles from Mr Bloom's precincts.

It was fortunate perhaps the day was so early; even the most phlegmatic of rural constables might look a little askance at a motorist desperately defying the speed limit in a purple dressing-gown and red morocco slippers. But I was innocent of robbery, for in exchange for these articles I had left behind me as valuable a jacket and a pair of brown leather shoes. I wonder what they will fetch at the sale? I wonder if Mr Bloom would have offered me Mr Champneys's full £300 *per annum* if I had consented to stay? He was sorely in need, I am afraid, of human company, and a less easily prejudiced ally might have been of help to him in his extremity. But I ran away.

And it is now too late to make amends. He has gone home – as we all shall – and taken his wages. And what troubles me, and now and then with acute misgiving, is the thought of Miss Algood. She was so simple and so easy a prey to enthusiasm. She dabbled her fingers in the obscure waters frequented by Mr Bloom as heedlessly and as absorbedly as some little dark intense creature on the banks of the Serpentine over a gallipot of 'tiddlers'. I hate to think of any of 'them' taking her seriously – or even otherwise; and of the possibility also, when she is groping her way through their underworld, for she never really found it in this – the possibility of her meeting him there. For whatever Mr Bloom's company in his charming house may have consisted *of* – and here edges in the obscure problem of what the creatures of our thoughts, let alone our dreams, are 'made on' – and quite apart too from Mr Bloom's personal appearance, character, and 'effects', my chief quarrel with him was his scorn of my old harmless family friend. I would like, if only I could, to warn her against him – those dark, affectionate, saddened, hungry eyes.

THE GAME AT CARDS

I T WAS THE EVE OF CHRISTMAS, SPARKLING AND CLEAR, AND THE charcoal-burner, having finished his work for the day, returned to his hut. He had built it in a glade at the upper edge of a wide green valley – hollow as a saucer, but encircled by dense forests, above which mountains towered into the light of the evening sky. The charcoal-burner's hive-shaped mound of chestnut wood had been covered in with its last turves that afternoon. He had kindled the sticks within, and now the red fire had begun slowly gnawing its way inch by inch through the logs of fragrant wood. He ate up his supper of black bread and onions, took a last long look at the weather, and went to bed.

When he awoke next morning snow had fallen. The beams of his hut were frosted with its radiance. He got up and looked out on a world made beautiful as a dream. The reflected light struck up into his lean wizened face and so dazzled his bright blue eyes that he could scarcely see for the splendour. Everywhere around him the snow lay soft as wool – its crystalled surface marked only by the steppings of birds and the footprints of little animals that had been abroad before daybreak. Strange sight now indeed was the snow-mounded hillock of burning chestnut wood, with its frail plume of smoke going up into the air. Nothing else stirred in that shining quiet.

With a bundle of fir branches the charcoal-burner brushed away the snow in front of his hut, then lit a fire a little within the mouth of it, where there was a hole in the roof for the smoke to go through. And while the fire was burning up he prepared his pot for his midday meal. It soon began simmering over the flames, and he sat idle for a little, watching the distant forests and the untrodden mountains under the pale low blue of the sky. It was bitter cold.

About the middle of the morning, as he was lifting the lid of his pot, he thought he heard voices. Glancing up over the smoke, he looked out and, sure enough, two strangers were approaching the hut along the narrow snow-covered track from the forest. They must have followed the high mountain road. As they came near, the charcoal-burner continued to watch them and was astonished. For the countenance of one of these strangers, who was a little in front of the other, was such as he had never seen before, unless in a dream. Yet it seemed he had known it since he was a child.

The sun burned clear, though almost heatless, in the sky, and the hoar-frost sparkled beneath its beams as he watched them. And when the two strangers had greeted the charcoal-burner, he not only bade them welcome to his hut and his fire to rest and warm themselves, but he also asked them to share his soup, and to forgive him that it was no better, since it was all he had. They thanked the charcoal-burner warmly and sat down, for they had been journeying since dawn.

While they talked together the charcoal-burner thrust more sticks under his pot and, as they fizzed and crackled, he stirred up the soup, wondering meantime – however little he had himself – how he could possibly make it go far enough for three hungry men, even though he had thrown in the last remnants of his store of meal and sweet roots. He was preparing to take it off the fire when, glancing up, he saw a third traveller – a fur hat drawn down low over his thick red hair – approaching the hut. But this man was walking alone. Now the charcoal-burner longed to invite this stranger too to share his pottage, and especially because he looked a man solitary by nature and one who had seen evil days. But how make his soup go round? While he was considering this, his face all wrinkled up, he turned towards the first of the travellers who had come. Their eyes met, and the other smiled and said, 'He is a friend.'

After that the charcoal-burner hesitated no longer. He at once hastened out over the snow, brought the solitary traveller to the hut, and sat him down, and even though in a little while, by twos and threes, other wayfarers appeared and joined the company already there, he had no more misgivings, but made them welcome one and all. And it seemed to him that, however much water he added to his smoking pot to help make the soup go round, the soup itself was none the worse for it. It not only smelt good in the sharp winter air, but to judge by the faces of the newcomers it seemed to taste good too. And it was astonishing how far what little black bread there was had gone round. They all made cheer together and enjoyed to the full the charcoal-burner's fire and hospitality.

When the sun, already low in his December arch, had sunk behind the mountain-tops, and dusk had fallen on the eastern forests and a few stars had pierced into the sky, the charcoal-burner found that there were no less than thirteen travellers gathered about his blazing fire – for he counted them. And never had any man on earth better company than he that Christmas evening. Cramped though the shelter of his hut might be, none of them seemed to be out in the cold and none hungry, and every one was well content. He had given them all he had and was as happy as a king.

Whenever the charcoal-burner raised his eyes and looked at the stranger who had first spoken with him, he marvelled. And whenever the gaze of this stranger's eyes met his own it seemed to the charcoal-burner as if the very secrets of his heart were reflected in those depths, and they smiled each at the other.

When it was so dark over the forest that the least stars of Orion showed needle-clear in the moonless sky, and the Dog Star shook like a basket of gems beneath them, one of the strangers, whose name he had heard – and that was Peter – beckoned to the charcoal-burner, and he followed him into the snow a few paces from the hut. Peter stooped close to the charcoal-burner in the starshine and said:

'There is One within who, in thanks for the food and shelter you have given us and for your welcome, would show you his kindness. Wish, and the wish shall be granted you.'

The charcoal-burner looked at Peter dumbly and shook his head.

'It was more than grace enough,' he said at last, 'that he should take of me the little I had to give, and I want nothing.'

But still the stranger, called Peter, pressed him to name his wish. 'I am doing my Master's bidding,' he said. 'Wish now, if only for courtesy's sake. For it is already dark, and we must journey on.'

The charcoal-burner frowned and scratched his head in dismay. He looked across the frozen snow-capped forests towards the western mountains, now cold and leaden in the fading twilight, and could think of nothing. Nothing – except only his pack of playing cards. They seemed to have fluttered into his head out of nowhere, and try as he might he couldn't get them out again. He had had this pack of cards since he was a boy, and to amuse himself in the long hours be spent alone in the forest had often played merely against himself as 'dummy'. And when any chance traveller came his way he would play a game with him before they lay down to sleep. His cards were the joy of his life.

So the charcoal-burner tried and tried again to think of a wish, but could remember nothing but his cards. At last he looked up boldly and blurted out, 'Well, there's just one thing, and that is that whenever I play cards I shall always win.'

Peter looked at him in astonishment. Of all wishes in the world this was the last he would have expected. Nevertheless his Master had bidden him give the charcoal-burner anything he asked for. What should he do? The fire flames faintly lit up his bearded face as he stood in the dusk looking at the charcoal-burner in perplexity. Then he slowly turned his head and glanced through the entry of the hut. The stranger who had offered the charcoal-burner his wish was seated a little apart in the entry, while the others were talking together. At this moment he, too, glanced up at Peter, as if he had divined his doubts. And he nodded his head. So Peter said to the charcoal-burner:

'As it was promised you, your wish is granted. The Master wills it so.'

At this the charcoal-burner felt a sudden shame, and turning aside, pretended to be busying himself without heed of his guests over his mound of smouldering chestnut wood, while they themselves made ready to leave him. And each one of them in turn, as he stood there stooping and scrabbling with his hands, came to bid him farewell, and to thank him for his hospitality. Except only he who had come third of the company, who lifted his hands as if in farewell, but came no nearer. And the stranger who had come first was the last to go. And he himself brought with him the old pack of cards which he had found in the hut, and himself put them – smilingly – into the charcoal-burner's hands. The charcoal-burner looked up at him, and there was a star shining between the stranger's head and his shoulder, and above that head hung the three middle stars of Orion. The stranger smiled again, and the charcoal-burner was left alone.

Now, though the charcoal-burner had long since left behind him the days of his childhood, for a time he felt utterly desolate and forlorn. It had been such a happiness to welcome the travellers. But they were long since out of sight; even their voices had ceased to sound in the still cold air. His fire threw a rosy light over the snow; he was alone. He returned to his hut, sat down, and with his heart thumping under his ribs dealt out two hands of cards. Then he lifted his face towards the sky and said, 'This time I will win.' And he played and beat dummy. Then he played a second game, lifted his head and said, 'This time dummy shall win for me.' And sure enough dummy did. All was fair and square, and so things went on. As Peter had promised him, whenever he played cards with his grimy pack – and he would sometimes tramp off to the nearest village tavern for a game with his old cronies – he always won. He delighted in playing more and more, until at last his skill seemed almost as extraordinary as his luck.

In time, simply because he knew he would always win, he would say so before he began to play. But this did not prevent either friends or strangers from playing with him, for men are so made that they do not believe such things. For this reason the charcoal-burner kept his stakes low when he played cards. For first, having no wife or children, and nearing old age, he had not much use for money or chattels. And next, he remembered the look on the stranger's face, and as often as not played for love on that account.

Still, when he played now and then in the town against a rich man – for the fame of him had gone abroad – he would play for good high stakes and would win. It seemed only proper that now and then he should win something really handsome, after the kindness shown to him by the stranger. But when he played against anyone poorer than himself he would whisper secretly to his cards: 'Hark'ee, my pretty men, that man yonder – though for this game only is me, me myself.' Then he would lose, but never very much.

So the years went by, until, as with all men soon or late, he came at last to know that he would not be likely to live much longer. And as he sat one night, first telling his fortune, and then dealing his cards for a solitary game with himself, he thought again of that Christmas morning many years ago. He had hoped, and even expected, that some day the strangers would return, and had even gone so far as to prepare and keep by him a little store of food in case they should be his guests a second time. Then he would entertain them more worthily. But they had never come his way again. Indeed, it is said that they never come the same way again; that to meet them one must follow them.

And the charcoal-burner, drawing near his end, when he remembered how he had been promised any wish he could think of, and how in his folly he had thought only of his cards and what little good he had done with them, was suddenly grieved in mind. He brooded for many days; his face puckered up with his thoughts, his eyes almost hidden beneath his black eyebrows. And at last he said to himself, as he had already said many times before: 'There stood you, and there stood he. And of all things stark stupid in your crazy old noddle you could think of nothing but a greasy old pack of cards! Ay, and even when he gave you your wish, what in heaven have you done with it!'

There and then he could bear himself no longer. He went down into the forest – though he was that night halfway up the mountainside – and, following an unknown track, came in the darkness to a city in the valley. And he asked the Watchman, whom he met with his lantern in the streets, if he knew of any wicked man in the city who was lying near death. 'For you must understand,' he said, 'that I am a wicked man too, considering, as you might say, the little I have done, and that badly. All I want is just to ease any poor creature like myself for a few minutes before we both have to go the same way; ay, the dark way. Even talking can be a comfort.'

The Watchman looked at him and thought he was mad.

'See here,' cried the charcoal-burner, gripping the Watchman's shoulder with his hand, 'when the last journey's coming near, you too will *know* what you want. At least, I hope so.'

And the Watchman, to humour him – for he spoke fiercely in the dark shadow of the narrow street by the small light of the lantern, and not even the sound of any wayfarer's footsteps to be heard – told him that at this very moment a Jew – a lawyer – lay dying in his great house at the other end of the town.

'And a wickeder old long-nosed skinflint,' he said, 'you never set eyes on.'

At this the charcoal-burner rejoiced, and with his stave in his hand went off at once and knocked at the Jew's door. He stood in the porch, the moonlight shining upon him there, and knocked again. For at first the Jew's servants, who were feasting and carousing, knowing that their master, even if he heard them, was now helpless and could do nothing, and could take nothing away with him, had paid no heed to his knock. But one came at last and opened the door, and not clearly seeing the charcoal-burner – himself being frowsy with too much eating and drinking – and thinking he might be a messenger sent by the doctor or apothecary, let him into the house.

So the charcoal-burner shuffled up the marble stairs, taking care not to lay his hand on the gilded hand-rail or to brush the gilded balusters as he went upwards, and he came into the room where the dying Jew lay in his bed. As he had foreseen, indeed as he had hoped, there sat a crookback stranger beside the bed, very still, and mantled up close in a high black hood like a cowl. He seemed to be watching the Jew, as a hungry cat watches at a mouse's hole.

When the charcoal-burner pushed open the door and looked into the room he did not so much as glance up at him, but seemed to know already that he was there. The charcoal-burner was sure of this. He felt in his very bones that this motionless figure (who seemingly had not even so much as stirred his head under his hood) not only knew who he was, but where he had come from, and what he had come for. The charcoal-burner began to tremble a little, whereupon, from under his ragged cloak, he at once fetched out his pack of cards and called out as loud as he could to the stranger: 'See here! Here we are, you and me: play me a game before this old Jew dies.'

The stranger sat motionless. 'What stakes?' he said.

The charcoal-burner said: 'That old man's soul is soon to be going onwards, and his body will be left behind – and you may be going *with* him.'

At this the stranger stooped in with his shoulders a little, like a falcon, and nodded his head, but he did not look at the charcoal-burner.

'Well,' said the charcoal-burner, 'when I play cards I always win. I warn you.'

'Hmph!' said the black stranger.

'And if,' the charcoal-burner went on, 'you play with me and I win, then the stake is that you leave this old Jew to me and get away back to where you came from. But if by ill-luck *you* win – which you won't – then on the stroke of midnight you shall have not only what is left of that groaning old cadaver in the bed, but me too for company on your way home; for I'm soon to be going the old Jew's way myself.'

The stranger never stirred, but from beneath the black habit he wore softly thrust out his hand. And the charcoal-burner put the pack of cards into it. So they sat down together, facing one another, on two gilded chairs covered with bright blue silk tapestry and on either side of a little table beside the rich Jew's bed. Then the stranger shuffled the cards; the charcoal-burner cut them; and the stranger dealt them. They played steadily, their eyes fixed on the cards and their mouths tight shut. And the charcoal-burner won.

The stranger said, 'Again!' The charcoal-burner, who, for the shivering and fever in his own body, tried in vain to keep his teeth from chattering, looked towards the old Jew in the bed. His eyes were shut, and as he breathed his breast rose and fell quick as the beat of a bird's wings. The charcoal-burner leaned over and gave him to drink, then turned towards the cards again, for he knew there was no time to be lost. And again he won. The stranger sat hunched up in his black habit, and so icy cold he seemed by nature that the charcoal-burner could feel the presence of him near by, though otherwise the very air around him seemed to be on fire. And the stranger cried, 'Yet again!' and shuffled the cards.

'Ay!' cried the charcoal-burner, 'but this, mind you, is the last.' He cut the cards; the other dealt; and they played. They played so fast and furiously that the charcoal-burner's knees knocked together under the table and the sweat ran down his face. But at last he won.

At this his enemy suddenly lifted his whole length clean out of the chair on which he had been sitting, stooped close across the table over the cowering charcoal-burner, fixed on him one appalling glance from under his hood, flung the cards into his face, and went out.

He was gone; the room was empty except for the dying Jew upon the bed. And it was now bitterly cold, as though an endless night were approaching. The charcoal-burner stumbled across to the chair by the bedside, and putting out his hand, groped under the sheet for the hand of the old Jew, leaving his cards scattered upon the floor. And the darkness drew on....

*

After a space of time, of which he knew nothing, the charcoal-burner found himself journeying in a strange country serene and fair, the like of which he had never seen before, not even in a dream; and it was evening. His heart was light as air, and happy beyond words to tell. And, pace for pace beside him, walked a stranger almost of an exact likeness to the old Jew that had died upon the bed, and yet in one thing his companion was not like the old Jew, for he, too, seemed to be happy, and to be stepping as lightly over the daisied grass as the charcoal-burner himself.

So they came together to the gates of Paradise. And the charcoal-burner rapped with his stave on the gate, just as he had rapped with his stave in the moonlight on the door of the Jew. And Peter thrust open the little spying grille or peephole in the great door and looked out, and there came an outburst of distant music on the air. Such was the gift of Peter's memory that he knew the charcoal-burner at once, and greeted him kindly. But the Jew fell back at the sight of Peter, and shrank into himself till he looked utterly small and mean, cowering behind his friend. But Peter had caught sight of him and paused, even as he laid his hand upon the latch of the gate. And he said to the charcoal-burner: 'What is that little black creature you have there, hiding behind you?'

'In the place where I come from,' said the charcoal-burner, 'this man was a Jew.'

'So, too, was I,' said Peter. 'Was he a good Jew?'

'No, he was a wicked Jew. But I say "was" not "is".'

Peter said: 'What else was he?'

The charcoal-burner, remembering what had been told him by the Watchman before he went on his way to the Jew's house, answered truthfully, 'He was a lawyer.' Then Peter said: 'Come in yourself, charcoal-burner, none so welcome. But you must come in alone.'

The charcoal-burner looked earnestly at Peter but never stirred. He stood where he was, and at last he said: 'Do you remember the cards, sir?'

At this Peter's bearded and wrinkled old face looked for a moment almost as young as a boy's, and he smiled in the light that was around him, and said, 'Ay.'

And the charcoal-burner said: 'With those cards I played at the last a cheating, black-avised stranger for this old man, and won. He was the stakes. Three times I played – and the air, cold as ice, yet burnt up as if with fire. And three times I won. It sucked the very marrow from my bones. I can't come in without my friend.'

Peter turned his head away for a moment, deep in thought, then once more peered out through the grille at the spirit of the wicked old Jew, huddling there beyond and behind the charcoal burner, with his hooked nose, and his dark eyes glancing restlessly to and fro as he listened to this talk between them. At last Peter spoke in a voice so low that the Jew could not hear, and said: 'Being your friend, we should like him to come in. But there is no room here for such as he.'

'Ah,' said the charcoal-burner, 'that was not what I said when you and your friends came to my hut that Christmas morning long ago.'

At this Peter's face grew more troubled and perplexed than ever as he stood with his eyes still fixed on the Jew – and with little satisfaction. Then the charcoal-burner, looking in his turn through the grille of the door and into the light beyond, saw by a mercy the other Stranger who had been first of the company to greet him from over the mountains and had sat with him in the hut beside his fire and given him his wish. Bitter cold it had been that day.

Yet the look that passed between them now was as if this memory they shared of even as long ago as that were of the coming of Spring on the very outskirts of Paradise. And the charcoal-burner, shaken with joy, turned a little towards the old Jew as if to say, 'See, this is my friend!'

At last Peter himself, seeing the charcoal-burner's eyes fixed on the light beyond, also turned his head – yet still unwillingly – and looked over his shoulder as if to ask a question. And just as when they had made the compact over the cards, the Stranger within smiled at the charcoal-burner, then at Peter, and nodded his head. So Peter laid his hand upon the latch and opened the gate; and the charcoal-burner and his friend passed in together.

CREWE

WHEN MURKY WINTER DUSK BEGINS TO SETTLE OVER THE railway station at Crewe, its first-class waiting-room grows steadily more stagnant. Particularly if one is alone in it. The long grimed windows do little more than sift the failing light that slopes in on them from the glass roof outside and is too feeble to penetrate into the recesses beyond. And the grained massive black-leathered furniture becomes less and less inviting. It appears to have been made for a scene of extreme and diabolical violence that one may hope will never occur. One can hardly at any rate imagine it to have been designed by a really *good* man!

Little things like this of course are apt to become exaggerated in memory, and I may be doing the Company an injustice. But whether this is so or not – and the afternoon I have in mind is now many years distant – I certainly became more acutely conscious of the defects of my surroundings when the few fellow-travellers who had been sharing this dreadful apartment with me had hurried out at the clang of a bell for the down train, leaving me to wait for the up. And nothing and nobody, as I supposed, but a great drowsy fire of cinders in the iron grate for company.

The almost animated talk that had sprung up before we parted, never in this world to meet again, had been occasioned by an account in the morning's newspapers of the last voyage of a ship called the *Hesper*. She had come in the evening before, and some days overdue, with a cargo of sugar from the West Indies, and was now berthed safely in the Southampton Docks. This seemed to have been something of a relief to those concerned. For even her master had not refused to admit that certain mysterious and tragic events had recently occurred on board, though he preferred not to discuss them with a reporter. He agreed, even with the reporter, however, that there had been a full moon at the time, that, apart from a heavy swell, the sea was 'as calm as a millpond', and that his ship was at present in want of a second mate. But the voyage of the *Hesper* is now, of course, an old tale many times told. And I myself, having taken very little part in the discussion, had by that time wearied of her mysteries and had decided to seek the lights and joys and coloured bottles of the refreshment room, when a voice from out of the murk behind me suddenly broke the hush. It was an unusual voice, rapid, incoherent and internal, like that of a man in a dream or under the influence of a drug.

I shifted my high-backed ungainly chair and turned to look. Evidently this, the only other occupant of the room, had until that moment been as unaware of my presence in it as I of his. Indeed he seemed to have been completely taken aback at finding he was not alone. He had started up from out of his obscure corner beyond the high window and was staring across at me out of his flat greyish face in unconcealed stupefaction. He seemed for a moment or two to be in doubt even of what I was. Then he sighed, a sigh that ended in a long shuddering yawn. 'I am sorry,' I said, 'I supposed—'

But he interrupted me – and not as if my company, now that he had recognised me as a fellow creature, was any the less welcome for being unexpected.

'Merely what I was saying, sir,' he was mildly explaining, 'is that those gentlemen there who have just left us had no more notion of what they were talking about than an infant in the cradle.'

This elegant paraphrase, I realised, bore only the feeblest resemblance to the violent soliloquy I had just overheard. I looked at him. 'How so?' I said. 'I am only a landsman myself, but...'

It had seemed unnecessary to finish the sentence – I have never seen anyone less marine in effect than *he* was. He had shifted a little nearer and was now, his legs concealed, sitting on the extreme edge of his vast wooden sofa – a smallish man, but muffled up in a very respectable greatcoat at least two sizes too large for him, his hands thrust deep into its pockets.

He continued to stare at me. 'You don't have to go to sea for things like that,' he went on. 'And there's no need to argue about it if you do. Still it wasn't my place to interfere. They'll find out all right – all in good time. They go their ways. And talking of that, now, have you ever heard say that there is less risk sitting in a railway carriage at sixty miles an hour than in laying alone, safe, as you might suppose, in your own bed? That's true, too.' He glanced round him. 'You know where you are in a place like this, too. It's solid, though—' I couldn't catch the words that followed, but they seemed to be uncomplimentary to things in general.

'Yes,' I agreed, 'it certainly looks solid.'

'Ah, "looks",' he went on cantankerously. 'But what *is* your "solid", come to that? I thought so myself once.' He seemed to be pondering over the *once.* 'But now,' he added, 'I know different.'

With that he rose and, dwarfed a little perhaps by the length of his coat, sallied out of his obscure corner beyond the high window and came to the fire. After warming his veined shrunken hands at the heap of smouldering cinders in the grate under the black marble mantelpiece – he seated himself opposite to me.

At risk of seeming fastidious, I must confess that now he was near I did not much care for the appearance of this stranger. He might be about to solicit a small loan. In spite of his admirable greatcoat he looked in need of a barber, as well as of medicine and sleep – a need that might presently exhibit itself in a hankering for alcohol.

But I was mistaken. He asked for nothing, not even sympathy, not even advice. He merely, it seemed, wanted to talk about himself. And perhaps a complete stranger makes a better receptacle for a certain kind of confidence than one's intimates. He tells no tales.

Nevertheless I shall attempt to tell Mr Blake's, and as far as possible in his own peculiar idiom. It impressed me at the time. And I have occasionally speculated since whether his statistics in relation to the risks of railway travel proved trustworthy. *Safety first* is a sound principle so far as it goes, but we are all of us out-manoeuvred in the end. And I still wonder what end was his.

He began by asking me if I had ever lived in the country – 'In the depps of the country'. And then, quickly realising that I was more inclined to listen than talk, he suddenly plunged into his past. It seemed to refresh him to do so.

'I was a gentleman's servant when I began,' he set off; 'first boot-boy under a valet, then footman and helping at table, then pantry work and so on. Never married or anything of that; petticoats are nothing but encumbrances in the house. But I must say if you keep yourself *to* yourself, it sees you through – in time. What you have to beware of is those of your own calling. Domestic. That's the same everywhere; nobody's reached much past the cat-and-dog stage in that. Not if you look close enough; high or low. I lost one or two nice easy places all on that account. Jealousy. And if you don't stay where you are put there's precious little chance of pickings when the funeral's at the door. But that's mostly changed, so I'm told; high wages and no work being the order of the day; and gratitude to follow suit. They are all rolling stones nowadays, and never mind the moss.'

As a philosopher this white-faced muffled-up old creature seemed to affect realism, though his reservations on the 'solid' had fallen a little short of it. Not that *my* reality appeared to matter much – beyond, I mean the mere proof of it. For though in the rather intimate memories he proceeded to share with me he frequently paused to ask a question, he seldom waited for an answer, and then ignored it. I see now this was not to be wondered at. We happened to be sharing at the moment this – for my part – chance resort and he wanted company – human company.

'The last situation I was in' (he was going on to tell me), 'was with the Reverend W. Somers, M.A.: William. In the depps of the country, as I say. Just myself, a young fellow of the name of George, and a woman who came in from the village to char and cook and so on, though I did the best part of that myself. The finishing touches, I mean. How long the Reverend hadn't cared for females in the house I never knew; but parsons have their share of them, I'm thinking. Not that he wasn't attached enough to his sister. They had grown up together, nursery to drawing-room, and that covers a multitude of sins.

'Like *him, she* was, but more of the parrot in appearance; a high face with a beaky nose. Quite a nice lady, too, except that she was mighty slow in being explained to. No interference, generally speaking; in spite of her nose. But don't mistake me; we had to look alive when she was in the house. Oh, yes. But that, thank God, was seldom. And in the end it made no difference.

'She never took to the vicarage. Who would? I can hear her now – Blake this, and Blake that. Too dark, too vaulty, too shut in. And in winter freezing cold, laying low maybe. Trees in front, everlastings; though open behind with a stream and cornfields and hills in the distance; especially in summer, of course. They went up and down, and dim and dark, according to the weather. You could see for miles from those upper corridor windows – small panes that take a lot of cleaning. But George did the windows. George had come from the village, too, if you could call it a village. But he was a permanency. Nothing much but a few cottages, and an outlying farmhouse here and there. Why the old brick church lay about a mile away from it, I can't say. To give the Roaring Lion a trot, perhaps. The Reverend had private means – naturally. I knew that before it came out in the will. But it was a nice fat living notwithstanding – worked out at about fifty pounds to the pigsty, I shouldn't wonder, with the vicarage thrown in. You get what you've got in this world, and some of us enjoy a larger slice than we deserve. But the Reverend, I must say, never took advantage of it. He was a gentleman. Give him his books, and tomorrow like yesterday, and he gave no trouble – none whatever.

'Mind you, he liked things as they should be, and he had some of the finest silver I ever lay finger on; and old furniture to match. I don't mean furniture picked up at sales and such like, but real old family stuff. That's where the parrot in the family nose came from. Everything punctual to the minute and the good things *good*. Soup or fish, a cutlet, a savoury, and a glass of sherry or madeira. No sweets – though he was a lean, spare gentleman, silvery beard and all. And I have never seen choicer fruit than came from his houses and orchard, though it was here the trouble began. Cherries, gages, peaches, nectarines – old red sun-baked walls nine or ten feet high and a sight like wonder in the spring. I used to go out specially to have a look at them. He had his fancies, too, had the Reverend. If any smoking was to be done it must be in the shrubbery with the blackbirds, not under the roof. And sitting there in his study, sir, he could detect the whiff of a cigarette even in the furthest of the attics!

'But tobacco's not *my* trouble, never was. Keep off what you don't need, and you won't want it when you can't get it. That's my feeling. It was, as I say, an easy place, if you forgot how quiet it was – not a sound, no company, and not a soul to be seen. Fair prospects, too, if you could wait. He had no fancy for change, had the Reverend; made no concealment of it. He told me himself that he had remembered me in his will – "if still in his service". You know how these lawyers put it. As a matter of fact he had given me to understand that if in the meantime for any reason any of us went elsewhere, the one left was to have the lot. But not death. *There,* as it turned out, I was in error.

'But I'm not complaining of that now. He was a gentleman; and I have enough to see me through however long I'm left. And that might be for a good many years yet.'

The intonation of this last remark suggested a question. But my confidant made no pause for an answer and added argumentatively, 'Who *wants* to go, I should like to ask? Early *or* late. And nothing known of what's on the other side?' He lifted his grey eyebrows a little as if to glance up at me as he sat stooped up by the fire, and yet refrained from doing so. And again I couldn't enlighten him.

'Well, there, as I say, I might have stayed to this day if the old gentleman's gardener had cared to stay too. *He* began it. Him gone, we all went. Like ninepins. You might hardly credit it, sir, but I am the only one left of that complete establishment. Gutted. And that's where these fine gentlemen here were talking round their hats. What I say is, keep on this side of the tomb as long as you can. Don't meddle with that hole. Why? Because while some fine day you will have to go down into it, you can never be quite sure while you are here what mayn't come back out of it.

'*There'll be no partings there* – I have heard them trolling that out in them chapels like missel-thrushes in the spring. They seem to forget there may be some mighty unpleasant *meetings.* And what about the further shore? It's my belief there's some kind of a ferry plying on that river. And coming back depends on what you want to come back *for.*

'Anyhow the vicarage reeked of it. A low old house, with lots of little windows and far too many doors; and, as I say, the trees too close up on one side, almost brushing the glass. No wonder they said it was what they call haunted. You could feel that with your eyes shut, and like breeds like. The Vicar – two or three, I mean, before my own gentleman – had even gone to the trouble of having the place exercised. Candles and holy water, that kind of thing. Sheer flummummery, I call it. But if what I've heard there – and long before that gowk of a George came to work in the house – was anything more than mere age and owls and birds in the ivy, it must badly have needed it. And when you get accustomed to noises, you can tell which from which. By usual, I mean. Though more and more I'm getting to ask myself if any thing is anything much more than what you think it is – for the time being.

'Same with noises of course. What's this voice of conscience that they talk about but something you needn't hear if you don't want to? I am not complaining of that. If at the beginning there was anything in that house that was better out than in, it never troubled me; at least, not at first. And the Reverend, even though you could often count his congregation on your ten fingers, except at Harvest Festival, was so wove up in his books that I doubt if he'd have been roused up out of 'em even by the Last Trump. It's my belief that in those last few weeks – when I stepped in to see to the fire – as often as not he was sitting asleep over them.

'No, I'm not complaining. Live at peace with who you can, I say. But when it comes to as crusty a customer, and a Scotchman at that, as was my friend the gardener, then there's a limit. Mengus he called himself, though I can't see *how,* if you spell it with a z. When I first came into the place it was all gold that glitters. I'm not the man for contentiousness, if let alone. But afterwards, when the rift came, I don't suppose we ever hardly exchanged the time of day but what there came words of it. A long-legged man *he* was, this Mr Menzies; too long I should have thought for strict comfort in grubbing and hoeing and weeding. He had ginger hair, scanty, and the same on his face, whiskers – and a stoop. He lived down at the lodge; and his widowed daughter kept house for him, with one little boy as fair as she was dark. Harmless enough as children go, the kind they call an angel, but noisy, and not for the house.

'Now why, I ask you, shouldn't I pick a little of this gentleman's precious fruit, or a cucumber for a salad, if need be, and him not there? What if I wanted a few grapes for dessert or a nice apricot tart for the Reverend's luncheon, and our Mr Menzies gone home or busy with the frames? I don't hold with all these hard and fast restrictions, at least outside the house. Not he, though! We wrangled about it week in, week out. And him with a temper which once roused was past all reasoning.

'Not that I ever took much notice of him until it came to a point past any man's enduring. I let him rave. But duty is duty, there's no getting away from that. And when, apart from all this fuss about his fruit, a man takes advantage of what is meant in pure friendliness, well, one's bound to make a move. Job himself.

'What I mean to say is, I used occasionally – window wide open and all that, the pantry being on the other side of the house and away from the old gentleman's study – I say I used occasionally, and all in the way of friendliness, to offer our friend a drink. Like as with many of Old Adam's trade, drink was a little weakness of his, though I don't mean I hold with it because of that. But peace and quietness is the first thing, and to keep an easy face to all appearances, even if you do find it a little hard at times to forgive and forget.

'When he was civil, as I say, and as things should be, he could have a drink, and welcome. When not, not. But it came to become a kind of habit; and to be expected; which is always a bad condition of things. Oh, it was a thousand pities! There was the Reverend, growing feeble as you could see, and him believing all the while that everything around him was calm and sweet as the new Jerusalem, while there was nothing but strife and agrimony, as they call it, underneath. There's many a house looks as snug and cosy as a nut. But crack it and look inside! Mildew. Still, our Mr Mengus had "prospects", up to then.

'Well, there came along at last a mighty hot summer – five years ago, you may remember. Five years ago, next August, an extraordinary hot summer. And an early harvest – necessarily. Day after day I could see the stones in the stubble fields shivering in the sun. And gardening is thirsty work; I will say that for it. Which being so, better surely virgin water from the tap or a drop of cider, same as the harvesters have, than ardent spirits, whether it is what you are bred up to or not! It stands to reason.

'Besides, we had had words again, and though I can stretch a point with a friend and no harm done, I'm not a man to come coneying and currying favour. Let him get his own drinks, was my feeling in the matter. And you can hardly call me to blame if he did. *There* was the pantry window hanging wide open in the shade of the trees – and day after day of scorching sun and not a breath to breathe. And there was the ruin of him within arm's reach from outside, and a water tap handy, too. Very inviting, I'll allow.

'I'm not attesting, mind you, that he was confirmed at it, no more than that I'm a man to be measuring what's given me to take charge of by tenths of inches. It's the principle of the thing. You might have thought, too, that a simple honest pride would have kept him back. Nothing of the sort; and no matter, wine or spirits.

I'd watch him there, though he couldn't see me, being behind the door. And practices like that, sir, as you will agree with me, can't go on. They couldn't go on, vicarage or no vicarage. Besides, from being secret it began to be open. It had gone too far. Brazen it out: that was the lay. I came down one fine morning to find one of my best decanters smashed to smithereens on the stone floor, Irish glass and all. Cats and sherry, who ever heard of it? And out of revenge he filled the pantry with wasps by bringing in over-ripe plums. Petty waste of time like that. And some of the greenhouses thick with blight!

'And so things went, from bad to worse, and at such a pace as I couldn't have credited. A widower, too, with a married daughter dependent on him; which is worse even than a wife, who expects to take the bad with the good. No, sir, I had to call a halt to it. A friendly word in his ear, or keeping everything out of his reach, you may be thinking, might have sufficed. Believe me, not for him. And how can you foster such a weakness by taking steps out of the usual to prevent it? It wouldn't be proper to your self-respect. Then I thought of George; not compromising myself in any way, of course, in so doing. George had a face as long as your arm, pale and solemn, enough to make a cat laugh. Dress him up in a surplice and hassock, he might have been the Reverend's curate. Strange that, for a youth born in the country. But curate or no curate, he had eyes in his head and must have seen what there was to be seen.

'I said to him one day, and I remember him standing there in the pantry in his black coat against the white of the cupboard paint, I said to him, "George, a word in time saves nine, but it would come better from you than from me. You take me? Hold your peace till our friend's sober again and can listen to reason. Then hand it over to him – a word of warning, I mean. Say we are muffling things up as well as we *can* from the old gentleman, but that if he should hear of it there'd be fat in the fire; and no mistake. He would take it easier from you, George, the responsibility being mine."

'Lord, how I remember George! He had a way of looking at you as if he couldn't say *boh* to a goose – swollen hands and bolting blue eyes, as simple as an infant's. But he wasn't stupid, oh no. Nobody could say that. And now I reflect, I think he knew our little plan wouldn't carry very far. But there, whatever he might be thinking, he was so awkward with his tongue that he could never find anything to say until it was too late, so I left it at that. Besides, I had come to know he was, with all his faults, a young man you could trust for doing what he was told to do. So, as I say, I left it at that.

'What he actually did say I never knew. But as for its being of any use, it was more like pouring paraffin on a bonfire. The very next afternoon our friend came along to the pantry window and stood there looking in – swaying he was, on his feet; and I can see the midges behind him zigzagging in a patch of sunshine as though they were here before my very eyes. He was so bad that he had to lay hold of the sill to keep himself from falling. Not thirst this time, but just fury. And then, seeing that mere flaunting of fine feathers wasn't going to inveigle *me* into a cockfight, he began to talk. Not all bad language, mind you – *that's* easy to shut your ears to – but cold reasonable abuse, which isn't. At first I took no notice, went on about my business at my leisure, and no hurry. What's the use of arguing with a man, and him one of these Scotchmen to boot, that's beside himself with rage? What was wanted was *peace* in the house, if only for the old gentleman's sake, who I thought was definitely under the weather and had been coming on very poorly of late.

"'Where's that George of yours?" he said to me at last – with additions. "Where's that George? Fetch him out, and I'll teach him to come playing the holy Moses to my own daughter. Fetch him out, I say, and we'll finish it here and now." And all pitched high, and half his words no more English than the mewing of a cat.

'But I kept my temper and answered him quite moderate and as pleasantly as I knew how. "I don't want to meddle in *anybody's* quarrels," I said. "So long as George so does his work in this house as will satisfy *my* eye, I am not responsible for his actions in his off-time and out of bounds."

'How was I to know, may I ask, if it was *not* our Mr Mengus who had smashed one of my best decanters? What proof was there? What *reason* had I for thinking else?

"'George is a quiet, unbeseeming young fellow," I said, "and if he thinks it's his duty to report any misgoings-on either to me or to the Reverend, it doesn't concern anybody else."

'That seemed to sober my fine gentleman. Mind you, I'm not saying that there was anything unremidibly wrong with him. He was a first-class gardener. I grant you that. But then he had an uncommonly good place to match – first-class wages; and no milk, wood, coals or house-rent to worry about. But breaking out like that, and the Reverend poorly and all; that's not what he thought of when he put us all down in his will. I'll be bound of that. Well, there he stood, looking in at the window and me behind the table in my apron as calm as if his wrangling meant no more to me than the wind in the chimmeny. It was the word "report", I fancy, that took the wind out of his sails. It had brought him up like a station buffer. And he was still looking at me, and brooding it over, as though he had the taste of poison on his tongue.

'Then he says very quiet, "So that's his little game, is it? You are just a pair, then?"

"'If by pair you're meaning me," I said, "well, I'm ready to take my share of the burden when it's ready to fit my back. But not before. George may have gone a bit beyond himself, but he meant well, and you know it."

"'What I am asking is this," says our friend, "have you ever seen me the worse for liquor? Answer me that!"

"'If I liked your tone better," I said, "I wouldn't say how I don't see why it would be necessarily the *worse*."

"'Ehh? You mean, Yes, then?" he said.

"'I mean no more than what I say," I answered him, looking at him over the cruet as straight as I'm looking at you now. "I don't ask to meddle with your private affairs, and I'll thank *you* not to come meddling with mine." He seemed taken aback at that, and I noticed he was looking a bit pinched, and hollow under the eyes. Sleepless nights, perhaps.

'But how was I to know this precious grandson of his was out of sorts with a bad throat and that – seeing that he hadn't mentioned it till a minute before? I ask you! "The best thing you and George there can do," I went on, "is to bury the hatchet; and out of hearing of the house, too."

'With that I turned away and went off into it myself, leaving him there to think things over at his leisure. I am putting it to you, sir, as a free witness, what else could I have done?'

There was little light of day left in our cavernous waiting-room by this time. Only the dulling glow of the fire and the phosphorescence caused by a tiny bead of gas in the 'mantles' of the great iron bracket over our heads. My realist seemed to be positively in want of an answer to this last question. But as I sat looking back into his intent small face nothing that could be described as of a helpful nature offered itself.

'If he was anxious about his grandson,' I ventured at last, 'it might explain his being a little short in temper. Besides… But I should like to hear what came after.'

'What came after, now?' the little man repeated, drawing his right hand gingerly out of the depths of his pocket and smoothing down his face with it as if he had suddenly discovered he was tired. 'Well, a good deal came after, but not quite what you might have expected. And you'd hardly go so far as to say perhaps that anxiety over his grandson would excuse him for what was little short of manslaughter, and him a good six inches to the good at that? Keeping facts as facts, if you'll excuse me, our friend waylaid George by the stables that very evening, and a wonderful peaceful evening it was, shepherd's delight and all that. But to judge from the looks of the young fellow's face when he came into the house there hadn't been much of that in the quarter of an hour they had had together.

'I said, "Sponge it down, George, sponge it down. And by good providence maybe the old gentleman won't notice anything wrong." It wasn't to reason I could let him off his duties and enter into a lot of silly peravications which in the long run might only make things worse. It's that you have to think of when you are a man in my position. But as for the Reverend's not noticing it, there, as luck would have it, I was wrong myself.

'For when the two of us were leaving the dining-room that evening after the table had been cleared and the dessert put on, he looked up from round the candles and told George to stay behind. Some quarter of an hour after that George came along to me snuffling as if he'd been crying. But I asked no questions, not me; and, as I say, he was always pretty slow with his tongue. All that I could get out of him was that he had decocted some cock-and-bull story to account for his looks the like of which nobody in his senses could credit, let alone such a power of questioning as the old gentleman could bring to bear when roused, and apart from what comes, I suppose, from reading so many books. So the fat *was* in the fire and no mistake. And the next thing I heard, after coming back late the following evening, was that our Mr Mengus had been called into the house and given the sack there and then, with a quarter's wages in lieu of notice. Which, after all, mind you, was as good as three-quarters a gift. What I'm saying is that handsome is as handsome does, and that was the Reverend all over; though I agree, mind you, even money isn't necessarily everything when there's what they call character to be taken into account. But if ever there was one of the quality fair and upright in all his dealings, as the saying goes, then that was the Reverend Somers. And I abide by that. He wouldn't have any truck with drink topped with insolence. That's all.

'Well, our friend came rapping at the back door that evening, shaken to the marrow if ever man was, and just livid. I told him, and I meant it too, that I was sorry for what had occurred: "It's a bad ending," I said, "to a tale that ought never to have been told." I told him too, speaking as quiet and pleasant as I am to you now, that the only hope left was to let bygones be bygones; that he had already had his fingers on George, and better go no further. Not he. He said, and he was sober enough then in all conscience, that, come what come may, here or hereafter, he'd be even with him. Ay, and he made mention of me also, but not so rabid. A respectable man, too; never a word against him till then; and not far short of sixty. And by rabid I don't mean violent. He spoke as low and quiet as if there was a judge on the bench there to hear him, sentence said and everything over. And then...'

★

The old creature paused until yet another mainline train had gone roaring on its way. 'And then,' he continued, 'though he wasn't found till morning, he must have gone straight out – and good-bye said to nobody. He must, I say, have gone straight out to the old barn and hanged himself. The midmost rafter, sir, and a drop that would have sufficed for a Giant Goliath. All night. And it's my belief, good-bye or no good-bye, that it wasn't so much the *disgrace* of the affair but his daughter – Mrs Shaw by name – and his grandson that were preying on his mind. And yet – why, he never so much as asked me to say a good word for him! Not one.

'Well, that was the end of that. So far. And it's a curious thing to me – though they say these Romans aren't above making use of it – how, going back over the past clears everything up like; at least for the time being. But it's what you were saying just now about what's *solid* that sets me thinking and keeps repeating itself in my mind. Solid was the word you used. And they look it, I agree.' He deliberately twisted his head and fastened a prolonged stare on the bench on which he had been seated. 'But it doesn't follow there's much comfort in them even if they are. Solid or not, they go at last when all's said to what's little else but gas and ashes once they're fallen to pieces and been put on the fire. Which holds good, and even more so, for them that sit on them. Peculiar habit that, too – sitting! Yes, I've been told, sir, that after what they call this cremation, and all the moisture in us gone up in steam, what's left would scarcely turn the scales by a single *hounce!*'

If sitting *is* a peculiar habit, it was even more peculiar how etherealising the effect of my new acquaintance's misplaced aspirate had been – his one and only lapse in this respect throughout his interminable monologue.

'Yes, they say that so far as this *solid* goes, we amount to no more than what you could put into a walnut. And my point, sir,' he was emphasising with a forefinger that only just showed itself beyond the long sleeve of his greatcoat, 'my point is *this* – that if *that's* all there is to you and me, we shouldn't need much of the substantial for what you might call the mere sole look of things, if you follow me, if *we* chose or chanced to come back. When gone, I mean. Just enough, I suppose, to be obnoxious, as the Reverend used to say, to the naked eye.

'But all that being as it may be, the whole thing had tided over, and George was pretty nearly himself again, and another gardener advertised for – and I must say the Reverend, though after this horrible affair he was never the same man again, treated the young woman I mentioned as if he himself had been a father – I say, the whole thing had tided over, and the house was as silent as a tomb again, ay, as the sepulchre itself; when I began to notice something peculiar.

'At first maybe, little more *than* mere silence. What, in the contrast, as a matter of fact, I took for *peace*. But afterwards not so. There was a strain, so to speak, as you went about your daily doings. A strain. And especially after dark. It may have been only in one's head. I can't say. But it was there: and I could see without watching that even George had noticed it, and *he'd* hardly notice a black-beetle on a pancake.

'And at last there came something you could put word to, catch in the act, so to speak. I had gone out towards the cool of the evening after a broiling hot day, to get a little air. There was a copse of beeches, which as perhaps you may know, is a very pleasant tree for shade, sir, at a spot a bit under the mile from the back of the vicarage. And I sat there quiet for a minute or two, with the birds and all – they were beginning to sing again, I remember – and – you know how memory

strays back, though sometimes it's more like a goat tethered to a peg
on a common – I was thinking over what a curious thing it is how
one man's poison is another man's meat. For the funeral over, and all
that, the old gentleman had thanked me for all I had done. You see
what had gone before had been a hard break in his trust of a man,
and he looked up from his bed at me almost with tears in his eyes.
He said he wouldn't forget it. He used the word substantial, sir; and
I ought by rights to have mentioned that he was taken ill the night
of the inquest; a sort of stroke, the doctor called it, though he came
round, I must say, remarkably well considering his age.

'Well, I had been thinking over all this on the fringe of the woods
there, and was on my way back again to the house by the field-path,
when I looked up as if at call and saw what I take my oath I never
remembered to have seen there before – a scarecrow. A scarecrow –
and that right in the middle of the cornfield that lay beyond the
stream with the bulrushes at the back of the house. Nothing funny in
that, you may say. Quite so. But mark me, this was early September,
and the stubble all bleaching in the sun, and it didn't look an *old*
scarecrow, either. It stood up with its arms out and an old hat down
over its eyes, bang in the middle of the field, its back to me, and its
front to the house. I knew that field as well as I know my own face
in the looking-glass. Then how could I have missed it? What wonder
then I stood stock still and had a good long stare at it, first because,
as I say, I had never seen it before, and next because – but I'll be
coming to that later.

'That done, and *not* to my satisfaction, I turned back a little and
came along on the other side of the hedge, and so, presently at last,
indoors. Then I stepped up to the upper storey to have a look at it
from the windows. For you never know with these country people
what they are up to, though they may seem stupid enough. Looked

at from there, it wasn't so much in the middle of the field as I had fancied, seeing it from the other side. But how, thought I to myself could you have escaped me, my friend, if you had been there all through the summer? I don't see how it could; that's flat. But if not, then it must have been put up more recently.

'I had all but forgotten about it next morning, but as afternoon came on I went upstairs and had another look. There was less heat-haze or something, and I could see it clearer and nearer, so to speak, but not quite clear enough. So I whipped along to the Reverend's study, him being still, poor gentleman, confined to his bed, in fact he never got up from it; I whipped along, I say, to the study to fetch his glasses, his boniculars, and I fastened them on that scarecrow like a microscope on a fly. You will hardly credit me, sir, when I say that what seemed to me then most different about it – different from what you might expect – was that it didn't look in any ordinary manner of speaking, quite *real.*

'I could watch it with the glasses as plain as if it had been in touch of my hand, even to the buttons and the hat-band. It wasn't the first time I had set eyes on the *clothes,* either, though I couldn't have laid name to them. And there was something in the appear-ance of the thing, something in the way it bore itself up, so to speak, with its arms thrown up at the sky and its empty face, which wasn't what you'd expect of mere sticks and rags. Not, I mean, if they were nothing but just real – real like that there chair, I mean, you are sitting on now.

'I called George. I said, "George, lay your eye to these glasses" – and his face was still a bit discoloured, though his little affair in the stableyard was now a good three weeks old.

'"Take a squint through these, George," I said, "and tell me what you make of *that* thing over there."

'George was a slow dawdling mug if ever there was one – clumsy-fingered. But he fixed the glasses at last, and he took a good long look. Then he gave them back into my hand.

"'Well?" I said, watching his face.

"'Why, Mr Blake," he said, meaning me, "it's a scarecrow."

"'How would you like it a bit nearer?" I said. Just off-hand, like that.

'He looked at me. "It's near enough in *them,*'" he said.

"'Does the air round it strike you as funny at all?" I asked him. "Out-of-the-way funny – *quivering,* in a manner of speaking?"

"'That's the heat," he said, but his lip trembled.

"'Well, George," I said, "heat or no heat, you or me must go and have a look at that thing closer some time. But not this afternoon. It's too late."

'But we didn't, sir, neither me *nor* him, though I fancy he went on thinking about it on his own account in between. And lo and behold, when I got up next morning and had slid out of my bedroom early, and went along into the corridor to have another glance at it, and – believe me, sir, as you looked out into the morning the country lay as calm and open as a map – it wasn't there. The scarecrow, sir. It wasn't there. It was vanished. Nor could I get a glimpse of it from downstairs through the bushes *this* side of the stream. And all so still and early that even there from the back door you could hear the water moving. Now who, thinks I to myself, is answerable for *this* jiggery-pokery?

'But it's no good in this world, sir, putting reasons more far-fetched to a thing than are necessary to account for it. That you *will* agree. Some farmer's lout, I thought to myself, must have come and moved the old mommet overnight. But, that being so, what was it ever put up for? Harvest done, mind you, and the crows, one would think, as welcome to what they could pick up in the stubble – if they hadn't picked it all up already – as robins to house crumbs. Besides, what about the peculiar looks of it?

'I didn't go out next day, not at all; and there being only George and me in the vicarage, and the Reverend shut off in his room, I never remember such a holy quiet. The heavens like a vault. Eighty-four in the shade by the thingamy in the verandah and this the fourth of September. All day long, and I'll vouch for it, the whole twenty acres of that field, but for the peewits and the rooks running over it, lay empty. And when, the sun going down, the harvest moon came up that evening – and that summer she showed up punctual as a clock the whole month round – you could see right across the flat country to the hills. And the night-jars croaking too. You could have cut the heat with a knife.

'What time the old gentleman's gruel was gone up and George out of the way, I took yet another squint through the glasses from the upper windows. And I am ready to own that something inside of me gave a sort of a *hump*, sir, when, large as life, I saw that the scarecrow was come back again, though this is where you'll have, if you please, to go careful with me. What I saw the instant before I began to look, and to that I'd lay my affidavit, was something moving, and pretty rapid, too; and it was only at the very moment I clapped the glasses on to it that it suddenly fixed itself into what I already *supposed* I should find it to be. I've noticed that – though in little things not mattering much – before. It's your own mind that learns you before what you look at turns out to be what you expect. Else why should we be alarmed by this here *solid* sometimes? It *looks* all so; but *is* it?

'You might be suggesting that both shape and scarecrow too were all my eye and Betty Martin. But we'll see later on about that. And what about George? You don't mean to infer that he could borrow to order a mere fancy clean out of my head and turn it into a scarecrow in the middle of a field and in broad daylight too? That would be the long bow, and no mistake. Ay, and take it in some shape for what we *did*! No. Yet, as I say, even when I first cast eyes on it, it looked too real to be real. So there's the two on the one side, and the two on the other, and they don't make four.

'Well, sir, I must say that from that moment on I didn't like the look of things, and never have I shared a meal so mum as when George and me sat to supper that evening. From being a hearty eater his appetite was fallen almost to a cipher. He munched and couldn't swallow. I doubt if his vittles had a taste of them left. And we both of us knew as though it had been printed on the tablecloth what the other was thinking about.

'It was while we sat there, George and me alone, him on the right and the window opposite, and me on the cupboard side in what was called the servants' hall, that we heard some words said. Not what you could understand, but still, words. I couldn't tell from where, except that it wasn't from the Reverend, and I couldn't tell what. But they dropped upon us and between us as if there was a parrot in the room, clapping its horny bill, so to say, motionless in the air. At this George stopped munching for good, his face little short of green. But except for a cockling up inside of me, I didn't make any sign I'd heard. After all, it was nothing that made any difference to *me*, though what was going on was, to say the least of it, not all as it should be. And if you knew the old vicarage you'd agree.

'Lock-up time came at last. And George took his candle and went up to bed. Not quite as willing as usual, I fancied; though he had always been a glutton for his full meed of sleep. You could notice by the sound of his feet on the stairs that he was as you might say pushing of himself on. As for me, it had always been my way to sit up after him reading a bit with the Reverend's *Times*. But that night, I went off early. I gave a last look in on the old gentleman, and I might as well mention – though dilatory isn't the word for these doctors, even when they *are* called in in reasonable time – I say a nurse had been sent for, and his sister was now expected any day from Scotland. All well there, and him lying as peaceful on his bed as if the end had come already. Well, sir, that done, coming back along the corridor I blew out my candle and stood waiting. The candle out, the moon came streaming in, and the outside from the window lay spread out beneath me almost bright as day. I looked this ways and I looked that ways, back and front; but nothing to be seen, nor heard neither. Yet it seemed not more than one deep breath after I had closed my eyes in sleep that night that I was stark wide awake again, trying to make sense of some sound I'd heard.

'Old houses – I'm used to them; the timbers crinkle like a bee-hive. But this wasn't timbers, oh no! It might maybe have been wind, you'll say. But what chance of wind with not a hand's-breadth of cloud moving in the sky, and such a blare of moonlight as would keep even a field mouse from peeping out of its hole? What's more, not to know whether what you are listening to is in or outside of your head isn't much help to a good night's rest. Still I fell off at last, unnoticing.

'Next morning, as George came back from taking up the breakfast tray, I had a good look at him in the sunlight, but you couldn't tell whether the marks round his eyes were natural – from what had gone before with the other, I mean – or from *insommia*. Best not to meddle, I thought; just wait. So I gave him good morning and poured out the coffee and we sat to it as usual, the wasps coming in over the marmalade as if nothing had happened.

'All quiet that day, only rather more so, as it always is in a sick-room house. Doctor come and gone, but no nurse yet; and the old gentleman I thought looking very ailing. But he spoke to me quite cheerful. Just like his old self, too, to be sympathising with me for the double duty I'd been doing in the house. He asked after the garden, too, though there was as fine a bunch of black grapes on his green plate as any out of Canaan. It was the drought was in his mind. And just as I was leaving the room, my hand on the door, he mentioned one or two compliments about my having stayed on with him so long. "You can't pay for that out of any Bank," he said to me, smiling at me almost merry-like, his beard over the sheet.

'"I hope and trust, sir," I said, "while I am with you, there will be no further fuss." But I had a surety even as I said the words that he hadn't far to go, so that fusses, if come they did, didn't really much matter to him. I don't see how you would be likely to notice them when things are drawing to a last conclusion; though I am thankful to say that what did occur, was kept from him to the end.

'That night there came something sounding about the house that wasn't natural, and no mistake. I had scarcely slept a wink, and as soon as I heard it, I was on with my tail-coat over my night-shirt in a jiffy, though there was no need for light. I had fetched along my winter overcoat, too, one the Reverend himself had passed on to me – this very coat on my back now – and with that over my arm, I pushed open the door and looked in on George. Maybe he had heard my coming, maybe he had heard the other, I couldn't tell which, but there he was, sitting up in bed – the moonlight flooding in on his long white face and tousled hair – and his trousers and braces thrown down anyhow on the chair beside it.

'I said to him, "What's wrong, George? Did you hear anything? A voice or anything?"

'He sat looking at me with his mouth open as if he couldn't shut it, and I could see he was shaken to the very roots. Now, mind you, here I was in the same quandary, as they call it, as before. What I'd heard might be real, some animal, fox, badger, or the like, prowling round outside, or it might not. If not, and the house being exercised, as I said, though a long way back, and the Reverend gentleman still in this world himself, I had a kind of trust that what was there, if it *was* anything, couldn't get in. But naturally I was in something of a fever to make sure.

'"George," I said, "You mustn't risk a chill or anything of that sort" – and it had grown a bit cold in the small hours – "but it's up to us – our duty, George – with the Reverend at death's door and all, to know what's what. So if you'll take a look round on the outside I'll have a search through on the in. What we must be cautious about is that the old gentleman isn't disturbed."

'George went on looking at me, though he had by this time shuffled out of bed and into the overcoat I had handed him. He stood there, with his boots in his hand, shivering, but more maybe because he felt cold after the warmth of his sheets than because he had quite taken in what I had said.

'"Do you think, Mr Blake," he asked me, sitting down again on his bed, "you don't think he is come back again?"

'*Come back*, he said, just like that. And you'd have supposed from the quivering of his mouth I might have stopped it!

'"Who's, George, come back?" I asked him.

'"Why, what we looked through the glasses at in the field," he said. "It had his look."

'"Well, George," I said, speaking as moderate and gentle as you might to a child, "we know as how dead men tell no tales. Let alone scarecrows, then. All we've got to do is just to make sure. You do as you're bid, then, my lad. You go your ways, and I'll go mine. There's never any harm can befall a man if his conscience is easy."

'But that didn't seem to satisfy him. He gave a gulp and stood up again, still looking at me. Stupid or not, he was always one for doing his duty, was George. And I must say that what I call courage is facing what you're afraid of in your very innards, and not mere crashing into danger, eyes shut.

'"I'd lief as not go down, Mr Blake," he said. "Leastways, not alone. He never took much of a liking to me. He said he'd be evens. Not *alone*, Mr Blake."

'"What have you to fear, George, my lad?" I said. "Man or spectre, the fault was none of yours."

'He buttoned the coat up, same as I am wearing it now, and he gave me just one look more. It's hard to say all that's in a fellow-creature's eyes, sir, when they are full of what no tongue in him could tell. But George had shut his mouth at last, and the moon on his face gave him a queer look, faraway like, as if all that there was of him, this world or the next, had come to keep him company. I will say that.

'And when the hush that had come down on the house was broken again, and this time it *was* the wind, though away high up over the roof, he didn't look at me any more. It was the last between us. He turned his back on me and went off out into the passage and down the stairs, and I listened until I could hear him in the distance scrabbling with the bar at the back. It was one of those old-fashioned doors, sir, you must understand, just loaded with locks and bolts, like in all old places.

'As for myself, I didn't move for a bit. There wasn't any hurry that I could see. Oh, no. I just sat down on the bed on the place where George had sat, and waited. And you may depend upon it, I stayed pretty quiet there – with all that responsibility, and not knowing what might happen next. And then presently what I heard was as though a voice had said something – very sharp and bitter; then said no more.

There came a sort of moan, and then no more again. But by that time I was on my way on my rounds inside the house, as I'd promised; and so, out of hearing: and when I got back to my bedroom again everything was still and quiet. And I took it of course that George had got back safe to his...'

Since the fire had faded and the light of day was gone, the fish-like phosphorescence of the gas-mantles had grown brighter, and this elderly man, whose name was Blake, I understood, was looking at me out of his white, almost leper-like face in this faint gloom as steadily almost as George must have been looking at him a few minutes before he had descended the back stairs of the vicarage, never, I gathered, to set foot on them again.

'Did you manage to get any more sleep that night?' I said.

Mr Blake seemed to be pleasingly surprised at so easy a question.

'That was the mistake of it,' he said. 'He wasn't found till morning. Cold for hours, and precious little to show why.'

'So you did manage to get a little sleep?'

But this time he made no answer.

'Your share, I suppose, was quite a substantial one?'

'Share?' he said.

'In the will...?'

'Now, didn't I tell you myself,' he protested with some warmth, 'that that, as it turned out, wasn't so; though why, it would take half a dozen or more of these lawyers to explain. And even at that, I don't know as what I did get has brought me anything much to boast about. I'm a free man, that's true. But for how long? Nobody can stay in this world here for ever, can he?'

With a peculiar rocking movement of his small head he peered round and out of the door. 'And though in this world,' he went on, 'you may have not one *iota* of harm to blame yourself for *to* your-self, there may still be misunderstandings, and them that have been deceived by them may be waiting for you in the next. So when it comes to what the captain of the *Hesper*—'

But at this moment our prolonged *tête-à-tête* was interrupted by a thickset vigorous young porter carrying a bucket of coals in one hand, and a stumpy torch of smouldering brown paper in the other. He mounted one of our chairs and with a tug of finger and thumb instantly flooded our dingy quarters with an almost intolerable gassy glare. That done, he raked out the ash-grey fire with a lump of iron that may once have been a poker, and flung all but the complete con-tents of his bucket of coal on to it. Then he looked round and saw who was sitting there. Me he passed over. I was merely a bird of passage. But he greeted my fellow derelict as if he were an old acquaintance.

'Good evening, sir,' he said, and in that slightly indulgent and bantering voice which suggests past favours rather easily earned. 'Let in a little light on the scene. I didn't notice you when I came in and was beginning to wonder where you had got to.'

His patron smirked back at him as if any such trifling human attention was a peculiar solace. This time the porter deliberately caught my eye. And his own was full of meaning. It was as if there were some little privy and ironical understanding between us in which this third party was unlikely to share. I ignored it, rose to my feet and clutched my bag. A passenger train had come hooting into the station, its gliding lighted windows patterning the platform planks. Alas, yet again it wasn't mine. Still – such is humanity, I preferred my own company, just then.

When I reached the door, and a cold and dingy prospect showed beyond it, I glanced back at Mr Blake, sitting there in his greatcoat beside the apparently extinguished fire. With a singularly mournful look, as of a lost dog, on his features, he was gazing after me. He seemed to be deploring the withdrawal even of my tepid companionship. But in that dreadful gaseous luminosity there was nothing, so far as I could see, that any mortal man could by any possibility be afraid of, alive or dead. So I left him to the porter. And – as yet – we have not met again.

A REVENANT

I T WAS AN EVENING IN NOVEMBER; TOO EARLY IN THE YEAR, that is, for winter coughs to have set in. And coughs to the lecturer are like reefs to the mariner. They may wreck his frail craft. So extreme indeed was the quietude in the Wigston Memorial Hall in which Professor Monk was speaking that if he had remained mute for but a moment, even the voice of the gentle rain that was steadily descending out of the night beyond upon its corrugated roof would have become audible. Indeed his only interruption, and it had occurred but once every quarter of an hour, had been a sudden, peculiar, brief, strident roar. On his way to the hall he had noticed – incarnadining the louring heavens – what appeared to be the reflected light from the furnaces of a foundry. Possibly it was discharging its draff, its slag, its cinders. In any case, a *punctual* interruption of this kind is a little dramatic; a pregnant pause, and it is over. Nor did it affect him personally.

The professor had read somewhere that on occasion a certain eminent mathematician will sink in the midst of one of his lectures into a profound reverie, which may continue for ten minutes together. Meanwhile his students can pursue at leisure *their* daydreams. But students are students, not the general public. He himself, while avoiding dramatic pauses, could at once read out loud and inwardly cogitate, and he much preferred a sober and academic delivery. He never allowed his voice to sink to a mutter or rise into a shout; he neither stormed nor cajoled, nor indulged even in the most modest of gestures. A nod, a raised finger, a lifted eyebrow – how effective at their apt moments these may be! He flatly rejected, that is, the theatrical arts of the alien – to let his *body* speak, to be stagy, oratorical.

He even regarded the bottle of water that stood on his reading-desk as a symbol rather than as a beverage. A symbol not, of course, hinting at any connection with sacred Helicon, but of the fact that his lectures were neither intoxicating nor were intended to be intoxicating. How many times, he wondered, had he repeated his present experience? Scores, at least. He had become at last a *confirmed* lecturer.

And yet, to judge by his feelings at this moment, he might almost have been a novice – a chrisom child. This was odd. The particular lecture he was engaged on – its subject the writings of Edgar Allan Poe – was one of his own favourites. He had delivered it at least half a dozen times, and always with a modest satisfaction. No more than just that. It owed, of course, a great deal to its theme; one that possessed an almost repulsive attraction for the queerest of readers. Anything about Edgar Allan Poe was edged with the romantic, tinged with the macabre – that strange career, its peculiar fruits.

Nevertheless, and not for the first time, as the professor stood alone up there on the platform, full in the glare of an arc-lamp suspended almost immediately over his head, he had become sharply aware not only that he was, with one single exception, the only human being present who was not sitting down, but also that he was the only human being present who was making a noise. The realisation, in this intensity at any rate, was new to him; and it made him a little uneasy. Not that he had much patience with members of his own calling who pretend they dislike lecturing. That must be affectation. He enjoyed it. But he would enjoy it even more, he sometimes mused, if he could carry off with him a clear and definite notion as to the *effect* of what he had been saying.

Any impression of this kind might, of course, prove sadly disillusioning, but it would at least be positive. As a professional man, that is, Professor Monk lived in a faint mist. It was not that he pined for encouragement. Certainly not. His appeal was to the intelligence rather than to the emotions. He aimed at nothing in the nature of what in his subject's native land is known as the 'heart-to-hearter'. He had views, and tried to express them; it would therefore be helpful to discover if they were shared or rejected. Such evidence was very scanty. Again and again when, his lecture safely over, the customary rattle of applause had followed its last word, he had sat speculating precisely how much of it was due to good manners and how much to a natural sense of relief. A sigh is so much less audible than the clapping of hands. *Any* physical reaction after one has been sitting cramped and mute for a solid hour is of course as instinctive as sneezing is after snuff. But English audiences are oddly inscrutable.

For this reason he had more than once been tempted to insert in his paper a sentence or two that he himself felt confident was shocking, or even to leave out all the negatives on any particular page, all the *nots* – just to see the effect. But even English audiences are less easy to shock than once they were. Besides... well – not tonight. His only desire at the moment was to get finished, to have done. An unfamiliar longing had swept over him to go away, and never come back. Oh, for the wings of a dove, he was sighing with the Psalmist. And he knew why.

It was not the hall itself that was to blame. Lecture halls are much alike. Sunday-schoolish in atmosphere, they usually resemble railway waiting-rooms in their general effect. The fierce light beating into his spectacled eyes and on to his high conical brow was a slight embarrassment – it dazzled if it did not daze. He was accustomed to that too, however. After all, lecturers must be seen, even if they are not heard. He wished again what he had often wished before – that so-called house-decorators, when engaged on places of public assembly, would choose for their paint other tints than a dingy duck-green edged with a chocolate brown. Why, again, should the chairs selected suggest an orphanage? Were they assumed to be the only certain means of keeping listeners awake?

Still, this was all in the usual way of things. There was no walk in life without its vexations. As for his chairman, all that he could see of *him* at the moment was a puckered ecclesiastical boot. Simply, however, because he was motionless, he was not necessarily either inattentive or asleep. And what if he was? He himself had a genuine sympathy for chairmen. They were usually far too busy men, and tired. He had shared their trials and temptations. Nor had he the faintest hint of a complaint to make against his audience. He would have preferred, naturally, the farthest few rows of chairs to look a little less vacant; but this was a compliment to the occupants of the rest. All those who had come had stayed, and – though owing to his glasses he was unable to see them very distinctly – those who had stayed had been markedly attentive. He remembered a facetious friend once gravely asserting that it is impossible to thin a lecture down too much, and that, if it is to be appreciated to the full, at least one attempt at the jocular is essential every quarter of an hour. Make them laugh; it clears the air. That, however, was not his own method. He had neither thinned nor temporised, nor tried to amuse. Moreover, everybody was listening; no one had laughed; the theory was absurd. Then what was wrong?

Immediately in front of him and at the end of the room a circular white-faced clock hung midway above the two low, rounded arches which led out of the hall. Its hands now pointed to fourteen minutes to nine. The end then was in sight. And so, lowering his head a little, and pausing an instant, he ventured to take a second long, steady look at what he was now perfectly well aware had been the cause of his disquietude – a solitary figure who was standing (almost like a statue in its niche) within the left of these two doorways.

This person had been the only latecomer. At one moment the alcove was vacant, at the next *there* its occupant was. He must have sallied in out of the night as furtively as a shadow. The lecturer much preferred latecomers to early-goers. The former merely suggested the impracticable – that he should begin again; the latter that it was high time to stop. There was no doubt, however, that this particular listener had been a little on his nerves. Once having vaguely descried him, he had been unable to forget his presence there. Why stand? And why stand alone? He should himself have had the audacity to beckon him in. A warm word of welcome would have been by far the most politic method of – well, he might almost say, of accepting his challenge.

Unfortunately, any such word was now too late. Motionless in the dim light – his dark voluminous cloak around him, and hat in hand – there the stranger stood, leaning indolently the while one foot crossed over the other, against the hollow of the arch. The attitude suggested a pose, but, pose or not, he had not altered it. The glare of the arc-lamp in the professor's eyes, his very uneasiness indeed, prevented him from clearly distinguishing the distant features. But the turn and inclination of the head, the perfect composure, the attitude, vaguely arrogant, of a profound attentiveness – everything suggested that this particular individual was either wholly engrossed in his own thoughts, *or* in what he was listening to. The latter should have been a consoling reflection. But, alas! one may be engrossed in destruction – as was Nero when Rome was burning, as is always the Father of Lies, and the angel of Candour. Well what of that? Like the professor himself, he had come, he would go; and that would be the end of the matter.

It was nonetheless a little odd that of all those present none seemed to have become aware of this conspicuous interloper. Yet he was obviously a stranger in these parts. What chance could have summoned him in? Not necessarily the woeful November weather. For as the professor all alone had come walking along on his way to his lecture through the drizzling lamp-lit streets, he had passed by not only a flaming picture palace, radiant with seductive posters, but the vestibule of a dingy dejected little theatre – which appeared a good deal more inviting, nonetheless, than the spear-headed railings and dank brick wall of the cobbled alley which led into the Memorial Hall.

There were, then, rival attractions in the town. If so, why had this theatrical-looking personage not taken advantage of them? Or was he himself one of a company of touring play-actors idling his time away until the call boy claimed him for the second act? Had he ventured out of his green room for a breath of air, or for a draught even more exhilarating? Why again is it that extremely actual things in appearance may at times so closely resemble the imagery of sleep? But what folly were all such speculations. Nevertheless, Professor Monk had continued to indulge in them, and with an amazing rapidity, while he continued to read his paper. To satisfy them was quite another matter.

His voice – and he enjoyed this scrupulous resonant use of it – his voice rang on and on, sounding even louder than usual in his own ear by reason perhaps of this attack of what might be called psychic indigestion. Nor was he aware of any suddenly revealed reason to be distrustful, let alone ashamed, of his paper. When looking it over he had taken the opportunity of re-reading some of the stories, most of the poems, and an essay or two. He had consulted here and there one of the more recent lives. Its actual composition had taken him a good deal more than a week; and it was at least systematically arranged. In four parts, that is: (*a*) the Environment; (*b*) the Man; (*c*) the Tales and Poems; (*d*) the Aftermath. Even if he had been able to extemporise he would have preferred to keep to the written word. It was a safeguard against exaggeration and mere sentiment.

As, tall, dark, steel-spectacled, and a little stiff, he stood up there decanting his views and judgements, it ensured that he said only what he meant to say, and that he meant only what he said. He disliked lectures that meander. He preferred facts to atmosphere, statements to hints, assumptions, 'I venture's', and dubious implications. He detested theorising, fireworks, and high spirits. The temperamental critic is a snare. And though poetry may, and perhaps unfortunately, *must* appeal to the emotions and the heart, the expounding of it is the business of the head. Besides, a paper simply and clearly arranged is far easier to report. He hoped that his audience would go away with something definite in their minds to remember, though he was not so sanguine as to suppose that they would remember much. 'Hammer, hammer, hammer,' he would laugh to himself, 'on the hard high road!'

Until this hour indeed it was highly probable that many of them had never read, even if they had ever heard of, much more of Poe's writings than *The Pit and the Pendulum*, and possibly *The Bells*. Others may have accepted him merely as the melodramatist of *The Maelstrom,* or *The Cask of Amontillado,* the sentimentalist of *Annabel Lee,* the cynic of *The Masque of the Red Death,* and the fantast of *The Fall of the House of Usher.* A few of the more knowledgeable might have stigmatised him not only as a gross sensationalist, of little character and no morals – and an American at that – but something of a poseur and a charlatan. This was a view, he confessed, that had been shared by no less distinguished a compatriot of Poe's than the great novelist, Henry James, who had dismissed his work as a poet in three contemptuous words – 'very superficial verse'. Yes, and thrillers are thrillers and shockers shockers, whether they are old or new. He himself could not agree with so sweeping a verdict, but he would not disguise the facts.

It would be only too easy indeed, he had declared, to treat the subject of Poe in what might be called a pleasing, persuasive, and popular fashion. He had tried to avoid that, to be frank and just without becoming censorious. He had admitted that to look for lessons, instruction, spiritual insight, and what in his own country is called uplift, in the career and writings of the author of *The Premature Burial, The Black Cat,* or such poems as *The Conqueror Worm* and *Ulalume,* was like looking for primroses and violets fresh with dew in a funereal wreath of artificially dyed *immortelles.* And though he would agree – and here he had cast a deprecatory glance at his chairman – that it was a lecturer's office to expound rather than to indict, he could not avoid a dutiful word or two on the ethics of his subject. He had expressed his agreement with Longfellow that life is both real and earnest, that books are more than merely a drug, an anodyne, a solace, a way of escape. Poets, too, have their specific value, and, unlike Plato, he would certainly not dismiss them from his Ideal Republic. 'Not bag and baggage!' Nonetheless poetry is in the nature of honey. It is not a *diet.* He himself was of opinion that a delight in beauty cannot be considered a substitute for the desire for knowledge, an excuse for any laxity of moral fibre, or for the absence of any serious convictions. And he had no wish to be partisan. However that might be, poets themselves, though they secrete this enticing honey, have not always proved themselves the best of bees. Their characters and their conduct, alas! are seldom as impeccable as their syntax.

A man's style, whether in prose or verse, in some degree, of course, reveals that man himself. And Poe on the whole wrote well. But we must be careful. A style that may be good from a merely literary point of view is not necessarily the work of a good man, nor is a bad style necessarily the work of a rascal. Otherwise, how few men of science – philosophers even – would escape damnation! Though again, what a man writes may reflect himself, as in a sort of looking-glass, it does not necessarily reflect the complete self. By no means, surely, is the whole of Burns in his love lyrics. Was even *Paradise Lost* all Milton? If so, the less Milton he. Byron, Baudelaire, Horace, Herrick, had they nothing of heart, mind, and soul but what was imaged in their writings? What then of Poe?

The professor had confessed impatience with the iridescent *veil* theory of poetry. Did the worn-out slogan Art for Art's Sake, if examined closely, mean anything more profound than pudding for pudding's sake, or plumbing for plumbing's sake? Nor is a poem as a poem the better or worse for having been written at an age when most young people prefer the excitements of cricket or basketball; are, in fact, in Matthew Arnold's words, young barbarians at play. Genius may sometimes manifest itself in precocity; nonetheless, such a poem as Poe's *To Helen,* which he professed to have written at fourteen, must take its place with the rest of his work. It must stand or fall on its poetic merit.

Nor again, the lecturer had insisted, is any piece of literature the richer or more valuable for having been composed in an attic, in wretched circumstances. Not for a moment had he conceded that between poetry and poverty there is only the difference of the letter V – 'The viol, the violet, and the vine' – that sort of thing. Men of imagination may be naturally sensitive, delicately poised, easily dejected – it is the price they pay for so precious an inheritance. But is it too extreme a price? Even Robert Louis Stevenson – an artist to his finger-tips – had not excused the man of genius the obligation of meeting his butcher's bill. Indeed he had said harsher things than that. Chaucer proved himself a man of affairs; Shakespeare made a handsome fortune and retired in his later forties to his birthplace; Robert Browning in the prime of life was occasionally mistaken for a prosperous banker; Westminster Abbey was at this moment positively surfeited with poetic remains. And that is hardly the Valhalla of the disreputable.

But even as a child Poe had been perverse and self-willed. And certainly in the brief months he spent at Jefferson's beautiful and serene University of Virginia, and in his even briefer career as a cadet in the lovely natural surroundings of West Point – though every allowance of course should be made for the young and the gifted – he had without question shown himself arrogant, fitful, quarrelsome, unstable. Had he been the reverse of all this, which of its better qualities would be missing from his work?

There was, of course, the other side of the account to consider – Mangan, De Quincey, Coleridge. One could hardly, alas! think of their writings dissociated from certain weaknesses not merely of constitution but of moral fibre. Mangan had died in poverty in deplorable circumstances in the same year as Poe himself, 1849; and this too was the death-year of Beddoes, while Emily Brontë had died only the year before – a strange eventuality, since there was much in common between them all – ill health, adverse fortune, extremes of mood and imagination. But Branwell's habits rather than her own were Emily Brontë's scourge, and the tragic and morbid end to Beddoes's career seemed to be proof of 'a sadly unstable mind'.

On the other hand, virtue, the lecturer was bound to confess, is not the prerogative either of the Stock Exchange or even of the

Church; and our public-houses, our workhouses, and other abodes of the unfortunate and the unwise are thronged with human beings incapable even of scribbling a limerick or of rhyming *dove* with *grove*. In other words, it is by no means only the rarely gifted that are responsible for all the failures in life.

Poe's two years as private soldier, corporal, and sergeant in the American Army, though it had been an experience forced on him, had proved him capable of endurance, discipline, and responsibility. He had been sober and diligent, and had won the respect of his officers. No man of genius need be the worse off for *that*! In after years he had remembered the experience with sufficient tolerance at least to make its surroundings the scene of one of the best, one of the most original, and, even better, one of the least bizarre of his short stories: *The Gold Bug. The Gold Beetle,* as we should say. And though the writing of verse and even of poetry is seldom fated to be much more than its own reward, fiction may well be.

One of Poe's earliest stories, indeed, had won him a substantial prize; and it was only editorial discretion that had prevented him from carrying off a prize for the best poem also. 'Your *Raven,*' wrote Elizabeth Barrett from her sick couch in Wimpole Street, 'has produced a sensation... Our great poet, Mr Robert Browning, was struck much by its rhythm.' There was little indeed to suggest that Poe had any extreme aversion to becoming a popular writer. Again and again success – and 'I mean,' the professor had emphasised, with a tap of his finger on the desk, 'I mean *material* success' – had been within his grasp. Yet his feeble fingers had refused to clutch at it.

Nonetheless, the professor had refused to ally himself with those who maintain that to be popular is a proof of mediocrity. There were great books whose appeal is universal. Poe's triumphs, however, had been brief and very few. It could hardly be otherwise with a writer so egregious and idiosyncratic.

In spite of a personal charm and fascination almost hypnotic in effect, even at times on those of his own sex, Poe utterly refused to tolerate any opinions or convictions contrary to his own. He was obstinate and contumelious, scornful of the workaday graces that so sweeten human intercourse, and – to change the metaphor – *oil* the wheels of life. In his youth he had been treated harshly perhaps, had been denied what no doubt he regarded, but quite erroneously, as his rightful inheritance – his foster-father's fortune, for example; but he had failed to profit by so drastic a lesson. It could scarcely be said that it was the mere hardships of destiny that had prevented him from rivalling in general esteem even Longfellow himself, who, whatever his failings, seems to have been consistently true to his principles, was accepted as the laureate of his own people, and was a man of as many simple and homely qualities of head and heart as he was nobly leonine in appearance. And *he,* again, had made a fortune!

To compare, moreover, Poe's work with Emerson's was like comparing a neglected graveyard, dense with yew and cypress under the fitful lightings and showings of the moon, with a seemly, pro-portionate, if unadorned country parsonage, in the serene sunshine of a transatlantic morning in May. Man for man, Poe had not the virtues of Emerson, and Emerson had neither the exotic gifts nor the failings of Poe. Let us acknowledge it then. If in literature there is such a thing as the diseased, and even the sordid, why not attempt to exemplify them, even though it was exceedingly difficult to define them? The professor had, rather tentatively, made the attempt.

On the technical side of Poe's work, he had himself always realised that his appreciation had been less full and less penetrating than it might have been. Here his lecture had skipped a little. But had it been otherwise how many of his listeners – those rows of silent faces – would have continued to listen? There were children among them. One little girl had a slumbering infant in her arms! Temper then the wind to the shorn lamb. Craftsmanship, artistry, he had announced, however, is vital alike in prose and verse; but you cannot really separate words from what they say. And the highest art is the concealment of art; and, beyond that, the concealment of the concealment. Could this be said of Poe's technique? Is not rather one of the chief defects of his poems their flawless mastery of method? Poe, it seems, had never *lisped* in numbers, but (quite apart from his own account of the composition of *The Raven*), we know how laboriously many of his later numbers came.

Still, if writing is an art, so also in its modest way is the compiling of a lecture. The professor had dealt briefly with what he described as Poe's mere tricks as a versifier, his verbal repetitions, his childish delight-in the jingling of rhymes, and in emphatic metres. He had referred to his theory and practice of lyrical brevity – and there is no such thing as a *poem* that cannot be read and enjoyed in the course of half an hour. There was, he agreed, a measure of truth in this, but surely it is a question for the reader to decide – the reader, say, of the *Iliad,* the *Divine Comedy,* the *Prelude.* For his part, there could not be too much of a good thing. He had agreed also that the primary impulse of poetry is the sharing of pleasure rather than the teaching of lessons. But there are various kinds of pleasure, they are of differing values; and poems whose chief appeal is to the senses – whether they are in the nature of a stimulant or a narcotic – should for that very reason be examined in the light of reason.

He had, however, left that examination to his listeners, and instead had specified where and when and to what end certain of the poems had been written – *The Bells,* for example, which from being a few lines enshrining an idyllic and rapturous moment in the company of the charming but minor poetess, Mrs Whitman, had gradually been expanded by the poet into the rather heady masterpiece of its kind now only too familiar. It had been not only easier but more practical to do this than to attempt a close analysis.

Apropos of Mrs Whitman, he had broken off to refer to the poet's rather numerous infatuations and attachments, or one might almost say *de*tachments – those fleeting and even fugitive Egerias – from the lovely and doomed Mrs Stannard, the original of his Helen and the idolatry of his boyhood, to the ladies to whom each in turn in his later years he had proposed – and indeed almost insisted on – marriage: after the death, that is, of his young wife Virginia. Like many other poets, Poe had loved at times unwisely and by no means always too well. He had sipped deep of the cup of feminine adulation – whatever its sediment might be. Scandal in consequence had not spared him, nor even slander, but for the most part it had left him unscathed.

The professor had referred in this connection to the poet's child-like, ethereal, camellia-pale Virginia, 'the tragic bride of but fourteen summers', whose brief life, with all the recurrent horrors shared by them both and incident to her fatal disease, had been but a protracted journey to an early grave. And that said, how could he but also refer to Poe's humiliating dependence on his more than motherly mother-in-law, Mrs Clemm? Muddie, as he called her, to whom he wrote letters as naturally affectionate and commonplace as most of his correspondence tended to be high-flown.

There were indeed episodes in Poe's life which it would be futile to pass over, and impossible to condone – dismal lapses, even apart from those due to physical disability and the ravages of drugs. Truth imposes on us the obligation to record what only sympathy and indeed humility can help us to understand. Nonetheless, he had tactfully, regretfully refrained from bestowing that scrutiny on 'the dark side of the poet's career' which one is apt to fix on a drop of ditch-water seen through a microscope. Not that Poe himself had spared others. As a critic alike of humanity and of literature, his bias was on the side of severity; he despised a fool, ridiculed failure, had no mercy on his enemies, and little patience with aims and ideals contrary to his own. Whatever the value of his writings might be, in Poe's eyes 'an inferior poem was little short of a crime'. An arrogant assurance of his own powers was alike his weakness and his strength.

Unlike Poe himself, however, the professor had endeavoured to be moderate. As briefly as possible, he had told of the poet's last few sombre and disastrous days at Baltimore, that final ignominy when he had been found in a high fever, half naked, and scarcely sane, in the clutches of political miscreants who had confined him merely in order that he should serve their purpose at the voting booth. He had spoken of the horror and solitude of his death in the public hospital, that last forlorn cry of: 'Is there any help?... Lord help my poor soul!' He had lamented that all this had occurred within a few hours of the first occasion in the poet's life when, restored to the Elmira whom in his early days he had loved and been cheated of, promise for the future had never seemed for him so fair, so full of hope, and rich with opportunity.

And as he said the words, a sudden overwhelming billow of mistrust had swept over the lecturer's soul. It was as if a complete flock of geese were disporting themselves on his grave. Why, in heaven's name, instead of perhaps a glimpse of Goya's serene yet appalling picture, *The Pest House,* had Rembrandt's curiously detached study, *An Anatomical Lesson,* flickered at this moment across his mind? And this when his paper was on the point of completion – fourteen minutes to nine?

Solely, it seemed, by reason of the presence of this one silent stranger yonder, who, as he himself raised his eyes from his desk to peer at him over his spectacles, had answered him look for look, scrutiny for scrutiny, a moment before. The lecturer had made no statement he was ashamed of; nothing false, nothing even dubious. And yet his words seemed to have lost their savour. But however that might be, he reminded himself that one cannot by mere wish to do so blot out the past. The mind itself must be its own sexton beetle. One cannot unsay the said, even in a lecture. The very attempt would be ludicrous. He was being fanciful. He was falling a victim to what he cordially despised – the artistic temperament! So late in life! He had come to lecture, yet to judge from this sudden disquietude, he was being 'larned'. Well, he must hasten on. Life, like a lecture, is a succession of moments. Don't pay too extreme an attention to any one or two; wait for the end of the hour.

'I think perhaps,' he was declaring at this moment, 'the most salient, the most impressive feature of Poe's writings, as with Dean Swift's, though the two men had little else in common, is his own personal presence in them. Even in his most exotic fantasies, some of them beautiful in the sense that the phosphorescence of decay, the brambles and briars of the ruinous, the stony calm of the dead may be said to be beautiful; some so sinister and macabre in their half-demented horror that if we ourselves encountered them even in dream we should awake screaming upon our beds – even here the sense of his peculiar personality is so vivid and immediate that, as we read, it is almost as if the poet himself stood in the flesh before us – in his customary suit of solemn black, the wide marmoreal brow, the corrosive tongue, the saturnine moodiness.

'Flaubert's ideal of the impersonal in fiction indeed was utterly beyond Poe. His presence pervades such a tale as *The Pit and the*

Pendulum, The Cask of Amontillado, or *The Tell-tale Heart* no less densely than it pervades his *William Wilson,* his *Masque of the Red Death,* his *Ligeia,* and *The Haunted Palace.* This may in part be due to the fact that his was a mind at once acutely analytical and richly imaginative. This is a rare but by no means unique combination of what only appear to be contradictory faculties. Incapable of compromise, Poe had remained preposterously self-sufficient, self-immolating, and aloof; and, in spite of occasional gleams of sunshine, a moody, melancholy, and embittered man. He was thus alike the master and the victim of his destiny. If not a positive enemy of society, there is little to suggest that – apart from literature – he was ever much concerned with the social problems, causes, principles, and ideals of his own time and place. With some justification perhaps – as events have proved – he distrusted democracy, detested the mob, and he warned his fellow-countrymen of the sordid dangers incident to an ignorant republic. These views nonetheless were those of an egotist rather than an aristocrat. By birth he was of little account – the son of a mere travelling actor.

'Nor, though he had, it is true, been brought up in the traditions of a gentleman of the Southern States and abhorred all New Englanders, was he by any means a giant among pygmies. Longfellow, Emerson, Washington Irving, Bryant, Whittier, Thoreau, Oliver Wendell Holmes were in varying degrees his contemporaries; and, first cousin to him, in mind if not in blood, Nathaniel Hawthorne. Since, too, *The Gold Bug,* like *The Murders in the Rue Morgue,* is one of the earliest tales of its genre in English, and *Treasure Island* is one of its remoter offspring, one might add Fenimore Cooper. He had lived, that is, in one of the Golden Ages of English literature – not that of our own day, the Brass.

'As for J. R. Lowell, an admirable critic of the widest range, in his knowledge alike of books, men, and affairs, though he was responsible for the caustic summary of Poe's work as three-fifths genius and two-fifths fudge, he was one of his closest and loyalest friends.

'I am not,' announced at last the professor, wearily, and never before had he been so tired of the sound of his own voice, 'I am not a mathematician, and cannot check Professor Lowell's vulgar fractions. But even if allowance be made for the fact that here in England even the parochial are inclined to sneer at the provincialism of all things American, it must be remembered that for years Poe was anathema, a man accursed among his own people. And it is certainly not in this country that since his death his work has been neglected. It had *not* been a beneficent influence' – the professor had once more assured his audience; and that not merely because 'it is easier to imitate fudge than works of genius. What a man does, however, must not mislead us in our judgement of what he *is*. Poe was a round peg in a square hole. The wise and the prudent in this world make the best they can of these conditions. Not so this ill-fated, saturnine, sinister poet. Whatever our debt to him may be, *he* flatly refused to follow their example.'

During the pause that completed this sentence – perhaps a tenth part of a second – some imp in the professor's mind engaged in a violent argument with him as to which kind of peg and in what kind of hole he was himself just now; and then reminded him that pegs and holes may be of many shapes other than merely square or round – ovals, hexagons, oblongs, polygons. But he knew this imp of old, and dismissed him.

And now his lecture, which for the first time in his placid career had been little short of a martyrdom, was all but over. Though his air and manner conveyed no symptom of what was in his mind, hotly debating, ill at ease, dejected, not a little indignant, he had come to his peroration. Yet once again he lowered his head for a final fleeting glimpse of the stranger in the doorway, and ejaculated the few sentences that remained.

The last syllable had been uttered. His task was done. He had shut his mouth. For an instant he stood in silence facing his listeners – an intellectual St Sebastian – no less mute and more defenceless than an innocent in the dock. At the next he had turned stiffly, had gravely inclined his head in the direction of his chairman, and had sat down. He crossed his legs, he closed his eyes, he folded his arms. Though the electric vibrations of the hideous arc-lamp over his head continued to quiver beneath his skull, though a vile disquietude still fretted his soul, he had come back safely into his shell again. A moment before he had been a public spectacle; now he was private again; his own man and all but at liberty. Even better, he had ceased to criticise himself.

He was listening instead to his chairman, a smallish man in a clerical collar, and, in spite of that clerical collar, attired in a suit of a cloth much nearer grey than black. He had a square head, square shoulders, square hands, and a plain, good-natured, eager, and amusing face. Those hands were now in rapid motion in a mutual embrace one of the other; and, with enviable ease and fluency, he was assuring his audience how much they had all been instructed and entertained. He was rapidly confessing, too, that he had himself come to the meeting that evening knowing very little of Mr Edgar Poe's works. The name was familiar – but some of us hadn't much time for fiction. So far as he himself was concerned, life *was* real and earnest. He had, it is true, taken a hasty glance at a page or two of what appeared to be a very clever and harmless tale entitled *The Purloined Letter,* and believed he could recite then and there the first few lines of *Annabel Lee, not* by the way to be confused with an old wholesome favourite

of his, *Nancy Lee*. Their lecturer, however, had not, he fancied, mentioned this particular piece, and had passed over this story, though
he had referred to others that were concerned with an even graver
crime than that of pilfering, nay – let us give the dog the name he
deserves – *stealing* a letter. He meant, brutal murder. There were far
too many murders in the fiction of our own day. On the other hand,
an orang-outang, whatever its extremes of conduct may be, has not
been given a conscience. He is not *morally* responsible. Man, whether
his descendant or not, *is*.

Tales of crime were, alas! very prevalent in these days, much too
prevalent, he feared. Quite respectable and well-educated people
not only read but wrote them. They were yet another symptom
of the unrest of the age. The professor had, of course, referred
to America – the United States. Was it to be credited that in that
great English-speaking country the harmless if slightly colloquial
expression, 'Taking a man for a ride', actually signified consigning
a fellow-soul into eternity? On the other hand Mr Edgar Poe, he
gathered, could not be held responsible for the present sad state
of Chicago. He understood he was a Virginian, a Southerner, and
though one of the tales mentioned by the professor bore what he
feared was the only too appropriate title, *MS. Found in a Bottle,* the
poet, it seemed, had lived not only prior to the Civil War, but long
before the days of Prohibition. That, however, was only a blessing
in disguise. For in view of what the lecturer had said of Mr Poe's
sad and afflicting end, they must remember that those responsible
for the Volstead Act had *meant* well. There were tragedies in every
life, skeletons in every cupboard. And the lecturer's subject was no
exception. As for his marriage with a wife then only fourteen years
of age, though no doubt it is true that Juliet in the play was also of
equally tender years, she was emphatically not Romeo's first cousin.

He himself could not approve of this arrangement. We mustn't run headlong into wedlock.

Then, again, he heartily agreed with the lecturer that the piece *To Helen* was a remarkable feat for a lad in his early teens – *most* remarkable. But he deplored any suggestion that *all* lads of fourteen should be encouraged to be equally precocious. There were dangers. Even, too, though a man may be his own worst enemy, he may yet attain renown as a writer. Poe himself had. Nevertheless he implored them one and all to remember that it is better by far for ever to hold one's peace than to write, however attractively, what it may some day be too late to recall. That solemn thought, he gathered, was their lecturer's urgent lesson to them this evening.

Before, he concluded, before inviting that stronghold of their society, Miss Alibone, to propose a vote of thanks to Professor Monk, he would like to announce that at their next meeting their old friend Mr Alfred Okes, so busy in so many fields, was to talk to them on the subject of conchology – the science of seashells, from the whelk to the conch – the latter being famous in mythology, though it was frequently mispronounced. And on *that* occasion there would be lantern slides.

'I ask you, sir' – he suddenly rounded on the professor with the most tactful and endearing of smiles – 'I ask you, sir, to accept our heartiest, our most cordial thanks for your most entertaining, informative, and, I will add, even edifying discourse. We have been well fed.'

The professor unsealed his tired eyes, looked up, smiled a little wanly, and hastily pocketed his paper. In a few minutes, the hall already nearly empty, he had followed his chairman down the five well-worn, red-druggeted steps into the ante-chamber. There he was welcomed by a row of empty wooden chairs, a solid grained table, a copper-plate engraving in a large black frame over the chimneypiece of a gentleman in side-whiskers, whose name, owing to the foxed condition of the print, he had been unable to decipher, and the ashes of a fire in the grate. It had been feebly alight when he arrived. It was now dead out. Why did this seemingly harmless chamber at this moment resemble the scene of a nightmare? He could not tell. His chairman seemed to be finding nothing amiss with it. He was adjusting his grey woollen muffler, he had bidden him a hearty good-night, he had turned away, adding jovially over his shoulder, as he hurried forth: 'Ah, Professor Monk, here's a little friend to see you – eager no doubt to drink at the fountain-head. Come in, my dear' – and was gone.

The little friend, however, who was now beaming at the professor from under a dark felt, medallioned school-hat and from behind gold spectacles straddling a small, blunt, resolute nose, was in fact anxious only to secure his autograph and still more anxious to discover if he could possibly be related to Miss *Mima* Monk, the famous film star. 'It's the same name, you see,' she said, 'that's why.'

Alas! the professor was compelled to confess, he had no relatives in the neighbourhood of Los Angeles. He opened the little green and gold birthday book, and turned a little wearily to November 8, to read: 'Words are the only things that last for ever. – *William Hazlitt.*' The child watched him as he made the dot after his sedate signature a little more emphatic.

'We've learned some of Mr Poe's poems in class,' she was assuring him breathlessly. 'I think it's *lovely*. Our teacher says *The Bells* is meant to sound like real bells – it's all imitation.'

'Yes, indeed,' the professor replied, 'it is called onomatopoeia.'

'Omonatopoe-oe-oeia,' she trebled after him like a wren, and with yet another coy and beaming smile had taken her book and departed.

Her footsteps, it seemed, had suddenly quickened into a scamper, then she too was gone. The professor sighed, and rose from his chair. And then, suddenly transfixed, with one arm actually halfway through the sleeve of his antiquated mackintosh, he turned, realising that what he had vaguely foreseen and apprehended had come to pass.

The gentleman in the black cloak until this moment unperceived in the shadow at the turn of the door had advanced into the room, and was now confronting him from the other end of the varnished table. The glass-shaded electric lamp that hung between them shed a lustre almost as of alabaster on his pallid face and wide prominent forehead – a pallor intensified by the darkness of his long hair, the marked eyebrows, the small moustache. He was a man seemingly aged about forty, rather under the middle height, and spare, but he carried himself with an air of elegance, a trace even of the foppish. His black beaver hat clasped between his delicate hands, he remained silent and motionless, his chin, the least vigorous of his finely cut features, lowered upon his black satin stock, his dark luminous grey eyes fixed on the professor's face. There was a peculiar abstraction, even vacancy in their depths – a slightly catlike appearance, as if they were not wholly in focus; and this, in spite of the intense regard in them – a regard which brought to the professor's mind a phrase he had read somewhere – 'they seemed to shed darkness in that place'. And though they expressed no hostility, and Professor Monk had the advantage in stature, he was finding it difficult to meet them. They were strangely *occupied* eyes. Besides, the hall outside was now not only silent but empty; and it was atrociously cold.

The imp within his mind had begun chattering again. 'He stoppeth one of three', was echoing in the professor's consciousness. Why *The Ancient Mariner*? The cold, perhaps. Meanwhile, he realised that he must break *this* ice. His silence was becoming discourteous. He glanced again at his visitor, and was again sharply reminded that he bore a striking resemblance… To what? To whom? There had been no pause in which to collect his thoughts. The professor met many strangers; how could he be expected with all the good will in the world to recall always either themselves or their names? Names are at best but labels.

'*Er* – good evening—' he began – but a low, insistent voice had broken in on him.

'Where *is* this place?' it was inquiring.

'This place? '*Where?*' exclaimed the professor. 'Wigston, you mean?'

'Wigston – ah, yes. And England?'

The professor continued to listen, the prey now of another kind of discomfort. There are degrees of eccentricity – and he was alone.

'*That* was my impression,' the other was saying. 'And these people' – he raised his hat in a peculiarly graceful gesture towards the doorway – 'these people were not completely ignorant of the subject of your address?'

'Indeed, no'; a deprecating smile had crept into the professor's face; 'though we mustn't of course expect—' But he was not allowed to complete his sentence.

'And you yourself must have been deeply interested in your theme to venture on compounding a complete lecture upon it. Fifty-three minutes in all!'

'Indeed, yes,' interjected the professor warmly.

'I see.' The stranger paused. 'I observed that the date on the notice-board facing the street is 2nd November, and the year 1932. You will realise that I have myself come some little distance. There are – difficulties. But it was rather the name than the date which attracted

me. Edgar Allan Poe's, I mean, and your own, too, of course. I fear
I cannot compliment you upon its appearance.'

'My name!… Oh, yes, the street?' said the professor.

'Rain so sooty-dark upon a scene so dismal, the niggardly glare,
the stench, and what might be described as the realism of it all!
You yourself perhaps are unfamiliar with Virginia – Richmond,
Charlottesville, the South. You are from Oxford, perhaps? Has that
ancient seat of learning also endured of late the ravages of change?'

The slim erect figure had bowed slightly – with a deprecating
politeness. The professor shook his head. 'No, not Oxford; London,'
he said.

'Ah, yes, London. I am from…' But at this moment, unfortunately,
the neighbouring foundry had once more metallically ejected its slag,
and the word was lost. 'So Edgar Allan Poe' – his visitor pronounced
the syllables as if they were in the nature of a sarcasm or even a jest –
'so Edgar Allan Poe is remembered even in this benighted town?'

'Remembered!' cried the professor. 'Why, yes, indeed. My whole
intention was to suggest for what reason he should be remembered.
The acoustics of the hall, perhaps—'

'But, indeed,' the stranger was assuring him, 'I heard perfectly.
I was engrossed. Engrossed. A host of remote memories, echoes,
speculations returned into my mind. But I have ventured to intrude
on you, not to pay compliments which you might find wearisome,
but in the hope that you will allow me – even at this late day and
hour – to ask you one or two questions.'

The professor's dark eyebrows expressed a faint surprise. 'As a
matter of fact—' he began.

'Oh, yes,' the visitor hastened to add, 'I was aware that your chairman had invited questions – with a disarming cordiality indeed. But
though, professor, you had remarkably attentive listeners, you will

agree perhaps that they were rather passively receptive than actively critical. That was my *impression*. There is an old saying: Every time a sheep bleats it loses a mouthful. Well, yours at least never bleated. Apart from that, however, there are questions it may be more courteous to ask in private. Such as mine. May I continue?'

'By all means.' The professor's eye ranged furtively over the intensely unoccupied row of hard-wood chairs. 'Won't you sit down?'

'Thank you,' said the stranger; 'when I disagree I prefer to stand. I have come, as you see, unarmed, except in respect of the tongue. We are on equal terms, then, though you might perhaps agree that in matters of the mind one solitary question may be almost mortal in effect. First, then, am I justified in deducing from what you have said that one word would summarise your own personal attitude towards the man of letters you have lately been dissecting: the word "scorn"? You were at pains, I admit, to disguise it, to salve in one sentence the wound given by another. But the tone, the flavour, the accent – I could not be mistaken. And is not scorn, professor, a dubious incitement for the critic, the expounder, the appreciator of any artist and his work? Moreover, it is one thing to despise a fellow-creature, another to malign him.'

'Malign!' cried the professor. 'My sole aim and intention was to tell the truth.'

'Ay, and so you dragged the well. And I am now enjoying the flavour of its dregs. You had ninety-eight listeners this evening. I myself counted them. You gave me plenty of time – between your ideas, I mean. That was fortunate. Your *poet*, let me inform you, once read his *Eureka* – an essay in the imaginative synthesis of philosophical and scientific thought which you evaded so skilfully by the mere mention of it – he read, I say, his *Eureka* – his mistress jewel – on a stormy night in a bitterly cold hall in Richmond before an audience of only sixty souls in all. It occupied two hours and a half. You and your hungry little flock, then, had not only the easier ordeal, but also a less difficult subject-matter. Apart from the title of your paper, you divided it into four parts: The Environment; the Man; the Tales and Poems; the Aftermath. Am I right? Superficially, that is a simple and lucid arrangement. Did you keep to it? Hardly. Again and again, like the moth to the candle – or shall we say, to the star! – you returned to the poet's private life, to his unhappy childhood, aureoled, in your own pinchbeck phrase, "with the chameleonic hues of romance". To the follies and misfortunes of his youth, to his failures, his poverty, his bereavements, his afflictions of body and mind, and what you supposed to be his soul – to his miserable death. Well, we live and die, and must leave posterity to do its best – and its worst – with us. But was it necessary to regale your docile and ignorant audience with allusions to the poet's young mother, the forsaken, penniless actress, and to *her* vile, tragic death in a filthy tenement when he himself was a child? I grant you his Helen. She even reminded your quick wits of Troy. But what of his simple-minded and afflicted sister Eulalie? What of exhuming into the light of night the very remains of his ever-youthful and long-suffering Virginia – to pry and peer into *their* sacred secrets? You used the word morbid. Whose was the morbid, yes, and the sordid, when you declared that those poor relics had actually lain concealed awhile under the bed of one of her husband's besotted biographers? The ashes of Annabel Lee, forsooth! And selfless and faithful old Mrs Clemm, *her* mother, *his* more-than-mother, with her basket of broken meats collected from door to door to save her loved ones from starvation. And the poet's cloak, that in those icy winters in New York had to serve by day as a protection for his own wretched back, and by night as a coverlet for his dying Virginia's bed. You used the term, tragedy, professor;

why did you turn it into a melodrama? Is there to be no humanity or decent reticence concerning the life of a man who is dead, mainly because he was a writer? Is *every* poet at the hands of *any* showman doomed to suffer again and again the pangs of a Monsieur Waldemar? I ask you – I put the question.'

'Let me repeat,' said the professor frigidly, 'you have misjudged my intention. You imply that a man's circumstances in life have no relation to his actions, to his principles, to his ideals. I deny it. Knowledge aids understanding. How else explain, excuse, condone?'

'Condone! It was, then, with the same compassionate aim that, having condensed a lifetime of forty years – not an exorbitant allowance – into a sensational and appetising quarter of an hour, you dealt with the *man*? It was perhaps your passion for moderation that persuaded you only to hint at such words as mountebank, ingrate, wastrel, fortune-hunter, seducer, debauchee, dipsomaniac. Hints serve better. But words, professor, have the strange power of revealing not merely what a man consciously intends to say, but what, perhaps unknown to himself, he means and feels. And the simplest of your listeners can have been in little doubt of that. I confess to perplexity. Have the poets themselves ever claimed to be saints? Have the most exemplary of them ever professed to be anything but sinners? Name me one poet, one imaginative writer even, of any account, whom you yourself suspect of believing that his failings as a man in any sense or degree *aided* his genius. They may profess it – but not within themselves! Oh, yes, I agree that a man's writings indelibly reflect him and all of him that matters most. And since your poet's are all that is left of him in this world, and they alone are of lasting value, should we not look for him there? Did you attempt to depict, to describe, to illuminate that reflection? No: for that would have needed insight, the power to divine, to re-create. *You* are a stern and ardent moralist, professor. But since when has the platform become a pulpit? It needs, too, little courage to attack and stigmatise the dead.'

The stranger's wandering gaze had returned slowly to the professor's face. 'Provided, of course, you are confident that dead he will remain. Nonetheless it seems to me a rather paltry amusement – carrion stuff.'

'I say again,' cried Professor Monk hotly, 'truth was my aim. I resent this attack. It is beside the point.'

'For my part,' said the other, 'I resent nothing. I am here merely to "drink from the fountain-head". But even if we admit that from his childhood up, as a human being, gentleman, and Christian, your poet fell far short even of the happy mean, is there no other standard by which to judge him? The decalogue he shared with every man, and, like most men, and many professors, he would long since have been forgotten if he had not proved himself – I will not venture to say worthy of remembrance, but – defiant of oblivion. What he *might* have done even in spite of his miseries and weaknesses, his tortured nerves and treacherous body – *that* no man can declare. But in respect, professor, to what he actually *did* – as an artist, a man of letters, a poet? Does that suggest that he ever consented to sell the smallest fraction of his soul for bread, or wine, or – brief anodyne against a world which he himself had no hand in creating – even drugs? Did he condescend to write down to his readers; or, worse, up? Did he betray his intelligence; prostitute his mind; parade his heart? Did he even attempt to improve the *shining* hour? You would agree that the writer in his solitude must obey scruples, hold fast to an aesthetic probity, serve with a forlorn devotion in a cause which the generality of men know nothing of. But *his* laws are unwritten laws. Not that I suggest that your victim even in this was blameless – far from it. But you yourself seem never to have been aware of such an ordeal. You made pretty play with the artistic temperament – with your morbid, and your moody, and your melancholy, and your misanthrope – but of the artist's *conscience* not one word.'

'Even if your allegations were not grossly exaggerated,' said the professor, 'surely there is little novelty in such a notion, and I had to consider my listeners.'

'Had the poets,' said the other, 'put their faith solely in novelty and considered only their listeners, there would have been no *Paradise Lost*, no *Hamlet*, and a few of the Greek tragedies. Surely only an artist's *best* is worth his trouble? And that being so – heaven help him – can he, *need* he care who shares it? Let me repeat, I am not defending Mr Poe, God forbid; he is gone long since, as your genial friend the minister on the platform would put it, to his account. It could be only then in the strangeness of some sepulchral dream that he could or would return to a world he little liked, and was little liked by. But all this apart – these dingy relics, I mean, the unsavoury events of his life and the invaluable lessons to be derived from them: what conceivable concern had they with the very subject of your paper?'

The slate-grey eyes peered out dark with anger from behind the glass of their spectacles. 'Subject?'

'It has escaped your memory, it seems. Read your own handbills then. "The *Writings* of Edgar Allan Poe".'

'That is a quibble.'

'It is essential. Your better nature gave you the title of your paper. Your worse followed the easier, the more appetising, the more popular, the charnel-house treatment of your theme.'

A pallor almost as extreme as that of his visitor had spread over Professor Monk's features. A hatred of this stranger, a hatred not the less bitter for being now innocent of contempt, was stirring in his mind. His glance fell from the fixed eyes to the thin satirical lips and thence to the delicate hands, but he realised that this petty effort to appear indifferent had woefully failed him. 'I consider,' he managed to say, in a low, hardly articulate voice, 'I consider this is an outrage and an insult.'

'That may well be so,' responded his visitor, with a hardly perceptible shrug of his cloaked shoulder. 'And I believe if your poet were here – I mean, professor, in the flesh – that he too would not hesitate to agree with you. But let us be honest for a moment. Apart from other writers – Thomas Lovell Beddoes and a Miss Brontë – you mentioned James Clarence Mangan, hinting that possibly Poe himself definitely stole, cheated him of his technique. Did you produce one single syllable in proof of this? And if you had, when, may I ask you, were poets forbidden to gild the silver they borrow? You said that Poe shared with these writers something of their dreams, their visions, their frail hopes and aspirations. How far did you inform us regarding the meaning, the source, the value and reality, quite apart from the fascination of those dreams? Poe's complete mortal existence was a conflict with his woe of spirit, his absorption in death and the grave, his horror of the solitude of the soul, of the nightmares that ascended on him like vultures from out of the pit of hell when he lay on his hospital death bed. What do *you* know of these? What will your listeners find of comfort, of reassurance in your academic mouthings and nothings when *they* come to face their terrors of the mind, *that* unshatterable solitude?

'My only speculation is not concerning which of the authors you mentioned you know least about, but what conceivable satisfaction you found in reading their books. And believe me, my dear professor, your groping remarks on poetic technique were nothing short of fatuous. Not only can you never have written a line of verse yourself, unless perhaps as an inky schoolboy you thumped out a molossus or a spondee or two on your desk, but you can never even have read with any insight the poet's essay on the subject. Indeed, what is your definition of poetry? Did you refer to his? It is deplorable enough that you have confused the imagination, that sovereign power, that divine energy, with a mere faculty. Reason, yes. But is not man's feeblest taper, like the sun itself in heaven, a *dual* splendour – of heat *and* light? Are you aware that you made no use of the word intellect, or divination, or afflatus, ay, and worse, even music? Did not Poe himself maintain that "in enforcing a truth, we must be simple, precise, terse. We must be cool, calm, unimpassioned. In a word, we must be in that mood which, as nearly as possible, is the exact converse of the poetical"? That, you may claim, was a mood you endeavoured to share. But did *he* never share it? Was opium or Hippocrene his aid in that? How then can you justify your commendation of that vain piping wiseacre Emerson, who in his own practice suggested that poetry is skim-milk philosophy and flowery optimism cut up into metre, and dismissed all else as jingle? Or your half-hearted rejection of Mr Henry James's shallow gibe, "very superficial verse". Is beauty the less admirable because it is skin deep? I know little of Mr James, but assume from what you yourself said of him that one might as justly dismiss his fiction as sillily super-subtle psychology. Was *he* a devotee of the Muses – of Music? *Music*, let me quote again, "music when combined with a pleasurable idea, is poetry; music without the idea is simply music; the idea, without the music, is prose, from its very definiteness."'

'Who said that?'

'Ah! Is it sense or nonsense?'

'I had an hour,' muttered the professor tartly, 'not all night.'

'And what virtual service,' continued his visitor more genially, 'is there in comparing poems different in aim, in kind, and in quality?

Has not even the ass its own niche in the universe? Is not every work of art – yes, even your own lecture – something single, unique; and are these precious comparisons anything better than mere mental exercises? Heaven forbid, and heaven forbids much, that I should legislate in such matters. My mere question is, how can *you*? Believe me, while what you told us of creative insight – invention as you called it – might set any sensitive human heart aching with despair, your remarks on the art of writing were nothing short of a treason to the mind. They were based on inadequate knowledge, and all but innocent of common-sense. Have you ever read that Poe never *laughed*? Perhaps not. And you had no reason to notice that one at least of your listeners refrained even from smiling, though on my soul I can imagine no moment in which he would be more bitterly tempted to indulge in the cachinnation of fools than in this.

"'Questions" – questions! I awaited in vain the faintest intimation that our poet was perhaps the first of his kind to foresee the triumphs and the tyranny of modern science; that he was no mere groping novice in astronomy, physics, and the science of the mind. Creature of darkness his imagination may have been: but was there no light in his *mind*? If you could meet him face to face, professor, at this moment, here, now – I ask you, I entreat you to confide in me, would you deny him the light of his reason? Would you? You might even try to forgive his extravagances, his miseries; you might even agree that even four-score years of purgation could hardly serve to annul the habits of a lifetime; and that yet in spite of his discordant nature, his self-isolation, he was happier in the solitary company of his own miserable soul than... But I must refrain from being wearisome. I will burden you with but one more quotation:

"'We have still a thirst unquenchable... It belongs to the immortality of man... It is no mere appreciation of the beauty before us, but a wild effort to reach the beauty above... to attain a portion of that loveliness whose very elements perhaps appertain to eternity alone..."

'Those tears, then, that respond to poetry and music are not from "excess of pleasure, but through a certain petulant, impatient sorrow at our inability to grasp *now*, wholly, here on earth, at once and for ever, those divine and rapturous joys of which, *through* the poem, or *through* the music, we attain to but brief and indeterminate glimpses." These words, professor, though you are evidently unaware of it, were Edgar Allan Poe's. And I – I myself have as yet found no reason to retract the conviction of their truth.'

Professor Monk's apprehension that his visitor, if not positively insane, was far from 'normal', had become a certainty. Their eyes, or rather the sentinels that look out of them, had met again. Who goes *there*? they had cried one on the other. And again it was the professor's that had returned no countersign. But dislike – a transitory hatred even – of his censor had fallen away into a sort of incredulity. That he should have consented to such a catechism. That a mere lecture should have led to this! He had been hardly troubling indeed to follow the meaning of the last remarks he had heard. His sole resource was to mutter that though he was grateful for his visitor's suggestions, it was clear that they would never see eye to eye in these matters, that the hour was growing late, and that he must be gone. He even managed to grimace a slant but not unkindly smile. 'We live in two worlds,' he said, 'you and I, and I fear we shall never agree. Nonetheless, and though you prefer to doubt it, I share your interest and delight in poetry, and, within strict limits, your admiration of Poe.' He cast a forlorn glance towards his hat perched in solitude upon a chair. 'We shall at least, I hope,' he added, 'part friends.'

'So be it,' replied his visitor, drawing his cloak more closely around him, raising slowly his heavy head.

> 'The cock he hadna crawed but once,
>> And clapped his wings at a',
> Whan the youngest to the eldest said,
>> Brother we must awa'…

'I also must be gone. We have met by chance. Let us not make it a fatality. By just such a chance indeed as that in your dreams tonight you may find yourself in regions such as our poet described, and may not, I fear, find much comfort in them. So, too, this evening, I found myself – well, here: in a region, that is, which it is your own excellent fortune to occupy and which is yet of little comfort to me. Is there not a shade of the Satanic in these streets? But what are waking and dreaming, my dear sir? Mere states of consciousness; as too in a sense is this, your world of what you call the actual, and the one that may await you. Opinions, views, passing tastes, passing prejudices – they are like funguses, a growth of the night. But the moon of the imagination, however fickle in her phases, is still constant in her borrowed light, and sheds her beams on them one and all, the just and the unjust. We may meet again.'

The dark, saturnine head had trembled a little, the weak yet stubborn mouth had stirred into a faint smile as the stranger thrust out an ungloved hand from beneath his cloak over the varnished wood of the table. Professor Monk hesitated, but only for a moment. Critic though he might be, and so not by impulse a man of action, he was neither timid nor unforgiving. His fingers met an instant the outstretched hand, and instantly withdrew, not because he had regretted the friendly action, but because of the piercing cold that had run through his veins at this brief contact. A sigh shook him from head to foot. A slight vertigo overcame him. He raised his hand to his eyes. For an instant it seemed as though even his sense of reality had cheated him – had foundered.

And when he looked out into the world again his visitor had left him. At last he was indeed alone. He stayed a moment, still dazed, and staring at nothing. Then he glanced at his mute typescript on the table, and then furtively into the grate. He paused, musing. His fingers fumbled in his waistcoat pocket, but encountered only a penknife. It was in part with a penknife, and when seated in his winter house before a burning fire, that King Jehoiakim had destroyed the Prophet Jeremiah's manuscript. But though, unlike the angel's little book in *Revelations,* the professor's paper was no longer sweet on his tongue, and there were a few dead coals at hand, he had no matches. His evening had wearied him, but this vile altercation seemed to have sapped his very life. Had he changed his views concerning the genius of Poe as a writer? – not by one iota. As a man? He had always, he realised, disliked and distrusted him; now he hated him. But this was immaterial. An absurd conviction of his own futility had shaken and shocked him. Life itself is a thing of moments, the last being its momentary apex. And *now* he felt as dead and empty as some sad carcass suspended eviscerated from a butcher's hook. By a piece of mere legerdemain in this cold and hideous room his view of himself and even of his future had completely changed. The pattern in the kaleidoscope – was that then nothing but a trick? A few dull fallen fragments of glass now, and no pattern at all? Being a man of habit and purpose and precision, Professor Monk was well aware that a drug, however potent, and whatever its origin, wears out at length its own effects. So with this evening's enterprise; he might, he *would,* soon be his own man again. But meanwhile… well, he would await the morrow, when perhaps his second thoughts would be less impetuous – and he himself less hideously cold.

He stooped awkwardly for his hat, and as he did so caught a glimpse of the little wizened, warty, bent-up old caretaker peering in at the doorway. 'Ah, there you are, sir,' he was assuring him, with the utmost friendliness. 'I was beginning to think you had passed out without my seeing you. They do sometimes. No hurry, sir.' Professor Monk hesitated; then paused; while yet again the adjacent foundry discarded its slag.

'Which way did that – er – gentleman go?' he inquired.

'Gentleman, sir? I've set eyes on no gentleman. Except for one of them saucy young schoolgirls from St Ann's half an hour ago, I see them all come along out together like rain out of a gutter-pipe. And the Reverend Mortimer hard at heel after them. It's fine now, sir, and starry, but the wind's rising. I have been talking with a friend.'

'Ah, yes. Thank you!' replied the professor. But it was well under his breath that he repeated, 'Ah, yes.'

THE GUARDIAN

T HERE ARE, I AM WELL AWARE, MANY EXCELLENT PEOPLE IN
this world who shun anything in the nature of the tragic in connection with *children*. And particularly if it carries with it what they
consider to be a strain of morbidity. My own conviction, nonetheless,
is that childhood is a state of extremes; alike of happiness and of
unhappiness. And I speak from my own knowledge – derived from
observation and experience long before this 'psychiatry' became a
craze – when I say, not only that some of the saddest, gravest, most
dreadful and most profound experiences in life may occur in our earliest years, but that, *if* they do, the effects of them in after-life *persist*.

I am not a mother. I am what is called 'an old maid'; but even 'old
maids', I assume, are entitled to their convictions.

I might first explain that I am the last of my family. In my earlier
years I had three sisters. Philip was the only son – and a posthumous
child – of the youngest of them – Rachel. And his mother was the
only one of us to marry. What opportunities the others had to follow
her example is nothing here to the point. At all events, they remained
single. My sister's choice was a tragic one; her head was at the mercy
of her heart. Her husband was a man who may be described in one
word: he was wicked. He was selfish, malicious and vindictive, and
the moment I saw him I warned my sister against him. But in vain.
He failed even to contrive to die respectably. I mention this merely
because his character may have some bearing on what I have to relate.
But what, I can hardly say.

Philip was born three months after his father's death. In spite of
the grief and affliction which my poor sister had endured during the

brief period of her married life, there appeared to be nothing amiss with *him*. Nature goes her own way. He was a quiet and tractable child, although he was subject to occasional outbreaks of passion and naughtiness. He was what is called a winning little boy, and I loved him very dearly. He was small for his age and slenderly built. In his earlier years his hair, and he had a long and narrow head, was of a pale gold – straw-coloured in fact; but it darkened later to a pretty lightish brown, and was very fine. Hairdressers frequently remarked on this. He had a small nose, and deep-set but clear grey eyes of a colour seldom seen in company with *that* coloured hair. He looked delicate, but was in fact not so.

This appearance – and he was by nature a sensitive and solitary child – suggested effeminacy. But since in his case it implied only fineness and delicacy of mind as well as of body, it was nothing but a tribute to him. I consider it a poor compliment to a *woman*, at any rate, to be regarded as mannish and masculine. Let us all keep to what we *are* and as much of it as possible. On this account, however, I counselled his mother to send him to no school until he was in his ninth year. She herself was inclined to be indulgent. Still, I am a great believer in the influence of a good home-life on a young child. Affection is by no means always a flawless mentor; but I know no better. And as my sister, still a young woman, had been left badly off, I had the pleasure and privilege of paying for Philip's education.

I selected an excellent young governess with a *character*. She taught him, five mornings a week, and with ease, the usual elements; and I especially advised her to keep as far as possible to the *practical* side of things. His own nature and temperament would supply him with the romantic. And that I regarded with misgiving. Later, he was sent to what an old friend of mine assured me was a school – a preparatory school – where even a sensitive and difficult child might have at least every opportunity of doing well and of being happy.

His first reports – and I had myself insisted on being taken over the whole school, scullery to attics, and on having a few words *alone* with the matron – were completely promising. Indeed, in his third term, Philip won a prize for good conduct – a prize that in these days, I regret to hear, is disparaged, even sneered at. Not that rewards of this kind are necessarily an enduring advantage – even to the clever. Much depends, naturally, on what is meant by goodness.

Now, in my view, it is a mistake to screen and protect even a young child too closely. Mind; I say, *too* closely. I am no believer in cosseting. A child has to face life. For this he has been given his own defences and resources. Needless to add, I am not defending carelessness or stupidity. I remember seeing at a children's party a little girl in a flimsy muslin frock and pale blue ribbons – a pretty little creature, too – who exhibited every symptom of approaching measles. Shivery, languid, feverish, running at the eyes and nose – the usual thing: and I kept her by me and I warned her nurse. But it was too late. Thirteen children at that one small party eventually fell victims to this stupidity. As with risks to physical health, so with mental ailments and weaknesses.

Night fears and similar bogies may be introduced into a young and innocent mind by a silly nurse-maid or by too harsh a discipline, or perhaps by an obscure inheritance. They may also be *natural* weeds. When I was a girl, even I myself was not entirely immune from them. I dreaded company, for example; was shy of speaking my own mind, and of showing affection. I used both to despise and to envy the delicate – the demonstrative; and even on a summer's day was always least happy in the twilight. Least at home. The dark, on the other hand, had no terrors for me. As events proved, such fears not only affected Philip a good deal more than they affect most children, but with a peculiar difference. Indeed, I have never since encountered a similar case.

Towards the end of December in that year he came as usual to spend his Christmas holidays with me. This was an arrangement with which my sister willingly complied. But I had only suggested it; I never made demands. His trunk was taken up to his bedroom, and we sat down to tea, at which my cook, who had been many years in my service, provided for him a lightly boiled egg – and I have never encountered even an old man who did not regard a boiled egg with his tea as a delicacy! As he sat facing me at the tea-table and in the full light of the lamp, I noticed at once that he looked more than usually pale. His face was even a little drawn and haggard. And 'haggard' is hardly a word one would willingly use in relation to a child. But it is the right word. Moreover, his clear but wearied eyes were encircled with bluish, tell-tale shadows. *That* meant bad nights!

'You are not looking very well, Philip,' I said. 'You don't seem to be hungry after that long journey. What time do you go to bed? Do you have any supper? Are your lessons at school worrying you? Have you perhaps got into hot water with one of your masters?… No, I don't think *that*!' As far as I can remember, these were the harmless and unprying questions I put to him. Like most children, he made no attempt to answer them. I didn't expect him to; I intended to *glean*.

'Thank you, Auntie Caroline,' he assured me twice over, in his usual rather prim manner, for he was a demure little boy, and I object to *artificial* baby talk. 'Thank you, Auntie Caroline,' he said, 'I feel very well. And I came out third or fourth in everything but French and Arithmetic. I was all but top in English.' And then, after a pause, while I continued to smile at him, he added that at times he had not been *sleeping* very well. 'I – often lie awake at night. And it goes on, you see, Auntie Caroline, sometimes into the day.' Strange: I failed even to ask him what precisely he meant by that 'it'.

'Well, Philip,' I said, 'that I think we can easily remedy,' although I had also failed to understand all the child may have meant by the words, *goes on*. 'You must have plenty of fresh air in your bedroom, and a sufficiency of blankets: a glass of hot milk with a little water, and a biscuit for supper; and in case you happen to wake up, Pattie (my excellent parlour-maid) shall see that there is a night-light in your soap basin. Do you have a light in your bedroom at home?'

'Yes, Auntie,' he said, 'but not at school. And it's not a night-light. It's just a bead of gas. It's blue; and sometimes when I have woken up in the middle of the night, I thought it was an eye looking at me out of the dark. But, of course, it wasn't an eye. It was only a bead of gas.'

'Well, it shall be a night-light,' said I. 'No one could mistake *that* for an eye, Philip?'

The next day at luncheon I thought he looked a little better. This, to be precise, was two days before Christmas. It was our first day 'Holidays Feast', as we used to call it; and luncheon consisted of roast chicken and vegetables, followed by a nice baked custard and some stewed prunes. In those days the small tart French prunes were still obtainable. Philip was exceedingly fond of bread sauce, and if it is not too richly flavoured, that is wholesome enough too. He steadily improved in looks during these holidays, and enjoyed his usual pantomime and one or two little Christmas parties. Nonetheless, I noticed that whatever his spirits might be during the day, he became far less talkative at the approach of evening.

A little girl, the daughter of a neighbour whose name it is needless to mention, would sometimes come with her nurse to play with him. She was one of those apple-cheeked, nice-mannered, sensible little girls who in these times seem so rare. During the early afternoon the two children would be perfectly happy together; but towards night-fall, when the day began to droop, Philip's spirits would perceptibly languish. He would then only pretend to play, and at tea it was Rosie and I who talked; though I am sure that in her childish fashion she did her best to persuade him to come out of his shell and to smile again. But a child of seven who refuses to eat a slice of plum cake when he is neither ill nor homesick must be troubled in *mind* or already sick; I knew that and kept my eyes open; and presently the trouble came out.

When Rosie was gone, Philip took a picture book – a Christmas present – and sat down on a stool by the fire, while I resumed my knit-ting. A cautious glance or two at him soon revealed the fact that he had ceased to read, although his eyes remained fixed upon his book. With a sigh he would begin again: and yet again his attention would wander. That night I twice visited his bedroom. He lay quietly asleep, his night-light burning on the wash-stand. In the small hours I fancied I heard a cry. I listened, nothing followed; and I left my bedroom door ajar. Next morning, after breakfast, he trod by accident on my cat's tail. It proved to be a *fortunate* accident – at least, for Philip. Animal and child, they were on excellent terms with one another, but at the sudden exasper-ated squeal from the startled animal he was peculiarly affected, began to tremble, and suddenly burst into tears. Now *that* I regarded at once as an unmistakable symptom of nervous trouble. I waited until the table had been cleared, then I called him to me and said, 'Philip, you must have had bad dreams last night. Pattie had not forgotten your night-light, I hope?' This, I am afraid, was a prevarication.

I see him now, in the holland overall which he always wore at meal-times and was then outgrowing, standing in front of me, his hand in mine, on the fur rug by the brass fender. A portrait of his maternal grandfather, whom he clearly resembled and who was not only a hard-working clergyman but a scholar, hung over the chimneypiece above his head. The light of the window – and it was a healthy, frosty, wintry morning – shone full upon his face.

'No, Auntie,' he replied, 'I had the light.' But as he stood looking up at me I noticed that his eyes had begun to move away, as if involuntarily, towards the right, and that it was with an effort that he turned them towards *me* again; and then it was too late for him to suppress a faint expression of alarm on his pale, delicate features. What does this mean? thought I.

'Is anything frightening you now?' I inquired. Colour crept into his cheek, and a sob shook him. He nodded.

'In this very room?' said I, and searched with my glance the corner of it towards which he had turned. Nothing whatever was there that could account for his apprehension; no more unusual object, at any rate, than a bust of Cicero on its pedestal by the book-case – a precious possession of my dear father's. But with a child, one never knows.

'What's troubling you now?' I said. 'Tell me, Philip.' And I spoke in a quiet easy voice, gently fondling his small fingers.

'It's what, Aunt Caroline,' he replied. 'I see.'

'See where?' I pressed him. 'Look at the bright, sparkling garden – at the trees and the hoar-frost on their branches, thick almost as snow. Darkness, you know, Philip, can only remove that out of *view*. They themselves remain the same – no enemies there. Just as we two remain the same – light or no light. Is there perhaps anything troubling your *mind*? Look at Puss, now. He knows as well as I do that what happened just now was nothing but an accident.'

'It's not in the *room*,' he told me. 'It's – it's inside. It's when I look right over – and turn my eyes this way, Auntie Caroline.' They hardly wavered. 'It began a long time ago; but – it's only sometimes.'

'What is only sometimes?' I said. 'At night, too?'

By dint of careful questioning, I discovered at length that what troubled him was no more, as I thought at the time, than a mere fancy. He told me that when he turned his eyes as far as their orbits admitted in a certain direction – and after recent experiments of this kind he had ventured to do this very seldom – he perceived a shape, a figure there. A something dark, small and stunted, I gathered, with humped shoulders and bent head, and steadily scrutinising him. I was dismayed. Mere fancy or not, it was no wonder that a child so sensitive should be disturbed by so strange an unpleasant an experience as this, even if it were a pure illusion.

'Now tell me, Philip,' I coaxed him. 'Here we are, alone; just you and me. Aren't you perhaps imagining what you see? If we try, we can at once see your mother. In our minds, I mean. Can't we? But that too would be imaginary. And next moment she is gone. There *can* be nothing. Look again.'

'Oh, Auntie!' he exclaimed, throwing his arms round my neck and bursting into tears again; 'it's like that horrid, horrid Satan.'

This, I confess, alarmed me, but I showed nothing of it.

'And who has been talking to you of Satan?' said I.

'Nobody, nobody,' he cried passionately. 'I saw it in a book.'

'Ah!' said I. 'Only in a book! Just a picture. That's where it comes from, then.'

'Yes, Auntie,' he sobbed, '*now*. But what I am telling you of was before that, *before* I saw it in a book.'

I was intensely anxious to comfort the child, and assured him yet again that all this could be only fancy, that no more than a mere dream may haunt one's memory even in the full light of the day, that God protects the young, that the innocent have nothing to fear. And I took care to say no more than I believed. 'Now, be brave. Just try,' I said, 'try once again.'

'But you see, Auntie,' he lamented, 'it isn't always *there*. And oh! I can't. I daren't!…'

Well, my very worthy family doctor came to see him. He declared the child was run down, highly strung, and so forth. That I knew. He prescribed Parrish's Food, and suggested, somewhat to my surprise, that he should be given half a glass of port wine every morning and afternoon. Still, when I ask for what I believe or have reason to hope will be good advice, I *take* it. And trusting that this treatment would soon mend matters, I refrained from writing to his mother. Matters did mend. We made no further reference, not the faintest, on either side, to what had troubled him. Not for some little time. Never reawaken trouble!

Little seemed amiss for a year or two. Philip spent his tenth birthday with me, and then contrary to my own conviction, but seeing how much better and more confident he was looking, I asked him in a jocular fashion, when his favourite pudding – a jam roly-poly – was on the table, I asked him if he had ever been troubled again with those old fancies of his. He knew at once to what I was referring, and met the question very gallantly, as I thought.

'Yes, I am now and then,' he said, 'but now I never really look. He's *there*; but I think unless I tried hard, I shouldn't see him. And at night – well, you can't help what dreams come, can you, Auntie?'

But how different were voice, manner, air, by comparison with the previous year. This being so, it was on my lips to counsel him to make the attempt then and there. Also to tell him of a mysterious belief in what are known as guardian angels. But – although I have no wish to be uncharitable – few even of those of us who share this belief *seem* to pay any active heed to it, and in the fear that he might perhaps be laughed at on this account at school, I refrained. The adult, alas, is not always courageous enough concerning his convictions on behalf of childhood.

'Well!' I said. 'We all have our little troubles, Philip, and we must do our best to learn to face them.' He smiled at me. We understood one another. 'Pattie,' I said, 'give Master Philip another slice of that excellent pudding.'

On reflection, it astonishes me that it never at any time occurred to me to consult an oculist. That might at once have put things right. Even people of excellent common-sense may occasionally be the prey of illusions – ghosts and similar nonsense. Charles Wesley, for example. And how easy it is, on a slight pretext, to give shape and meaning to what is purely the work of fancy. Hasn't the famous poet Shakespeare a passage in one of his plays concerning 'airy nothings' or some such words? Even the best, the most skilful of oculists – and I should have chosen a good one – might very well have ascribed the child's fancies to a disordered liver, to those floating specks we may observe when we look at a whitewashed ceiling. As for many of these mental specialists who are so much in evidence nowadays, I have, I confess, very little patience with them, or belief in them. Again perhaps I am wrong. But tampering with a child's mind is a dangerous experiment; and if it is put in the wrong hands, it may prove as clumsy an operation as that of a schoolboy using a penknife to repair his watch. And it will have much the same result.

There is one small thing I ought to add. I had discovered that this figure, this skulking shape, which Philip professed to 'see' at certain times, was not always *stationary*. Also, that the hump at the shoulders *appeared* to be that of folded wings which, on one occasion at least, he told me, were lifted (like a raven's or a vulture's); as we see in Gustave Doré's illustrations to the poet Milton's *Paradise Lost*; or is it Dante? But there again, a picture no doubt accounted for this.

The following year Philip did admirably at school. He had one illness from which he completely recovered. He still *looked* none too robust, but this was merely 'looking'. He was a thoroughly nice, straightforward, pleasant English boy, not easy at making friends, but able to make good ones; which is all the battle. And I am thankful to say that he seemed to have inherited no adverse characteristics from his father. Nonetheless, all my confidence, all my hopes for him – and words could not express my feelings even now, so many years after what followed – were doomed to be shattered.

A few weeks after his twelfth birthday, June 7th, I received a telegram from his headmaster. Only six words, which shocked me more than I can say: 'Please come at once. Grave illness.' 'Grave'; that one word was enough. When, within twenty-four hours of the receipt of this message, I arrived at the school and was at once closeted with the headmaster, he told me, to my consternation, that Philip, two nights before, had made an attempt to run away.

'To run away?' I repeated, blindly, eyeing my informant. 'Philip? Why? Where to?'

I could see by one or two little signs that in spite of his restrained manner and carefully chosen words, he – the headmaster, Mr Morgan, I mean – had been shaken by what had occurred. And I had no intention of being unjust. I was merely seeking the *facts*. Indeed, a few such questions soon made it clear to me that this statement was not precisely in *accordance* with the facts. That Philip had intended to make this attempt there seemed to be little doubt, since an old discarded rope from the gymnasium had been discovered hidden away behind his Sunday clothes in his locker.

What seems actually to have happened was this. For reasons unknown, the poor boy had recently been neglectful of his school work. Nothing more serious than inattention and a tendency to absent-mindedness – to daydreaming. That far-away look in the eyes which I knew so well. He had got into trouble, too, for leaving food on his plate. Loss of appetite, I suggested. On the other hand, there had been no hint of positive unhappiness, and certainly not of deliberate wrong-doing. Nor, it seems, had he confided what he intended to do to any living soul in the school, not even to his closest friend or chum, a freckled, honest-looking boy named Ollitt.

On the previous Tuesday, nonetheless, a few minutes before midnight, without awakening or disturbing any one of the four boys who shared his dormitory with him, he must have risen from his bed, opened the window, and crept out on to the narrow ledge of stone beyond it. It was, as I remember myself, a quiet and lovely night, the more serene for its moonlight. No rope had been used; that was certain. That had remained in his locker. 'If he had been awake – even partially awake,' I argued silently, 'why no rope?' The headmaster continued to look at me, but we found no words to express our feelings.

My own conviction – and I see no reason to change it now – is that, aroused, perhaps by some evil dream, Philip had been 'walking' in his sleep. There was no breath of wind that night – nothing that could have alarmed the poor boy. And yet, the vivid moonlight, perhaps an inward realisation of danger, something must have broken in on his sleeping mind, and aroused him – and then, no doubt, a frantic and desperate struggle to climb back into safety again. But in vain. The child, only, please God, half-conscious of his surroundings, and still under the influence of his dreams, had fallen headlong on to the flagstone path beneath the dormitory window. Within a few minutes he had been found there, unconscious, terribly injured. How little hope there was of his recovery was revealed by the headmaster's face as we sat together, both of us fallen silent again. He himself was in no way to blame; no one was to blame; and without hesitation I then and there said so...

I was taken into the sickroom – a whitewashed, cheerful, sunny room. There was a glass of flowers on the table – pinks, I remember. The room contained five beds. Beside the furthermost of them, to the right of the other doorway and in a little cubicle, a dormitory maid was sitting – the matron herself having left the room only a few minutes before. She appeared to be reading to herself, with lowered head, from a book. She was a pale-faced little thing, looking younger than I learned she actually was – with her fair straight hair, and quiet, grey eyes. Indeed, she was little more than a child. At sight of me, she shut her book, rose from her chair, curtsied – a thing seldom seen nowadays from girls of any class – and left the room.

My dear boy lay on his back, mercifully out of pain for a while. He was tranquil, seemed to be asleep, or on the verge of being so. I sat down in the vacant chair and watched him. But that afternoon I had no word with him. During the next morning, he was in charge of the trained nurse that had been sent for. But I was allowed to sit with him again immediately after luncheon. His mother could not arrive until the next day. And then, it was feared, she would be too late. He had not heard me cross the room and slip quietly into the chair beside his bed. He lay with closed eyes, deathly pale, his head moving restlessly on his pillow. And as with sickened heart I sat watching him, his lips began to mutter, and the eyeballs beneath the closed lids to waver.

Whether he was sleeping or waking there was only one interpretation of the expression – sorrow, and, as I fancied, fear. I could not bear to see it. 'Philip,' I whispered, stooping over him. His features instantly became motionless.

Otherwise there was no sign that he had heard. He was listening; caught up, it seemed, by some acute expectation. The grey eyes slowly opened and met my own. It was too late. The faint smile of welcome with which he now greeted me could not efface the darting piercing disappointment that had first been revealed in their depths. 'Dearest Auntie Caroline,' he whispered after a moment's pause, putting out his hand to me. 'Am I very ill?'

I smiled again, and bent and kissed the bloodless fingers. 'There, my dear,' I said. 'Lie quietly; all will be well. And there is no need in the world to say anything unless you wish.'

The doctor himself had warned us that the boy was not to be crossed in anything. And I realised what that meant. In the brief, broken talk between us that followed, he confessed that he had some days before made up his mind to run away. To his mother I admit, not to me; and then he had decided otherwise.

'Why, Philip? What had made you so unhappy?' I ventured.

'*Not* unhappy,' he assured me. 'I was too happy. But – but, you see, it was no use. It never *could* be.'

This completely perplexed me. But how ask a child why he is *happy*! 'Then there was nothing – I was with you a while when you were asleep, my dear – there was nothing on your mind; nothing to be afraid of?'

Yet again the eyes turned restlessly in their sockets. 'Afraid, Auntie!' he said. 'Oh, no. I don't mind *that* now. Nothing to be afraid of now, I mean. It's still there; but now – it doesn't matter.' And what I saw in his face at this moment was certainly neither dread, nor terror, nor even misgiving, nothing of that – but a grieved, profound, unutterable longing and pining.

'Listen, Philip,' I said; 'your mother will soon be here, very soon.'

'That's lovely,' he replied. But to my consternation – since I can truthfully say I had never in act or thought stood between them – there was *something* – a tone, an accent – wanting even in that 'lovely', however sincerely it was meant. What then else could he be pining for? What could I do – or say – to rest his mind, comfort him? I pondered in vain.

The plain whitewashed room was radiant with light. It was a beautiful summer morning; the airs at the window ebbed in, sweet with the flowers of the garden and the smell of new-mown hay. Out of the distance came the noise, the voices, of the boys in the playing-fields... A day of darkness, leaden clouds and pelting rain would have been easier to endure. At that time I had already steeled myself to many things in this world; but a life, I can truthfully declare, was slipping away far from me more precious than my own. I was a stranger to all this. I had never, except once before, felt helpless and forsaken. But how console a child with *that*!

And then, as if in direct answer to the question, the fallen narrow face on the pillow had suddenly become still again. The eyes beneath the leaden lids had moved to their extreme angle – away from me. And this, at the sound of a footstep. The door opened; I looked up.

It was the little dormitory maid. She had come to tell me that my sister had arrived, and would I join her in the headmaster's study. I looked at her – her face vaguely recalled some old picture I had seen. It was a quiet face, not pretty, but fair, with an unspoilt, remote look in her eyes. For an instant I could not reveal my thoughts. I was intensely reluctant to go. I smiled at her as best I could. 'Then I can commit my nephew safely to *you* for a few moments?' I said.

She turned to look at him – as I did. And – how describe what I saw? There was no expectation now, no foreboding, or pining in the face on the pillow. No trace of these. But a look fixed on her as near human ecstasy as mortal features are capable of. I detest anything even resembling sentimentality; but my heart seemed to clap-to in my body. No expression on any human countenance, not even of hopeless grief or anguish, has ever affected me so acutely. Nor had I realised until that tragic moment – nor have I ever either more than once shared – its inward meaning. But there was not the least doubt of it. The poor child was in love.